D0761828

TIME SPRINGS ETERNAL

Dr. Givon,
Thank you for your help
with my research on this book.
It's much different from the one you
sent me, but I hope did done the
life people justice in it.

Rutherford Case

TIME SPRINGS ETERNAL

❧BOOK 1 OF THE TIME SPRINGS ETERNAL SERIES❧

Rutherford Case

TAVA Mountain Publishing

TAVA Mountain Publishing
Melbourne, FL

Paperback: 978-1-953667-19-9
EPUB: 978-1-953667-02-1

Library of Congress Control Number: 2020917024

First paperback edition November 2020.

Cover art by Becky Fox (innervsion@gmail.com)
Layout by TAVA Mountain Publishing

For my ancestors, particularly the women
who forged the path I now walk

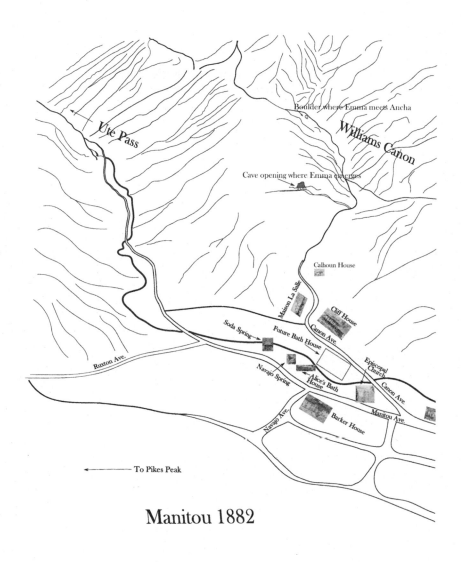

Manitou 1882

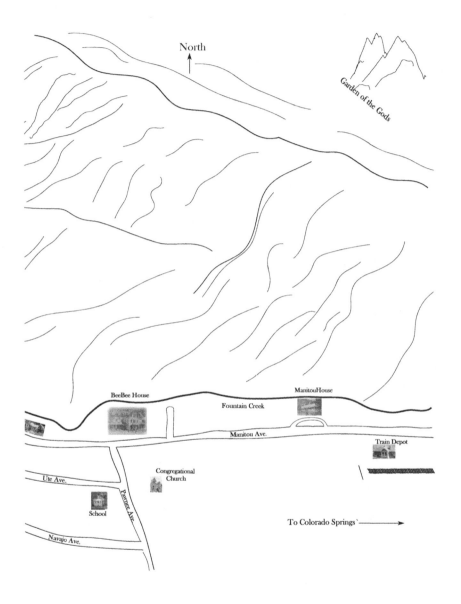

North

Garden of the Gods

BeeBee House

Fountain Creek

ManitouHouse

Manitou Ave.

Train Depot

Ute Ave.

Congregational
Church

Pawnee Ave.

School

To Colorado Springs ⟶

Navajo Ave.

Acknowledgements

I am convinced no one creates alone. Certainly, I don't. My friends Kim, Diana, Donna, and Carol kept the spark of the idea of this book alive even when I did not, then handed it back to me like a cared-for child when I was ready. My aunt Jeanie and cousin Elvira encouraged me along the way. Diana and Jeanie read as I wrote and provided me with helpful perspective. My life partner, Dean, allowed me the time and space to write and also provided valuable feedback on the drafts. Becky Fox captured the premise beautifully in the cover art.

I'd especially like to thank the experts that helped me. Local Manitou Springs historians Deborah Harrison, Lynn Beckner, and John Posusta, provided invaluable information and resources to me. This book would not exist without their help. It was through John that I was able to find Dr. Harriet Leonard's (the inspiration for Dr. Alice Guiles) great-great-granddaughter. She helped me confirm what I had learned about Dr. Leonard and get a sense of what life was like for her in the nineteenth century. I would also like to thank Dr. Thomas Givon, who wrote the book, literally, on the Ute language.

Thanks to all these people for joining me in the adventure!

✿ PROLOGUE ✿

The sun shining through the light blue curtains gently woke Emma. She rubbed her eyes and reached for Paul, only to find he was already out of bed, clamoring in the kitchen of their small apartment. As she sat up, he came into the bedroom with a tray holding a plate of avocado toast, coffee, and one red rose in a bud vase.

"Your breakfast, Miss Quinn."

"What a surprise! What's the occasion?" Emma arranged a pillow behind her for support.

"Well, since you are leaving for Colorado this afternoon, I wanted to make our last few hours special," Paul grinned.

"This is so sweet, thank you!" Emma accepted the tray. "I appreciate the attention, but I'll only be away a few days." Emma patted Paul's side of the bed. "Come lay beside me while I enjoy this treat. Oh, and hand me my phone so I can take a picture of this and post it so my friends can see what a wonderful man I am marrying!"

"I know, but I'll miss you anyway," Paul handed Emma her cell phone from the nightstand and lay next to her. "I'm sorry I can't go with you, but this deadline is looming large." Paul turned toward Emma and propped himself up on his elbow. "But the bonus I'll get if I finish on time will more than pay for our honeymoon." He smiled and gently brushed Emma's cheek with his finger.

"I understand. And really, it's better that it's just me and the girls this time. You can't help pick out the wedding dress, anyway." Emma nudged him with her elbow and winked. "Andrea and Randy have my schedule packed full. We have lots of details to finalize."

"It seems early to me. Our wedding isn't until May."

"Yes, but you know the Broadmoor Hotel is in high demand, and it's the job of my bridesmaids to keep me on track." Emma was flying from their place in northern Virginia to Colorado Springs, her hometown and where Emma and Paul planned to marry. Perhaps August was a bit early for the stated purpose of the trip, but Emma was happy to use it as an excuse to spend some time with her childhood friends and to get away for a while.

Aside from her dream wedding at the Broadmoor, Emma wasn't a romantic. Quite the contrary. She was fiercely independent. From early adolescence, she decided she would never depend on anyone for anything—not financially, not to define her self-worth, not to determine her priorities, not anything. Watching her single mother give up all her dreams as she struggled to support them on an administrator's salary had taught her that. Emma had focused on her education and on studying something that would earn a good living. She had graduated with honors in electrical engineering and had been working for a large government contractor since leaving college six years ago. Even if engineering was not her first passion, it

2

had provided her with more than adequate income and had brought her to Paul, her first real love. They had met at the University of Colorado their senior year when they were on the same senior project team. Both were career-minded and ambitious. They agreed to move together to northern Virginia, where now their careers were well underway. Emma had become a system engineer at her company, and Paul was now a superstar senior account manager at his. Together their futures looked bright, and they had agreed it was now time to take the next step in their relationship. They had become engaged a month ago.

"I want to give you something before you leave." Paul said, opening the nightstand drawer and pulling out a small box.

"Paul, you know how I feel about engagement rings. I really don't want one."

"Yes, I know. This isn't an engagement ring." Paul opened the box and showed Emma the ring inside. Emma felt strangely transfixed as she gazed at the large, tear-shaped cabochon surrounded by a setting of silver swirls and spirals. The cabochon was an opalescent blend of greens and golds.

"Oh, it's wonderful! What kind of stone is it?" Emma took it from the box and found that it fit the index finger on her left hand.

"I don't know. It belonged to my great-great grandmother. Remember I told you she was Native American? I always imagined her tribe must have crafted it."

Emma knew the significance this ring held for Paul. His entrusting it to her was a deeper sign of his commitment than a store-bought diamond engagement ring could ever be. She looked up from the ring and met Paul's gaze with her deep blue eyes. "Thank you, Paul. I understand what a gift this is. I will treasure it, as I do you." She kissed him tenderly.

.

ꙮ CHAPTER 1 ꙮ

Emma woke in absolute darkness. She struggled to remember where she was. Laying awkwardly on dry, dirt-covered stone, she felt her backpack under her, still snugly strapped to her waist and shoulders. She sat up carefully, slowly straightening out her arms and legs from an unnatural position. She yelled out, "Hello? Can anyone hear me?" Only a slight echo answered.

"God, what happened?" Emma thought as she felt around her, feeling only dirt and cold rocks. She reached behind her head and felt the large knot forming behind her right ear, her hair damp and tacky from the bloody wound. She looked at her hand or tried to, but the dark was so absolute, she could see nothing but black. She gingerly stood up, taking care not to hit her head on any obstacles made invisible by a darkness thicker than ink. She staggered from the dizzying pain in her head and reached out blindly to balance herself. Her hands landed on a wall of large rocks and rubble.

"Andrea? . . . Randy?"

No one answered.

Emma carefully removed her backpack and found the water bottle she had filled that morning. The water was cool and soothing over her parched throat. She carefully returned the water bottle and put her backpack back on. She struggled to recall her last memory as she leaned against the ragged wall.

"We were in the cave. We felt the ground shake and heard a rumble." Cave of the Winds—she was in Colorado. Emma remembered Andrea and Randy suggesting they tour the cave as a break from wedding planning. Horrified, Emma realized there must have been a collapse. *"What happened to them?"* She knelt down and felt along the ground, hoping to find them nearby, but terrified of finding them dead. She reached back to her backpack and pulled out her phone for some light, but the battery had run down. It wouldn't even turn on. She groped in her backpack and found her recharger, but she could not find the cord.

"Help! Help! Is anyone there!" she screamed as she desperately groped the rubble wall that blocked her way, trying to find an opening. All she found was where the wall of debris met the smoother, solid side of the cave chamber. Inch by inch, Emma walked along the wall of the chamber, testing each step and placement of her hands before putting her weight down, praying she did not step into an abyss.

Absolute darkness.

Absolute silence.

Absolute terror.

"Think Emma, think. You've gone five arm spans from the rubble blockage." Emma had taken care to track the distance she had traveled in case she needed to backtrack. As she reached her left arm out to feel ahead, her hand felt the wall curve away, as though into a passage or nook—or a bottomless pit. Emma

could feel her pulse and hear her heartbeat quicken. "*I don't want to lose my bearings. Where will this wall lead me?*" Emma paused and rested her cheek on the wall before deciding whether to continue around the curve. Desperate and feeling the panic returning, Emma closed her eyes and thought, "*Keep calm Emma, keep calm. You need your wits. Don't panic.*"

Emma opened her eyes. She focused on her breathing until she felt her heartbeat slow to a more normal rate. As her eyes continued moving randomly in the darkness, they lighted on something that was not black—almost indiscernibly not black, but not black just the same. She hoped it was external light.

Emma continued her way around the curve of the wall, carefully toward the weak light. She kept her gaze locked on it, not wanting to lose track of it for even a second. As she came closer, her gaze moved up to keep the light in view. She went another two arm-spans when the light disappeared.

"*I know it was there. I know it. Where did it go?*" Emma moved back an arm's reach and saw the light return. "*There must be a rock blocking the light as I move closer,*" Emma thought.

When Emma groped ahead, she felt more rubble. Her only option was to scale it and find the dim light, which she prayed was a sign of an opening out of the cave. She felt for a place where she could find purchase for her feet as she pulled herself up the rubble wall. At one point, the rock she reached for gave way, and she nearly fell. The climbing became easier after about seven feet, as the collapse seemed to curve away from Emma into a steep slope. At that moment, Emma saw the light again.

"*There it is! Oh, thank God, I see it!*" Emma kept her eyes fixed on the guiding light as she began to pull rocks carefully away to clear a path toward it, acutely aware that by doing so, she may cause the rocks to break free and crush her. Was it her imagination, or was the light growing dimmer? "*What's *happening? The light is fading! It must be getting dark! Then that must be an opening out of the cave if I can only free myself before darkness sets in."* Emma urgently pulled the debris out of her way, trading caution for speed. Finally, she removed a stone that made the area of light large enough for a small dog to get through.

"Hello! Hello! Help me! Please someone, help me!" Emma cried desperately as she kept pulling rocks and brushing crumpled stones out of her path, the area of light growing larger (and dimmer), but still too small to crawl through.

Suddenly, a rock came free and fell away, and the light doubled in size. *"Oh, I can get through that. I know I can!"* Emma pulled off her backpack and pushed it ahead of her as she crawled along her belly on the top of the collapsed debris. When she reached the opening, she pushed her backpack out and heard it hit the ground quickly. She hoped that meant she had a solid place to jump out of the hole and that it was not a far drop. As her head emerged from the opening, her eyes squinted closed as they adjusted to the abrupt change in brightness from the cave. She blinked quickly and saw that it was only a few feet to the ground. She pulled herself out of the cave and fell onto the ground, arms first.

The first thing Emma felt was profound relief to be out of the cave. The next thing she felt was pain. Her eyes burned from adjusting to the late afternoon light, which compared to the darkness of the cave was like looking into a spotlight. Her jeans jacket and flannel shirt had protected her arms somewhat, but she could feel the abrasions underneath and knew there would be bruising. Most of all, her head ached, and her vision was blurry.

Her cell phone was dead. She fished deeper in her backpack for her recharger cord and found it improperly stored in a small side pocket. She plugged her phone into the recharger and turned on the power. No signal. Figuring she was in a dead spot, which was not uncommon in the mountains, she began walking to find a signal or, barring that, someone to help. Emma had emerged from the cave onto a wide ledge facing southwest. The sun was setting to the west, behind the mountains, and she could see the tip of Pikes Peak, covered with snow. Emma looked toward Manitou Springs, where she saw buildings and lights, though sparser than she expected. Her concern now was to get help for her friends and anyone else who might be trapped in the cave. A short distance down the path from the ledge, Emma came to a dirt road, which she recognized as the path to Williams Cañon, and followed it toward town. Emma fought dizziness and nausea as she stumbled down the road. Where was the highway? Where were the cars, the buildings, the power lines? Nothing looked right. *"Could I be dreaming all of this?"* thought Emma.

Emma could not get her bearings. After she had walked about a mile, she came upon a large building—obviously a public building—and staggered through the main entrance where she grabbed the arm of a young man rushing by. "Please, I need help!" Emma cried. "My friends and I were in Cave of the Winds when it collapsed. I made my way out, but they are still there. I need someone to go rescue them!"

"Yes, ma'am!" he said, out of breath, "Everythang's a right mess, what with the earthquake. We're dealin' with the confusion as best we can. I'll let 'em know. But yer hurt bad yerself! Come, let me find yer a place to sit 'till I can git someun to hep ya."

"There were three of us, counting me, plus our guide. I don't know how many others might be trapped there," Emma said, as the young man took her backpack and ushered her to an upholstered armchair in the lobby of what appeared to be a quaint hotel. He looked quizzically at the backpack as he placed it next to the chair. "Yes ma'am," he said. "Rest yourself here, and I'll git hep."

"Oh, I think I'm going to be sick," Emma groaned. The young man ran to the corner of the room and brought Emma a brass vase. *"Is this a spittoon?"* she wondered.

"Here ya go, ma'am. Use this if ya need to. I'll git the doc as soon as I can."

"Thank you! My name is Emma!" Emma called to him as he ran out the front door.

"I'm Zack, ma'am!" he yelled back over his shoulder. And with that, Emma promptly bent over and vomited in the vessel.

Emma held her hand against her head and leaned back into the chair. The nausea was overwhelming, and the dizziness only made it worse. She bent back over and put her head between her legs, but then her head throbbed dreadfully. She needed to lie down, or she thought she'd faint. She knew she was filthy, and that her head was bloody, so she laid down on the wooden floor and put her head on her backpack. As she drifted off to sleep, she hoped when she woke, she'd find this had all been a strange, bad dream.

❀

Low voices buzzed around her as Emma slowly became aware of her pain again. She was lying on a cot under a cotton sheet. She had evidently received medical attention. She was clean, her head bandaged. Someone had rolled her shirt sleeves up over her elbows to apply a light gauze wrapping over her abrasions. When she turned her head, it hurt. When she lifted her arms, they hurt. Her whole body was stiff and sore. She looked around and saw that she was in a large room. She assumed it was the dining room of the hotel she had come to for help. The tables and chairs were stacked to one side to make room for about a dozen cots. She lay between two of them. A man moaning in his sleep occupied the cot to her left. Gradually, Emma remembered escaping the cave and trying to find someone to help rescue her friends. As the memory came back to her, her heart pounded. "Hello?" she called out weakly, "Hello?"

A middle-aged woman dressed in a simple brown calico dress with a long skirt and long sleeves came to the end of her bed. Over the dress, she was wearing a white cotton apron with deep pockets on either side, and around her neck was an odd-looking stethoscope. She wore her reddish-brown hair, lightly streaked with gray, in a high bun. Her face was rather angular, especially her square jaw, and her mouth and nose were rather small for her face. Her hazel eyes, however, exuded calm and intelligence. "I am glad to see you are awake. I was worried about your head wound," she said. "I am Dr. Guiles. What is your name?" She asked as she walked to the side of the cot and began taking Emma's pulse.

"Emma Quinn," Emma answered, puzzled at the Doctor's appearance.

"Do you mind answering some questions for me, Miss Quinn?" Dr. Guiles asked.

"No, of course not, but can you tell me, do you know how my friends are?"

"We sent some men to look for them, but we have heard nothing yet."

Emma fell back onto her pillow and winced, frustrated.

"Can you tell me what day it is?" The doctor continued.

Suddenly a man yelled out, "Doc!, Doc! We have Carson. He's badly hurt!"

"Over here, Jim." Dr. Guiles quickly motioned him to the empty cot to Emma's right. Emma watched as Jim and another man carefully laid Carson down. "Oh heavens, he has a severe

11

head wound," Emma heard the doctor say as she leaned over the man. Then the doctor let out a sigh. "I'm afraid he's dead, Jim."

"We were as careful and gentle as we could be, Doc. We found 'im up on the Williams Cañon trail, not far from the entrance to the cave where we were lookin' for them folks that young lady said was trapped there. I reckon the earthquake caused a rock to fall on 'im." Jim said.

"I'm sure you were careful, Jim. You didn't kill him; he's been dead a while. You and Carl did your best, and you did the right thing bringing him to me, but if you could take him to the mortician, I would be grateful. There is nothing more I can do for him."

"Okay Doc. We didn't find any signs of them other folks in the cave. It's too dark out now, we will have to keep lookin' for 'em tomorrow, first thing."

Emma felt her stomach lurch and a pang in her chest as panic for her friends set in. This earthquake was more serious than she realized if it was causing rocks to fall and kill people. She couldn't stand the thought of Andrea and Randy being cold and trapped in the absolute black darkness of that cave. Were they okay? Were they dead? She tried to get out of bed, though she had no idea what she was going to do once she got up. She cried out as the act of sitting up sent a jolt of pain through her head. Dr. Guiles turned back to her cot. Emma snapped, "Why have they stopped looking for my friends? Surely they can use flood lights and cameras and other emergency equipment to continue the search at night!"

Dr. Guiles looked at Emma and frowned slightly. "They are doing what they can, Miss Quinn. I understand you are worried, but I need you to be calm. Now, can you try to answer my questions? I want to make sure you are not seriously injured. I don't want to lose another patient tonight." Dr. Guiles helped

Emma get settled back into the cot and made her as comfortable as possible. "Now, can you tell me what day it is?"

Emma seethed, frustrated by her helplessness. She sighed deeply and tried to respond to the doctor. "I'm not sure. It was Saturday when we went into the cave. I think that was yesterday—maybe the day before. I'm not sure how long I was unconscious in the cave or how long I've been asleep here. What day is it?"

"It's Tuesday."

"It can't have been three days!"

"What year is it?"

"2019"

"I'm sorry? What did you say?" Dr. Guiles stared at Emma.

"2019," Emma repeated. Emma wondered if she had been in a coma for years and was now in some kind of strange new world where women dressed like pioneers again. "Why? If it isn't 2019, what year is it?" She asked.

"Miss Quinn, today is Tuesday, November 7, 1882."

✌ CHAPTER 2 ✍

Emma stared back at the doctor. "What? That's impossible.
It's ridiculous! I must be in a coma. This is all nonsense—
all of it! All I know is that there was a cave-in at Cave of the
Winds. My friends and I were touring it with a guide when we
heard and felt a low rumble. The next thing I remember is
waking up in the dark in the cave. I couldn't find my friends. I
found my way out, and here I am, trying to get someone to go
find them before they DIE in there!"

"There was an earthquake, Miss Quinn." Dr. Guiles agreed,
calmly. "It was severe enough to cause many rock slides in the
area and minor damage to some buildings in town. It appears it
also caused a cave-in at Cave of the Winds, as you say. They have
accounted for everyone they knew to be in the cave before the
earthquake. Still, the men will look for these people you say are
there. To be honest, your presence is a bit of a puzzle. No one at
Cave of the Winds has a record of you being there."

Emma stared up at the ceiling. "*What in holy hell is going on?*" she thought. Grasping for a thread of reality, she looked down at her hands and saw the ring Paul had given her on her left hand, giving her immediate comfort.

"Please, can I have my cell phone? I want to call Paul—my fiancé. I have to tell him what happened, that I'm okay."

"I am afraid I have no idea what you are requesting, Miss Quinn. You have a severe concussion, and you have some nasty scrapes and bruises. Your concussion is causing confusion. Once you heal up a bit, things will become clearer. I want you to stay here and rest for a while. We will sort it all out, don't worry."

Emma lost her patience. "Dammit! I am not confused or crazy. My two best friends are trapped in a cave. My fiancé does not know where I am or that I am safe. By now, he must have heard about the earthquake here and is no doubt trying to reach me. Please, just hand me my backpack—it's here somewhere, right?" Emma propped herself up and looked around.

"Yes, it's here." Dr. Guiles reached under Emma's cot and handed it to her. Looking quizzically at it, Dr. Guiles asked, "What's that material it's made from?"

Emma grabbed the bag, "The same thing most of them are made of: nylon." Emma unzipped a pocket and pulled out her phone and recharger, still connected by the cord, and turned it on. Still no signal.

In stunned silence, Dr. Guiles stared at the items in Emma's hands. She'd never seen anything like them before. A thin, rectangular case with a glass top covered a lighted, color image of Garden of the Gods, the rock formations near town. A cord, also of a mysterious material, connected the case to a larger black case, which had a small, blue light emitting from its side. "May I see these?" she asked Emma.

Emma thrust them at the doctor. "I'm still not getting a signal." As Dr. Guiles inspected Emma's phone, she saw the words "no signal" in small letters in the top corner. She thought back to Emma's clothes. Her outfit was common for many men around the area—all the miners wore Levi Strauss waist overalls. But she had never seen a woman wearing them, and she had never seen a woman wearing a flannel shirt. The girl's shoes and socks were the strangest of her attire. At the time Emma arrived, the doctor had had more urgent concerns than to pass judgement on Emma's clothing, but now, taken with these other things . . . "Miss Quinn," the doctor slowly marveled, "I am beginning to believe you are neither confused nor crazy. But now we have a bigger problem."

Dr. Guiles put Emma's things back in the backpack and placed it back under the cot. She stood at the end of the bed and called out for her assistant, "Sarah! Could you come here, please?"

"Yes, Mother?" Sarah was Dr. Guiles's daughter. "What do you need?"

"Please go get Claire. Miss Quinn here needs a place to continue her recuperation. She is well enough to leave here, and we may need the cot for others hurt in the earthquake," the doctor ordered.

"Surely. I'll go fetch her right away," Sarah said.

Dr. Guiles turned to Emma and said as calmly as she could, concerned about how Emma would react, "Miss Quinn, I am going to trust you. I believe you are telling me the truth as you know it. I don't understand how it can be, but the evidence is clear that something unusual is happening here. I know you have no reason to trust me, but I am asking you to. I am asking you to trust me when I tell you it is November 7, 1882. Trust me when I tell you I have never heard of 'nylon,' and I have never seen anything remotely like the things you have in your bag. Assuming we are both telling the truth, then somehow you have come from the year 2019 back to the year 1882. Is time travel possible in your time?"

Emma gaped at the doctor. If she had not felt confused or crazy before, she was feeling so now. *"What in God's name is going on?"* Emma thought. She lay there with her frozen gape for a moment. "No. No. No. No," Emma shook her head, only to stop when she found that it hurt. "No, I'm not buying any of this. What is this? Some kind of secret military experiment? Are you trying to learn what people do under impossible conditions? Do they go crazy? Do they become homicidal? Do they curl up in a ball and suck their thumb? No. This is NOT real. THIS IS NOT REAL!!"

As she feared, Emma's reaction was hysteria. Dr. Guiles realized this was not good for Emma. Not medically or otherwise. If Emma continued blurting out about how she was from the future, it could lead to all kinds of unforeseeable problems. What Emma—and the doctor herself—needed was time to sort things out and come up with a plan. The doctor rushed to her medicine bag and prepared an injection of chloral hydrate. She managed to inject Emma without assistance while Emma was consumed by her fit. Emma quickly calmed, and soon she was in a deep sleep. "Good heavens," the doctor muttered.

Dr. Alice Guiles was a physician in Manitou, and although she was fully trained, her circumstances had never required her to respond to an emergency before today. She had to admit to herself that the experience was exhilarating. But nothing in her training had prepared her for Emma, thought Alice, as she checked on the other injured people in the impromptu infirmary. Except for poor Carson, she expected all of them to make a full recovery. She had one broken arm, one sprained ankle, and half a dozen cuts and scrapes. She decided it was time to release them and make room for any more victims, including, perhaps, Emma's friends. She came to Billy

Bowman's bed. Billy had broken his left arm falling out of the loft at the livery when the earthquake caused him to lose his balance. "Hello Billy," the doctor said, "How's that arm feeling?"

"It's a bit achy, Doctor," Billy answered, looking down at the plaster cast the doctor had put on his forearm, "but I reckon I'll be okay."

"No doubt you will be perfectly fine in a few weeks. You will heal quickly. Just don't poke and prod at it, and in the meantime, try to keep it relatively clean. I've sent for your father. You may go home with him as soon as he arrives."

She was writing orders for Billy's father when Claire La Salle came up to her, touching her sleeve to get her attention. "Alice, Sarah sent for me. She said something about one of your patients needing a place to rest?" Claire was Alice's dearest friend. In Manitou, everyone was from somewhere else, the town being so new. Alice had come here from Keokuk, Iowa, where she had earned her M.D. Claire was from New Orleans. Tuberculosis, the "white plague," brought them both to Manitou. Both women had hoped to help cure the sick. Sadly, neither's hope was satisfied. Yet, had it not been for these circumstances, Alice and Claire may never have become friends.

One could hardly find two women who were more different. Alice was calm, cerebral, logical, methodical, dispassionate even. Claire was what Alice labeled a 'featherhead.' Claire violated all of Alice's cerebral rules. She fancied fortune-telling, spiritualism, and strange, witchy-voodoo things that were pure nonsense as far as Alice was concerned. But Claire was also empathetic, generous, tolerant, and open-minded—all qualities this situation called for. Alice looked up at her friend. Claire's curly light-brown hair was its usual disheveled mess, pinned more or less in a bun at the back of her head. Her dark brown eyes were large, ever so slightly too far apart, and always opened a bit too wide, making her look pleasantly surprised all the time. Her nose was short and rather rounded at the tip, but not unattractive. Her lips, full and wide, were her best feature. Claire was a mess, but Alice was very fond of her. "Yes, Claire. I'm glad you're here. You will not believe the story I have to tell you."

※

Of course, Claire had no trouble at all believing Alice's story. "Oh, this is fantastic!" Claire exclaimed. "A woman from the future? It's so exciting, Alice!"

"Yes, but it poses some problems, doesn't it? She does not believe me when I tell her it is 1882, so she is shouting out all sorts of things that will make her sound like a raving lunatic to most people. We need to get her to a safe place until we can prove to her in what time she really is. And then, we need to prepare ourselves for her reaction."

❧ CHAPTER 3 ❧

Harriet and Claire agreed to move Emma to Claire's boarding house to finish her recuperation. Emma was still very groggy from the sedative Alice had given her as they put on her strange socks and shoes, then wrapped her in a couple of wool blankets to prepare her for the walk.

"Where're you takin' me?" Emma mumbled while Alice struggled to get her shoe onto her left foot.

"We are taking you to my dear friend Claire's boarding house. You need a day or two to recover from your head injury. You will be safe and comfortable there." Alice replied.

"For heaven's sake, where is her coat, Alice?" Claire barked as she looked around Emma's cot.

"She only had that denim jacket."

"In November?"

"Who knows what the weather was like on her day in the future?"

"Oh, right."

"I d'n wanna go t' boarding houz," Emma slurred, leaning against Alice. The two women struggled to get Emma onto her feet and steady. They braced her on each side around the waist, threw her arms across their shoulders and held onto her wrist with their other hand. It was awkward, but the distance was not far—just across Cañon Avenue. The darkness offered the women cover as they guided Emma as quickly as possible to the boarding house.

"Let's put her in my bedroom," Claire said. "That way no one will see us, and we don't have to climb the stairs."

"Yes, that would be the best. You should be with her in her condition." Alice agreed.

"I'll sleep on the sofa, so I'll be here if she needs anything."

They managed to get Emma to the side entrance of Claire's boardinghouse, which led to Claire's private living area. Claire's quarters were small, comprising three rooms: a living area, Claire's bedroom, and another room where Claire did activities like reading cards and holding seances. Alice glanced with disapproval at the "reading room" as they continued to Claire's bedroom, where they guided Emma to the bed and got her settled once more. Emma fell back asleep almost at once. Fatigued from the effort, Claire and Alice looked at her with their hands on their hips, wondering what they were going to do. "Would you like a shot of whiskey, Alice?" Claire asked as she looked sideways at her friend.

"Yes, I very much would." Alice replied dryly, then heaved a deep sigh.

Alice sat across from Claire, who lounged on her pink velvet sofa, each sipping their whiskey. "Honestly, Claire, your furniture looks like it came from a brothel," Alice observed.

"That's because it did, ma chèrie, and I adore it. It came from a bordello in New Orleans. Madam Bellefleur was the madam there, and she taught me all about the occult."

Alice looked around the room she had spent so many hours in with her dear friend and had to admit it gave her a bit of a headache. The sofa was in front of the large window that faced the street, set-off on either side with end tables, each of which held a kerosene lamp. The red silk lampshades had purple tassels. In front of the sofa and chair was a simple, round mahogany occasional table under which a rug with a floral motif in shades of blue and rose covered the wooden floor. The transit windowsill above Alice's chair held various knick-knacks, including what looked to Alice like a voodoo doll. The large front window had red velvet curtains with gold fringe. The parlor stove on the far wall opposite the front window kept the room reasonably warm. Beside the stove was an armless chair, draped with a crocheted afghan in a striped pattern of blue and green. On the chair's needlepoint cushion sat Claire's cat, Lulu. "Yes, well, it has been a long day for us all," Alice said. "I must be getting home. It will likely be a long day tomorrow as well. Thank you for taking Emma in, Claire."

"Well, of course, what else could we have done?" Claire said. "How much longer do you think Emma will sleep?"

"Between the concussion and the sedative that I gave her, she should sleep through the night." Alice set her empty glass on the table and walked to the door.

"I will let you know when she is up in the morning, and maybe we can sort things out."

"Yes, please do. Goodnight," Alice said as she let herself out.

Claire took the afghan off the chair, disturbing LuLu in the process. "Sorry, love," Claire said to the cat, who looked over her shoulder at Claire, disapprovingly. Claire returned to her gaudy sofa. As she drifted off to sleep, she prayed they'd find a way to help Emma.

❋

Emma woke with what felt like the worst hang-over of her life. Her mouth was dry. Her tongue felt too thick. Her head ached. Even turning over in bed made her dizzy. She opened her eyes slowly to find the room barely lit by the early morning light. The room was small and felt even smaller because it was eclectically over-furnished. The bedframe was ornate wrought iron featuring scrolls and grape vines with large leaves. The small table beside the bed was a dark brown wicker and held several small glass bottles of perfumes, oils, and cremes. One bottle reminded Emma of the one from the TV show "I Dream of Jeannie" that she watched as a child. The lamp was stained glass—could it be a Tiffany lamp? Emma doubted it. The small wardrobe looked Spanish with its ornately carved painted doors that brightened the room with yellow, red, purple, and orange. The dressing table had an ottoman cushion of electric blue satin. A small washstand was wedged in between the dressing table and wardrobe. Emma struggled to remember how she got there. Images of darkness, a hospital cot, and a vague impression of walking in the cold flashed through her mind. She recalled the strange doctor dressed like a pioneer who said it was 1882 and felt a pang of anxiety as she remembered her friends were trapped in the cave.

Emma threw the covers off and stood up, only to sit down again as the wave of dizziness overcame her. She lowered her head, holding it in her hands. She needed her phone. She needed Paul. She needed to find out if her friends were okay. She slowly raised her head and just as slowly stood up. Well, she wasn't in the ad hoc infirmary any longer, that was clear. She was still in the clothes she was wearing when she woke there, though. Emma went to the door and opened it to find a living room decorated similarly to the bedroom, occupied by a woman lounged on a sofa, holding a calico cat.

23

"Oh, Good morning! I'm so glad you're up!" The woman said, putting down the cat and walking toward Emma, reaching out to take her hands. "My name is Claire La Salle. I'm Alice's—Dr. Guiles's that is—friend. She asked me to let you stay here while you recuperate from your head injury. I am happy to do so." Claire saw the lost, confused look on Emma's face. "Please, have a seat," she motioned to the armchair. "I imagine you have a lot of questions. I'll answer them if I can."

This was the first time Claire had really been able to see Emma. She was a striking woman. Her short, wavy hair was nearly black with just a hint of brown warmth, which contrasted dramatically with her fair skin. She was of medium height and frame, and looked quite fit. Her features were dainty and well-formed, but all paled in comparison to her eyes. She had the largest, darkest blue eyes Claire had ever seen. They hardly seemed natural.

Emma took the seat Claire offered. "I don't know what's going on. Have they found my friends? Are they okay? Has anyone called Paul, my fiancé, to let him know what's happened? Why was I sent here? I remember the doctor saying something about it being 1882, but that can't be. Is this some sort of an experiment? What the hell is going on?"

The guileless expression on Emma's face and the puzzled tone of her questions caused Claire to feel a stab of pity for the girl. She didn't know where to begin. "I have a pot of coffee here," Claire stalled. "Would you like some? How do you take it?" Claire gestured toward a porcelain pot shaped like a peacock that was sitting on the table between them.

"Yes, please, coffee would be great. I drink it black."

Claire reached for another cup and saucer from the shelf on the wall, poured the coffee, and handed it to Emma. Emma took a sip. "Thank you," she said, looking at Claire expectantly.

"Yes, well, bear with me while I take your questions in

turn." Claire began. "They were going to resume looking for your friends as soon as it became light enough, so I expect they are searching now. Alice knows you are anxious to learn that they have been found and are well, so she will send word as soon as there is news. As for Paul: I assume you are asking if anyone has telephoned him, and the answer to that is no. Was he also in Manitou?"

"No, he did not travel with me. He stayed home in Virginia."

Claire considered the implications of this. She wasn't sure how or why Emma was in this time and not her own. Were more people coming from the future? Contemplating this was more than Claire cared to deal with, so she focused on Emma. "You asked why you are here. You were in a make-shift clinic at the Cliff House dining room. Injured people were brought there after the earthquake yesterday. Dr. Guiles says that you have a concussion and need a few days to recover. The Cliff House is not prepared to keep people in their dining room for days, so we brought you here last night while you were still in a stupor from the sedation Dr. Guiles gave you." Claire paused as she thought about how to approach the matter of Emma being back in time. She silently prayed for help.

"Another reason we wanted to bring you here has to do with your last question. None of us understands any better than you do, but I swear to God and all that's holy, the year is 1882. When you discovered it last evening, you couldn't accept it and became distraught. Dr. Guiles gave you a sedative, but she feared for your safety. You were talking about things that made little sense to us. You had items in your bag that were strange. You were accusing people of experimenting on you. Alice decided the best thing would be to find a place for you that was secure and discrete until we could sort things out. So here you are."

Emma took all this in silently. Claire waited anxiously for her reaction. Would she become hysterical again? Violent? Catatonic? It was hard to guess, because Emma just sat and stared off, as though she were accessing memories in her mind. Finally Emma said, "I remember being with my friends, Andrea and Randy, touring Cave of the Winds with a guide. It was just the four of us in a chamber. A formation that the guide called 'flowstone' fascinated me, so I lagged behind as they walked on. It was then I remember hearing a low rumbling sound and feeling the ground vibrate. The next thing I remember is waking in the cave in complete darkness, cold and stiff, with this knot on my head. I couldn't find my friends, but I did find a way out of the cave, so I went for help. I remember thinking things looked different, but when I got out of the cave, I saw Pikes Peak, and that gave me my bearings." Emma paused, thinking, *"Pikes Peak is real. Pikes Peak can't be faked or manufactured to simulate another time. So, I am in a coma of some sort, dead, or I really am back in 1882."* Then, aloud to Claire, she continued, "You said there was an earthquake here yesterday?"

"Yes, it was a big one. It shook all the buildings, caused things to shake off shelves in some places and minor damage to the livery, I know. It caused some rock slides in the hills, too. A falling rock apparently killed a man named Carson White. As far as I've heard, his was the only death. The rest of the people hurt suffered relatively minor injuries, yours being perhaps the worst."

Emma continued her thoughts, frowning every so often. Claire sensed the threat of another emotional crisis had passed and relaxed a little. "My heavens, you must be famished," Claire said. "Let me fetch you some breakfast. It's usually bacon, scrambled eggs, toast with jam, and coffee. Molly cooks for us here, and she keeps it simple. After you eat, we'll see about getting you some suitable clothes."

"Yes, I am kinda hungry," Emma said absently, still deep in thought. Then her eyes came back into focus and she looked at Claire, "but I don't eat bacon, thanks."

As Emma waited, she gazed through the big front window. A man on a horse road slowly by. Emma noticed there were no electrical lines running along the dirt road. She knew the Manitou Springs of 2019 like the back of her hand, having grown up less than ten miles away in Colorado Springs. The town was littered with electrical lines. *"Am I really back in time?"* Emma thought, but the weight of the words was beyond her ability to comprehend.

Emma heard the hall door open. Claire walked in carrying a tray, which she sat down on the table. "Here you are, Emma. Please, eat," Claire said.

The food smelled wonderful to Emma, who was hungrier than she had realized. "Thank you," she said, reaching for the buttered toast. She spread the jam on heavy and took a bite. Claire had served her a large portion of scrambled eggs. She was not a big fan of eggs, but when she took a bite, she found them surprisingly good and ate them enthusiastically. She had been a strict vegetarian for several years, but once she started her career and had to travel frequently for work, she found it difficult to manage. She compromised with "no mammals," although she still felt guilty about how the food industry treated all animals. She thought vaguely about how it was probably hard to get avocados in 1882.

"I know these hills, these mountains. I grew up here." Emma took a sip of coffee to wash down the eggs. "I don't think the land can be faked," she added softly. "If I'm dreaming, I can't seem to wake." She paused again. "So for now," she looked at Claire, "I guess I have to accept what you are telling me—that I am in the year 1882."

Claire was as concerned about Emma's lack of emotion

now as she had been earlier about her potentially hysterical reaction to her situation. She studied the expression on Emma's face, hoping for some insight into what the young woman was feeling. Emma just stared into space.

"We need to get you something suitable to wear," Claire said, focusing Emma back to the present. "The clothes you have will draw attention and be hard to explain. I have a dress you can wear for now. We may need to pull it in a bit here and there, but that's not a problem." Claire went into her bedroom and came out with a dress and some undergarments. The dress was a solid, dusty rose light wool. Over a dozen little buttons led up to a high collar with ruffles of cream cotton. The cuffs of the long sleeves were similarly trimmed. The undergarments were all white cotton and consisted of a chemise, a corset, and bloomers. "I know it isn't fancy, but it is comfortable and warm," Claire said, handing the clothes to Emma. "You may use my bedroom to dress. Call out if you need me to help you."

Emma took the clothes into the bedroom and shut the door. She held up the bloomers to see how to put them on, only to discover they were open at the crotch. "What the . . .?" Emma said out loud. Why were they crotchless? It seemed out of character for Claire to have crotchless underwear, much less to lend something like that to Emma. "Claire?" Emma called.

Claire opened the door. "Yes?"

"Are you sure this is the underwear you meant to lend me?" Emma said, holding up the bloomers.

"Why yes, is there something wrong with them? They've been laundered."

"Well, uh, they don't seem to have a crotch."

"That's right. None of them do."

"Really? That's normal?"

"Yes!" Claire laughed. "How else are we to answer nature's call easily?"

Emma stared at Claire. She had no idea bloomers were normally crotchless. But now that Claire mentioned it, it would make using the bathroom easier given how cumbersome the rest of the clothing was. "Oh, sure, of course."

"Do you need anything else?" Claire asked.

"No, I think I can manage."

Emma put on the bloomers and chemise. She inspected the corset. Corsets were making a comeback in 2019, but Emma wasn't interested in following the trend. They looked like horrid things to wear. This one was no different. It laced in the back and had hooks and eyes in the front. It fit under her breasts, lifting them up in a way that rather pleased Emma, she had to admit. The corset was snug, but with a little effort, she hooked it together. She knew the back lacing could be used to pull it tighter, but she was content to wear it as loosely as possible. She pulled on the dress, which was about a size too big for her, but she decided it was comfortable as it was. She smoothed the skirt down and walked into the sitting room.

"Oh, you look fine in that dress, Emma!" Claire exclaimed. "The color suits you. But you have no shoes. Oh dear, I'm afraid all I have are some rather worn ones. I hope they fit." Claire rushed to her bedroom and came back with a pair of "granny boots," ankle high, with black lace and short, clunky heals. They were, like the dress, too big for Emma, but after she put on her socks, they fit well enough. She stood up to let Claire inspect her. "Yes, you look just fine, Emma." Claire smiled.

Shortly after Emma had dressed, a knock came to the door of Claire's private entrance. When Claire opened the door, Dr. Guiles entered quickly and before she could ask about Emma, saw her sitting there in Claire's clothes. "It's encouraging you're up and dressed. And how do you feel this morning, Emma?"

"My head still hurts, but I feel much better now that I've eaten." Emma replied.

"Well good, because we have a lot to discuss. I'm afraid things have become rather complicated."

ॐ CHAPTER 4 ॐ

"You mean more complicated than my being from the future?" Emma asked wryly.

"So, you believe it now? Well, that's progress. How did you convince her, Claire?"

"I didn't. Pikes Peak did."

"I see." Alice said, although she didn't. "Unfortunately yes, more complicated than that." Alice came in and took a seat on the sofa. "The men have come back from searching Cave of the Winds. They searched for where you found your way out and discovered a narrow hole you presumably came out of. They carefully opened the hole more so they could get anyone they found out. They searched the immediate area well, assuming you would not have been too far from your friends when the earthquake happened."

"No, I wasn't. They had walked ahead only a short distance when the collapse happened." Emma interrupted.

"Yes, they thought you all would be close together. They

looked thoroughly and found no one."

Emma's first thought was that she was glad for her friends. They apparently escaped the phenomenon that caused her to be sent back in time. But she did not know if they were safe. Were they sent to a different time, or had they been unaffected? Were they hurt? Were they alive? She may never know, and there was nothing she could do about it. She felt helpless.

"Emma, the people at Cave of the Winds say they have accounted for everyone who went into the cave yesterday. They can't explain why you are saying you were there. And there's more." Alice looked up at Claire. She hesitated to go on, knowing how much Emma was coping with.

"What? What is it, Alice?" Claire asked.

Alice let out a sigh and continued. "Mr. Millard came to me late last night, after I got home."

"Who is Mr. Millard?" Emma asked.

"He is the mortician here in town." Alice explained.

"What did he want?" asked Claire.

"He thought Carson's head injury was suspicious. There was more than one wound to his head, and Mr. Millard thought it unlikely that if the injury was caused by a falling rock, it would have resulted in repeated strikes. He came and asked me to return with him and have a closer look. When I examined Carson's head more closely, it appeared that it had been hit repeatedly—at least five times—in essentially the same place. It is suspicious. It rather looks like it was an intentional beating." Then Alice added, "I believe Carson was murdered."

"Oh, my lord, that's terrible!" Claire said, taking a seat on the chair near the stove. "Poor Carson. Who would have done such a thing?"

"Yes, that's the question, isn't it? And to further muddy the waters, when the men returned from their search, they said that the opening where Emma escaped from the cave was very near where they found Carson yesterday. It won't be long before Levi comes asking questions. Emma, we must devise a plausible story for how and why you are here. This is a very small town, and too many people know about you and your cry for help for your friends, who seem non-existent."

"And who is Levi?" Emma asked.

"Levi is the town marshal." Alice answered.

"He's also my brother-in-law," Claire added. "My departed sister Daphne's husband."

Emma again felt a wave of overwhelm. This was too much. She couldn't deal with it. She sat motionless in her chair, not knowing where to turn or what to do. She looked at Alice and said, "What am I going to do?" And then more excitedly, "Can't I just tell people the truth? They will believe me. You did, Doctor."

"Call me Alice, dear, and yes, I believed you because of the strange things you had in your bag and your matter-of-fact manner in referring to things I did not understand. But we must consider the implications of this. Time travel? What might the result be for the future if people know this is possible? Emma, do you have any insight? Do people routinely time travel in your day?"

"No, they don't. There are novels that incorporate time travel in their plots, and many movies and TV shows exist where the concept figures in. In these stories, there is always a concern that somehow the future will be altered by people coming back in time and changing the course of history. Yes, I suppose we need to think about how we proceed."

"TV? Movies?" Claire inquired.

"Oh, right, these things don't mean anything to you, yet. I guess I need to be more careful about what I say."

"Which only further supports my point. We need a story to explain Emma. Claire, could you bring us some refreshments, and we'll sort it out?"

Claire went to the kitchen for another pot of coffee and some cake. The women sat at the small table in Claire's reading room and drank and ate while plotting out a cover story for Emma. It had to be simple and hard to verify, but it had to account for Emma's presence and her claim of trapped friends.

"Okay, let me see if I've got it straight now," Claire said. "Emma is my distant cousin from New Orleans. She recently lost her family in a house fire and had no near relatives left. She telegrammed me from Denver, telling me what had happened and that she was in the area for a few days on her way further west to find work. I responded, inviting her here to stay with me and help at the boarding house, at least until she could make other plans."

"There will be questions. Who are these friends she is referring to? When did she get here? How did she get here?" Alice pointed out.

"We can use my head injury as an excuse. I traveled by train to Colorado Springs and you picked me up, Claire. I went exploring the next morning and found an entrance to the cave, so I ventured in to have a look when the earthquake happened. I suffered a head injury, and it caused trauma, confusion, and a bit of amnesia, which is now dissipating." Emma offered.

"Yes, some of that would work to help explain the reference to these 'friends,' but Claire would not have come to pick you up in Colorado Springs when the train comes all the way to Manitou now." Alice added.

"Okay, then I took the train all the way here." Emma said.

"No, no, this isn't going to work." Claire shook her head and waved her hand back and forth. "Levi would know all of this ahead of time, being my brother-in-law." She sat for a moment, thinking, and then said, "We are going to have to tell him the truth."

The three women looked at each other. "She's right." Alice concluded, then sighed. "We are going to need him on board to make this story work."

The women resigned themselves to the fact that they were going to have to trust at least one more person to the truth. It was fortunate that it was Levi. Levi Warwick had been married to Claire's sister, Daphne. They had all come to Manitou from New Orleans, seeking the cure for Daphne's tuberculosis. The fresh, dry, sunny weather and the healing properties of the mineral springs in the area were thought to help people recover from the illness. Daphne's disease had progressed too far, however, for the cure to help, and she had died the year before. But Levi and Claire had fallen in love with the natural beauty of Manitou and had decided to make it their home. As a woman and someone who dabbled in the occult, Claire enjoyed the relative tolerance of the town, especially as compared with the other places outside of New Orleans she had been in the United States. Levi took solace in the rugged outdoors, the isolation, and solitude the west provided.

"We will be able to trust him, won't we?" Emma asked.

"Levi is a bit of a stickler for truth. Frankly, he can be self-righteous. But I believe he will understand the gravity of this situation once we explain it to him." Claire answered.

"I really don't think we have a choice." Alice added.

By the time the women had devised their story, it was noon. "I have to get back to the Cliff House and see about releasing the rest of the injured. The hotel wants its dining room back as soon as possible," said Alice, taking her leave.

"Come on, Emma." Claire gathered up the dishes. "I'll show you around. I have a room you can use. It's really meant for a resident cook, but Molly lives elsewhere in town. It's small, but it's furnished and next to my reading room. I can unlock the door and you can share my quarters."

"Thank you, really," Emma responded. "I can't tell you how grateful I am for your and Alice's help. Why are you being so kind to me?"

Claire turned and looked at Emma. "Emma, I don't understand it, but you are here for a reason. God plopped you right down in my path. It's my duty to Him to do what I can for you. That is what's needed of me right now."

Claire's boarding house, rather unimaginatively called *Maison La Salle*, was on the west side of Cañon Ave. across from the Cliff House Hotel. It was a two-storied clapboard building, painted light blue with dark blue trim around the windows and gables. The four rooms and two suites on the second floor could accommodate eight residents, but Claire told Emma only five people were currently renting there. The first floor was the common area, except for Claire's private quarters and the room reserved for the cook that Emma would now use. To the left of the front hallway was a large parlor. The parlor had a sitting area featuring a long sofa in a paisley brocade of copper and brown and three green striped upholstered chairs separated by end tables with kerosene lamps. Three large windows faced the street, letting in an abundance of natural light. The middle of the room featured a heavy oak card table, behind which was a small sideboard on which sat two crystal decanters holding amber liquid. A set of matching tumblers and stemmed glasses sat beside the decanters. An upright piano stood against the wall next to an arched opening separating the parlor from the large dining room at the back of the house where all the boarders ate. A narrow passageway ran behind the staircase from the dining room to the kitchen. From the kitchen, a door led to a little fenced-in yard. Emma caught a quick glance at two structures at each back corner of the yard. At the far side of the kitchen was the door leading to the room for Emma.

It was small and simply furnished. Against the corner was

a twin bed with a plain pine headboard and quilted patchwork cover. Next to the bed was a little nightstand for a lamp. An armless chair in the corner near the foot of the bed provided a place to sit while dressing or to look out the window. Against the wall opposite the window was a small dresser, and hung on the wall next to that was a rod, presumably for hanging clothes. A washstand with a plain white porcelain washbasin and water pitcher stood on the other side of the dresser. A second door led to Claire's reading room. The best thing about the room was its proximity to the kitchen, which provided warmth.

"I know it isn't much, but I think you will be comfortable here, at least for a while." Claire said.

"It's perfect." Emma said. She was just relieved that she didn't have to worry about food and shelter immediately. She would, however, need to find a way to earn her keep as soon as possible. She was not accustomed to depending on anyone, and she wasn't planning to start now. "If you don't mind, Claire, I'd like to rest for a while."

"Of course! I imagine you are still not feeling yourself. I'll just leave you here. I will unlock the door to my quarters. Feel free to come in when you are ready."

"Thanks. I really do appreciate all you are doing for me."

৵ CHAPTER 5 ৵

Emma lay on the bed and stared at the ceiling, glad to be alone. She ran through all that had happened and still found it hard to understand, let alone accept. How had this happened? Was it real? For now, she would have to act as though it was—real or not. What alternative did she have? If she was right about how she came to be back in 1882, then she did not see a way to reverse the event. The unique and random conditions that seemed to have caused her unintentional time travel—two earthquakes happening at the same place but at different times—could hardly be replicated. For all she knew, the phases of the moon and position of the stars factored in, too. Even if she knew the cocktail of electromagnetic fields, frequencies, and who knows how many other variables that resulted in her displacement, the technology to recreate them was not available. It became clear to Emma that she was stuck where she was.

She thought about Paul, and tears welled up in her eyes.

What was happening on his end? She must be missing in 2019, or did she somehow splinter off, leaving half of herself there to continue on? Part of her hoped so, that she and Paul would have a happy life together. Emma looked down at her finger and saw the ring Paul had given her. She thought it was unlikely that she would be living in two different times. As the tears rolled down the sides of her face, she ached at the thought that she would never see him again, that they would never hold one another again, make love again. She wept, the grief becoming real. It didn't matter that the weeping was making her head hurt again. She couldn't control it; she didn't care to.

❀

Emma heard a knock on the door to Claire's quarters. It took her a moment after she opened her eyes to remember where she was. She must have cried herself to sleep. "Yes?" Emma answered.

"Emma, dear, Alice and Levi are here," Emma heard Claire's voice through the door. "Levi would like to talk to you. Do you think you can speak with him?"

Emma considered saying no, but that would only delay the inevitable. She would have to face things sooner or later. "Yes, I suppose so. I'll be right out." Emma first went to the kitchen, where a hand pump at the sink provided her with cool water to splash on her face. She knew her eyes were puffy and swollen from crying. She was an ugly crier. Maybe that would afford her some sympathy, she thought, as she walked back through her room and into Claire's sitting room.

Claire looked sympathetically at Emma. "Emma, let me introduce you to Levi Warwick, the marshal here in Manitou. Levi, this is Emma Quinn."

The man standing before Emma made a little bow with his

head. "I'm pleased to meet you, Miss Quinn," he said, holding his bowler hat between his hands. Levi appeared to be in his early or mid-thirties. He was just over six feet tall and solidly built. He had a closely cut beard that revealed a well-defined chin and jaw. His eyes were brown, and he had thick, long eyelashes, giving his eyes a deer-like appearance. He was very handsome, but Emma barely noticed in her present state.

"Thank you, likewise," she said.

"If you don't mind, could we sit down? I have some questions to ask you," Levi said as he gestured toward the sitting area.

"Sure."

Everyone, Alice and Claire included, found a seat. Emma felt their solidarity with her as she situated herself in the armchair.

"Alice and Claire have been filling me in on how you arrived here yesterday," Levi continued. "It's quite a story. Forgive me if I'm finding it hard to believe."

"Yes, it does seem far-fetched," Emma agreed, "I'm having trouble believing it myself."

"Do you have any proof that you are from the future?" Levi asked.

"Show him, Emma. Show him those things in your bag," Alice interjected.

"Claire, I think I left my bag in your bedroom. May I go get it?" Emma said.

"Yes, of course."

Emma returned with her backpack. She opened it and retrieved her cell phone and battery pack. Levi watched with wonder while she turned on the battery pack and then the phone.

"May I see that?" Levi asked in wonder.

Emma handed it to him. He saw the same image of Garden

of the Gods that Alice had seen the day before. But the message on the phone said, "Swipe up to unlock."

"How do you unlock it?" Levi said.

"Here, give it to me. I need to show it my face."

Levi handed the phone back to Emma, who held it in front of her face, unlocking it. She then handed it back to Levi, who took it and inspected it again, dumbfounded. "What does this do?"

"It does all kinds of things. It has completely changed the world. I'm not sure how much I should tell you, honestly, about what it is capable of. Maybe if I just show you some of what it can do, it would convince you I am from another age." Emma reached for the phone. She lifted it up and pointed it at them and said, "Say something, Claire."

"Say something? What? What should I say?'

"That's good enough." Emma lowered the phone. Levi, Claire, and Alice gathered around her to see the device. Emma hit another button, and they could see Claire standing next to Alice and Levi. They could see themselves move and hear Claire's voice. They were all stupefied. "Here, I'll show you some pictures." Emma opened her photos, which showed thumbnail images of her pictures. She had hundreds, maybe thousands, but she showed them only the most recent ones. "See. I took these yesterday, as we were beginning our tour of the cave. This is a selfie with me and my friends Andrea and Randy. They are—well, they were—to be my maids of honor at my wedding." She opened a picture of herself and two other young women smiling broadly, one holding up a peace sign. She felt a sharp pang in her chest. "And this one is Paul, my fiancé." She swiped right and showed a selfie of her and Paul taken just before she left for her trip. She felt herself growing more upset. "And here's a picture of the breakfast Paul made for me before I left for Colorado," at which point Emma broke down again into tears.

"Now, now," Claire said, putting her arms around Emma. "I know it's terribly difficult. Levi," she said more harshly to her brother-in-law, "Can't you see how hard this is for Emma. Is it really necessary to put her through this right now?"

Levi sat, stunned at what Emma had just shown them, trying to make sense of it. He could not find an explanation for what he had seen. As unbelievable as it was, for now he would accept that she was telling the truth. He answered, "Yes, I can see how it is difficult, and I am sorry, I truly am. Please don't think I'm being an ass, Claire, but a man has been killed. From the future or not, she was in the same area at approximately the same time as the victim when he was killed. I must question her."

"Oh, an ass is the least of the things you are, Levi!" Claire exclaimed.

"It's okay," Emma said, wiping her eyes. "Aside from being from the future, I have nothing to hide."

Levi handed her his handkerchief. Emma thought, *"Really? Men really carry handkerchiefs and hand them to weeping women in the nineteenth century?"*

"Thank you, Miss Quinn," Levi continued. "Now, immediately after you made your way out of the cave, did you see anyone?"

"No, and I was looking because I wanted to find help for my friends, who I thought were still in the cave. I didn't see anyone until I entered the lobby of that hotel."

"She went to the Cliff House, Levi," Alice clarified. "Zack and one of the other workers brought her to the dining room, where we had set up an area to tend to the injured. She had fallen unconscious. I determined she had a concussion."

"Then is it possible she saw something and has forgotten?" Levi asked.

"It's possible, but not likely given that she generally

remembers what happened."

Levi turned back to Emma. "Is there anything you saw or heard that might be relevant?"

"No, nothing."

"This is ridiculous, Levi. Think about it. Why would a woman, thrown back in time through some random natural phenomenon, fight her way out of a cave, wounded, and kill the first person she sees? What would her motive be? She needed help for God's sake," Alice argued.

"Calm down, Alice," Levi said, "I agree Emma is highly unlikely as our murderer. I just wanted to make sure she didn't have important relevant information." He stood up, reached for his hat, and said, "I will leave you now. Thank you, Miss Quinn, for answering my questions. I know you are having a difficult time, and for that I am sorry."

"And you agree to keep Emma's secret? To go along with our story?" Claire asked Levi.

"For now, yes," he answered and then quietly showed himself out.

The women looked at each other, wondering for how long they had won Levi's loyalty in maintaining the story. "We can count on him to keep your secret," Claire asserted.

"You mean until he is given a reason not to," Emma said, "He did not seem too happy about it."

"It's a shock for him, too. He needs a little time for it all to sink in. Once he thinks about it and realized the consequences of having it become common knowledge that you are from the future, he will be as committed as we are to keeping this secret. He is a man of high integrity, and he takes his oath to protect seriously," Claire said.

"Yes, I agree. He will come around," Alice added, "Now, if you don't mind Emma, I'd like to examine your injuries and change your bandages. Then I'm needed at the coroner's inquest."

Emma and Alice went into Emma's room, leaving Claire alone in her parlor thinking of Levi's reaction. She was very fond of Levi. He had been the best husband to her sister anyone could expect. He was a man of duty, and when Daphne became ill, he did not hesitate to move them to this place where the doctors said she had the best chance at recovery. Daphne was Claire's younger sister by four years. Their parents had died two years before their relocation to Manitou from the yellow fever that went through New Orleans, leaving the sisters with a modest income. Claire had decided to come along with Levi and Daphne. She had her reasons.

※

"Sit still, Emma," Alice commanded.

"I'm sorry, I'm just feeling so restless." Emma replied, "I don't know what to do. I can't believe what is happening to me. What will I do? I have no one, nothing. Everyone and everything I've ever known, everything I've ever worked for, all my plans and dreams—they are all gone, all at once. It's like I've died, Alice, but I'm still here. I wish I had died. It would have been better."

"Nonsense," Alice said as she put some kind of ointment on Emma's abrasions and wrapped new gauze around her forearms. "I understand that this is a tragedy for you. You have every right to be in shock and to grieve. But you must also have faith, my dear. You are NOT dead, so all is not lost."

Alice sounded like Emma's grandmother, Emma thought, ruefully. Emma's maternal family was from Wyoming, and they took life as it came, stoically. She remembered the time her grandmother said, "Dying's not the worst thing that can happen to you," as they sat by her grandfather who was in a coma,

44

wasting away with only days to live, Emma now agreed. Dying wasn't the worst thing. This was worse.

"The knot on your head is smaller. You will be as good as new in a few days, Emma." Alice closed her medical bag. Emma just stared at the wall. Alice could think of nothing else useful to say, so she quietly left.

A few moments later, Emma came out of her daze. Feeling at a loss what to do with herself, she decided she needed some fresh air. She walked through the kitchen and was standing beside the stairs that led to the second floor when she heard voices coming out of the large common parlor.

"I was sorry to hear about Carson, Josiah, but now that the election is over, and it looks as though our people will prevail, our project can go forward. I hope you'll carry on with the plans," she heard a male voice say.

"Thank you. Carson was a good friend and partner. Of course, I will complete the project as planned, Mr. Albright," the other man, presumably Josiah, responded.

"Good, then take this as a down-payment. There will be more to follow as the project progresses."

Emma ducked back into the kitchen to avoid being seen. She peeked around the corner and saw a man, nicely dressed, walk out the front door. She didn't see his face, but he appeared to be in his fifties, if not older, tall and broad. The other man, who was about her age, walked up the stairs. She heard his footsteps come to a stop as a door opened and closed on the second floor. It seemed someone named Josiah lived in Claire's boardinghouse and had worked with Carson White.

Emma went back through the kitchen into the small yard. It was mostly dirt and rocks, but sparse dead weeds crunched under her feet as she walked. A small flock of hens pecked at the ground around Emma's feet, herded by a rooster prancing around proudly. The coop where they lived was off to the right

45

of the yard while the outhouse was off to the left. Emma wrinkled her nose at the resulting combination of smells. No wonder the eggs were so good, though. These hens probably had laid the ones she had for breakfast that same morning. She looked up and saw a clear, blue sky. *"What am I going to do?"* she thought. She stood for a moment as though waiting for an answer, but not getting one, turned and walked back into the kitchen.

"Oh, hello! May I help you?" said a short, matronly woman as she put wood into the stove.

"Nnno," Emma stammered an answer, then collected herself and added, "I'm Claire's cousin, Emma, from New Orleans. I've only just arrived to stay with Claire for a while." Emma hoped she was convincing.

"I see. Well, I'm pleased to meet you, Miss. I'm Molly, the cook. I knew Claire had a guest at breakfast. She didn't say who." Molly looked at Emma and her bandages inquisitively, but Emma thought the least said the better.

"I was just passing through to my room," Emma gestured to the door as she awkwardly walked by Molly. Once in her room, she leaned against the door and let out a deep breath. It was going to be tough passing herself off as Claire's cousin, a woman from the nineteenth century.

Emma paced around her room like a caged animal, restless and helpless. She sat on the bed and looked out the small window. She stood again and opened each drawer of the dresser, just for something to do. They were all empty. She went to her backpack and retrieved her phone, unlocked it, and scanned through her pictures. She saw pictures of her friends in Virginia during the Memorial Day cook-out. She saw a picture she had taken last Christmas of her mother, grandmother, and uncle in the living room of her grandmother's house in Colorado Springs, next to the Christmas tree they had just decorated. She saw the photo she had taken of her cats, surrounding Paul on his recliner, a wide grin on his face. They were all out of reach to her now, and she sobbed. She sobbed the way she had sobbed when she lost her beloved dog when she was fourteen. She sobbed the way she had when her grandfather died.

Molly heard the sobbing and stopped chopping vegetables. Who was this girl, Emma? What was her story?

❧ CHAPTER 6 ❧

When Emma had once again cried herself out, she ventured into Claire's sitting room. She found Claire there, crocheting a doily, her cat Lulu sitting next to her on the pink velvet sofa. Emma came over and pet Lulu, who pushed against Emma's hand and slowly closed her eyes with pleasure. Claire put down her needlework. "I've invited Alice and Levi to join us for dinner. We can eat in my reading room. I thought we all should get better acquainted."

"Yes, I suppose we should," Emma said absently as she continued to pet Lulu.

"She likes you. She doesn't like many people."

"I love animals," Emma murmured. The cat was the most familiar thing she'd experienced since she woke in the cave. The cat began purring loudly.

Claire felt a tug of empathy for Emma. She longed to comfort her, but didn't know how best to do it. Just then there was a knock at the door. Claire opened the door while Lulu ran for her bedroom. "Good evening, Levi," she greeted her brother-in-law.

"Good evening, dear," he said, walking through the door and giving Claire a quick peck on the cheek. "Good evening Miss Quinn," Levi nodded toward Emma. He could see that she had been crying. Her eyes were swollen, but that did not hide their striking deep blue color. It was no wonder Emma was grieving. Levi knew something about grief himself. Even though he had lost the thing most dear to him, he had not lost *everything* dear to him. Emma had, and he could not imagine that.

"Please, call me Emma. We are supposed to be family of sorts, right?" Emma said softly.

"Quite right, Emma, and you should call me Levi." Then turning back to Claire, Levi added, "I saw Alice not far behind me," at which point Alice whisked through the door and plopped down on the armchair.

"Honestly, Levi, I am quite exhausted trying to catch up to you."

Claire laughed at her friend, "I'll let Molly know we are ready for dinner. Go ahead and have a seat at the reading room table." She walked to the kitchen as the rest of the party gathered around the table. Shortly, Claire and Molly returned with the plates already filled with the simple meal Molly had prepared. Claire took her seat and said a brief prayer of gratitude.

After dinner, the four gathered in the sitting room, enjoying a cup of coffee. Emma found the boiled brew rather strong and did not care for the grounds she kept feeling in her mouth, but she was grateful for coffee—it felt normal.

"How did the inquest go?" Claire asked Levi.

"Straight-forward, really." He said. "Once Alice gave her testimony, and the jury had a look at poor Carson, the verdict was that the manner of death was head trauma from repeated strikes from a blunt object—most likely the rock found near his body—from person or persons unknown. In short, homicide. So I now have an official investigation on my hands. It's going to be difficult given the lack of witnesses and the chaos going on because of the earthquake."

"It seems like a crime of opportunity to me," Emma said. "If the weapon was the rock, it is unlikely that the murder was planned. It is more likely that whoever did it decided on the spot. Something must have triggered them. Did Carson have enemies that you know of?"

Claire, Alice, and Levi looked at each other, surprised at Emma's assertiveness. She had been so quiet and reserved at dinner. "Yes, that does seem the likely case," Levi said, "as far as I know, though, Carson was well regarded by all who knew him. He was a landscape architect. He and his partner, Josiah Turner, have been working on the plans for a modern new bath house and park over by Navajo Spring. The developer, Frederick Albright, hired them for the job."

"Is Fredrick Albright a large, tall man?" Emma asked.

"Yes." Levi answered.

"And Josiah is a boarder here, isn't he, Claire?"

"Yes, but how did you know?" Claire asked

"I overheard them talking in the parlor this morning. It sounded like Albright was optimistic that the project could go on now that the election was over, and he wanted an assurance from Josiah that the plan would go forward despite Carson's death." Emma added, "Albright gave Josiah an initial payment with promises of more to follow as he made progress. Have you done a victimology on Carson yet?" Emma asked Levi.

"Victimology? I am not familiar with that word." Levi replied.

"It is when you investigate the victim to discover who and what their family, associates, business dealings, and so forth are to get a picture of who would want to kill them and why." Emma explained, eagerly. "For example, if it was an opportunistic killing, triggered by a strong emotion, then Carson probably knew the person who killed him—possibly well. So, whom did he know who could have been with him at the time? I would start with his family, then friends, then associates—work my way from those who were closest to Carson to those less close. They call it 'circles of acquaintances.'"

Again, Levi, Claire, and Alice looked at each other, not knowing what to make of Emma's apparent understanding of how to go about a murder investigation. "And how to do you know so much about this subject, Emma?" Alice asked.

"Well, I watch . . . I mean I've read a lot of books on it." Emma corrected herself before mentioning television. She did not want to explain how many hours of true crime television shows she had watched in her life. She did not want to explain television.

"They write a lot about this in the future?" Alice continued.

"Yes, quite a lot," that, at least, was true.

"Very interesting," Levi said. "That begs the general question, who is Emma Quinn, really? I am curious to know more about you, Emma." Levi gazed steadily at her, waiting for her response.

Emma took a deep breath. How did she even begin to describe her life without overwhelming them? In any given day of 2019, she was exposed to more information than they were in an entire year, maybe ten. She had the Internet, for heaven's sake—nearly all the world's knowledge at her fingertips. She had a Twitter, Instagram, and Facebook account that she monitored every day. And yes, compared to people in the nineteenth century, she was an expert in criminal investigation. Unfortunately, most of the technology that enabled it wasn't yet developed.

"I was born in Colorado Springs in 1992. I went to college and studied engineering at the University of Colorado, Boulder. I work in Reston, Virginia, near Washington, D.C., for a company that develops systems for the United States military. I read a lot, including books on solving true crime. It's a genre, 'true crime.'" Then, her voice fading, "and I am engaged to be married in a few months to Paul."

Again, Claire, Alice, and Levi shared more disbelieving stares. It was Alice who collected herself first, saying thoughtfully, "Levi, perhaps Emma could be of value to you in your investigation."

"I don't see how. No one knows her, and she's a woman." Levi said bluntly, taking a sip of his coffee.

"Oh Levi, use your imagination," Claire chimed in. "She may not be able to do the footwork, but she may be able to advise you. You aren't too proud to allow a woman to do that, are you?"

"It's not a matter of pride, Claire, it's a matter of fact. It is not proper." Levi held Claire's stare.

"It's okay, Claire. Levi is right," Emma interjected. "I am not part of law enforcement even in my day, much less in this one." Emma, resuming her reserved demeanor, added, "I'm feeling tired. If you don't mind, I will excuse myself for the night." She stood up and quietly left the room.

Claire and Alice both gave Levy a look to kill. "What?' he said defensively.

"You can be a stupid, insensitive lout sometimes, Levi Warwick." Claire scolded.

"Well, that's rather harsh, Claire," Levi defended himself, "I was merely being truthful."

"Emma is clearly an intelligent woman," Alice said, "We can't imagine what she might know that could be helpful in conducting your investigation, Levi, but that's not even the point. She has nothing, no one. She needs something to do—to help her adjust."

Levi sighed. "Something tells me Miss Quinn is going to be the bane of my existence."

❧ CHAPTER 7 ❧

Levi woke at dawn the next morning, and the first thing he thought of was Emma. Well, not Emma exactly, but her eyes—so remarkably blue. He also thought she had made an excellent point about how to proceed with the murder investigation. He did not know a lot about Carson, but he did know Carson lived with his brother, Thomas. He also knew that he was partnered with Josiah Turner, another landscape architect who rented room and board from Claire. He decided to start with Thomas.

Thomas White, known in town as Tommy, was the head chef at the Cliff House. The Cliff House was one of five large, modern hotels in Manitou. General William Palmer and Dr. William Bell founded the Colorado Springs Company in 1871, foreseeing the opportunity that the expanding rail road infrastructure afforded, and began developing Manitou into a world-class resort town. It was their plan to exploit the mountain scenery, featuring Pikes Peak and the various mineral springs clustered at the base of Williams Cañon, to entice tourists from the east. The Cliff House was the second major hotel built to accommodate all the visitors the town had quickly attracted. Levi found Tommy in the kitchen, directing the activities of the staff.

Tommy was Carson's younger brother by less than two years. They looked strikingly similar, each having straight hair the color of wet sand, a rounded nose, and light blue opaque eyes. Each had a jaw that was rather weak, resulting in an egg-shaped head. The most noticeable difference was their height. Carson was a few inches shorter than Tommy's six feet. "Tommy?" Levi said to get his attention. Tommy stopped instructing the staff and looked at Levi. "Hello Marshal. I expected you would be around soon."

"I am sorry about Carson," Levi extended his hand to offer his condolences. "He was a fine man, truly . . . and I am sorry to interrupt you, but could I have a word?"

"Thank you," Tommy said, shaking Levi's hand. "There's an office we can use just outside the kitchen. Follow me." Tommy led Levi to a small office with a simple oak desk and chair. Opposite the desk, there was an even simpler pine chair. Tommy sat at the desk. "Please, sit, Marshal."

Levi and Tommy were acquainted, as were most residents of Manitou, but did not know each other well. Levi was happy to have Tommy address him as Marshal, especially given the reason for his visit. The authority of the title would make the discussion easier.

"I imagine it is even more difficult for you now that Carson's death has been ruled a homicide. Do you know of anyone who would want to harm him this way?"

"No, Marshal. That Carson was murdered comes as the biggest shock of my life. I thought everyone held him in the highest esteem, as I did." Levi saw Tommy clenching his teeth, his jaw muscles contracting each time.

"Well then, if you don't mind, I'd like to know who his closest friends and associates were. His manner of death indicates he was likely killed by someone he knew."

"I have been wracking my brains asking myself who would have done this to Carson. I've never known a less offensive person in my life. His integrity and honesty were always a model to me." Tommy looked down at his hands folded in front of him on the desk. Levi waited patiently, and when Tommy remained silent in his thoughts, he pressed on.

"Yes, well, perhaps if you could simply go through those who knew him, it would be a place to start," Levi prodded gently.

"There's Josiah Turner, of course. Josiah is Carson's business partner. They have not been working together very long, really. Mr. Albright hired them to plan and build the park area around the new bath house. Carson trained with Frederick Olmsted's firm in New York City—that's where we came from— and Josiah had come from Chicago. He had worked with John Blair there before Blair came to Colorado Springs. Blair was aware of Carson's work through his association with Olmsted and he thought Carson and Josiah were both talented and complimentary in their skills. He encouraged them to submit a plan to Albright for the bath house project to launch their landscape architecture firm. When Albright selected their design, they moved here to finish the details with the building architect and oversee the project once it is underway."

"Yes, I heard about the bath house project. It sounds like a major undertaking. How long have you and Carson been in town, then?"

"We've been here about six months. We are sharing a little house on Manitou Avenue. I was fortunate enough to get my chef training from the great Charles Ranhofer of Delmonico's in

New York City. When Carson had the opportunity to come to this new resort town in the west, I decided it was an opportunity for me as well. I had a dream of having my own restaurant, but . . . well, things are complicated in New York. I thought my chances would be better here, and Carson welcomed the idea of us coming together. We have always been close. The Cliff House eagerly hired me when they learned of my credentials. They wish to outshine all other hotels in Manitou, and I aim to help them."

"Yes, 'The Saratoga of the West,' as they call Manitou," Levi reflected.

"Oh, believe me, Manitou outshines Saratoga as far as its natural beauty and mineral springs go. Coming out here was the best decision I have ever made. The opportunity is endless. All that's needed is a bit of capital."

"Was Carson interested in helping fund your aspirations to have your own restaurant?"

"Not specifically. I am saving for it, and we both stand to inherit a bit from our father that will help, too."

"It's unfortunate to have to lose your father to fund your dream."

"It is unfortunate, I agree. My father has not been well this last year, and I am not sure how much longer we will have him with us."

"And he is still in New York City?"

"Yes, he was too unwell and not at all interested in joining us here. Our older married sister is still there and looks after him."

"Is there anyone else you know of who knew Carson well?"

"Anna Calhoun, of course."

"Anna Calhoun, the banker John Calhoun's daughter?"

"Yes. She and Carson had recently become engaged, although no announcement has been made. I think it is general knowledge, though."

Levi felt embarrassed that he was not aware of this. As marshal, he probably should be more attuned to the social news than he was. He preferred his own company and considered discussing the business of others mostly gossip, which he avoided. "That seems a rather quick courtship." He observed.

"They took an immediate liking to each other. I don't know that it was love at first sight, but it was close. I know Carson was smitten the first time he met her."

"Had they set a date for the wedding?"

"No. I think that is why they had not announced it yet. Carson wanted to get the bath house project done. It would help fund his new family and also launch his business. I think Anna understood and agreed with Carson. I do think it was to be in the late summer, as soon as possible after the bath house opened."

"I see. That seems entirely sensible," Levi commented. "Can you think of others close to Carson?"

"We've been here such a short time. Other than myself and Josiah, whom Carson liked very well, he had no real friends here. He worked closely with Mr. Albright, of course, and the architect Mr. Ellis, but as far as I know, those were strictly business relationships."

"What did Carson do in his free time?"

"Well, he spent most of it with Anna, frankly. He occasionally played billiards. He also enjoyed exploring the area. He was always walking in the hills, convinced he would find yet another wonder, like a yet undiscovered spring or another cave! I hoped he would discover gold," he added with mild amusement, "But his focus was more on the natural beauty. He had quite fallen in love with it here."

Levi thought about the solace that the mountains, rock formations, and clear, blue skies had given him since he lost his beloved Daphne and felt a camaraderie with Carson. He wished he had known the man.

"Tommy, it is my duty to ask you where were you the day Carson was killed, around the time just before the earthquake?"

"I was here at the hotel in the wine cellar doing inventory."

"Was anyone working with you? Can anyone verify your activities?"

"I was working alone that afternoon. It was known we needed to get an order in by the end of this week if we were to have it by Thanksgiving. I telephoned the order to our agent in Colorado Springs yesterday. We are expecting a full house for Thanksgiving. I was looking forward to it as a festive start to the holiday season, but now . . ." Tommy's voice faded and his gaze turned inward. He took a deep breath and added, "I hope I've answered your questions, Marshal. I must get back to the kitchen now, if you don't mind."

"Of course, thank you for your time and help."

Levi left the hotel through the front entrance, which faced southwest. He could see snow-covered Pikes Peak behind rugged foothills of red rocks, dotted with pine trees. It was a brisk morning, with a light breeze that ebbed and flowed like the tide. The sky was pale blue behind bright clouds that were reflecting the morning sun in shades of yellow and pink. It promised to be another one of the beautiful days that caused Levi to make Manitou his home. *"Oh Daphne, it is so beautiful here today, my love,"* He thought. He took another moment to appreciate the day, then turned and walked down the steps with purpose.

Manitou was a small town with about 450 permanent residents, or at least residents that were not tourists. Many were transient and would come and go with the tourist season because Manitou was strictly a tourist town. Most industry and commercial business were in the larger nearby town of

Colorado Springs. One did not need a horse or carriage in Manitou because everything was within an easy walk. Colorado Springs was five miles away, but now that the Denver and Rio Grande railroad had built the spur between Colorado Springs and Manitou, one did not need a horse or carriage to get there, either. Levi planned to take the next train into Colorado Springs to visit the office of the bath house architect, Mr. Ellis. Josiah Turner also worked out of that office, and Levi preferred to interview him there rather than at their shared boarding house residence. He had some time to kill before the next train, so he stopped at the billiards hall. If Carson enjoyed playing billiards, Levi might learn something there.

Frank Bowman was the proprietor at the ten pins and billiards hall next to the Manitou House Hotel. It was one of two such establishments in town, but the only one open in November. Levi found Frank wiping down the bar at the back of the hall. He had always liked the proprietor, despite the frequent number of times he had had to keep him in the town jail cell for the night due to too much drink. Frank had a poet's spirit that contrasted with his rough looks. He was a tall, slender man with unruly salt-and-pepper hair and a thick mustache that balanced out his bushy dark eye-brows. His straight back and nimble body reflected a level of health and vigor that his weathered, lined face defied. He and Levi had one thing in common: both had lost their wives to tuberculosis. In Frank's case, he had been left with his son, Billy, to raise alone.

"Good morning, Frank," Levi said cheerfully as he walked to the back of the hall, "how is Billy's arm doing? Healing well, I hope."

"Well, howdy, Levi. Good to see ya this mornin'. Billy's doin' fine, but he don't know it. He's complainin' like he'd lost the dang arm." Frank picked up a glass from beside the sink and wiped it clean of spots before placing it on the shelf.

Levi smiled and let out a little laugh, "I can only imagine that he is milking his infirmary for all it's worth to avoid doing any hard work at the livery."

"I believe you've hit the nail right square on the head there," Frank agreed as both men laughed. "To what do I owe the pleasure of your company this fine mornin'?"

Levi pulled up a stool and sat down. "I suppose you've heard about Carson White?" he began.

"Yes, it's a shocker. Who would want to hurt Carson? I never met a nicer fella."

"Well, Frank, that's what I am trying to find out." Levi surveyed the billiard hall. The late-morning sun cast bands of light through the windows, making the floating dust in the air sparkle. "I understand Carson enjoyed billiards. Did he come in often?" Levi turned his gaze back to Frank.

"Not as much lately, but when he first came to town, he was in here two or three times a week." Frank put another glass on the shelf. "Once he and Anna started courting, though, I saw less and less of him." Frank stopped his work, threw his rag over his shoulder and leaned against the bar with both palms. "I guess that's to be expected."

"When was the last time you saw him here?" Levi reached for a toothpick from the shot glass container on the bar.

"Well, let's see," Frank stopped and thought, "I guess it would have been last Friday. He came in after supper time with Josiah."

"Did anything noteworthy happen, do you recall?"

"I don't know about noteworthy, but they'd been here a coupl'o hours when John Calhoun came in lookin' for Carson."

"John Calhoun? Anna's father?"

"No, John junior, Anna's brother."

"Do you know what he wanted?"

"No, but I noticed they seemed to be disagreein' about

61

somethin'. I couldn't hear what they were sayin' but their arms were wavin' and they were pretty animated. At one point, Josiah stepped in between 'em, seemin' to try to settle things down. John left in a huff, and shortly afterward, both Carson and Josiah left. It really didn't seem like much at the time."

"I see." Levi pictured John Calhoun, Jr. He would have to add him to the list of people to talk to. "And aside from that, do you know of anyone who had a bone to pick with Carson?"

"Not at all. Like I said, he's one of the nicest fellas I ever knew. He was an ace billiard's player and could have easily hustled anyone who came in, but he didn't. He just played his game straight-up. I don't know of anyone who felt different about him."

"Well, thanks for your time, Frank," Levi stood up and picked his hat off the bar, placing it on his head, "and tell Billy to stop sand-bagging!"

Frank laughed. "Sure thing, Levi."

Levi walked out of the darkness of the billiard hall into the bright day. His eyes stung from the sun and the dry, cold breeze coming up the valley towards the canyons. The warmth of the sunlight penetrated Levi's black wool coat, warming him even as the breeze chilled his face. He could see the train depot on the other side of Manitou Avenue. The late morning train from Colorado Springs was just coming to a stop, bringing in supplies and winter visitors, the lifeblood of the town. Fewer visitors came in the winter, but the relatively mild climate and unsurpassed natural beauty of the area still attracted hundreds of tourists, even this time of year. Manitou had an image as a high-end resort to protect. Murder simply would not do, especially an unsolved murder. Levi felt the pressure mound in his chest. He had to find Carson's killer—and soon.

ᐔ CHAPTER 8 ᐕ

The five-mile railroad spur between Manitou and Colorado Springs took about twenty minutes to travel. It would have been a shorter trip if the train did not stop in Colorado City. Levi wished it didn't, not because of the travel time it consumed, but because Colorado City was the exact opposite kind of town from what Manitou aspired to be. Colorado City was flavored by its roots as a gateway to the mining towns, complete with rowdy saloons, gambling houses, and brothels. The clientele Colorado City attracted were, well, low-brow, compared with the relatively affluent members of society Manitou appealed to—or wanted to. Levi sat quietly in his seat, looking forward to avoid eye-contact, as the passengers from Colorado City boarded. A townsman wearing a well-worn Stetson sat down beside Levi, removing his hat to display his greasy fine hair, lightly salted with gray. He smelled of stale tobacco and whiskey, probably from the night before. Levi's body tensed as his fellow passenger settled in.

"Howdy, Marsal," the man said, glancing uneasily at Levi's badge.

"Howdy." Levi replied without looking at the man. Both men seemed content to stop the conversation there.

Levi was glad for the fresh air provided by the short walk from the Colorado Springs train depot to Mr. Ellis's office on Pikes Peak Ave. *Mr. W. F. Ellis, Jr., Architect and Civil Engineer* was etched on a brass plate on the door leading to the staircase to his second-floor office. At the top of the stairs was a second door with a glass panel, on which was painted the same declaration. Levi glanced inside, seeing a young man bent over a drafting table. He turned the handle and walked in.

The man looked up at Levi and gently placed his drafting pencil against the lip of the table. If it hadn't been for the man's short-cropped full beard and bushy mustache, Levi would have taken him for a youth not more than nineteen. But Levi knew Josiah was closer to thirty. "I was wondering when you'd be by," Josiah said calmly.

❁

Emma woke to the sound of birds chirping. The familiar sound was comforting until she opened her eyes and remembered where she was . . . and when. She lifted her head off the soft feather pillow and was pleased that it did not immediately throb, although when she touched the wound, it was still sore. She needed to use the outhouse, but she was warm under the blankets and dreaded the ordeal of preparing for the task. Still, she would rather do that than use the pot under the bed. She heard a loud bang from the kitchen and smiled to herself when a woman's voice muttered an expletive she couldn't quite make out. Reluctantly, Emma rose from bed and changed into the dress Claire had given her as quickly as she could, motivated by the cold and the urgency of nature's call. She gently opened the door to the kitchen and peeked out to see if the coast was clear. Molly was standing at the sink, wringing out a large rag. The movement of the door caught her eye.

"Good morning, Miss Quinn," Molly said cheerfully, "you're up early. I hope I didn't wake ya with all that racket I made. That pot of water just slipped right out o' my hands. Now there's water everywhere."

Emma saw the pot sitting on the big pine table and a pool of water on the floor. "I was already awake. Please, call me Emma." Emma walked through the door. "I just need to dash to the outhouse. I can help you clean up afterwards."

Molly turned back to the puddle. "This? I can manage this." She said as she dropped the rag to the floor and stepped on it with her foot to blot up the water. "Breakfast will be ready soon. Will you be joining us in the dining room this morning?"

"I suppose so, if that's where Claire will be eating." Emma answered vaguely, walking carefully around Molly and the mess.

"She usually eats with the boarders. She says the more folks feel like family, the more likely they are to stay."

"Yes, that's probably true," Emma agreed as she made her way by Molly and rushed out of the kitchen.

"Ugh, I have got to get my act together," thought Emma as she made her way back from the outhouse. *"I can't avoid people forever. I have to get comfortable with my cover story. I just need a little more time."* She took a deep breath and stepped back into the kitchen. Molly was rolling biscuit dough out on the table. The wood in the stove burned strongly, heating the room as well as the oven. Emma felt a rush of panic, not knowing what to do or how to act. "I really am not feeling well, Molly. I think I'll have my breakfast in Claire's rooms after all, if you don't mind."

65

"Of course. I'll bring you a plate when it's ready. No bacon, I remember." Molly said as she watched Emma step quickly through the kitchen and back into her room. *That little gal is so strange,"* Molly frowned and pursed her lips, thoughtfully.

Emma paced her little room, rubbing her arms vigorously. Her teeth began chattering, even though she was not particularly cold. "I'm going stir-crazy," she said aloud. She looked at her bed, still unmade, and decided she could take care of that, at least. Afterwards, she sat on her neatly made bed and stared out the window, listening again for the birds, but the sun was now up and they had gone about their morning. She ventured into Claire's reading room and stood quietly, waiting for signs that Claire was up and about, but the quarters were silent. Emma opened the top drawer of the sideboard against the wall and found a tin box of cards. She took the box and sat down at the table, thinking she'd entertain herself with a game of solitaire, but when she looked at the cards, she realized they were not poker or bridge cards. There were too few of them, and they did not look familiar. One had a picture of a fox, with an insert illustration showing the nine of clubs. The next showed a snake, with an insert of the Queen of clubs. Emma was lost in her musings about what the cards were for when a voice startled her.

"I see you've found my fortune-telling cards," Claire said from the doorway to her parlor.

"I'm sorry. I shouldn't have been snooping. I was restless and looking for something to do. When I found these, I thought I'd play solitaire, but ..." Emma quickly stacked the cards together and put them back in the tin box they had come in.

"I have a poker deck here," Claire pulled the middle drawer out and reached for the deck, trading it for the one Emma held.

"I really am sorry."

"Don't give it a thought. This whole thing must be awful for

you. I understand you need something to do, to distract yourself
for a while. I am going to see about breakfast. Would you like to
join us this morning in the dining room?"

"I told Molly I wasn't feeling well and that I'd eat here, if
you don't mind. I don't know how to behave, Claire. I am afraid
I won't be convincing telling people I'm your cousin. I don't
trust myself around people." Emma looked up at Claire, her
brows pulled tight together and her chin quivered. Big tears
rolled down her cheeks. Claire pulled Emma to her feet and gave
her a hug. It was all she could think of to do for the girl. She
could not insult Emma by telling her it was going to be all right.
They both knew it might not be. Emma accepted the hug for a
moment, then pulled away. "I'm okay. I just need some time."

"I'll tell you what: I need to take care of breakfast, but
afterwards, let's sit down and practice your story. We'll work it
out until we are sure we have it straight. Then you will be more
comfortable getting out among people."

"Yes, okay. Yes, I think that would help."

❀

Emma and Claire spent the morning rehearsing Emma's story.
They were cousins, but not first cousins. They did not want the
connection to be too close. Emma had also lived in New
Orleans. Her family owned a bookstore. There had been a fire
that killed her family. Emma herself had been in the fire, but
had escaped with only scorched hair (explaining her
unfashionably short style). The fire had destroyed everything,
though, including the shop. Having no family left, Emma had
withdrawn what little money they had in the bank and headed
west. When she arrived in Denver, she telegraphed Claire that
she was in the area for a few days. Claire had responded with an
invitation to come stay with her in Manitou—at least until she

got back on her feet. Claire and Levi had met Emma in Colorado Springs the night before the earthquake and brought her to Manitou.

"Yes, I think this will work." Emma said after they had gone over the story several times.

"It is simple, and the less complicated, the better. Now, will you agree to join the tenants for dinner tonight? It will become suspicious if you continue to avoid everyone. Levi and I will be there, as always, and I'll invite Alice for moral support."

"Levi is always at dinner?"

"Why yes, unless he has another engagement. He and my sister, Daphne, lived in the large suite here at the boarding house. Levi still does."

"I am sorry you lost your sister, Claire. I imagine you miss her."

"Yes, very much. She died from tuberculosis last year. That's what brought us all here. We hoped the climate would heal her. She improved for a while, but in the end, it wasn't enough to cure her." Claire fell silent.

Emma faltered for something comforting to say, but words seemed inadequate. She brought the topic back to the present. "I'll agree to dinner, but can we still have breakfast here in your quarters? I need some time to prepare my mind for the act I must perform this evening."

"Of course we can," Claire said gently.

❀

After breakfast, Emma left Claire's quarters and headed up Cañon Avenue towards Williams Cañon, back to where she had emerged from the cave. She found the opening, which had been enlarged by the men who came searching for the friends she had claimed were still trapped there. She easily climbed back into the cave. The light reached into the chamber, allowing Emma to see where she had been entombed. There was no one there. Dark shadows melted into even darker spaces where the light could not reach. Emma had no intentions of venturing into those spaces. The terror of being trapped in the darkness was too acute. She stood in the chamber and looked at the cave walls. The flowstone formation she had been admiring before the earthquake was visible beside the rubble left afterwards. She reached out and touched it. *"Did this have a role in the time portal formed during the earthquake?"* Emma wondered. She detected nothing unusual emanating from it. She came back out of the cave and continued looking around outside of the opening. She couldn't tell which rocks had recently fallen and which ones had been there for an eon, though the steepness of the terrain made it likely that many of them had fallen the day of the earthquake. People had been in the area since then, so she knew it was unlikely she would find anything useful at the scene. She wasn't even sure exactly where Carson had been discovered, but she looked anyway.

She finished combing the area and found nothing noteworthy. She walked down from the cave ledge to the dirt road that led to town, but she decided to turn away from town and walk farther up the floor of the canyon. The clear morning air invigorated her. The sun warmed her skin. The rocks, so rough and jagged, reflected reds, yellows, and browns against the green and gray of the pine trees and the deep blue sky. The vegetation was mostly dried, but some brush was still green, turning red. With a shift in the wind, Emma could smell the balsam in the air. She saw a thick stand of pines a bit further on and, wanting to bathe in that scent, walked toward the pines. She turned past an enormous boulder and stopped dead. Twenty feet away from her, a bear was clawing on the trunk of a large ponderosa pine.

He stopped clawing and looked at her. Emma couldn't move. She couldn't breathe. The bear was enormous, fattened up for hibernation. He pushed against the tree and landed on four paws, letting out huffs of warning. Emma remained frozen. He then turned, showing Emma his impressive profile. She hoped he would just walk away, not seeing her as a threat, because she still could not move. The bear then turned back toward Emma and lurched, causing Emma to flinch. This agitated the bear further, and he stood up on his hind feet and grunted. Emma thought she might faint from fear when she heard a loud whoop and holler, "Yah! Yaaah! Yaaah! Yah!" and a vicious bark from a dog. From behind her, a blur of movement passed by, heading straight for the bear. A man and a dog ran toward the bear, the man waving his arms and a large branch from a tree, both man and dog making all the noise they could. The bear came back down on all paws, turned, and ran into the stand of trees, disappearing into a thicket of brush.

The man turned to her. His nut-brown skin was smooth over high cheekbones and a flattened nose. His black hair fell in two braids at his ears. His almond-shaped brown eyes pierced through Emma, clearly thinking her a fool. His dog came and sat at his feet and gave Emma the same look. The man was Native American. A Native American who had just saved Emma's life. Emma's knees began to shake as the paralyzing fear faded and adrenaline took over. She swallowed and tried to find her voice.

"Thank you," she said weakly, "I think you saved my life." She leaned against the boulder to steady herself. The man shook his head and walked past her, returning to wherever he had come from. "Kwiyaghat!" he called, and the dog ran after him. Emma watched as they rounded the curve in the path. She collected herself and went after them, but by the time she got to the curve, they had disappeared into the rocks. She looked for a moment, hoping to see them, but they had disappeared.

Emma walked as fast as she could back to the boarding house. She was still shaken from her bear encounter, but she was more affected by her encounter with the indigenous man. She entered Claire's parlor, breathing heavily.

"My God, where have you been?" Claire demanded, "You disappeared, and I was worried sick about you!" She stopped when she saw the look on Emma's face. "What's happened?"

Emma sat on the sofa, catching her breath, "I was nearly attacked by a bear, but a Native American man saved me."

Claire just stared at Emma, wide-eyed. After a moment she heaved a deep sigh, put her hands on her hips, and shook her head slowly.

"Are there still Native Americans living here? I thought they had already been run out by 1882."

"The last of the Utes were relocated to reservations in Utah last year, but Ancha wouldn't go. He lives in the foothills here."

"By himself?"

"Yes. We see him from time to time, but he keeps to himself. He doesn't cause any trouble, so he is tolerated."

"He's *tolerated*?" Emma asked, raising her voice, "*He* is tolerated?" Emma threw up her arms, exasperated.

"Yes." Claire repeated, puzzled by Emma's reaction, "Why, what did he do to you?"

"He saved my life, that's what he did, though I have no idea why. If I were him, I'd have let the bear eat me."

"What a horrible thing to say! Why would you say that?"

"Because we took everything from him and his people. We *stole* everything!" Emma yelled and, seeing Claire did not understand, ran to her sad little room and slammed the door. Claire, stunned by Emma's reaction, sat on the sofa and stared toward Emma's room. *"God, this is going to be harder than I imagined,"* she thought.

※

Emma threw herself face down on the bed and pounded the pillow with both fists as she screamed in frustration. She turned over and looked up at the ceiling, her eyes darting from corner to corner. She hardly knew herself anymore. It wasn't like her to be this emotional, to lose control. But she had lost control, hadn't she? There was no denying it. How much control had she ever really had? Had it always been an illusion? An illusion now shattered into a million pieces. Her life before now had been on plan, with no major hiccups. She had a good home and loving family; she had her education, a high-paying job, a wonderful man, a bright future. Everything had gone according to plan until now, but how much was because of her and how much due to providence? She had thought her life had been determined by good choices and hard work, but now . . . well, here she was through no intention on her part.

"So now what are you going to do, Emma? Who are you going to be now that your world had been destroyed?" The thought brought her mind back to the Native American Claire had called "Ancha." His world had been destroyed, too, and in ways that wouldn't be clear for many years. He had saved her, even though her people had taken everything from him. She sat up, having made a decision.

She went into the kitchen, where she found Molly stirring a pot of chicken and dumplings over the stove.

"That smells delicious, Molly," Emma said, smiling.

"Why thank you, Miss Quinn." Molly looked up and gave Emma a wide grin, exposing crooked teeth, except for the missing left canine and lower bottom tooth to its right.

"I wonder, do we have any fruit of any kind?" Emma asked.

"We have some apples in the root cellar," Molly said,

nodding to the narrow stairs in the corner of the kitchen. "You can have a couple of those, but don't take more. I need them for my pie."

"Thank you, Molly." Emma turned to go down the stairs. "I am looking forward to that pie." Emma found the apples in the cellar and took the best two she could find. It wasn't much, and for all she knew that blasted bear would get to them before Ancha did, but she wanted to try to let him know she appreciated what he had done for her.

She put on the cloak hanging by the kitchen door and went as quickly as she could to the boulder where she had encountered Ancha. She arranged the apples on a flat spot on the boulder and placed sprigs from a nearby evergreen around them, hoping Ancha would understand the gesture. She did not linger, not relishing running into any more wildlife that day.

❧ CHAPTER 9 ❧

L evi did not want to face facts. He wouldn't have pegged Josiah for a killer, but after what he'd learned, he wondered if it could have been anyone else. Why would Josiah have told him he was the last one to have seen Carson alive if he was the murderer? Levi was floundering, and soon the El Paso sheriff, Sheriff Dana, would want to know where things stood. He gently knocked on Claire's door. A friendly face would be welcome.

"Hello Levi," Claire smiled and stood aside to allow him to come in.

Levi removed his hat as he walked through the door. Claire took his hat and hung it on the peg on the wall.

"You look like you've lost your best friend," Claire observed.

"I'm just feeling discouraged with investigating Carson's murder." Levi sat in the armchair and clasped his hands between his legs, leaning forward. "I spoke to Tommy, Frank

Bowman, and Josiah. It appears Josiah was the last one to see Carson alive. I just can't believe he would hurt him, though. And all this poking around Carson's business. I feel like I'm intruding on a dead man's life. I have no idea what to do. There are no witnesses, so how can I prove who killed him?"

Claire stood beside Levi and placed her hand gently on his shoulder. "Are you hungry? I could find you some cold meat and biscuits—maybe with some honey?"

"Yes, that would be welcome, Claire, thank you."

Claire came back with a tray of cold fried chicken, biscuits, honey, and a pot of tea. "I'm glad you stopped by, Levi," she said as she set the tray down on the coffee table. "I want to talk to you about something." She poured Levi a cup of tea, stirring in three lumps of sugar to appeal to his sweet tooth, and handed him the cup. She waited until Levi had taken a bite from the chicken. "I appeal to you to reconsider allowing Emma to help with your investigation. I know, I know," she added quickly, seeing that Levi was about to protest, "you don't think it's appropriate, and I know there are issues to work out, but if she does it behind the scenes, perhaps she can be of help. She needs something, Levi. I am concerned for her well-being. She is an intelligent, educated woman with nothing to do right now but dwell on her situation. It isn't good for her."

Levi swallowed. "Solving a murder is a serious matter, Claire, not something to be used as a diversion from one's troubles. Why are you making Emma your problem, anyway? She is a stranger to you. She may even be dangerous herself for all you know. Are we *sure* she is telling us the truth?"

"God put her in my path, Levi It's His choice, not mine, that I help her. I've been able to observe her. I believe her. She needs friends right now, and that's what I intend to be."

"You and your God! Where was he when Daphne got sick and suffered, only to die? Where was he when your parents did the same? Where was he when . . ." but Levi caught himself before he went too far. "What do you owe your God?"

Claire gave Levi a long, steady look. "I don't know God's plan, Levi. I only know when I'm being called to act. I'm being called to act now, and I think you are, too, if you'd just open your mind some. What harm would it do to let her help? No one needs to know."

"A lot of harm if she's the one who killed Carson."

"Oh, for heaven's sake. You don't really believe that, do you?" When Levy didn't answer, Claire added, "Well, even if it were true, what better way to get a read on her than to engage her in the process?"

Levi sighed. He knew Claire. Claire would not give up once she thought she was right, and she surely thought she was right about this. He didn't need any more problems. He would be better off going along with it, for the time being. "Very well, Claire. I'll give it a try and see where it leads."

Claire gave him a wide grin and patted his hand. "Let me fetch her."

Not finding Emma in her room, Claire went on to the kitchen. "Have you seen Emma, Molly?" She asked the cook, who was bent over the open stove, gently placing her apple pie in the oven.

Just then, Emma came through the door. She returned the cloak to its hook and turned to Claire. "I'm glad you're here. I need to talk to you."

"Yes, yes, by all means. But Levi is here now and needs a word."

Claire returned with Emma, who sat down in the chair by the stove. She looked at Levi, waiting for him to start the conversation. When he didn't, she said, "Claire said you wanted to speak to me?"

Levi gave Claire a scolding glance for putting him on the

spot, then said, "Um, yes, Emma. I took your advice about how to investigate who might have killed Carson, but I must say, I don't see how it will lead anywhere. Without witnesses, I don't know how we will ever be able to prove who killed him. Claire here thinks you may still be able to help. I am willing to see if that's true, if you are agreeable."

"Yes, sure, if I can, I'm willing."

Levi was at a loss what to say next. He let truth be his guide. "I am not sure how to begin."

"Well, who did you talk to today, and what did you learn?" Emma prodded.

"I spoke to Tommy White, Carson's brother; Frank Bowman, the proprietor at the ten pins and billiard hall by the Manitou House; and Josiah Turner, Carson's partner. I learned that Carson is engaged to Anna Calhoun."

"Everyone knows that!" Claire interjected

"Well, *I* didn't, Claire," Levi admitted, annoyed. "May I continue?"

"Yes, of course," Claire muttered.

"Also, Carson and John Calhoun, Jr., Anna's brother, had an argument Friday evening at the hall. Josiah was there at the time and said it wasn't anything serious. Anna had sent John to get Carson out of there. Seems she felt his time was better spent with her."

"Humph, that doesn't surprise me." Claire said.

"What do you mean?" Levi asked

"Let's just say Anna requires a lot of attention and leave it at that, shall we?"

"Claire, I can't work with innuendo. If you have nothing material to add, please keep your opinions to yourself."

Having been chastised a second time, Claire stood up and left the parlor through the door to the boarding house hall, saying as she left, "I have chores to see to."

Levi signed and looked at his hands, still clasped between his knecs. Emma prodded him again. "What else did you learn?"

"It seems Josiah was the last person to see Carson alive."

"Well, that's significant. At the very least, it helps build a timeline. What did Josiah say?"

"He said he and Carson were scheduled to meet Mr. Albright on the ridge off the trail to Williams Cañon to talk over the plans for the landscaping of the bath house. They wanted to have a vantage point that would help Mr. Albright see their vision. The whole area where the bath house will be can be seen from there, along with the immediate surroundings. Mr. Albright never showed up, though, so after a while, they decided the meeting was a bust. Josiah says he left Carson there, alive and well. Right after Josiah got back to town, the earthquake hit. Josiah says he heard about Carson the next day. I just don't see Josiah as a killer. I have seen him often here at the boardinghouse. I've eaten with him in the dining room many times over the last few months. He is a likable young man, polite, friendly. He doesn't drink too much or indulge in the vices Colorado City has to offer, like some around here do."

"I'm not sure good character is enough to exonerate someone in this case," Emma said, her eyes flashing interest, "since it appears to have been a crime of passion and opportunity. Also, it is common that either the last person to see the victim alive or the first person to discover them dead turns out to be the killer. Is there any way Carson could have angered Josiah enough to murder him?"

"I just don't see Josiah getting that riled up over much of anything. His temperament is so even."

"We all have our breaking point, Levi. We don't know the whole story yet. But you are right not to jump to the conclusion that it's Josiah. There are still several people you have yet to interview. It's likely you will learn more. Why, for instance, didn't Mr. Albright make the meeting? How long before the earthquake did Josiah leave Carson? Did anyone see Josiah after the meeting?" Emma stood up and walked to the chest of drawers, opening one, then another of them.

"What are you looking for?"

"Paper and something to write with."

"I think Claire has something in her reading room." Levi said as he walked into the other room. Emma heard the squeak of a drawer open and close. Levi stood in the doorway, holding paper and a pencil. "Maybe it would be easier to work in here."

Emma joined him at the reading room table. He pushed the paper and pencil towards her, raising his eyes to meet hers, expectantly. Emma again thought of a deer as she looked into Levi's deep brown eyes, adorned by those extraordinarily thick, long lashes. He raised his brows and gave his head a quick nod, encouraging her to begin.

"Okay, so let's start with Carson's closest circle." Emma listed Tommy White, Josiah Tucker, Mr. Albright, John Calhoun, and Anna Calhoun. "So far, you have only talked to two of them. We need to verify their stories and talk to the others on this list before getting too discouraged." Emma put two headings at the top of the paper: *Opportunity* and *Motive*. "Perhaps we can at least start eliminating people."

"You are right. I haven't completed my interviews, so we may still find justice for Carson." Levi felt energized to continue his investigation to wherever it may lead.

❧ CHAPTER 10 ❧

Emma felt energized, too. She had something to focus on now, work to do. After Levi left, she went looking for Claire and found her in the boarding house parlor, dusting the furniture.

"Claire, I need to talk to you, do you have a minute?" Emma asked anxiously.

"Yes, let me just finish up in here. I'll meet you in my parlor."

Emma returned to Claire's quarters to wait, pacing around the small parlor, planning. She spun around when she heard Claire come into the room. "Claire, now that Levi has agreed to let me help him with his investigation into Carson's murder, I'll need a place to work. Can I use your reading room as a war room?"

"A war room?" Claire frowned.

"I'm sorry. That's a term in my day, in my line of work, for a space a team uses to work out a plan, or to perform a task requiring close collaboration. I need space where I can tack up paper—oh, paper!" Emma paused, thinking. "Is there a butcher in town?" Emma was moving around the room, animated with a sense of urgency.

"Well, I suppose I can spare the room for a while. The nearest butcher is in Colorado Springs, but we have plenty to eat here, Emma."

"I need butcher paper. I need some long sheets of paper I can write on." Emma swept her arm in front of her like she was opening a curtain, then, realizing she had no means to pay for anything, and remembering what she had wanted to talk to Claire about when she returned from her outing, added, "I need to start earning my keep around here, Claire. Let me do something to pay my way. I can clean. I can help Molly in the kitchen, preparing meals and cleaning up afterwards. Or, I could get a job in town and pay you room and board. I can do anything that needs doing."

"Slow down, Emma." Claire pressed her palms towards the floor. "You are making my head spin. I see that you need things, so let's take a trip into Colorado Springs tomorrow and do some shopping. As for a job, you are still recovering from your accident. There is no rush."

"But all the things I need cost money, Claire, and I intend to provide for myself. I can't take advantage of your generosity forever."

"I have the means to help you get on your feet, Emma. Please, let me help you. I understand you want to pay your way, and I am sure there are opportunities for you to earn sufficient wages for your needs soon enough. Let's take one thing at a time. May I suggest we concentrate on preparing for your 'coming out' dinner?" Claire added with an amused smile.

"Coming out dinner?' Emma frowned, puzzled. Then she realized that Claire's term had an entirely different meaning than in Emma's time. "Oh, yes. Yes, I would like to have a good, long bath, wash my hair. Do you dress for dinner?"

"Not especially, no." Claire answered, "But I may have something else you can wear. I just need to make a trip to the attic. And you might enjoy a mineral bath at Alice's bath house. That should refresh you. I don't know why I didn't think of it sooner."

"Alice has a bath house?"

"She leases it from the Colorado Springs Company, but she is the proprietress. The bath house is on the other side of Fountain Creek, next to Navajo Spring." Claire motioned Emma to come look in the direction she was pointing out the front window. "You will find it easily. It's a long, wooden building. If you are interested, go ahead. I'll meet you there with some fresh cloths."

Emma was intrigued by what she would find at the bath house. She took the footpath that led from Cañon Ave. to the bridge that crossed Fountain Creek, the creek that ran down the center of Manitou. Emma stopped on the bridge to take in the view. She marveled at how unspoiled the area around the creek was compared with her time. There were no large structures in the area between Manitou Ave. and Cañon Ave. A rustic pavilion marked the spot where Soda Spring offered up its effervescent mineral water. A large boulder marked the location of Navajo Spring. They were two of eight natural mineral springs open to the public in Emma's time. Emma was not sure how many were known in 1882, but she knew it was the main reason people had come to Manitou. It was called Manitou Springs in her day because of these famous springs. Even though the buildings familiar to Emma were not there, the hills and mountains were like old friends. Pikes Peak was well-covered with snow that reached down into the foothills. Manitou's relatively mild weather, even in the winter time, kept the snow from reaching town. Here at the creek bed, scrub oaks and rocks littered the land. Manitou Ave. gave Emma some sense of bearing, and she spotted the Barker House at the corner of Manitou Ave. and Navajo Ave. It was smaller than it would later be with additions, but she was glad to recognize it.

Just to the left of Navajo Spring was the building Claire had described. The long, narrow clapboard building looked more like a large shed, weathered and uneven. It looked like it had been there long before the mere ten years Manitou had been a town. The door at the end of the building had a sign hanging over it that read: *Mrs. A. S. Guiles, M.D. ELECTRICIAN*. Emma knocked twice and heard a muffled "come in." She opened the door to find Alice sitting at a simple wooden table, writing in a ledger illuminated by a kerosene lamp, as the small window provided insufficient sunlight.

"Why hello, Emma!" Alice said, laying down her pen, smiling.

"Hi!" Emma walked in and shut the door. "Claire suggested a mineral bath might be good for me and sent me your way." Emma looked around at the room, skeptical about the idea. It seemed a rather shabby operation. The small room that served as an office and reception was furnished by the table, two wooden spindle chairs, and a glass-fronted cabinet against the far wall. A narrow hall at the back of the room led down the length of the building. "I'm curious, though. I see you call yourself an 'electrician' on your sign. I'm not sure I understand what that means."

Alice's serious expression lifted into a bright smile before she began, "Yes! I use electricity as a medical treatment for various conditions, like back pain, rheumatism, other chronic diseases."

"Like electric shock treatment?" Emma asked, surprised.

"Shock! Heavens no, I take all precautions to avoid any

danger of that to my patients. I can show the electric bath to you another time, perhaps. I do not recommend it for you. Your injuries are from physical trauma, not disease. A hot mineral bath, however, would be very beneficial for you, followed by a cold-water plunge. Let me get the bath ready for you. Have a seat while you wait."

Emma's curiosity about the 'electric bath' was piqued, but she was glad Alice was not recommending it. She was not confident it was safe. She was very much looking forward to a hot bath, mineral water or not. She heard some banging sounds and the sound of water pouring, then footsteps on the wooden floor signaling Alice's return.

"Follow me," Alice said, motioning for Emma.

Emma followed Alice into the narrow hallway, walking past little rooms to the right, each holding a wooden bathtub, raised, but set half-way into the floor. Alice gestured to Emma to enter the next-to-last room. The small bench and two hooks on the wall provided a place for patrons to undress and hang their clothes. A shelf next to the tub held a large towel. The tub was filled with steaming water.

"The water comes from the Navajo Spring." Alice explained. "I heat it using the boiler at the end of the building. It's hot, but try to tolerate it. I'd like to have a look at your abrasions before you get in the bath to make sure they have healed enough to be in the water."

Emma removed her dress and hung it on a hook to allow Alice to examine the scrapes on her forearms. Alice removed the thin layer of gauze from each arm. "Good, they are healing nicely," Alice said. "Don't soak them too long. From here on out, they need dryness and air to finish healing. You are done with the bandages." Alice took the old bandages and walked to the doorway. "I'll let you know when you have been in long enough. The cold-water plunge will be ready for you then," Alice turned back to Emma as she walked out the door. "Do you need anything else?"

Emma would have liked soap, but she knew it was not that kind of bath. Hot water would have to be enough. "No, I think I am good."

Alice shut the door, leaving Emma alone. She finished undressing and gently lowered herself into the water, which was as hot as any hot tub she'd ever been in. She noticed a drain plug at the end of the tub that allowed the tub to drain straight onto the ground. "Ahhh," Emma sunk into the water and rested her head at the end of the tub, closing her eyes. This was the best she had felt since arriving back in time.

❀

Alice was looking out the tiny window of her bath house office, wondering what Emma could tell her about how medicine had advanced over the years, when she saw Claire coming toward the bath house, carrying a bulky bundle wrapped in a blanket. She opened the door to let Claire enter.

"Thank you, Alice. These are some fresh clothes for Emma." Claire plopped her load on the table. "Oh, it's been quite a day." Claire sighed and took a seat, smoothing her skirts. She reached up to her unruly hair, tucking the errant locks behind her ears, and looked at her friend with the wide-eyed expression she always wore. "A bear nearly mauled Emma, but on a high note, I persuaded Levi to engage Emma in his investigation into Carson's murder. She seems quite eager to help." Claire decided not to mention the outburst Emma had had after her bear encounter, or more accurately, her encounter with Ancha. "And maybe the best part, Emma has agreed to join me and the rest of the boarding house tenants for dinner this evening. I do hope you will join us. Emma could use the support. We spent the morning practicing her story, but I think she is still a bit nervous. I am, too, to be honest."

As usual, Claire had packaged so much into her brief statement, Alice hardly knew where to start unraveling it. "A bear? How dreadful! She didn't mention it. I am gratified to hear Levi is being open-minded. I would be happy to dine with you this evening. I just need to let Sarah know I won't be home for dinner." Alice glanced at the clock on the wall. "Oh! It's time to get Emma out of the bath. I'll bring her these clothes," she added, picking up the bundle.

"Very well, then. I'll see you soon, Alice, and thank you for all you are doing for her."

❧ CHAPTER 11 ❧

Emma felt like a new woman. Her experience at the bath house had left her feeling fresh and rejuvenated. She liked the change of clothes Claire had brought her very much. The light and dark blue striped wool skirt was gored and flowed nicely as she walked. The cream blouse buttoned up the front and had lace on either side that continued around the collar and at the wrists. A jacket of material matching the skirt finished the ensemble. Unlike the first dress Claire had provided her, these clothes fit Emma as though they were made for her. She had a little spring in her step as she walked back to the boardinghouse. She was starting to feel like herself again.

Back in her room, Emma found more clothes hanging on the rod mounted to the wall. She looked through the garments, which were of excellent quality. In the dresser drawers, she found additional underclothes. *"Where had these clothes come from?"* She had brought back the clothes she had been wearing before her bath, wrapped in the blanket Claire had used. She sat the bundle on the bed and reminded herself to ask Claire about how to launder them.

Where would she be without Claire and Alice? Her imagination wandered, considering the alternative ways her being thrust back in time could have played out. Most of them did not end well. Perhaps Claire was right. Perhaps Emma was here for a reason. Could being drawn in to a murder investigation be it?

She went into the reading room and pulled her notes and pencil out of the drawer. She sat down to capture some thoughts on the case, but did not get anywhere. *"We simply need more to go on,"* she thought. She heard a gentle rustle at the threshold to the parlor.

"Emma, it's time for dinner. Are you ready?" Claire said softly.

Emma took a deep breath. "I'm not sure, but I'm as ready as I ever will be, I suppose."

They joined Alice in Claire's parlor and went together into the boardinghouse parlor, where the other tenants had gathered for casual socializing before dinner. Emma saw Levi in the back of the room, pouring a glass of whiskey. He stopped in mid-pour when he saw Emma. He squinted at Emma and put the lead crystal decanter down firmly on the sideboard, looking decidedly displeased. Emma felt her stomach drop.

"Everyone, I'd like to introduce you to my cousin, Miss Quinn, from New Orleans." Claire announced to the room. The tenants looked questioningly at one another—everyone but Levi, who continued glaring at Emma. Josiah was the first one to respond.

"Welcome, Miss Quinn," he said brightly, setting his drink on the table and reaching out to take Emma's hand. She reached out to him, and he made a brief bow over her hand.

"This is Mr. Josiah Turner, Emma." Claire said. "He hails

from Chicago." Claire turned to the next person queued behind Josiah, "and this is Mr. William Stewart, who works at the livery and has been a tenant with me from the beginning, isn't that right Mr. Stewart?"

"Yes ma'am! I was the very first tenant. This is the finest boarding house in town. Miss Quinn, glad to make your acquaintance," William said, smiling and shaking Emma's hand enthusiastically. "Please, call me Willy."

Emma took an immediate liking to Willy. His wiry frame exuded energy; his gestures were quick and sure. A long, full mustache overwhelmed his lean, narrow face. His ready smile went all the way to his hazel eyes, making them squint almost closed. "Nice to meet you, Willy," Emma smiled as Willy continued shaking her hand.

"And next to Levi are Mr. Graham, who manages the bookstore in town, and Miss Sully, who is a laundress at the Manitou House, one of the finest hotels in town."

Emma nodded to the two, "Nice to meet you, both." They nodded back, expressing agreement.

"Well, folks, I see that Molly has put the chicken and dumplings on the sideboard. Let's go eat!"

As the party made their way to the dining room, Emma heard Levi behind her, whispering angrily to Claire, "Why is she wearing that?"

"Would you rather have it rot in the attic along with the rest of her things?" Claire whispered back. "Emma needs them, and they fit her perfectly. Levi, please, be reasonable."

Everyone seemed to defer to Emma, treating her like the guest of honor. Emma hesitated, not knowing what the established seating was.

"Here Emma," Claire gestured to the seat to the left of the head of the table nearest the sideboard, "Sit here next to me. Alice, please sit here on my other side."

Emma served herself from the sideboard and went to her seat. Josiah pulled it out for her. "Thank you, Mr. Turner," Emma said, smiling up at Josiah as he helped push her chair in. Josiah took the seat next to her. She waited while everyone got their meal and took their seats. Levi took his seat at the far end of the table, opposite Claire. Claire was the last to come to the table. She reached out for Emma's and Alice's hands. Josiah reached out and took Emma's other hand and bowed his head. Emma quickly followed suit while Claire said a brief grace. After the "Amen," Josiah gave Emma's hand a brief squeeze before letting go.

"When did you arrive, Miss Quinn?" Josiah asked amiably.

"Emma arrived Monday night, Josiah. She will be staying with me for the foreseeable future." Claire interjected.

"Aren't you the one that got hurt in the cave during the earthquake?" Willy added, "Are you all right?"

"Yes, I am fine, thank you, Willy. I'm afraid I don't remember much about it."

"You suffered quite a nasty bump on the head, Emma," Alice offered. "It's no surprise you don't remember clearly." Alice took a drink of water.

"Billy down at the livery said you were yellin' about some friends trapped in the cave, but Jim said they didn't find anyone when they went lookin'—aside from poor Carson, that is." Willy looked down sheepishly at his dish, then looked back up at Emma, expectantly.

"The injury Miss Quinn suffered caused a concussion, Willy. She was just confused." Alice said firmly.

"Surely Miss Quinn can speak for herself." Josiah offered, then paused. "Perhaps she would rather not talk about it."

Emma looked around the table at the various reactions. Willy was openly anxious to hear more. Miss Sully's sideways look at Emma betrayed her eagerness to know more, too. Josiah was too polite to show his interest, but his comment had a tacit question behind it. Only Mr. Graham seemed genuinely indifferent.

"Alice is right. I don't really remember anything. I'm not even sure I was ever *in* the cave," Emma lied. "I may have just been near it when a rock hit my head. I was sorry to hear about Mr. White, though. I understand he was murdered?" Emma wanted to change the subject away from herself, and she thought it might be instructive to see how the others reacted to the subject of Carson. She noticed Levi giving her yet another sour look. Josiah fidgeted in his chair.

"Yes, and I am investigating it, so it's best we don't talk about it." Levi said with finality, frustrating Emma's hope of learning more and causing an uncomfortable lull at the table.

"Claire tells me you had a close call with a bear today, Emma." He added, taking a large spoonful of food, chewing slowly.

"Oh my!" Miss Sully exclaimed, raising her brows, "That must have been horrifying for you, Miss Quinn."

"It was. I was literally petrified with fear." Emma's aggravation with Levi growing with his every chew.

"How did you escape injury?" continued the laundress.

"The Native American man scared it away. Claire told me his name is Ancha." Emma reluctantly answered.

"The Indian?" snarled Graham. "What's he doing so close to town?"

"Why shouldn't he be so close to town, Mr. Graham?" Emma challenged.

"He shouldn't be here at all," Graham said, raising his voice. "His people were all moved to Utah last year. He should be sent along with them," he scowled.

Claire, seeing Emma take a deep breath to respond, interjected, "Molly made an excellent apple pie for dessert. Is anyone interested?"

"I'd love some, Claire!" Alice quickly answered.

"Lovely. Emma, perhaps you could help me in the kitchen?"

Emma's good mood from earlier was thoroughly eroded, her stomach now in a knot. "Yes, of course, Claire, I'd be happy to," and she followed Claire into the kitchen.

"Ugh!" Emma threw her napkin on the kitchen table in anger. "What is *wrong* with Levi tonight?"

"I'm afraid it's my fault, Emma." Claire said.

"Well, why is he taking it out on me, then?" Emma took plates from the shelf for the pie.

"I'm sure he doesn't mean to. I gave him an unpleasant surprise, it seems." Claire sliced the pie and began serving the pieces onto the plates. "The clothes you are wearing, the clothes I put in your room, they were Daphne's."

Emma rolled her eyes and lowered her shoulders, all the animosity melting away. "Oh, no wonder. I can see why that would upset him." She picked up two plates to take to the dining room.

"I feel foolish that I didn't think it through. I just thought you needed clothes, and Daphne had these beautiful things that might work for you. Daphne would have been happy that her things were going to good use! It never occurred to me how Levi would feel about it. I should have spoken to him first." Claire collected the rest of the plates, balancing one against her wrist and hand.

"You meant well, Claire, and I thank you. If it's too upsetting for Levi, I won't wear her things."

They returned to the dining room with the pie. "Would you like some, Mr. Turner?" Emma asked Josiah.

"Most definitely! Molly makes the best pie I've ever had." Josiah responded, smiling back at Emma. As he reached for the plate, his hand gently brushed hers, and she felt a flush go over her.

Emma sat down with her plate and looked over at Levi, feeling sorry for her earlier reaction. He had turned his glare to Josiah. He wiped his mouth, set down his napkin and said, "Tell Molly she outdid herself, Claire. It's been a long day, so I will excuse myself." He walked out of the dining room, leaving his pie untouched.

The remaining tenants filled the rest of the mealtime with tense silence, interrupted by murmurs affirming Molly's culinary skills and the clinking of forks and plates.

✌ Chapter 12 ✌

The next morning, Emma put on the too-large dusty rose dress Claire had lent her on her first day at the boarding house. Emma brushed the dust from the skirt and sniffed under the arms. The dress needed laundering, and she felt frumpy in it. She found a hairbrush in the dresser, which she guessed was Daphne's just like all the other things Claire had put in her room. Levi didn't need to know about the brush, at least. As she brushed her hair, she looked out of the little window in her room. It faced north, towards Williams Cañon. There were a few houses sparsely sprinkled between the boarding house and the canyon. Some of them were the Queen Anne style so much in vogue at the time and reminded her of doll houses. The road that ran in front of the boarding house, Cañon Ave., eventually became the footpath she had taken that first day after she escaped from the cave. It followed the bottom of Williams Cañon north for a couple of miles. Emma noticed she could see part of the ledge where she had emerged from the cave from this vantage point, unobstructed by buildings, towers, or Highway 24. Emma admired how the sun was shining on the slopes of the canyon and casting dark shadows in the crags of the rocks.

"Good morning, ladies." Emma entered the kitchen, finding Claire and Molly finishing preparations for breakfast.

"Good morning, Emma! Here, would you take this tray of potatoes to the dining room?" Claire handed Emma a large porcelain dish piled high with fried potatoes. She took them into the dining room and placed them on a mat on the sideboard. She heard heavy footsteps coming down the stairs. A moment later Levi stopped at the threshold.

"Good morning, Emma."

"Good morning," Emma mumbled, trying to make her way past Levi, but he did not yield.

"I'm glad you're here. I owe you an apology." He reached out and held her arm, gently.

Emma avoided his eyes. She was trapped in the narrow threshold, with Levi so close she could feel his soft breath against her cheek. "No, you don't. If you'll excuse me, I'm helping Claire get breakfast out."

Levi released her arm, but remained in her way. "I was rude to you last night. That was wrong of me."

"Claire explained your reasons. I understand."

"Please, look at me, Emma."

Emma kept her head down, but looked up at Levi, wanting the awkward moment over.

"Claire did the right thing, giving you Daphne's clothes. Of course she did. Please, I want you to have them and make good use of them."

Emma raised her chin slightly. "I'm not sure I can now, knowing they were Daphne's."

"Out of the way, you two, this pan is hot!" Molly came through with a large pan of eggs. Claire followed close behind her with the dish of fried, thinly cut steaks.

Claire picked up a bell sitting on the sideboard and rang it loudly. "Go ahead and eat," she said to Emma and Levi. "No sense letting the food get cold waiting for the others."

Emma and Levi served themselves and ate in silence as the other tenants filtered into the dining room. When Miss Sully came in, Emma asked her, "Miss Sully, do you take in laundry from customers other than guests at the hotel?"

"Oh, please, call me Christina," she giggled. "Yes, I do take in laundry from others. I have to charge a bit more, of course, for use of the hotel's facilities." Christina took a big bite of eggs and smiled as she chewed.

"Emma and I are going into Colorado Springs today," Claire announced as she placed her napkin in her lap. She glanced up at Levi and added, "Emma needs some things. I thought it would be better for us to take the boarding house rig, Emma. We may have too much to carry back on the train." Josiah entered the dining room, wishing everyone a good morning as he sat down with his meal. "Ah, Josiah! I was just saying that Emma and I are taking the rig to Colorado Springs this morning. Would you like to ride with us?"

"That would be most pleasant, thank you."

"I mentioned it to Willy on his way out this morning, so he should have the buckboard ready for us as soon as we are done eating."

❀

Josiah sat between Claire and Emma on the buckboard's bench, driving the horse. Emma was glad to have another opportunity to talk to him. She was hoping to coax some useful information out of him about Carson.

"Another beautiful day, don't you agree, Miss Quinn?"

Josiah observed, making genial conversation.

"Yes, it certainly is. Not unlike my first day here, at least until the earthquake." She paused a moment, then looked sideways at Josiah. "I was sorry to hear about Mr. White. I understand he was your partner?"

"Yes," Josiah said quietly. "I will miss him as a partner and a friend. He was the talented one."

"Oh, I'm sure you are every bit as talented."

"I have technical knowledge, yes—about plants and various building materials and methods—but Carson had vision and artistic style. I am unsure of the future of the firm, frankly."

"The bath house project should put quite a feather in your cap, Josiah, it will continue, will it not?" Claire joined in.

"Indeed, it will. Mr. Albright came to me the day after Carson was killed to get my commitment to finish the project. I assured him that I would complete the job. As you said, it will help greatly in making a name for the firm, but I must confess, I am not confident I can do it without Carson."

"Nonsense, Josiah. I know you can do it," Claire encouraged.

"Did you see Carson the day he was killed, Mr. Turner?" Emma pursued, hoping she didn't put Josiah off with her questions, although that reaction might in itself be telling.

"I did. We voted that morning, then we walked around the bath house site. I had some preliminary drawings from Mr. Ellis, the architect, and we wanted to discuss our ideas for the landscaping ahead of a meeting we had planned with Mr. Albright that afternoon. We parted late morning with an agreement to meet up at Williams Cañon around half-past one o'clock. We had a scheduled meeting there with Mr. Albright at two o'clock."

"Why, that was shortly before the earthquake!" Claire exclaimed. "That was right around the time they think Carson was killed! You didn't see anything, Josiah?"

"No, nothing. Carson and I waited for Mr. Albright, but he never came. I left Carson there, it must have been about a quarter of an hour before the earthquake. I stopped at the Cliff House bar on my way back to town. That's where I was when the earthquake hit."

"Then you were probably the last person to see Carson alive." Emma observed.

"OH!" Claire cried, gripping the handrail to steady herself after Josiah hit a deep rut in the road. Emma reached out and grabbed Josiah's arm to keep her balance.

"Sorry ladies." Josiah steered the horse to a smoother part of the road. "But you were in the area at that time, too, were you not, Miss Quinn?"

"I was, but I had been knocked unconscious during the earthquake. My memory is still a bit fuzzy. I don't recall seeing anyone before that. It was nearly dark when I regained consciousness."

Josiah glanced at Emma, but she was not sure if it was to see if she would say more or to see if she was telling the truth.

"What made you think you had friends trapped in the cave?"

"Alice explained last night, Josiah," Claire reminded him. "Emma suffered a serious concussion and had been confused."

"Yes, I thought I was back in the fire, I think." Emma offered. Claire's glare communicated an unspoken *"What are you saying?"*

"Fire?" Josiah responded.

"My family was killed in a fire back home along with two workers from our shop who I considered friends. I had been out running errands. When I returned, I saw the shop was on fire. I ran in to save them, but it was too late. The fire singed my hair, but I was otherwise unharmed."

Clare looked off into the distance, trying to keep expressionless. Josiah's attention was focused on Emma.

"I am sorry for you, Miss Quinn. It seems you have been through quite a lot recently. My condolences to you on the loss of your family."

"Thank you, Mr. Turner. And please, call me Emma."

Josiah gave Emma a sympathetic smile, "And please call me Josiah."

Emma fell silent. She marveled at the sparsely populated countryside, which she would not have recognized at all were it not for the familiar rock outcroppings of Garden of the Gods, peeking out in the distance. The cliffs just east of that were where she knew Mesa Road and the Kissing Camels area would be one day. She preferred the land free of buildings and roads clogged with smog-producing vehicles. The road was dusty, but the air was clear and clean despite the smoke coming from the chimneys in town.

She touched the ring on her finger and thought of Paul with a pang in her heart. She missed him the way one misses a loved one who has died, with an ache born from knowing the person no longer physically exists—or in this case did not yet exist, and would not for more than one hundred years. She had been so consumed with recovering from her head injury and coping with the upheaval of being out of her time that she had not been able to grieve Paul. She felt her eyes well up. *"Not now,"* she thought. She took a deep, hesitating breath and pushed back the tears.

"I imagine Colorado City is calmer now than when you came through at night earlier this week." Josiah interrupted Emma's thoughts. "It can be quite raucous at night."

"It was an unusually calm Monday night." Claire diverted the conversation away from Emma. "At least when we came through."

"Yes," Emma agreed vaguely, still fondling her ring.

The rest of the journey passed uneventfully, the companions making casual small talk along the way. "Where would you like me to hitch the rig, Claire?" Josiah asked as he drove the wagon up Cascade Ave.

"Pikes Peak Ave. is fine, Josiah. We can walk everywhere we need to go from there." Claire instructed him.

Josiah stopped the horse at the corner of Pikes Peak and Cascade. "If you are going to be long, I'll take the rig to the livery and pick it up this afternoon. You can come to the office when you are ready to return home."

"Yes, that would be best, Josiah, thank you," Claire said, then turned to Emma and asked, "Where would you like to begin?"

"I really want some stationery supplies—paper, a pen, maybe a pencil."

"I know just the place: Eoff and Howbert. It's just around the corner." The ladies began walking east to the shops, most of which were on Tejon Street. Colorado Springs was a much larger town than Manitou and was centered at Pikes Peak Ave. and Tejon St. The buildings along Tejon St. looked straight out of a western movie. Many were wooden clapboard with false fronts to make them look bigger than they actually were. Some were constructed of brick. Most of the storefronts were sparce, but Emma found the stationers' storefront charming. A bay paned window, filled with books and open cases of writing sets, beckoned them into the shop. Emma saw copies of *Little Women* and *Far from the Madding Crowd,* along with other titles she did not recognize. She felt a thrill when she walked in and picked up a copy of Mark Twain's classic, *Adventures of Tom Sawyer,* admiring the blue cover embossed with black scrolls and gold stars.

"Oh my God, I can't believe it! A first edition! It's beautiful!

Claire, look at this book!" Emma could see how well-made it was, the signatures sewn, not glued. "And look at these illustrations!" Emma opened the book to find it sprinkled with engravings. "How much does this cost, I wonder?"

The young lady clerk standing nearby heard Emma and answered, "Two dollars, miss. Would you like it?"

Emma looked at Claire and whispered so only she could hear, "Oh, that seems kind of expensive, isn't it?'

"It's the going price for most novels here. You may find a better price in Denver." Claire whispered. Emma thought about the thousands of books she had downloaded on her cell phone—including the one in her hand—that she could not read if she wanted to save her battery for as long as possible. She carefully returned the book to the display. "No, thank you, not today."

Emma picked out a modest pen, a bottle of ink, some writing paper and a blank journal. "I'm so happy to have these writing supplies, Claire." Emma smiled at her package while the two continued their walk down Tejon Street. "And I will keep track of what I owe you for this and all the rest of the things you buy me today. I want to pay you back every cent."

Claire took Emma's arm as they walked. "I am not the least bit concerned about it," she assured Emma, though she knew Emma would not let it go. They stopped at a confectioner's shop and bought some lemon drops. Emma's face puckered as she sucked on one while she listened to Claire sweet-talk her butcher into giving them over two yards of butcher paper. He rolled it up and handed it to Claire, scratching his head because he couldn't imagine why she needed it. After procuring Emma a pair of boots and a pair of shoes, they moved on to finding her some new clothes.

"There seem to be many more men's clothes stores than women's," Emma commented as they continued their stroll. "In my day, it's the exact opposite."

"Really? How interesting. Well, most women have their clothes made by seamstresses, and they usually work from their residences. Of course, with garment factories using sewing machines, and with the train system now connecting the country, more ready-made garments are available. You can even order by mail or, in some cases, telephone! It's really quite remarkable how things are changing!" Claire prattled.

Emma made a little smirk, thinking that Claire did not know the half of how things would change. How excited would Claire be if she had Amazon Prime?

"The emporium will have some clothes. Let's go there next." Claire pointed to the store on the corner.

In the store, Emma was shocked at the dearth of selection. "They don't have much to choose from here, and the prices seem high to me. Twenty dollars for this simple dress? How much are average wages?"

"It varies, but I think Mr. Graham makes about ten dollars a week working at the bookstore. I believe office workers make considerably more, especially if they can type."

So, this dress would be about two weeks' wages, Emma figured, if she had a job, which she did not. "I don't know how I'll ever be able to repay you for the shoes, much less clothes at these prices!" Emma, dejected by the reality of consumerism in the nineteenth century, dropped her hands heavily at her sides.

"You are right about the selection," Claire said, frowning. "What makes it worse is the solution is right in front of us, if only Levi would see reason."

"Actually, Levi spoke briefly to me this morning. He apologized for how he had acted last night and said you were right to give me Daphne's clothes."

"Well then, what is the problem?" Claire asked, exasperated.

"I am not sure I believe him, and I don't want to disrespect

Daphne's memory." Emma's little frown and pained look spoke volumes.

Claire guided Emma to an upholstered bench against the wall of the store. She sat next to Emma and took her hand. "See here, Emma. You did not know Daphne. I wish you had. She was the most wonderful woman. She was kind, generous, and sympathetic to the plight of others. During her life, she gave freely to those less fortunate than herself. Before she became ill, she worked tirelessly for charities, particularly those aimed at helping children. She would be appalled if she knew her beautiful clothes were moldering in an attic, being of no use to anyone." She paused, holding back tears. "I miss her every single day of my life. I will never have my sister back, but it's made worse knowing that she can't continue doing good in the world because of misguided thoughts that wearing her things would be disrespectful to her. Quite the contrary, stubbornly refusing to put her things to good use would be disrespectful. Please reconsider. The clothes are perfect for you, and you need them."

Tears rolled down Emma's cheeks, the grief in Claire's voice bringing hers to the surface. A tear fell on the hand that Claire was holding. "If you are sure, Claire . . ."

"Of course, I'm sure. Now, it's settled," and she gave Emma's hand a few quick, gentle pats.

Emma felt a heavy burden lift from her shoulders. She loved the clothes Claire had brought from the attic. She loved their style and the way they fit her. She loved that they smelled of cedar and lavender. She wiped the tears from her face with the back of her hand and smiled shyly at Claire. "Thank you. I will never be able to repay your kindness."

"Come, let's go have a late lunch. There's a restaurant just up the street a block or so. We will take our time and enjoy ourselves."

The New England Kitchen was just north of the opera house on Tejon St. "I didn't know we had had an opera house once." Emma said as they came upon the large building.

"Oh yes, we are quite proud of it! Why, just this last April, the Irish poet Oscar Wilde gave a lecture. I think it might have been too highbrow for many people here, but those who attended were impressed with him. Let's see what the announcement says is coming next." Claire pointed to the window displaying the upcoming events. "Look, Emma! '*Grand Spiritualistic Revival*, featuring the Miller brothers and Anna Eva Fay.' It's December fifth! I have always wanted to see Miss Fay. I understand she is phenomenal. Oh! I want to go, don't you?"

Emma could not very well say no in the face of Claire's enthusiasm. "Absolutely, I will go with you!" Emma said.

Claire clapped with glee.

❧ CHAPTER 13 ❧

Emma skipped dinner. The ride back to Manitou with Claire and Josiah had been pleasant enough, but now she wanted some time alone. She took out her cell phone and recharger and looked again at pictures of Paul. *"I don't know how to get back to you, Sweetie. I am not even sure it's possible."* She found her ear buds and played her favorite song, "In the Air Tonight," an "oldie" by Phil Collins, playing the air drums at the climactic moment, but it failed to cheer her. She wanted to spend the entire night listening to her music, but she had to conserve her battery. She heard commotion in the kitchen signaling dinner was over and reluctantly stashed away her modern artifacts.

"Can I help clean up?" she asked Claire as she entered the kitchen. "I can wash or dry, whichever you'd rather not do."

"Yes, thank you. Please wash. I can put things away as I dry. We missed you at dinner."

"I wasn't hungry after the big lunch we had." Emma rolled up her sleeves and pumped water into the sink. Claire scraped the dishes clean in a bucket before handing them to her.

"Good evening, Emma."

Emma turned and saw Levi standing in the passage from the dining room. "Good evening," she meant to sound pleasant, but it came out flat. She turned back to her chore.

"I was wondering if you were available this evening. I spent the day continuing my interviews, and I'd like to go over what I learned with you."

"Yes, as soon as I'm done helping Claire."

"Here, Levi," Claire handed him a rag. "If you dry while I scrape, we will be done quicker."

❀

"I believe him." Emma tacked a long piece of butcher paper on the wall of the reading room.

"Josiah is still our primary suspect." Levi tapped his finger on the table and took a sip of whiskey from his glass. "And I learned nothing today that would exonerate him."

"I was able to talk to him on the way to Colorado Springs, and he struck me as being genuinely sorry Carson was dead. In fact, I think he is worried that he can't do the bath house project without him."

"Yes, but as you have pointed out, it was likely done in the heat of emotion. One could later feel badly about it and still be guilty."

Emma sat down and leaned against her elbows. "You're right," she admitted. "So, did you learn anything useful today?"

"I spoke to the supplier in Colorado Springs. He verified that Tommy telephoned in the wine order about twenty minutes before the earthquake. Also, I went back to talk to Tommy, and he said he saw Josiah at the bar in the hotel just after he finished the call. The earthquake happened only moments after that."

"It seems Josiah is telling the truth about that, then." Emma took the pencil and drew a long horizontal line at the top of the paper. "Let's build a timeline."

Levi stood next to her. "The earthquake happened just after three o'clock that afternoon." She could smell the whiskey on his breath as he spoke. It was a pleasant oak scent.

"We still do not know precisely when Carson was killed. If Josiah was the last to see him alive, then the earliest he could have been killed is before the earthquake, say a quarter to three." Emma drew a vertical line and made a note. "He was found and brought to the Cliff House after I regained consciousness. We need to ask Alice what time that was. That will give us a window." Emma glanced at her notes on the desk. "Did you talk to John or Anna Calhoun today?"

"I spoke to John. He would not allow me to talk to Anna. She is distraught over Carson, it seems. She hasn't left her room since she heard of his death, and she is barely eating. His concern for her seemed quite sincere."

"I'm sure she is grief stricken. They were to be married, after all. They had their entire lives ahead of them." Emma sat back down, balancing her pencil between her fingers, wondering how Paul might be reacting to her disappearance. She grieved for him, but she believed he still lived, or would someday, and that was some comfort. She came back to the moment. "Did John say anything else? Where was he when the earthquake stuck?"

Levi leaned his forearms on the table, clasping his hands in front of him. "He had taken his mother to the dentist in Colorado Springs to see about a toothache."

"I still think it is important we talk to Anna. She might know something that proves significant."

"Carson's funeral is tomorrow. I plan to go. Perhaps you and Claire will come, too?"

"That's a great idea, Levi!"

Levi was surprised at her tone. She seemed to be looking forward to attending the somber affair, but he decided her reaction was likely because she was eager to continue the investigation. He pulled his pocket watch out and looked at the time. "Thank you for being a sounding board, Emma. I'll see you tomorrow." Levi got up to let himself out. Emma heard him say goodnight to Claire as he went through her parlor.

"Did you and Levi make any progress?" Claire asked, joining Emma at the table.

"It's hard to say. It appears that John Calhoun has an alibi." She pointed at the paper on the wall where she was developing the timeline. "I need to talk to Alice to get a better idea of the window of time when Carson could have been killed. The smaller the window, the more certainly we can eliminate people who have alibis." Emma paused, trying to capture a fleeting thought, but it evaporated. "Levi suggested you and I attend Carson's funeral tomorrow."

"Of course. I did not know him well, but he spent several evenings here, playing cards with Josiah, Willy, and Peter Graham. Certainly, I was well enough acquainted with him to want to pay my respects."

"Did Levi ever play cards with Carson?"

Claire let out a little laugh. "Levi? No, not hardly."

Emma frowned, puzzled by Claire's response. But before she could ask, Claire said, "It is getting late. I will bid you good night."

"Good night, Claire."

After Claire left, Emma lit a small candle from the kerosene lamp on the sideboard and then turned down the lamp. She used the dim candlelight to see her way to her bedroom and to light the lamp on her bed stand. She was relieved to get out of her dress, but it was chilly in her room. She relied on the heat from the kitchen and the parlor stove to warm her room, and this time of evening, the heat from those sources had waned. She happily shed the corset, but left the rest of her undergarments on and climbed into bed, snuggling under the wool blanket and quilted bed cover. She longed to read herself to sleep, but she had no book and would not use her cell phone for that purpose. She wiggled under the covers to warm up and missed Paul's warm body. A wave of sadness welled over her. Her thoughts turned to her friends Andrea and Randy. She prayed they were okay—that they had not been hurt during the earthquake and that they were in their own time, not lost like she was. Her family must be distraught, not knowing what had happened to her. She assumed she was missing in her time and that everyone was still looking for her. She missed them all, and her hope of ever seeing them again was dim. *"Cowgirl up, Emma,"* she told herself. *"You can't give in to the sadness."* She managed not to break down into sobs, but large tears ran down the sides of her face until she fell asleep.

Emma woke with a start. The room was dark and cold. Something had woken her, but all was silent. She scooted to the end of the bed, keeping the warm blankets around her, and looked out the window. She saw the Milky Way across the moonless sky. She saw a dim light in the blackness of the hills to the north and wondered if it was Ancha's fire light. A soft click of the kitchen door latch alerted her. Someone must have needed the outhouse. She looked at the stars again. They were beautiful. She had seen the Milky Way a few times in her life when she was out camping in Wyoming with her friends, but to see them from her bed, in town, was sublime. She looked again for the light in the hills but couldn't find it. Had she imagined it? She heard muffled footsteps going up the stairs and along the hall, but then all was quiet again. Fully awake now, she leaned over and retrieved her cell phone from her backpack, hidden under her bed. She just wanted to see Paul's face.

✑ CHAPTER 14 ✑

Emma shivered, blew on her hands and rubbed them together to warm them. She needed gloves. The morning light had not reached into the canyon and would not until nearly noon. She stood in front of the boulder where she had left the apples for Ancha. The apples were gone. In their place she found a single bear claw, attached to a beaded necklace by a sinew thong that made a loop at the top. She picked it up to admire the craftsmanship.

"I had a vision."

Emma spun around, startled by the voice behind her. There stood Ancha, his look boring a hole through her. She took a moment to collect herself. "A vision?"

"We are to be friends." Ancha continued his steady look. His dog came trotting up to his side and sat.

Emma set the necklace gently back where she found it. "This is beautiful. It's a bear claw, right?"

"It is for you."

"Oh! It's beautiful, but I couldn't accept such a fine thing. Did you get the apples? I know it wasn't much, but I wanted to thank you for saving my life. I should have brought something for your dog, too." Emma smiled at the dog. "He certainly helped. What's his name?"

Ancha walked to the boulder and took the necklace. He reached for Emma's hand and put the necklace in her palm, closing the fingers. "I had a vision. We are to be friends. This is for you," he repeated. "Dog's name is Kwiyaghat—means 'bear.'"

Emma looked down at the necklace. "Thank you. It is generous and kind of you." She was surprised at how comfortable she felt in the man's presence, even though his eyes seemed to see straight through her. He exuded a calmness that put her at ease. "I would like to be friends." She began shivering violently.

"Go back. Get warm," he said bluntly, then turned and walked back into the rocks, Kwiyaghat running after him.

She was too cold to call him back and learn more, but he had piqued her curiosity. She ran as best as she could in the walking skirt back to the boarding house, wondering, *What vision? What had it shown Ancha?"*

❋

"Is this appropriate for a funeral?" Emma asked Claire, spinning around in the dark plumb wool suit and black blouse.

"Yes, that is a perfect choice. It is cold today, so you will need a heavy cloak. You need a hat and gloves, too. There are several things I did not bring from the attic. Let's go get the cloak, and you can see what else is there you might want."

Emma had not had reason to go upstairs in the boarding house before. The staircase was steep and narrow; she wondered how they had moved the furniture in.

"As I mentioned before, I have six accommodations," Claire said as she climbed the stairs. "To the left of the stairs in the corner is Josiah's room and next to it, Willy's. The small suite opposite them is empty right now. Peter's room is toward the front to the right of the stairs, and Miss Sully's room is across the hall from his. Levi's suite is the corner unit."

Emma took a quick look around. "It's a nice place, Claire." And it was. The polished wooden hall floor, complimented by the tan and cream striped wallpapered walls, created a calm background. Each varnished door had a brass plate indicating the room number and was flanked by tulip-shaded kerosene lamp sconces to illuminate the tenant's entry. A window to the left at the end of the hall allowed sunlight in, which reached the length of the hall and ended at a sage green velvet upholstered bench at the far end. The door to Levi's suite was to the left of the bench. "Levi's suite is above the kitchen. I imagine that helps keep it warm," Emma observed, turning to follow Claire up the even narrower stairs to the attic.

"I should have brought a lamp." Claire lamented. The attic had small windows in the dormers, but they did not let in much light.

"It's okay. All I need right now is a cloak, a hat, and gloves."

"Yes. The cloak is hanging on that coat rack in the corner." Claire pointed to the far, dark corner of the attic. She knelt down in front of a large walnut chest and opened it. "Her black gloves are in here." The chest was cedar-lined and had a tray insert that rested on top. The tray held several pairs of gloves and scarves. "Here they are," Claire pulled out a pair of black kid leather gloves lined with wool with a single brass button at the wrists. "The hats are over here." Claire walked to a stack of hat boxes piled against the wall and began going through them, one by one, until she came to the hat she was looking for. "This one will work nicely, I think," she said, holding up a black, wide-brimmed beaver hat with a small flat crown and black ostrich plumes.

Emma took the hat, cringing that it was made from a beaver pelt. Well, it would be warm anyway, she thought ruefully. And as her mother frequently said, "Beggars can't be choosers." She would also add that ingratitude was the height of bad manners. "Yes, thank you," Emma said.

※

"My heavens, it's cold!" Alice exclaimed quietly as she joined Claire, Emma, and Levi outside the church.

"Yes, it's unfortunate," said Emma. "It makes it harder to observe the funeral attendees. I was particularly hoping to observe Carson's friends and family." Emma saw a man about her age escorting a young woman up the walkway. "Is that Anna?" She asked Claire.

"It is, poor dear. And that is John Calhoun, Jr., escorting her. The couple behind them are Mr. and Mrs. John Calhoun, Sr."

Anna was in full mourning dress. The veil over her face made it impossible to discern what she looked like, much less what her face may communicate. Her clothes were fine, and she carried herself with dignity. She was short and slightly built. Emma thought she looked doll-like, she was so diminutive. John tipped his hat to the group as he walked by, expressionless.

"Tommy said there would be a reception after the interment at the Cliff House," Levi told the ladies. "We may observe something there. I understand it will be quite elaborate."

"I didn't know the White brothers were so well-to-do,"

Claire said. "Ah, there is Josiah!" She waved to get his attention. He saw the group and walked toward them.

"Their father has some money, I believe. He and their sister could not come from New York in time for the funeral, of course. Perhaps they wired money. In any case, I'm sure Mr. Calhoun would make sure it was done properly for Anna's sake. He dotes on the girl, I understand," Levi shook Josiah's hand as he joined them. "Good afternoon, Josiah."

"We were just discussing the funeral reception." Claire explained to Josiah.

"Yes, you are quite right, Levi. Mr. Calhoun would make sure the reception is done right." Emma detected a slight tone of criticism in Josiah's tone. "It looks like everyone is gathering inside the church." He gestured for the ladies to walk ahead of him, offering his arm to Emma as she walked by. Levi brought up the rear of the group, watching the woman in his dead wife's clothes walk ahead with the other man.

❁

Most people had been at The Cliff House dining room for the funeral reception for some time, enjoying the food that Tommy White had arranged, when those who had attended Carson's interment arrived. They formed a short reception party, comprising only Tommy, the Calhouns, and Josiah.

"Come, let's pay our respects," Claire said, "and I will introduce you, Emma."

Emma was glad for the opportunity to meet those closest to Carson. She wanted a chance to form her own judgement of each of them. The stoic nature of people in these times made it harder to read them, but she still felt it was likely that one of them had killed the landscaper. They seemed to have lined up according to their relationship to Carson, starting with Josiah

115

and ending with Anna and Tommy.

"Miss Calhoun, please accept my deepest sympathy for your loss." Claire folded her hands in front of her and tilted her head, leaning forward slightly as she spoke to Anna. "May I present my cousin, Miss Emma Quinn. She came to us just this week from New Orleans. She, too, has suffered the profound loss of her family to a fire."

"I am sorry to meet you under these circumstances, Miss Calhoun," Emma said softly, lowering her head, then looking at the young woman in the veil. She could see only the shape of Anna's face beneath the black crepe.

"It seems we have mourning in common, Miss Quinn. I also extend my sympathy to you." Anna's voice was almost childish, high-pitched and lacking the richness of an adult's tone.

They were forced to move along to allow other guests to pay their respects. Claire and Emma joined Alice and Levi near the large fire place, each accepting a glass of wine offered by a passing waiter.

"May I join you?" Peter Graham approached the group.

"Of course." Levi turned to make room for Peter.

"It's certainly a well-done reception." Peter said, taking a sip of red wine. "The oyster pie was delicious. Did you try it?"

"Yes, the food is excellent. I'd expect no less from Tommy." Levi agreed.

"Look at how many people are here to pay their respects," Claire lifted her chin to indicate the long reception line. "I feel so badly for Anna, dressed in full mourning. It's so heavy."

"Unhealthy, as well." Alice added. "I hope she doesn't plan to stay in full mourning for long. It's fairly well-established that the dyes they use contain a dangerous level of arsenic."

"Oh my! Well, Alice, you should tell her!" Claire exclaimed.

"I doubt there is much risk that she will continue wearing

116

that veil after today." Peter said ruefully, smirking slightly.

"Why do you say so?" Claire's tone chastised Peter.

Peter turned his back to the reception line and leaned toward the group conspiratorially. "I understand that she is socially ambitious. She will be searching for a suitable replacement for Carson as soon as possible."

"What an uncharitable thing to say, Mr. Graham." Claire scolded. "Where did you get such an idea?"

"Truthfully, from Carson himself, though he did not put it in those terms exactly."

"Were you a close friend of Carson's Mr. Graham?" Emma asked.

"I wouldn't say so, no. I knew him mostly through our card games. We played several times at the boarding house, did we not, Claire?"

"Yes, I'd say you played about once a week—more often than that before Carson started courting Anna."

Emma turned her gaze to Josiah, still receiving people in line. He saw her looking at him and nodded, looking weary of his social obligation to accept condolences. She would have to find a way to discover what Josiah's opinion of Anna was. Maybe Willy, too, she thought, remembering that he also played cards with Carson. "I don't see Willy Stewart here." She noticed, looking around the room.

"He probably felt uncomfortable about coming." Claire speculated.

"Why would he feel uncomfortable?' Emma asked. Mr. Graham looked at her with raised eyebrows. The others looked surprised at her question.

"Willy works at the livery tending the horses." Graham said, obviously thinking that a sufficient explanation.

Emma just stared, not comprehending.

"This isn't Willy's usual social circle," Claire elaborated.

"He would likely feel out of place."

"I see." Emma said flatly.

"I'm surprised you are not in mourning, Miss Quinn, having just lost your parents." Graham seemed to take satisfaction in putting Emma on the spot. Emma remained silent, not knowing what the appropriate reaction was.

"I say, Peter, that is a rather insensitive comment." Levi came to Emma's defense. "Not only did she lose her family, she also lost her worldly possessions."

Levi's statement surprised Emma. She had not expected him to get so involved in her cover story. She had thought the best she could hope for was that he would not actively refute it. She gave him a small smile of gratitude.

"I apologize, Miss Quinn. I meant no offense," Graham said, begrudging his reprimand, then added, "I will excuse myself. I see someone I'd like to greet." He gave Levi a sideways glance and walked away, though it was not clear to whom he was referring as he wandered through the room.

"Honestly Claire, that man is insufferable," Alice scowled at Graham's back. "He thinks he is so superior, and on what basis, I ask you?"

"He fancies himself an intellect, I think," Claire said.

"Humph," was Alice's final word on the subject. Levi let out a soft laugh, amused by Alice's outspokenness.

"Alice, I've been working on determining the window of time when Carson could have been killed," Emma said, changing the subject. "I know about the earliest time he could have died, but I was hoping to get a better idea of when the latest time was."

"This is not the place to be having this conversation, Emma. I'll go back to the boarding house with you and we can discuss it there." Alice suggested.

❧ CHAPTER 15 ❧

"This is the timeline I'm developing," Emma said, pointing at the butcher's paper pinned to the wall of the reading room. Alice, Levi, and Claire sat at the table studying the details.

"You have the earliest Carson could have been killed as two forty-five in the afternoon," Alice observed. "But how do you know that?"

"That's when Josiah says he left Carson. Even if Josiah killed Carson, which I do not believe he did, that would be the earliest time." Emma explained.

"What if Josiah killed Carson earlier? We only have his word for the time of the meeting on the ledge at Williams Cañon." Alice pointed out.

"They expected Mr. Albright, so they were there a bit before the scheduled meeting. I doubt Josiah would have killed Carson when he believed Mr. Albright would appear any minute." Emma reminded them.

"Mr. Albright is in Denver today. I plan to talk to him

Monday. He will be able to verify if they had a scheduled meeting," Levi added.

"For now, let's assume Josiah is telling us the truth. What I was hoping to determine is the latest Carson could have been killed," Emma said to focus the discussion. "Alice, can you estimate how long Carson had been dead when the men brought him to the Cliff House that night?"

Alice thought for a moment. "When I examined him, he was pale. His hands were cold, but when I opened his shirt to check his heart, I noticed it was cooler than usual, but not like his exposed hands. I did not notice that rigor mortis had begun, but I regret to say I didn't do a thorough examination specifically for that purpose. It may have started, but I would say only just."

"What does that say about how long he had been dead?" Emma asked.

"It is imprecise, but I would say he had been dead at least two hours, perhaps as many as four."

"And what time was he brought to you?" Levi asked.

"It was right at half-past-six o'clock that evening."

Emma made a mark and labeled it to indicate when Carson was brought to Alice. "Four hours earlier would have been two-thirty, which is consistent with what we've assumed. It seems the most likely window is from two-thirty to four-thirty that afternoon. That is helpful, having such a narrow window."

Alice looked at the watch pinned to her jacket. "I must get home. Sarah will be starting dinner soon."

"Thank you for your help." Levi stood up to help Alice out of her seat. Claire went with her to show her out.

"Egad, it's cold!" Levi and Emma looked at each other and laughed, hearing Alice's exclamation coming from the other room.

"Yes, yes, so please be on your way, Alice, so I can close the door." Claire commanded.

They heard the door shut, the squeak of the parlor stove open, the pop and hiss of the fire, and the clank of the stove closing. Claire returned to the reading room.

"It is going to be frigid tonight, I think. Emma, you may want to sleep in the parlor tonight to keep warm. At the very least, keep your door open so the heat can have a hope of reaching your room. Levi, if you don't have your stove going, you'd better start the fire now if you want heat tonight."

Levi gave Emma an amused smile. "I know when I'm being dismissed." Levi stood and kissed Claire on the cheek. "Good afternoon, ladies."

※

Emma went into her room and changed into a more comfortable skirt and blouse. She found a warm shawl in the drawer and wrapped it around her shoulders. Gathering the pen, ink, and journal she had bought—or rather Claire had bought—she went into the reading room. She found Claire sitting at the table with the deck of cards Emma had found a couple of days earlier. "Are those tarot cards?" Emma set her writing things aside on the table. "Will you tell my fortune, Claire?"

"They are called Le Petit Lenormand," Claire shuffled the cards. I know they are not the exact kind that Mlle. Lenormand used, but they capture the essence. My teacher, Madam Bellefleur, studied under Mlle. Lenormand. You've no doubt heard of her?"

"I've never heard of either of them." Emma sat across from Claire.

"Really? Mlle. Lenormand is still famous even though she has been dead nearly forty years. She was Marie Antoinette's fortune-teller. She never married but was quite wealthy when she died. Her foolish nephew was her only heir, and he destroyed all her occult writings after her death. I am very fortunate to have learned from someone who knew her." Claire laid the cards on the table and looked at Emma.

A gust of wind rattled the window and stirred the curtains slightly, drawing the women's attention.

"It is getting colder outside. I fear tonight will be the coldest one we've had so far this season," Claire mused.

Emma, still looking at the window, thought of Ancha and Kwiyaghat, huddled together somewhere. "I hope Ancha will be all right."

Claire turned back to Emma. "It's commendable that you have compassion for Ancha, but I must warn you not to get too friendly with him, Emma."

Emma turned sharply back at Claire. "Why not?"

Claire was taken aback that more detail was necessary. "Well, isn't it obvious? He's an Indian."

"You don't strike me as the kind of person who would be racist, Claire?" Emma said, calmly. "What does his being an Indian have to do with anything? He gets cold just like any other human being."

"Well, of course he does. But his people have lived here forever. They know how to cope."

Emma shook her head, dismayed that Claire did not appreciate the irony of her statement.

"I'll read your fortune, Emma." Claire picked up the cards, hoping to divert the conversation. "What is your question?"

"Will I ever get back to my own time?"

Claire picked up the deck and handed it to Emma. "Shuffle a few times while you think of your question and then cut the cards."

Emma did as she was instructed. Claire re-stacked the

cards and laid out nine of them in a three-by-three array.

"How appropriate. 'The Ship' is in the center. This is the card of travel. There are three hearts and three spades, so they are balanced. There are only two clubs, but they are close to the Ship." Claire considered the other cards. Emma noticed the pictures on the cards. The one with a ring and the one with a bear captured her attention. Clair let out a sigh.

"What? What do the cards say, Claire?"

Claire looked up at Emma. "I wish they were clearer, Emma, but sometimes that's a good thing. It means the future depends more on our choices and actions."

"But what do they say?"

"*The Ring, The Star, The Bouquet, The Bear, The Ship, The Whip, The Anchor, The Moon,* and *The House.*" Claire named each card left to right and top to bottom. "They indicate that you were in a committed relationship that brought you happiness. A power beyond your control separated you. Going forward, you will need motivation and discipline to overcome obstacles. The path to success will not be easy, but you will gain stability. The Moon indicates recognition for your efforts. Ultimately, you will find home." Claire did not share with Emma that the cards also said she may be stuck in wishful thinking or fantasy, and where (or perhaps more accurately when) "home" was could not be determined.

"Yes, yes, that makes sense to me," Emma said. Emma pointed at the Bear. "What does this card mean? Can it be a person?" She thought of the real bear she had recently encountered—and Ancha.

"It represents power and force, sometimes a powerful person." Claire laughed a little and said, "It can also represent an actual bear!"

Emma leaned over the cards to get a better look at them, studying each picture.

"I would be happy to teach you more about reading cards, if you'd like." Claire offered.

Emma leaned back in her chair and smiled. "Maybe another time. Right now, I'd like to do some writing in my journal."

Claire gathered up the cards and closed her eyes as she shuffled them, preparing to do her own reading for the day. The parlor stove had warmed the reading room to a cozy temperature. The kerosene lamp augmented the late afternoon sunlight, making the room glow a light yellow-orange. Emma had a sense of domestic comfort, enjoying the quiet companionship the two women shared.

November 11, 1882

How strange to be writing that date. I still find it impossible that I'm back in time. I am the unluckiest person in the world to have gotten caught in a time portal produced by an earthquake. The odds of creating the exact conditions for that to happen must be astronomical! What are the variables? What is their relationship? Can they be replicated? How do I even begin?

I miss Paul desperately. I wonder what he is doing, how he is feeling. I wonder how my family is doing. Are they looking for me? Do they believe I'm dead?

I am grateful for Claire and Alice, though. I would be hopeless without them.

I wonder what Ancha's vision was and what he meant when he said that we are to be friends. Is it possible he can help me?

"Are you all right?" Claire asked.

"I just miss everyone," Emma wiped a tear from her face.

"Don't lose hope, Emma." Claire reached out and gave Emma's arm a gentle squeeze. The clock in the parlor struck five o'clock. "I'll be in the kitchen if you need me."

↝ CHAPTER 16 ↜

Emma ventured into the kitchen soon after Claire to find Molly finishing dinner preparations.

"Dinner will be ready soon, Miss Quinn." Molly wiped her hand on her apron and used it to insulate her hands as she opened the oven door. A waft of the savory scent of onions and carrots came drifting past Emma's nose, making her mouth water. How could she be hungry after indulging in all the food at the funeral reception?

"It smells wonderful, as does everything you make Molly. How can I help?"

Molly turned to Emma, looking uncomfortable. "Why Miss Quinn, you are a guest here."

"I am a poor relative, living off the generosity of my cousin. I mean to earn my keep here as best I can, and please, call me Emma."

Just then Claire walked in from the passageway to the dining room.

"Claire, please tell Molly to let me help her. I'll do whatever she needs me to do."

Claire turned to Molly. "If Emma wants to help, by all means let her, Molly."

"All right, Ma'am," Molly acquiesced. She looked around in search of what needed doing. "I suppose you could make the biscuits, Miss . . . I mean Emma."

"Absolutely! Where is your recipe?"

Molly gave Claire a long-suffering look that said, *She is going to be more trouble than she's worth.*"

"Perhaps Emma could set the table and help you get the dinner out," Claire suggested. Molly immediately looked relieved.

"Yes! I can do that!" Emma offered.

"Come with me, I'll show you were we keep the place settings," Claire said over her shoulder as she walked to the dining room.

"I'm not sure I know how to set a proper table, either, Claire." Emma whispered, standing next to Claire at the sideboard. Claire opened the top drawer and began taking out the silverware. Claire looked skeptically at Emma. "I know I must seem utterly useless to you," Emma continued in a quiet voice. "People aren't as focused on these things in my time. Heck, we hardly ever even eat at the table. We usually eat in front of the . . ." She caught herself just in time again. "window."

"The window? How strange," Claire frowned. "Well, we must start somewhere, then. How to set a table is as good a place as any."

Emma felt ridiculously inadequate. She could do differential equations, but she did not know how to make biscuits or set a table. What use will she be here and now?

Claire described what she was doing as she laid down one place setting. "We usually stack the plates at the end of the sideboard so folks can serve themselves there."

Using Claire's example as her model, Emma managed to set the rest of the place settings. Claire supervised and gave her a wide smile of approval when she finished.

"How about some music before dinner?" Claire suggested. She walked through the archway and took a seat at the upright piano. She lifted the lid and began playing "Reuben and Rachel."

"Oh, I know that one!" Emma exclaimed when she heard the tune. She stood behind Claire and sang along to the first verse and chorus. Claire didn't have the sheet music; she was playing the tune by heart. When Emma stopped singing, Claire stopped playing.

"Why did you stop singing, Emma? You have a beautiful voice!"

"I only know the first verse."

"Well, I'll teach you the words, my dear. Do you know 'Molly Darling'?"

"No. But I know 'Oh! Suzannah,'" Emma offered, hopefully.

"Hooray!" and Claire began playing the tune.

Both women laughed joyfully when they had finished singing. They both spun around when they heard clapping coming from the parlor.

"Bravo!" Levi said, his claps joined by Josiah's and Miss Sully's.

"Oh, do another song, please!" Miss Sully requested over her claps. "Miss Quinn, your voice is like an angel's."

"Dinner is served!" Molly called from the dining room, saving Emma the awkwardness of having to confess that, as far as she knew, she didn't know any other songs of the day.

Levi followed Emma into the dining room. "You do have a lovely voice, Emma."

"Thank you, Levi." Emma handed him a plate and took one for herself. Molly had put a large serving platter out that held the beef pot roast she had made. It was carved and surrounded by potatoes, carrots, and onions. Emma hesitated.

"Is something wrong with the roast, Emma?" Levi asked, looking at the platter.

"No, it's perfect, I'm sure." Emma realized then that she would have to revise her diet constraints. She could not expect Molly to accommodate her preferences when she was cooking for many, especially as she herself was a beggar of sorts. She took a slice of beef and surrounded it with the vegetables.

"Does the beef come from nearby ranches?" Emma asked, taking her seat.

"Of course," Claire answered. "We have the finest grassland in the state around Colorado Springs."

Emma supposed that the cattle were treated as well as the chickens in the backyard, enjoying the sunshine and grassland until their last day. They were circumstances she could accept, she decided, taking a bite of her dinner.

Molly customarily left immediately after serving dinner because she had a family of her own. Emma insisted on cleaning up after the boarders had finished eating. She wanted to be of some value to Claire. The task seemed straightforward, but Emma soon learned that it was not. She debated whether to heat water for cleaning, and after looking around the kitchen for soap and finding none, decided it would be necessary if she had any hope of getting the dishes and pots clean. She discovered the pot on the stove held water that was hot and assumed Molly had heated the water for cleaning purposes. *"Ugh, it's like I never knew how to do anything."* Emma said to herself. She sorted out which tubs to use and forged a plan for doing the task. As she scrubbed the pots, she heard muted piano music from the parlor and voices singing.

After she finished the dishes, she joined the tenants in the parlor. Claire was playing a quiet tune at the piano. Miss Sully was crocheting something, a headrest cover, perhaps. The heat coming from the parlor stove warmed the room almost uncomfortably. The men were gathered near the sideboard, enjoying an after dinner drink.

"Are you sure you won't join us for some cards, Levi?" Peter asked. Willy and Josiah waited hopefully for Levi's reply.

"You know I don't play, Peter."

"I just thought, now that Carson is gone . . ." Peter's voice drifted

"I'll play." Emma said, brightly.

"We play poker, Miss Quinn." Peter clarified politely.

"Texas hold 'em? Five-card stud? Seven-card stud? Black jack?" She asked, failing to see her mistake.

Everyone in the room seemed frozen in place. They looked at her as if she were standing there buck naked.

"Poker is wildly popular in New Orleans. Everyone plays it there, isn't that right Levi." Claire came to Emma's rescue.

Levi glared at Claire. "Not everyone, Claire."

"Very well, not *everyone*, but many," Claire said, laughing to lighted the mood. "I believe it started there, in fact, back before the Louisiana Purchase."

By then, Emma had put together that perhaps it was not proper for women to play poker and gamble in the nineteenth century. Also, she wondered how old all of the games she had mentioned were. She had never thought about it before. She tried to walk it back what she said. "Perhaps some of these are games my family came up with. I just took for granted everyone played them. As for gambling, I'd have to use toothpicks, as I have no money. I just thought since we are in the privacy of our boarding house . . ."

"I'm game to using toothpicks," offered Josiah, obviously

trying to be helpful.

"I'd be willing to, too," added Willy.

"Well, I hardly see the point of playing without a meaningful wager. It's really not poker without wagering." Peter grumbled.

Emma was irritated. She enjoyed poker, with or without money bets, and she just wanted a pleasant division.

"What about whist?" Josiah suggested.

"Oh, forget the whole damnable thing," Peter said. "I'm going to my room. Good night."

Everyone seemed to relax once Peter Graham had left the room.

"I'd play whist," Claire said. "Levi?"

"Yes, I suppose."

"I'm afraid I don't play the game, but I'd watch." Willy added.

"If you will remind me of the rules. It's been a while." Emma had never heard of whist, but fools jump in where angels fear to tread. She longed for some fun.

As it turned out, whist was similar enough to bridge or spades that Emma picked up on it quickly. She and Josiah formed one team, Levi and Claire the other. Claire agreed to keep score. During Levi's deal, Emma made small talk. "It's interesting how one person can change the dynamics of a group. The game had been poker, and the players, you," as she lifted her chin toward Josiah and Willy, "and Mr. Graham and Carson. Now it's whist, and the only common player is Josiah. All because Carson is, sadly, gone."

"Yeah, I'm gonna miss our poker games." Willy said, sitting between Josiah and Claire, peeking at their hands. "But this game whist looks right interestin'."

Josiah remained silent. Emma tried another tack to engage him. "Did Carson play whist, Josiah?"

"I can't say. The subject never came up. He was an ace poker player though." Then he laughed and said, "He wiped Graham out regularly, didn't he Willy?"

"Heck, yeah. Why the last time we played, Graham hinted Carson was cheatin'. I thought it was gonna end in a gun fight out on Cañon Ave.," laughed Willy.

Levi and Emma exchanged a quick glance.

"It was nonsense, of course. Carson was the most honest man I ever knew," Josiah added. "Graham was pretty mad, though."

"How much did Graham lose to Carson that night?" Levi asked.

Willy and Josiah looked at each other, considering the answer. "I'd say it was close to a hundred dollars," Josiah said.

"My heavens!" Claire exclaimed. "That's nearly three months' wages for Mr. Graham! I had no idea you fellows played such high stakes."

"We don't. Willy and I had cashed out long before. I'm not sure what possessed Graham to get so competitive. Then he started losing, but instead of cutting his losses, he kept playing. Carson suggested several times to call it a night, but Graham insisted they keep playing to give him a chance to win back his losses."

"How did he settle up with Carson? Surely he didn't have one hundred dollars at the ready?" Levi, sensing the importance of this discovery to his investigation, pressed the men.

"He wrote Carson an IOU." Willy offered.

"When was this last game?" Emma asked.

Again, Josiah and Willy looked at each other in collective thought.

"Well, it was last Saturday night, right Josiah, the Saturday before Carson was killed?"

"Indeed, it was."

↝ Chapter 17 ↜

The temperature that night fell well below freezing. Emma lay in her bed, keeping the door to the reading room open to allow the heat from the parlor stove in. She had wanted to talk to Levi about what they had learned about Graham, but the card game had run long and it was too late when everyone retired. She couldn't get warm, so she went to the parlor and lay on the sofa with her wool blanket. The stove kept that room sufficiently warm, at least. Claire's cat Lulu jumped up and snuggled against Emma, purring. Emma put her arm over Lulu and gave her a little squeeze. "I needed a kitty hug." Emma murmured to the cat as she drifted off to sleep.

"Wake up Emma." Claire gently shook Emma. "It's time to get up. Sunday is Molly's day off, so I have to fix breakfast before we leave for church."

Emma propped herself up on her elbow and looked around the parlor, feeling groggy and disoriented. It was still dark outside. Claire was holding a lamp over Emma's head.

"Yes, all right. I'll help you," Emma said sleepily.

Claire got the kitchen stove fire started. While they waited for it to heat, she began preparing the biscuits. Emma went out to gather eggs at the hen house. It was tricky, balancing the lamp and gathering the eggs, but she managed.

"Burrrhhh, it is freezing out there!" Emma complained as she walked into the kitchen. "I hope these eggs didn't freeze in the time it took me to walk back."

Claire laughed. "The fire is hot now. I'm heating some water if you want to use it to wash up before you dress for church."

Emma hesitated. She was not much of a church-goer, but there didn't seem to be any question that she would accompany Claire. It would give her an opportunity to observe her new community, she thought, putting a positive spin on it.

"Go get the water pitchers from our rooms and I'll fill them with hot water." Claire ordered.

Emma washed up at her washstand and dressed quickly. She returned to the kitchen and did her best to help Claire finish getting breakfast ready. She and Claire had just set the meal on the sideboard when Levi came down, dressed for church.

"Good morning, Emma, Claire." Levi served himself and took his seat.

Emma took the seat next to him. She leaned toward him and said with her voice lowered, "I wanted to talk to you last night, but I didn't have the chance. We must add Mr. Graham to our suspect list, don't you think? He is the first person who has an apparent motive, as far as we know."

"Yes, I agree," he answered, equally quietly. He took a breath to say more, but Willy Stewart walked in with a bounce in his step.

"Good mornin' ladies, Levi." Willy piled eggs on his plate and drizzled honey over his biscuit. He sat and poured a cup of coffee from the pot on the table. He had greased his hair back with pomade and waxed his mustache. Emma guessed he also planned to attend church. "Sure is cold outside, ain't it?" He took a big bite of eggs and smiled.

"Willy, last night you said Peter had signed an IOU for the money he owed Carson," Levi started

"Yeah, that's right."

"Do you know how long he had to pay it off?"

"Naw. But I do recall Carson sayin' somethin' about it going a long way toward a nice honeymoon for him and Miss Anna. So I reckon Carson wanted it afore the wedding."

"Let's clean up the breakfast dishes, Emma." Claire interrupted, consulting her lapel watch. "We can leave the biscuits and honey out for the others when they come down. Church starts soon."

❀

"I'm Catholic," Claire explained to Emma on their walk to the Congregational church. "But we only have mass on the fourth Sunday of the month this time of year. We have to share Rev. Byrne with the church in Colorado Springs. We meet in the schoolhouse on Ute Ave. Are you Catholic, Emma? Levi here goes to the Congregational church. So does Alice, so I join them on the Sundays I don't have mass."

Emma and Levi looked at each other and smiled at Claire's rambling. Emma took advantage of the fact and avoided answering Claire's question. Claire didn't seem to notice.

"All the 'society' people go to the Episcopal church because Dr. Bell is a member." Claire pointed to the Episcopal church as they walked down Cañon Ave. "Dr. Bell is from England, you know," Claire added as though it was an explanation. "Look! There's Anna and her parents. Looks like Mr. Graham was right about Anna shedding her mourning veil."

Anna and her parents were standing at the end of the walkway on the street, talking to the gentleman Emma thought was Mr. Albright. Levi, Claire, and Emma stopped to greet the group.

"Good morning, Mr. Calhoun, Mr. Albright," Levi said, extending his hand to each man. "Good morning, ladies." He nodded and reached for the brim of his boulder hat to greet them. "Terribly cold this morning, isn't it?"

"Indeed it is, Marshal." Mr. Albright agreed, looking curiously at Emma.

"This is Miss Quinn, Claire's cousin from New Orleans." Levi said, presenting Emma to Mr. Albright.

"It's a pleasure to meet you, Mr. Albright."

"This pleasure is mine, to be sure, Miss Quinn," Albright said, taking Emma's gloved hand and giving her a little bow.

"We missed you at Carson's funeral yesterday, Mr. Albright." Claire said pleasantly.

"Yes, I'm afraid I had business in Denver that could not wait. I returned on the late train yesterday evening."

While the small talk took place, Emma got her first look at Anna, who seemed unaware she was being observed. She was not a particularly pretty woman. She had heavy-hooded eyelids that drooped downward on the sides of her gray eyes. Her narrow, sharp chin pointed out well beyond her mouth, indicating, perhaps, a slight under-bite. Although she was still dressed in black, her veil was draped behind her head.

Anna became conscious of Emma's eyes on her. She turned to Emma and said in her childish voice, "Miss Quinn, I regret I did not have the opportunity to talk more to you yesterday. The reception went on so long. Perhaps we can provide some comfort to each other in our time of grief. You and Mrs. La Salle must come have tea with Mama and me next week. We can become better acquainted."

"I'd like that very much," Emma accepted.

"Good. Mama, would Tuesday be agreeable to you?"

"Of course, my dear. Miss Quinn, Mrs. La Salle, please join us then."

"We'd love to." Claire affirmed.

"Come ladies, it's too cold to tarry, and we will be late for church," Levi smiled and took Claire by the arm.

Emma looked over her shoulder as she followed and saw Josiah running up to Anna, offering her his arm as they went up the walkway and into the church.

❀

"I know Reverend Jones said we should love our neighbors as ourselves, but I just can't, I'm so mad." Alice stomped her foot on Claire's parlor rug with an unsatisfying silence. "I've been running that bath house for years, and now they tell me there is no position for me at the new one."

"What do you mean, my dear? They will have so many more guests, so much more to do, at the new one. And they will need an attending physician, surely." Claire motioned Alice to sit down before taking her own seat.

"All the high and mighty men of Colorado Springs and Manitou have decided it wouldn't do to have a female physician."

"Even for the ladies?"

Alice sat down and made an angry wave, as if to shoo the thought of the men like a fly. "To hell with them."

"Alice!" Claire scolded.

"I mean it, Claire. I'm as good a physician as anyone around—better than some, if you know what I mean."

"Oh, don't tell me they are asking Dr. Wilson to be the

resident physician! That would verge on criminal!"

"No, no, even they know better than that, but that isn't the point."

"So just stay at the old bath house. You have a lease for it, do you not?"

"Yes, with the Colorado Springs Company, the very one that owns the lease for the new bath house. They say they are going to convert the old one into a bottling plant. They're cancelling my lease as soon as the new bath house opens."

"I'm so sorry, Alice. You've been running the bath house ever since I've known you."

Emma listened to the two friends, trying to piece things together. "Can they break your lease like that? Don't you have it in writing?"

Alice's look said "silly girl." She went on to say, "The Colorado Springs Company owns this town, quite literally, Emma." Alice let out a breath. "I don't know what I am going to do. My family relies on me for income."

Claire bowed her head and looked at her hands folded on her lap, then lifted her eyes at Alice, embarrassed for her. This shifted when a devilish grin bloomed on her face as she lifted her chin. "What are you doing on Tuesday, Alice?"

"Why do you ask?"

"I think you should join us at the Calhoun's for tea. I'll send a note to Mrs. Calhoun with Molly asking if it would be all right."

"I'm sorry, Claire, but what does tea on Tuesday have to do with what we've been discussing?" Emma asked. It wasn't unusual for Claire to bounce from subject to subject, but this seemed an unusual non sequitur, even for Claire.

"I just think it would be pleasant if Alice joined us."

Alice shook her head, a bit frustrated with the conversation. "Yes, I suppose I could join you if you'd like, Claire." She looked at the clock. "I must be off. Sarah will have

Sunday supper ready soon." She gave Claire a kiss on the cheek.

"That sucks for Alice," Emma said after Alice had left.

Claire gave Emma a look of puzzlement. But she understood the sentiment, if not the words. "I don't know what things are like in your day, Emma, but in this place and time a hand full of rich men decide what happens. The best regular people like us can do is play to their weaknesses." Claire went to the stove and gave the fire a violent poke with the poker, stoking the flames.

❧ CHAPTER 18 ❧

After Emma had helped clean up from supper, she returned to her room. She wanted desperately to change into something warm and comfortable, like a pair of flannel pajamas and soft, fuzzy socks. She wanted to snuggle up in her bed with her journal and a pen that did not need to be dipped in ink every three or four words. She reached under the bed and pulled out her backpack, placing it on the bed next to her. She regretted that she had taken out most of the things she usually carried in it for the day trip to Cave of the Winds. Still, she thought she might find a pen or two stuck in one of the many little pockets. In one pocket she found some lip balm and hand wipes wrapped in individual packets. She found her plastic reusable water bottle in the main compartment. In the next pocket she found her wallet, which included her credit cards, ATM card, driver's license, and fifty-seven dollars in cash. The bottom of the pocket held another couple of dollars in coins. *"Fat lot of good all of this stuff is now,"* she thought. The cash, with the dates ranging from 2006 to 2017, wasn't even of any use to her. She reached deeper in the pocket, and it was ridiculous how happy she felt when she found a gel pen. She propped her feather pillow against the headboard and reached for her journal on the nightstand.

November 12, 1882

Paul, I wish I would wake and find these last few days had been a dream. I wish I'd wake and turn to find you sleeping next to me in our bedroom with the light blue curtains. Then, after we made love, I could tell you about the crazy dream I'd had.

Writing was not providing the comfort she sought. Her sadness overwhelmed her thoughts, so Emma put her journal down and returned the pen to her backpack. She opened the center pocket and pulled out the bear claw necklace Ancha had given her. She laid back in her bed, clasped the necklace in her hand, and held it to her chest. It calmed her to hold it.

❀

Emma's grandmother always did laundry on Mondays. Emma never thought much about it because her grandmother had a chore for each day of the week. But when Emma entered the kitchen Monday morning, Claire was walking in from the hallway, carrying bed linens and towels.

"It's laundry day, Emma," Claire dropped her armful into a large tin tub that sat on the kitchen floor. Molly was heating up a big pot of water on the stove. "The tenants put the clothes they want washed in a flour sack and leave it in the hallway.

141

They put any suits they want cleaned on the hook by their door. You could help us by bringing down each tenant's laundry and logging it so we can return each item to the proper owner." Claire opened a drawer from a cupboard and pulled out a ledger. "Don't forget to go through the pockets. Those men never seem to remember to empty their pockets."

Emma did as Claire requested, bringing each tenant's laundry down, being careful to keep them separate as she went through pockets and logged each item. Levi had left a silver dollar, three nickels, and a dime in his corduroy pants. Peter Graham had left a handkerchief that also needed laundering, embroidered with his initials, in his jacket. Willy's jeans pockets were empty. "Miss Sully didn't have any laundry set out." Emma said, as she moved on to the last pile.

"The hotel allows her to do her laundry there. I charge her a little less for her room and board since we don't do her laundry. Everyone benefits." Claire explained, pouring the hot water into the tub and pouring salt into the water. Molly sat a bottle of cheap gin and a stiff brush on the table, pulled a flour cloth rag from her waistband, and picked up Graham's jacket. She poured some gin onto the rag and dabbed an oily spot on the jacket.

Emma began going through the last set of clothing, which belonged to Josiah. His pants pockets and the pockets of the suit jacket were empty. He had also put out his dress overcoat. The side pockets were also empty, but when she reached into the lapel pocket, she felt a piece of paper. She pulled out a folded sheet of writing paper and set it aside. The paper fell off the table and landed slightly opened. Emma saw the start of the writing, *I, Peter Graham of Manitou, Colorado, owe* . . . Emma hesitated only a moment, checking to make sure Claire and Molly were not looking, before she opened the paper. The note read:

November 4, 1882

I Peter Graham, of Manitou, Colorado, owe Carson White, of Manitou, Colorado, the amount of one hundred twelve dollars ($112.00), to be paid in full by December 31, 1882.

It was signed with Graham's signature. Emma noticed a reddish- brown smudge on the lower left side of the note. She was no expert, but it looked like dried blood to her. How had Josiah come in possession of this IOU? If it was blood, whose was it? Emma folded it and put it in her own pocket to deal with later. She needed to think about what it could mean.

"Emma, fetch the other two tubs from the cellar and fill one of them with water to rinse the clothes in," Claire instructed.

"What is the other tub for?"

"You can put the clothes in them after you rinse and wring them out."

The three women engaged in idle chatter as they worked to clean the tenants' linens clothes. Molly removed spots from clothes that could not be immersed in water—things Emma would have taken to the dry cleaners. "My heavens, this stain on Levi's suit jacket does not want to come out. I'm going to have to pull out my special stuff." Molly went over to a shelf and brought down a tin. She opened it and sprinkled the powdered contents onto the spot she had been working on.

"I've been trying to get Molly to share the formula for her spot remover with me ever since she's worked here. She won't do it." Claire said, smiling at Molly.

"It's something my mother handed down to me, Ma'am. I consider it a family secret and job security." Molly laughed, clearly not sincerely worried.

Emma's hands were getting fatigued from wringing out the

143

water from the clothes. She looked with a sense of dread at the substantial quantity of undergarments, sheets, towels, and shirts left to do.

The rhythmic sounds of the washing, rinsing, and wringing was interrupted by the sound of the front door opening and slamming shut quickly, followed by quick, heavy boot steps coming down the hall. The women looked up to see Levi walking into the kitchen, an urgent expression on his handsome face.

"What is it, Levi?" Claire asked

"Josiah has been arrested for Carson's murder."

❧ CHAPTER 19 ❧

"How is this possible?" Emma looked across the reading room table at Levi. "You are the town marshal."

"Sheriff Dana had him arrested when he arrived at his office in Colorado Springs this morning." Levi paced back and forth in the room. "The sheriff asked his deputy to telephone me afterwards as a 'professional courtesy,' the deputy said."

"Well, they can't possibly have any proof, Levi. I mean, you are the one who has been doing the investigation, and you haven't found any, have you?" Emma got up and poured two coffees from the pot on the sideboard. She handed Levi one of them before taking a sip of hers, keenly aware of the folded paper in her pocket.

"No proof, no. But the deputy said it was a process of elimination. 'Who else could it be?' He said." Levi sat down and took a long drink from his cup.

Emma thought back to her ride into Colorado Springs with Josiah and Claire. He had been humble and seemed entirely sincere in his rendition of what had happened the day Carson was killed. She felt sure he had been telling the truth then, and his story had checked out to the extent they could verify it. She did not believe Josiah was capable of this crime, but how did the IOU fit in? She looked at Levi, who was still agitated, drumming his fingers on the table and wearing a pained expression. "What do you think will happen, Levi?" She asked him.

"I must admit, it does not look good for Josiah. I know the sheriff is under pressure by the influential businessmen in town—probably from the Colorado Springs Company—to find a resolution to this matter. Too much is at stake, not just for the future of the bath house project, but also for Manitou itself. He will very likely be tried for murder."

She kept the note to herself for the time being. It could only hurt Josiah, and she did not want to put Levi in a difficult position. Once he knew about it, he would be duty-bound to turn the evidence over. They needed time to complete their investigation. "Frankly, it seems to me arresting the last remaining landscape architect would put the bath house project more at risk of not completing on schedule. I don't understand why 'the powers that be' would want to do that. Today is the day you are interviewing Mr. Albright, so there is hope we could still learn something that will exonerate Josiah."

"They are instructing me to stop the investigation, Emma."

"Can they do that? Do they have jurisdiction?"

"Ultimately, yes. They are county law enforcement. Also, they have the backing of everyone of influence. I am appointed and at the mercy of those in power."

"Is that it, then? Are you satisfied that justice has been served? Because I am not—not by a long shot."

"I am not satisfied, but there's nothing else I can do without risking my position." Levi gave the leg of the table a frustrated kick. "Although I don't know what good it is being a law man if they won't let me do my job."

"Well, what about bail?"

"That will be up to the judge, of course, but it's possible he will be released on bail if he can come up with it."

"We have to think of something, Levi, to get Josiah out of jail and give us time to find out what really happened. He lives here, at the same boarding house as you. Can't you vouch for him and request he be released on his own recognizance?"

Levi considered her suggestion. "I am on good enough terms with the judge. I may be able to persuade him. I will certainly try."

"In the meantime, we will have to continue the investigation unofficially and discretely. It's ironic, really."

"I fail to see the irony, Emma."

"This frees me up to take part in the investigation now that it is no longer an official inquiry, and that may present some advantages."

Levi sat up in his chair and leaned his forearms on the table. "I understand your frustration, Emma, believe me. I don't like my authority being undermined. It damages my ability to keep the law. Even so, it may very well be that the right man has been apprehended. Don't assume that an unofficial investigation will lead to a different outcome. You may just learn differently."

"Well, I don't believe it." Emma leaned across the table toward Levi. "But even if it does, it will be because a complete, objective investigation took place and not a rush to judgement for political or economic expediency. I will be satisfied with the truth even if I don't like it. Come on, Levi, let's not give up on doing the right thing. Let's work together on this."

Levi saw the passion and earnestness in Emma's dark blue eyes. Her energy was contagious, as was her commitment to righteousness. He felt a mixture of excitements that invigorated him at the same time that it disturbed him. He had not felt this purposeful, this *alive*, in a long time. "By God, you are right." He hit the table flat-handed. "Let's do it. I will talk to Albright, and I think poor Josiah could use some of Molly's fine baked goods while he sits in the county jail."

❧ CHAPTER 20 ❧

Emma packed a basket of Molly's biscuits, a small jar of honey, and some apples and caught the afternoon train to Colorado Springs. Levi had drawn her a simple map for how to get to the jail on Vermijo and Cascade. She couldn't resist saying, "Ah, yes, the DMV is there now." She tried very hard not to talk about the future, but she didn't think there would be harm in that slip. Still, she needed to be vigilant for many reasons. A slip in front of the wrong people could have seriously negative consequences.

She was grateful that Colorado Springs was still small and most things were a short walk from the train depot. The day was sunny, as most days were in Colorado, and the terrible cold snap from a couple of days ago had passed. Emma enjoyed the walk alone and, aside from the dirty, dusty roads, she found that she preferred the small village feel of 1882 Colorado Springs over the concrete covered urban version she knew. She noticed that in the place that was to become the Antlers Hotel was a large building under construction. She couldn't remember when the original hotel had opened, but she knew it was in the 1880s sometime. She walked around to look at the front, realizing this must be the original hotel. It was at least one hundred and fifty feet long and half as deep, with four large dormers and a small, but tall, domed tower facing the front. The first two floors were of stone, as was a wall up to one dormer. The remaining floors were of wood. She felt a pang of nostalgia, confused by the backwards timeline she was now living. This building was so beautiful and had so much more character than the one that will occupy the same place, with the same name, in the twenty-first century. She took in the rest of Pikes Peak Ave. It had its charm, that was for sure.

Emma continued south on Cascade, picturing in her mind the map Levi had drawn her. Of course, nothing looked familiar, and at the next block she turned west. There she found a substantial stone structure with a sign designating it as the county jail. She walked into the dark building and saw a deputy sitting behind an oak desk, awkwardly pecking at a type-writer with his index fingers. He got the keys stuck in a cross-lock and muttered some vague profanity while he struggled to free them, getting black ink from the ribbon on his fingertips in the process. When he saw Emma, he stood to greet her.

"May I help you, Ma'am?" The deputy wiped his ink-stained fingers on his dark pants. He wore street clothes, but his badge identified him as law enforcement. His gray mutton chops covered his cheeks but failed to hide his jowls or the folds under his neck. Though he was scowling still, he had deep laugh lines at the corners of his eyes. Emma blamed the typewriter for his sour greeting.

"I am sorry to interrupt your work, Deputy."

"I welcome it, Ma'am. Them dang contraptions are supposed t' make our work easier, but I spend all my time fightin' with the thang." He turned and gave the typewriter another derisive look.

Emma smiled, wondering how the deputy would adapt to the Internet. "I'm here to see Josiah Turner. I've brought him some food. I live in the same boarding house as he, and the proprietor sent me."

The deputy rubbed his hand over his chin. He seemed reluctant to let Emma see Josiah.

"Here, you can see what I have in my basket." Emma pulled the cloth away to show him its contents. "It's not much, but we thought he might be hungry."

"We feed the prisoners, Ma'am." The deputy peered into the basket and looked under the apples. "But I don't see any harm in lettin' him have this to snack on between meals. You do know he's in for bashin' his partner's head in, killin' him?"

"Yes, of course. The town marshal, Marshal Warwick, also lives in the same boarding house. He told us."

"I thought the marshal lived at Maison La Salle."

"Yes, that's right."

"Don't a woman run that place?"

"Yes, that's right. Mrs. La Salle."

"But you said the proprietor sent you." The deputy turned to get the large ring of keys off a hook on the wall.

Emma frowned. What was his point? Then she realized her mistake. "I'm sorry. I misspoke. I meant proprietress, of course." Emma rolled her eyes. She would have to be more aware of gender-specific language.

"Follow me, Ma'am."

"It's Miss, Deputy. Miss Quinn. And you are Deputy . . .?"

"Ferris, Miss."

Deputy Ferris picked one key from the ring and unlocked a large metal door and opened it. He led the way down a corridor with small cells on either side. It was dark and musty.

The air was stale, and there was an unpleasant smell of humanness. Dim beams of light came from each cell and illuminated the dust motes in the air. Emma followed him midway down the corridor. He stopped in front of a cell to the left.

"You can't stay long, Miss."

"I understand. But could I have a moment alone with Mr. Turner? I have news for him from his friends of a private nature."

The Deputy looked around as though he'd left the answer lying someplace and had forgotten where. Finally, he looked reluctantly at Emma. "I suppose it will be all right, but only for a little while. I'll be right outside the door. Yell if you need me."

"Thank you, Deputy. I'm sure I'll be fine."

The deputy turned and walked back to the front office. Emma noticed he kept the door ajar.

"What are you doing here, Emma! This is no place for you!" Josiah whispered loudly as he came running up to the bars.

"It's no place for you, either, Josiah," Emma whispered back. She heard someone in a cell at the end of the jail having a coughing fit, followed by an expletive. "Here, I brought you some things to eat, including some of Molly's fantastic biscuits." Emma found she could not fit the basket through the bars, so she sat the basket down on the stone floor and gently gathered its contents in the cloth. She held the gathered top and pushed the parcel through the bars. Josiah reached to take it, covering her hand with his to keep the top gathered closed. Their eyes met. "It's awfully stuffy in here, and the smell is atrocious," Emma said.

"Thank you." Josiah let his hand linger on hers longer than necessary, but Emma did not pull away.

"Josiah, Levi said he would try to get the judge to release you on your own recognizance until the trial. In the meantime, we plan to continue investigating, unofficially, to see if we can exonerate you."

"You don't believe I did it, then?"

"I don't. I'm not sure about Levi, but he agrees you were arrested prematurely. Look, I don't know how much time the deputy is going to give us. Please, is there anything else you can tell me about that day on the ledge at Williams Cañon, the day Carson was killed? You said you were there well ahead of your meeting with Albright, and you stayed well after the appointed time. What did you and Carson talk about?"

Josiah walked to his bed slab and sat down, laying his bundle next to him. "We started off discussing the ideas Carson had for the landscaping, including the structural materials and the plants he imagined. We were hashing out what we wanted to propose to Albright. It didn't take long because we had already agreed on the design. It was more a rehearsal for how to present to Albright." Josiah hesitated, clasping his hands between his knees and leaning on his thighs.

"If that didn't take long, what did you do the rest of the time you were waiting?"

Josiah looked down at his hands, rubbing his thumbs against each other.

"Josiah, I want to help you. I don't believe you did this thing. If there is something more, please tell me."

"I don't see how it is relevant, Emma, and it was private."

Emma grabbed the bars. "Josiah. I respect your discretion, but we can't know what matters. What seems irrelevant to you might, when put into context, be the very key to making sense of what happened to Carson. Please tell me."

Josiah looked up at the wall standing only six feet from him. He stood up and walked back to Emma. He put his hands over hers on the bar and whispered. "We were killing time, looking down the valley where Manitou lies. I light-heartedly

153

said now that Graham owed him so much money, he and Anna could set a date to marry. He laughed a little. Then he took a deep breath and said, 'I love it here, Josiah. I want to make this my home. I want to walk amongst these hills and mountains and through Garden of the Gods. I want to get my inspiration from the natural beauty I see everywhere here.' I agreed it was the most beautiful place I had ever been. Then we mentioned the election and how we hoped the members of town council would continue supporting the bath house project. As it turned out, all the councilmen were re-elected, and they had always supported the project. Anyway, by then we agreed Albright was a no-show. I was ready for an afternoon drink, but Carson said he wanted to stay for a while. I invited him to join me at the Cliff House when he came back. I left him there."

"Is there anything else? Anything at all?"

Josiah shook his head as if to dislodge anything that he may have forgotten. "No, nothing. That's it."

Just then the deputy opened the door. "Miss, it's time for you to say your goodbyes."

"Just a minute, Deputy. We are almost done." Emma called back, then turned to Josiah. "Josiah. I was checking pockets this morning to make sure they were empty before doing laundry." She reached in her pocket and pulled out the IOU. "I found this in the lapel pocket of the overcoat you had set out." She opened it and showed it to him through the bars. "How did it end up in your pocket?"

Josiah looked at her in dismay. "I don't know."

"Miss Quinn! I insist. It's time to say goodbye!" The deputy yelled.

❧ CHAPTER 21 ❧

After dinner, Emma and Levi gathered in the reading room to compare notes from the day. They sat at the table with a decanter of brandy and two snifters. Emma poured each of them a drink and handed Levi his.

"What did you learn from Albright today?" Emma asked.

"I expected him to be vague and evasive. He usually is, but he was surprisingly forthcoming."

"Really?" Emma took a sip of her brandy.

"Yes. He said that he had every intention of meeting Carson and Josiah as agreed, but he received a telephone call summoning him to an emergency meeting with the board of directors of the Colorado Springs Company in Colorado Springs. He left immediately on horseback. He was in Colorado Springs when the earthquake hit, he said. I haven't had the chance to check out his story, but it is verifiable, so I expect it will prove true."

"Why didn't he send word to them that he was going to

miss the meeting?"

"He said that in his rush it just didn't occur to him. Later, when it did, it was too late to do any good."

"Hmmm."

"What?"

"Powerful men rarely do their own dirty work." Emma took another sip of her drink.

"Why would Albright want Carson dead? Carson was key to the bath house plans."

"Yes, that's what I thought, too, until someone, possibly the powerful men from the Colorado Springs Company you mentioned, pressured the sheriff to arrest Josiah. Is it possible Carson and Josiah discovered something that put the plans at risk?" Something tickled at Emma's memory that roused her suspicion, but she couldn't put her finger on it.

"Are you suggesting Albright arranged to be gone so that someone else could go to the Williams Cañon meeting and kill Carson? I don't know, Emma. That seems a rather long shot, don't you think? And if so, why not just kill them both? Why only Carson?"

"Maybe so they could frame Josiah for the crime and get rid of him that way."

Levi considered the theory for a moment, then shook his head. "I just don't think so. It seems far-fetched. My experience is that murder isn't that well-thought-out. As you yourself have pointed out, this seems to be a case of passion and opportunity, not pre-mediation."

"It would be handy if there were some way to spend time in Albright's office to see if anything suspicious is going on."

"I think your imagination is running away with you. Now, tell me what you learned from Josiah."

Emma showed her displeasure by scrunching up her nose at Levi, who, rather than feeling chastised, found it charming.

He had the sense to hide a smile.

"He seemed likewise truthful, although at first he was reluctant to tell me everything that happened."

"Did he say why?"

"He thought it was private and irrelevant, but I convinced him we couldn't know that. At any rate, he said he teased Carson about soon having enough money to set a date to marry Anna owing to his winning at polker with Graham. Then Carson said he intended to settle permanently here because of the natural beauty of the area. And then something about the election . . . That's it!" Emma suddenly realized what had been nagging at her.

"What?"

"Albright was concerned about the outcome of the election! He said something about it the day I overheard him and Josiah talking in the parlor. Josiah said he and Carson had talked about hoping they retained support for the bath house from the town council after the election, but he later learned everyone was re-elected, so whatever the threat had been, it was avoided. But no one knew the outcome of the election yet when Carson was killed. The election was still underway. Who ran who was not elected?"

Levi let out a soft, cynical laugh. "The same men always win town council. Hutchinson, Bell, Albright, BeeBee, Barker, and Nichol. John Calhoun ran, but he did not win. I can't imagine any of them would be against the bath house. The whole town will benefit from it. But the fact is this is a small community run by an even smaller number of men."

"Well, I'm not sure we made any progress today." Emma stretched her arms over her head. Her corset, which she wore as loosely as possible, still felt confining and kept her from getting a proper stretch and breath. "Ugh, I hate these damn things." She reached down to reposition the corset. She looked up at Levi, who was looking at her with his eyebrows raised to his hairline. "Why are you looking at me like that?"

"It is just that ladies don't usually act so casually in front of men."

Emma was tired and not in the mood for repressive Victorian attitudes. "For heaven's sake Levi, we are practically family, or pretending to be. Surely there are latitudes. If you think this is 'casual' . . ." She didn't know how to finish the thought.

"Yes?" Levi raised his eyebrows even higher.

"Never mind."

❀

Back in his suite, Levi poured himself a tumbler of whiskey and lit a cigar. He settled himself into his over-stuffed chair in front of the heating stove and put his feet up on the ottoman as he took a puff of his cigar. He reached for the photograph case that sat on the table beside his chair and looked at the picture of Daphne, the lamplight reflecting warmly on her dainty features. Her soft, honey blond hair and her smooth, ivory skin were forever beyond his touch. She had been so beautiful, so kind. He recalled when they were first married nearly ten years ago. She was full of life and laughter. She loved to play the piano and dance, but it was her kindness that had won his heart. She had died just over a year ago, and before that, she had been very sick for a long time. They had wanted a house full of children. Coming to Manitou had been a last desperate effort to restore her health and their dreams. He remembered what she had said when it was clear she would not recover and had but a short time to live:

"Levi, promise me you will go on, that you will not dwell in grief."

"I can't promise. I don't know how to live without you, Daphne."

"You must. Don't dishonor me by living an unhappy life. Yes, be sad, but not for long. Life is too short not to rejoice in every day. You are still young and healthy. You may still have a family."

"Stop!" Levi cried, taking Daphne's hand in his and kissing it, his tears falling. "I can't possibly imagine it. I won't."

Daphne had smiled weakly. "Perhaps not now, but one day you will be able to not only imagine it, but want it, and I want it for you." And then she had fallen asleep. She died a few days later, never lucid again because of the laudanum Dr. Guiles had mercifully given her to ease her pain.

He held the picture to his chest, tears once again running down his face from the bittersweet memories. *"Daphne, oh Daphne, how I loved you and love you still. These last few days I am feeling more interested in life than I have since I lost you, and I feel so disloyal. I don't deserve happiness when you were robbed of it."* Just then the wood popped loudly in the stove and let out a loud hiss.

❧ CHAPTER 22 ❧

The next morning after breakfast, Emma took her sponge bath. She looked at the heavy, cumbersome dress she had been wearing and had a visceral reaction. *"I am not putting on all these clothes. They are too confining."* She put on the clothes she had worn the day she emerged from the cave—no crotchless bloomers, no corset, just her comfy jeans, flannel shirt, and jeans jacket. She put the bear claw necklace Ancha had given her around her neck, and while Molly was out at the hen house, she snuck into the root cellar and grabbed a few apples, wrapped them in a tea cloth, and left the boarding house through Claire's private door. Maybe if she kept her head down, people would assume she was a boy. *"I need a cowboy hat,"* she thought. She walked up Cañon Ave. toward her and Ancha's boulder, as she had come to think of it.

She had not seen Ancha since the day of Carson's funeral, the day that the horrible cold snap had come. She had not had an opportunity to get away during the day since then to find out if he had made it through that frigid night okay. The only way she knew to contact him was through the boulder, so she hoped he was nearby, watching. In any case, she would leave him the apples to let him know she had been there.

She still felt wary as she approached the boulder, remembering the terror of her bear encounter. She felt silly, but she stomped the ground loudly as she walked up the canyon path and sang "Lions and Tigers and Bears, Oh My," hoping to warn any wildlife of her presence and avoid a repeat.

She reached the boulder and looked around, seeing nothing in the way of wildlife but birds flying through the sky. She laid the apples on the boulder. "Ancha?" She waited for a sign that he was nearby and had heard her. "Ancha, I've left you some apples. I hope you get them before an animal does." She waited. When she heard nothing, she ventured further into the canyon. She had always loved getting out into the mountains and had hiked almost every trail between Colorado Springs and Mueller State Park, including climbing Pikes Peak. In 2012, the Waldo Canyon fire had destroyed some of her most beloved landscape and threatened her grandparent's house on the northwest side of town. The damage the fire caused broke her heart. She thought about the trees she was looking at now and wondered how many of the smaller ones were the very same ones she had walked by at some point far into the future. She took a deep breath of gratitude for the freedom and solitude she felt in nature.

After she had walked about a mile, maybe more, she reluctantly turned around. In this moment she believed she was back in her own time. The land had not changed. The same kind of birds flew in the sky. The same types of plants grew through the crags in the rocks. The same sun shined down on her. If she could just stay here in the canyon, away from any other human beings, then she could feel like nothing had changed for a while, that time had little meaning. She vowed to spend more time hiking.

She heard a sound and stopped walking so she could hear it more clearly. She smiled when she realized it was the distant bark of a dog. "Kwiyaghat!" She called.

The mongrel came running toward her, his tongue hanging out in goofy happiness. He put his front legs against her thighs, wagging his tail enthusiastically, panting. She rubbed his ears and smiled down at him. "Hi there! I'm so glad to see you!" She looked down the path. "Where is Ancha, huh?" She kneeled down to continue giving Kwiyaghat a good rub-down.

"Kwiyaghat!"

Emma looked up. There stood Ancha. The dog broke from Emma's grasp and sat at his master's side. "There you are," Emma said as she stood up and brushed her hands together to get the dirt off. "I'm glad you're here. Did you see the apples I left for you?"

"Yes, thank you." Ancha looked Emma up and down. "You are dressed strangely."

Ancha's English surprised Emma; it came easily to him, and he had little accent. "Yes, well, I brought these clothes from home. They dress differently there."

He walked closer to her to get a better look. He reached out to touch her jeans jacket, which contained spandex. He looked down at her hiking shoes, which had several kinds of materials not yet invented. He looked back at her with squinted eyes. "Where is your home?"

Emma thought for a moment. She thought about the vision Ancha had had showing him they would be friends. They could both use as many friends as they could get. She thought about how much her people owed his people. She decided to be forthright with him. "This is my home, just not my time. I am from the future."

Ancha nodded slowly, as though what she said made perfect sense.

Emma saw a rock with a flat top behind Ancha. "Let's sit and talk." She lifted her chin toward the rock. Ancha looked over his shoulder in the direction of her gesture. He turned back to her and nodded. She led the way, and they sat.

"I love the necklace you gave me." Emma reached for the bear claw against her chest. "Did you make it?"

"I did not. A shaman gave it to me. My teacher."

Emma didn't know what to say. Why would Ancha give her something that had great value to him? He didn't know her. He had no reason to give her such a precious object. She looked at him. "I don't know what to say. This must be very valuable to you. I feel very honored, but I don't feel I deserve it. Why did you give it to me?"

"I had a vision."

"Yes, you mentioned your vision, but what did it show you?"

"I saw an eagle. The eagle carried a ring—the ring that you are wearing." Ancha pointed to the ring Paul had given her. "The eagle flew over a great bear. The bear raised up on its back legs, looked up at the eagle, and opened its mouth wide. The eagle dropped the ring into the bear's mouth and he swallowed it. Then, the bear split open and became a vast valley of hunting grounds," Ancha swept his arms open wide, "filled with buffalo, antelope, and deer. Flowers bloomed and grass grew in the valley. Clear water flowed in a river through it. My people lived along the valley and had plenty to eat and drink."

"I understand the end of your vision is desirable, but how do I figure in?" Emma asked.

"The vision is telling me that you are important. I do not know exactly how. It will become clear in time. The necklace will help us stay connected."

"You speak very good English. How did you learn it?"

"The Mormons taught me."

Ancha didn't seem to want to elaborate, so Emma let it go. She wished she remembered more about the history of the Utes from high school. Unfortunately, she wasn't taught much and remembered even less. She knew it didn't end well for them, though.

"You said a shaman was your teacher. Are you also a shaman?"

"Yes." Ancha was a man of few words.

Emma felt the need to show Ancha good faith. "Do you have any questions of me?"

"You say you are from the future. How far in the future?"

"I came from the year 2019." Kwiyaghat nudged his nose under Emma's hand, and she pet him.

"How did you get here?"

"I was in Cave of the Winds in 2019 when an earthquake hit. I was struck in the head with a rock and knocked unconscious. When I regained consciousness and got out of the cave, I was in the year 1882. That was last Tuesday. I understand an earthquake hit here that day as well. I think a combination of the composition of the rocks, the cave, and the frequency of the earthquakes formed some kind of time portal."

Ancha considered what Emma had said. "We have both lost everything."

The truth of his statement hit Emma with a sharp pang in her chest. "Yes, everything."

They sat in silence for a few moments. Emma scratched Kwiyaghat behind his ears. Ancha pulled an apple from the pouch at his side and pulled a knife from a sheath in his belt. He cut a segment of the apple and offered it to Emma.

"Thank you," she said. She took a bite from the piece as Ancha also took one from his portion. The comfortable companionship was inexplicable to her, but she enjoyed it. She swallowed and said, "Do you stay in this area? Can I always find you here?"

"No. I stay in a place no one knows. But I am here often."

"I'd like to know how to find you."

"Continue using the boulder. I can read, if you want to leave a note."

"Yes, all right." Emma wondered how easy that would turn out to be, but she accepted it for now. She looked up at the sky and realized she had been gone a long time. "I need to get back. I have an engagement this afternoon. Thank you, Ancha, for letting me get to know you better." She stood up and gave Kwiyaghat another pat on the head before walking back to town.

❧ CHAPTER 23 ❧

Emma did not see anyone on her walk back to the boarding house. She used Claire's private entrance again and was walking through the reading room to her bedroom when she heard a voice coming from behind her.

"Emma!" Claire shouted.

Emma stopped short in the doorway and turned to face Claire's obvious wrath.

Claire glared at Emma, taking in how she was dressed and the necklace around her neck. "For the love of God, why are you dressed like that? People will become suspicious. What is that around your neck?"

Emma glared back. Her blood was boiling. She was an adult. How dare Claire question her like she was a wayward teenager? She would not live as a criminal under house arrest. She inhaled deeply to inform Claire so and then remembered how dependent she was on Claire's charity. This frustrated her even more. She hesitated only a moment before adopting a contrite countenance.

"I'm sorry, Claire. It was risky, I see." She looked up plaintively at Claire. "But these clothes you wear, they are so confining, so oppressive! I can hardly breathe in them, much less move freely. I just wanted to take a walk in the hills and be comfortable."

Claire's shoulders relaxed a little, but she was not ready to let Emma off the hook entirely. "And the necklace? I don't recall you having it when you arrived."

Emma had the impulse to lie to Claire. It really wasn't her business. But honesty was the basis for good relationships, and Emma needed good relationships. Claire deserved the truth and a lesson in boundaries. "Claire, I will tell you, even though, with sincere respect, it isn't your business. The necklace was a gift from Ancha."

"What? He is giving you gifts now? Emma, this is highly improper." Claire put her fists on her hips. "You must return it, of course."

"I will do no such thing." Emma crossed her arms in front of her. "What happens between Ancha and me is our business, Claire. I appreciate your concern, but please recognize it is my decision."

"Decisions have consequences, Emma," Claire said with a cold calmness, "and not just for you, but for him and, frankly, the rest of us who have befriended you. Think about that. It will make all of our lives difficult if you are seen as becoming too sympathetic to Ancha or, worse, too *familiar*. Now, we must ready for tea with Anna and Mrs. Calhoun." Claire gave Emma a final disapproving look before turning into her bedroom and shutting the door.

Emma shut her own door and pounded once on it with her fists. *"I have to find a way to be self-sufficient. I can't live under Claire's control. I won't, no matter how kind and well-meaning she is. I have to find a means of income."* She turned to the clothes hanging on the rod next to her dresser and felt resentment grinding at her heart. Yes, they were fine—beautiful even—but they looked like strait jackets to Emma.

❀

The atmosphere was tense in Claire's apartment as the women washed and dressed for tea. Emma sat stiffly at the dressing table in Claire's room as Claire silently attempted to fix her hair, pulling firmly and jabbing hairpins this way and that to hold Emma's hair in position. "Good luck." Emma finally said, looking at Claire's reflection in the mirror. "My hair does as it damn well pleases."

"Much like its owner." Claire said, trying to hold a tendril in place with pins, to no avail. She threw her arms down and looked at Emma's reflection. They both burst out in laughter.

Emma turned toward Claire and took her hands. "Claire, I am sorry. I don't mean to bring you trouble. I can't tell you how deeply grateful I am for *everything* you have done for me, and I don't want to disrespect you."

Claire gave Emma's hands an affectionate squeeze. "I can't imagine how difficult things are for you, Emma. I imagine you and Ancha feel you have something in common, both being displaced as you are. But it is not a simple situation. Not everyone is happy that Ancha remains in the area. They will use any excuse to make the argument to force him away. It's for his sake as well as yours that I caution you."

"I know. I know you only want what's best for everyone. It just seems so unfair and unnecessary to have to worry about such things."

"Come, let's not argue. Let's be friends." Claire pulled Emma to a stand and gave her a hug. When they pulled away the tension was gone.

❀

Alice stopped by to walk with Claire and Emma to the Calhoun residence. Emma discovered as they walked that it was one of the large Queen Anne style houses she could see dotting the hills from the small window of her bedroom. She had always loved the doll house look of that style of architecture. There were few examples of it in Northern Virginia, or she would have encouraged Paul to consider it for their home one day—one day. She shook off the sadness of her situation and instead focused on getting through this social occasion successfully. As agreed, she would follow Claire's lead.

The covered porch wrapped around two sides of the house, supported by five square wooden pillars painted cream. The women walked up the stairs to the front door, and Emma gave the brass knocker three firm knocks. A maid answered the door. "Welcome ladies. Mrs. and Miss Calhoun are expecting you. Please, come in."

The maid took their cloaks and led them into the parlor, where Mrs. Calhoun and Anna sat doing needlework. They put their projects in baskets at their feet and stood to welcome their guests as they entered. Anna was still dressed in mourning, although she was no longer wearing a veil. Emma didn't know if that was significant or not, but she remembered Peter Graham's comment at the funeral. Was Anna anxious to move on and find another suitor? The octagonal-shaped parlor was ornately furnished. A chaise longue sat beneath one of the windows that made up three sides of the room. A large potted plant flanked each side of the chaise. The intricately carved fire place mantle featured stained glass windows on either side and one transiting high above the mantle. Statues and other curios rested on every surface. The sofa upholstery was a puce brocade with an ivy motif, which, against the yellow and white polka dotted armchairs, only slightly offended Emma's aesthetic. The fire blazing in the grate made the room feel entirely too close for Emma. She noticed that the windows provided views in three directions, including town and the hills toward Williams Cañon.

"What a lovely view you have here." She commented.

"Yes, and I have the same lovely view from my room," Anna said.

"I have long said I am jealous that our parents treat Anna as the resident princess." All the ladies turned to see John Calhoun, Jr., leaning against the doorway between the parlor and the sitting room, grinning with his arms casually folded across his chest. "Her room is like Sleeping Beauty's tower."

"Oh John, stop teasing your sister," Mrs. Calhoun scolded him, but not seriously. "Come, let's gather in the sitting room. Margie will bring us our tea there."

The party moved to the next room, which was smaller and less crowded than the first. An occasional table sat in front of an area with two sofas and four chairs, none of which matched.

Margie brought out a tiered plate of little cookies, scones, pecan tassies, and finger sandwiches that Emma later learned were tongue and sardine. Another tray held a large porcelain tea set.

"This is all very lovely, Mrs. Calhoun. Thank you so much for having us," Claire said.

"The pleasure is ours, Mrs. La Salle. We are most eager to make the acquaintance of your cousin, Miss Quinn." Mrs. Calhoun smiled at Emma, who bowed her head slightly in acknowledgement.

"I don't know if you've met my son, Miss Quinn. This is John Calhoun." She gestured to her son, who was sitting in the chair to Emma's right. He reached out for her hand, which she gave him.

"Pleased to see you again, Miss Quinn. I am sorry we did not speak more at poor Carson's funeral." He said, gently holding her hand and dipping his head.

"The pleasure is mine, Mr. Calhoun." Emma said. John Calhoun was young, no more than twenty-five. Still, he exuded the confidence born of privilege that was almost arrogant. He was of medium height, had a full beard, and a mustache that helped mask his pudgy cheeks. Emma wondered if it was unusual for him to be joining the ladies. She turned to Anna and, playing off John's mention of the funeral, added, "I want to express again my deepest sympathy to you over the loss of your fiancé, Miss Calhoun. I do know the grief is profound."

"Yes, it is devastating. I am sympathetic to your loss as well, Miss Quinn. It is awful losing my fiancé, but I cannot imagine losing my whole family and home, as you did." Anna looked kindly upon her mother and brother and slowly shook her head.

"How did you learn about Carson? I hope you were not alone." Claire said.

"John and I were here in the parlor. I was finishing the edging on the bed linens for my trousseau when Tommy came to tell us. At the time, we didn't know Carson had been murdered. It was awful enough as it was." Anna's eyes welled with tears.

"You weren't home, Mrs. Calhoun?" Claire asked.

"I was, but I was asleep. John had taken me to the dentist earlier that day, and the dentist gave me laudanum. I went straight to bed when we returned home." Mrs. Calhoun reached for her daughter's hand to comfort her.

Anna pulled a handkerchief from her sleeve and dabbed her eyes. "I have been collecting things in my hope chest ever since Carson and I became engaged. The pillow cases I finished that day were the last of the linens I had been working on."

Emma noticed the intricate edging and brightly colored embroidery on the fine cotton. In an attempt to lighten the topic, she said, "That's lovely, Miss Calhoun. May I see it?"

Anna looked down at her hanky and said, "Oh, this? Yes, of course," and she handed it to Emma.

The crocheted edging was of very fine thread and made a delicate embellishment to the hanky, on the corner of which was embroidered a peacock, its tail feathers fully open. The iridescent greens and blues of the feathers were highly detailed, requiring tiny stitches. Emma looked at the backside and saw that it was almost a perfect mirror of the front. She remembered her grandmother telling her that was the mark of skill. "It is remarkable, Miss Calhoun. You are quite talented." As she handed the hanky back to Anna, she noticed that Anna appeared embarrassed by the compliment. She was hugging her forearms against her body and slightly rubbing her elbows. She took the hanky and tucked it back into her sleeve.

"I quite agree, Miss Quinn!" Mrs. Calhoun said.

"Well, ladies, I don't want to wear out my welcome at your tea party." John stood up to leave. "I did, however, want to see you, Miss Quinn. I hope we will meet again soon."

"Mr. Calhoun, if I might have a word with you before you go?" Claire surprised the room by her request.

"Certainly, Mrs. La Salle, shall we go to the parlor?"

"Yes, thank you." Claire followed John's gesture toward the parlor, leaving Emma and Alice to carry the conversation, which neither of them were particularly prepared to do.

After an awkward lull, Mrs. Calhoun asked politely, "Dr. Guiles, how is business at the bath house?" She took a sip of her tea and a tiny bite of her pecan tassie while she waited for an answer.

"Very well, considering it's nearly winter. The tourist

patronage is lower, of course, but the locals from Colorado Springs take advantage of the quieter time. My electric bath is drawing a lot of interest."

"Yes, you may recall I came for an electric bath for my rheumatism. I rather think it helped. Perhaps I will come again for a maintenance treatment."

"I recommend you do them regularly for the best results. Once a month if you can manage it."

"Will you be offering them at the new bath house once it opens?" Anna asked politely.

Alice set her teacup down on the saucer. "I'm afraid not, Miss Calhoun. I have been notified that Dr. Fuller will be the resident physician at the new bath house. I gather he is not a proponent of electric baths or electric physicians, in general."

"How narrow minded of Dr. Fuller!" Anna exclaimed. "I understand the new bath house is expected to attract the wealthier segment of society from the east and even Chicago and St. Louis. I do hope so. There is a dearth of eligible men of good breeding in these parts."

"Anna! What a shocking thing to say!" Mrs. Calhoun reprimanded.

"Well, it's true, Mama. Carson was a rarity here. But once he finished the bath house project, he would have been able to name his price anywhere. We talked of moving to Chicago. We would have been a part of the growing segment of society that is self-made and highly respected." Anna began to tear up again.

"It may well be true, dear, but it is far too soon to be talking as though you are anxious to replace dear Carson. You must observe a decent mourning period."

Anna looked away, petulant. She pulled her hanky out again and dabbed her eyes, then reached for her teacup and a cookie.

"I apologize, ladies." Claire returned from the parlor and

took her seat. "I had some banking business to discuss with Mr. Calhoun." She turned to Mrs. Calhoun. "It must gratify you and Mr. Calhoun that your son is following in his father's footsteps in banking."

"Yes, quite," was Mrs. Calhoun's curt response. Clare looked around the room, trying to sort out what she had missed and why the room felt so uncomfortable.

❧ CHAPTER 24 ❧

It was twilight when the ladies made the short trek back to the boarding house. "What was so important that you had to leave Emma and me alone with the Calhoun ladies?" Alice demanded.

"I had banking business to discuss with John Jr., Alice. I had hoped either he or Mr. Calhoun, Sr., would be there today to save me a trip into Colorado Springs. The better question is what happened while I was out of the room?" Claire walked between Emma and Alice down Cañon Ave. the short distance back to the boarding house.

"Anna's lack of decorum embarrassed Mrs. Calhoun." Alice answered.

"Oh? In what way did Anna lack decorum?"

"She seemed to be too ready to move on from Carson's death. She was talking about how few suitable men there were in the area and that the bath house might attract a better class of visitors, alluding to potential suitors." Emma summarized as they walked into Claire's parlor.

"I think we could all use a nice glass of brandy, don't you agree?" Hearing no objections, Claire poured two drinks and passed them to her friends before serving herself. "That tea was fairly difficult, though the food was tasty." Claire took a long sip of brandy and sat on her sofa. Lulu jumped onto her lap and head-butted Claire's hand for some attention. "Things never became comfortable once I returned. I thought I had offended somehow. I am relieved to learn otherwise. I'm not surprised about Anna, really. She has always seemed a bit of a social climber to me."

"That's not very charitable of you, Claire. We know nothing about Anna or the Calhouns." Alice chided.

"Actually, I have socialized with the Calhouns on occasion. I see them at events at the opera house regularly, and I have attended parties at their home a few times. I do my banking with Mr. Calhoun. I have seen Anna enough to know she seeks to move up in society and rather looks down her nose at Colorado Springs and our little village. You're quiet, Emma. Is something on your mind?"

"I am just trying to reconcile what Anna said with something Josiah shared with me when I visited him in jail. Anna said that she and Carson were planning to settle in Chicago at some point, but Josiah said Carson had told him that he wanted to make Manitou his home."

"Oh, I can't imagine Carson would stay." Claire said. "There would not be enough work for him here, I shouldn't think. Perhaps he was just musing with Josiah."

"Yeah, you're probably right." Emma agreed.

The front door to the boarding house opened, and the ladies could hear men's voices from the main hallway. Emma ran to the hallway door and opened it.

"Josiah! You're free!" Emma ran up to Josiah and reached

for his hands. Emma turned to Levi, who was standing next to Josiah with a stern look on his face. "How did you do it, Levi?"

"I went to Josiah's arraignment and vouched for him. I told the court I would ensure he showed up for trial. The judge agreed to release him on his own recognizance."

"For which I will be forever in your debt, Levi." Josiah added.

"Yes, well, I see no reason for you to rot in that jail while you await trial. You are innocent until proven guilty, after all." Levi did not look entirely happy with the situation. Emma wondered if he still thought Josiah was the killer.

"You did the right thing, Levi." Emma affirmed.

"I'm starved, Claire," Josiah said. "Is there any food in the kitchen to which I could avail myself?"

"I'm sure there is. Emma and I did not eat dinner here ourselves. Let's go look and see what we can find for you."

Josiah gave Emma and Levi a brief nod of his head and followed Claire to the kitchen.

"Am I to be left to drink alone?" Alice asked from the threshold to Claire's parlor.

"Come join us, Levi." Emma said.

"No, thank you. I am hungry as well. I think I will find something to eat and retire for the night. It has been a long day." Levi headed for the kitchen.

Emma rejoined Alice in Claire's parlor. "I'm so glad they let Josiah out of jail. I knew Levi could persuade the judge."

Alice settled into the pink velvet sofa. "It surprised me that he had been arrested in the first place."

"Levi thinks those in power pressured the sheriff to make an arrest quickly, and since no other suspect has emerged, the sheriff said Josiah was guilty by process of elimination, essentially." Emma patted her lap to invite Lulu. The cat accepted the invitation and happily curled up.

Claire entered carrying a tray with cake and coffee. "I realized while I was in the kitchen that Emma has been with us a week, today! I thought we'd celebrate with a treat." She sat the tray on the occasional table.

"It seems much longer to me, frankly." Emma reached for her cake, upsetting Lulu. "So much has happened."

"I'm just glad your concussion was mild." Alice said. "You recovered quickly, and I can see no lasting ill effects. Do you feel well?"

"Yes. After the first two or three days, I felt much better. Now, I'd say I'm recovered except for some discoloration on my arms where the scrapes were."

"How are you feeling otherwise, Emma?" Claire asked. "I mean, I am grateful you have healed physically, but how are you *feeling*?"

Emma sat back in her chair and put her hands in her lap. "It's confusing. I miss Paul terribly, and my friends and family, but most especially Paul. But I've been so busy adjusting here, trying to learn how to function and find a way to be at least a bit useful, that it has distracted me from my grief. I feel it mostly at night when I am alone in my room and have time to reflect. Intellectually I understand that I am likely stuck in this time permanently, but it's difficult. The times are so different."

"In what ways?" Alice leaned forward and set down her cup.

"Well, that's the other thing that makes my situation hard. I wish I could tell you all about my time—the good and the bad— but I am not sure I should. I don't want to influence history by divulging too much. I guess it's a bit like when you read cards for people, Claire."

"Card reading is imprecise—not predestined. People can alter what the cards predict about the future by the choices they make, the actions they take. In your case, you *know* what happened, what will happen, at least generally."

"I don't know, perhaps Emma is right, Claire. Perhaps it is exactly like reading cards. But does it matter? Emma, dear, I am not sure you single-handedly can change the course of history. At least not in ways that matter in the long run. That's entirely too much responsibility for you to carry. It will be unhealthy for you to bear that burden by yourself for the rest of your life. Also, as Claire has pointed out to me, your being here with us in this time is as much a part of God's plan as anything else is. Yes, I agree that you are here for a reason that none of us understands, and because of that, it is no mistake that you have knowledge and insight we do not. It would seem counter-productive to withhold it, perhaps impossible, really."

"I agree wholeheartedly with Alice," Claire said. "I also feel strongly that the reason He brought you to us, to Alice and me, is so you would have friends who would have your interest at heart and not try to exploit you, friends you can trust and confide in without fear."

Emma looked at each of the women and smiled. Her heart swelled with the warmth of the gratitude she felt toward the women, her friends. She shifted in her seat, aware again of the pinching of her corset and the tightness of the clothes she was wearing. "Well, I can start by telling you the clothes women wear in my time are much more comfortable than these!" The women all laughed.

Just then there was a quiet knock at the hallway door. Claire opened it to find Josiah standing there, his head dipped slightly, looking bashful.

"Josiah! Is everything all right? Do you need something else from the kitchen?"

"No, no, I don't need anything, thank you, Claire. I was hoping to speak to Emma."

"Oh!" Claire turned to Emma, raising her eyebrows in

question.

"Yes, please, come in Josiah." Emma stood to greet Josiah, who seemed to be at a loss as to why he was there.

"Claire, dear, thank you for the brandy and the cake. I must be heading home now. My family will think I've fallen off the face of the earth." Alice stood and gave Claire a kiss on the cheek. She took her cloak off the hook, wrapped herself in it, and left.

"Come have a seat, Josiah. Would you like a brandy?" Claire offered.

"Yes, please." Josiah accepted.

Claire poured and handed Josiah the snifter of brandy. "I am rather tired. I believe I will retire to read for a while."

"Goodnight, Claire." Emma said. She turned to Josiah and waited for him to say something.

"Emma, I wanted to thank you for all that you have done on my behalf. I gathered from Levi that you felt strongly there had been a rush to judgement, and it was you who persuaded him to speak to the judge. I rather think I would still be in jail were it not for you."

"I only hope Levi can find the truth. I worry that if he doesn't find the killer, they will find you guilty at your trial."

"Yes, I fear that, too. Believe me, if I knew anything that would help my cause, I would tell Levi. Does he know that you found the IOU in my jacket pocket?"

"No. I don't feel good about withholding it from him, but he would be obligated to disclose the discovery to the prosecutor. Until he has discovered something in his investigation that might exonerate you, I will keep it to myself."

"And if he doesn't find anything?"

"Can you tell me how it came to be in your jacket pocket?"

"I don't know how it got there, Emma. I never use the lapel pocket of my overcoat, so I didn't check it the night before I put it out for laundering, as I did my other pockets. I don't know how—or when—it found its way there."

"Are you certain?"

"Yes, quite."

"Well, that suggests someone else, probably from the boarding house, put it there, doesn't it?"

"That is my thought as well. How else could it have happened?"

"We can rule out Levi. Willy and Miss Sully seem unlikely. By far the most likely person is Peter Graham, but how did he come by the IOU, and why would he put it in your pocket?"

❧ CHAPTER 25 ❧

In her room, Emma continued to puzzle over why Graham would have put the IOU in Josiah's pocket. How was it that Graham had the IOU, and what would his motive be for putting it in Josiah's pocket? Emma thought the most likely thing for Graham to do with it is burn it, but even that was unnecessary. Carson was dead, so the IOU was void. If it was to incriminate Josiah, it was an ill-conceived tactic. Carson could have given it to Josiah for safe-keeping. Josiah being in possession of it proved nothing, one way or the other.

"Exactly!" Emma exclaimed aloud. There was no reason for her to withhold her discovery from Levi. She would come clean with Levi and show him the IOU the next day.

November 14, 1882

It's been one week since I "arrived" here. Claire was kind to try to celebrate it, but I still feel that my life has been destroyed. Coping has kept me busy, I admit, but I would love nothing better than to be back in my own time, back to my life. But this is my life now. I am thankful for Claire and Alice. They have been true friends to me. I shudder to think what might have happened to me were it not for them. And there's also Ancha, whom I feel an inexplicable connection with. I've never known a Native American before. I feel a deep guilt over what the white man did to the Native Americans from the time we arrived from Europe. It hurts to look at him and know how bleak the future is for his people. I feel drawn to him though, and he believes our destinies are somehow linked. I plan to continue my friendship with him despite what Claire says. I only hope it doesn't damage my relationship with her too much.

✻

She had had an epiphany in the consciousness between sleep and wakefulness the next morning, and she was anxious to act on it. She needed to look her best. She fiddled with her hair, trying to get it into her version of a French twist, but to no avail. Her hair was hopeless. She finally pulled it all up to the top of her head and pinned it. She'd just cover it with her hat. At some point she was going to have to learn to fix her hair, she thought with a sigh. She put on the dark plum wool outfit she had worn to Carson's funeral. It was a good balance of style and seriousness, and it was warm. She had discovered it was another frigid day when she went to gather the eggs for breakfast. She fastened the hat to her head. *"Doesn't look half bad,"* she thought, looking in the mirror of her washstand. She pulled on the black kid gloves and walked into the parlor.

"Where are you going dressed to the nines?" Claire looked up from her mending. Lulu looked up from her curled position

183

next to Claire and stretched her front legs, then rolled onto her back.

"I am going to get a job, Claire. Don't worry, I will keep up with my chores here, but I need my own source of income."

"Are you sure, Emma? Do you feel ready? I mean, you are still healing from your injury and adjusting to these times."

"Yes, I'm sure. I will not adjust by hiding. I have to get out in the world and find my way. And as much as I appreciate your generosity, I can't take advantage of it indefinitely. I have to be able to take care of myself."

"I understand, although I wish you would be more patient with yourself. You seem to have something specific in mind."

"I do. It came to me as I was waking. I don't want to jinx it by talking about it." Emma bent down and gave Claire a peck on the cheek and Lulu a rub on her tummy. "I'll let you know how successful I was." She wrapped her cloak around her and headed out the door.

Levi had told her that Mr. Albright kept an office at the Manitou House, where he also lived. It was a hotel, but it was the nearest one to the train depot, so he rented a ground-floor suite of rooms out of convenience. He could get to Colorado Springs quickly, if needed, but he lived in Manitou, because soon he would need to be at the building site daily, once the bath house was under construction. It was to his office she was now heading.

Emma took in the sites along her short walk to Manitou House. The uncultivated land between Cañon Ave. and Manitou Ave. looked wild. Fountain Creek ran through the area, babbling loudly and flanked on either side by scrub oak, pines, boulders, and rocks. She could see the pavilion at Soda Spring and the big boulder that marked the location of Navajo Spring. A winding path meandered through and crossed the creek on the bridge Emma used to get to the bath house for her luxurious hot mineral bath. The only buildings in the large triangular area were Alice's modest bath house and the Episcopal church. Across from the church, on the other side of Manitou Ave., was the Barker House.

Most of the shops, boarding houses, and saloons were along Manitou Ave. Townspeople were milling about, tending to their daily activities, sweeping entryways, setting out produce and signs for sales of dry goods. Emma walked by the Eoff & Howbert Bookstore and saw Peter Graham through the window, arranging a book display. She took a mental note to stop by on her way back.

She walked by the Mansions Hotel, the largest hotel in town, called by the locals "the BeeBee House" after the proprietor. The large wooden structure went back a block and had a veranda that wrapped around the ground floor. Emma felt sad that most of these beautiful buildings had not survived to her day. They were grand and charming. The vision in front of her looked like a greeting card as a horse-drawn carriage pulled up to the front of the hotel.

Manitou was unique in western towns. It did not have the lawless reputations of other places like Dodge City, Virginia City, Deadwood, or Tombstone. It was meant to be a resort spa town, and an upscale one at that—one to rival those of Europe. While it currently fell short of that vision, it certainly stood apart as a special place. Emma knew it had bright days ahead. She took a deep breath of the cold morning air and walked into the Manitou House lobby.

"Excuse me," Emma walked up to the clerk behind the reception counter. "Could you tell me where I could find Mr. Albright's office?"

"Yes, Miss. It's down the hall, last suite on the right. Would you like me to ring his office and announce you?"

"Oh! Yes, I suppose that would be the thing to do." Emma

found herself surprised that the hotel had a telephone.

"May I tell him your name, Miss?"

"Yes, it's Miss Quinn, Emma Quinn, Claire La Salle's cousin."

The clerk picked up the earpiece of the phone sitting behind the counter and turned a crank. A moment later, he said, "Mr. Albright, Miss Emma Quinn, Mrs. La Salle's cousin, is here to see you." Emma heard a muffled voice on the other end of the line. The clerk replied, "Yes sir. I'll send her." He hung up the phone and turned to Emma. "Mr. Albright asks you to please come to his office."

"Thank you so much." Emma smiled and turned to walk down the hall. She came to the last door on the right and knocked. Mr. Albright answered the door.

"Miss Quinn! What a surprise to see you. Please, come in and have a seat." He stepped aside and gestured for Emma to enter.

Emma took a seat in the chair in front of Albright's desk. It was a simple oak desk, with a leather desk pad surrounded by a silver writing set that held a dip pen and bottle of ink, a box of "lucifers," sealing wax, and a brass seal. A large kerosene lamp provided ample light for writing, although the room itself had gas light sconces on either side of the door. Behind the desk was a short sideboard where a tea set and two decanters of liquor rested. The office was a corner room, and from the window above the sideboard, Emma could see the train depot.

"To what do I owe this honor?" Albright smiled genuinely and took his seat behind the desk. He interlaced his fingers and rested his hands on the desk pad.

Albright was a large man in stature and, coupled with his natural self-assurance, he commanded the room. Emma did not intimidate easily, but she felt her own confidence waver as she considered how to present her proposal. She decided the clear, direct approach would be best.

"I'll just come straight to the point, Mr. Albright. I have lost everything in the tragic fire that claimed my parents' lives. Not only have I lost them, which has left me deeply grieved, but also my worldly possessions and my means of an income. Cousin Claire has been generous and provided me with necessities and friendship, but I need to provide for myself. My family had a bookstore, which I helped run. I have useful skills, like managing business correspondences and bookkeeping. I can type. I thought perhaps I could be of service to you as you prepare to manage the bath house project and in your other business affairs. In addition to those capabilities, I have an understanding of electricity. My father's avocation was inventing, and he dabbled in the application of electricity. I was his assistant, as I myself had an interest in the field. While I am no expert, my basic understanding of such things may be of value to you." Emma maintained her eye contact with Albright, hoping she was exuding the right mix of competence, confidence, value, and humility.

Albright raised his eyebrows and turned down his mouth, considering what she had said. After a moment, he said, "I must say, I am taken aback by your forthrightness, Miss Quinn. I am not sure I've ever encountered it before in a woman."

Emma felt her stomach fall and a flush of embarrassment heat her face.

"I know the world is changing rapidly and women are entering the workforce in ways they never have before," Albright continued, "But you are a young and beautiful woman. Wouldn't your time be better spent finding a suitable husband and starting a family, especially since you have lost your own?"

Emma knew Albright intended no offense, but she felt her anger and frustration rise. She took a deep breath to calm herself. She needed to play her hand carefully. "Mr. Albright, I appreciate your concern for my future. I value my independence and feel I have a lot to offer the world if I am given the opportunity. If you have a need for my skills, perhaps you'd be willing to engage me on a trial basis. May I suggest a month? If after that time I have not demonstrated my worth, you may send me on my way with no hard feelings."

Albright smirked genially and shook his head. "You are indeed remarkable, Miss Quinn. If you were a man, I'd be a fool not to take you up on your offer. Any man with the determination and gumption you've shown would be sure to be an asset to my company." He hesitated and once again seemed to consider the idea. "Yes, all right, Miss Quinn. Why not! Let's give it a try. I admit I find it difficult to keep up with my correspondence, review plans, provide direction, and split my time between here, Colorado Springs, and Denver. I have some initiatives that require attention that may be well suited to you."

Emma suppressed her urge to express her surprise. "Thank you, Mr. Albright. I sincerely appreciate you giving me a chance to prove myself. I will do my best not to disappoint you. I am available to start immediately. When would you like me to begin?"

Mr. Albright stood, signaling the meeting was over. "Today is Wednesday. I need a day or two to think over how I might use your services. Why don't we start this experiment on Monday? Plan to be here at nine o'clock in the morning."

Emma stood up and held out her hand to shake Mr. Albright's. "Thank you, Mr. Albright! I look forward to it."

Mr. Albright hesitated a moment before gently shaking Emma's hand. "It looks like I have a lot to learn about today's modern woman," he smiled.

❧ CHAPTER 26 ❧

Emma was walking on air on her way back to the boarding house. She couldn't believe how easily her plan had worked, and she couldn't keep the grin off her face. It was the first time she had really felt like herself since she was sent back in time. She was so pleased with the outcome of her offer to Mr. Albright that she almost forgot to stop in at the bookstore where Peter Graham worked.

The shop was small, but bright and welcoming. The display at the large front window allowed ample sunlight through to illuminate the store, and several wall sconce lamps provided additional lighting so customers could browse the selection of books, pamphlets, periodicals, newspapers, and maps. The window display was simple, elegant. Imperial blue velvet, draped on the display shelves, provided a cozy nest for the newest and best-selling books. Interspersed between them were silver ink wells and pen sets, fine stationary, and other writing accessories. At the front of the shop was another display table with stacks of books strategically placed for effect. Toward the back of the shop were the shelves of other reading materials, blank journal books, writing paper and other stationary items similar to those featured in the window. The smell of paper and ink pervaded the air. In short, Emma loved the place. The clerk's counter was in the middle of the shop on the left side of the entrance. Sitting behind the counter on a three-legged stool, Emma saw Peter Graham, who had looked up at her when she caused the little bell above the door to ring as she entered.

"Miss Quinn! How nice to see you!" Graham stood and walked around the counter, smiling. "Can I help you find something today?"

Emma looked around the shop. "This is a lovely shop, Mr. Graham. My parents owned a bookstore in New Orleans." Emma paused, pretending to reflect on her loss. "I love bookstores. I visited the one in the Springs the other day. It is very nice, as well, but I think I prefer this one. I am surprised a town the size of Manitou can support it this time of year."

Graham followed Emma's gaze around the shop. "This one is owned by the same men as the one in the Springs, but I have control over its appearance and what we stock. I am flattered that you like it. I do rely heavily on the tourists for business. I usually close from December through March or mid-April, depending. This year I will close at the end of November." He looked back at Emma and clasped his hands in front of him, raising his eyebrows. "Was there something in particular you needed?"

"No. I was strolling town and saw you through the window. I thought if you weren't too busy, I'd stop and say hello." Emma smiled, trying to look disarming.

Graham laughed humorlessly. "Well, as you can see, I am alone, so I welcome your visit. I have no seat to offer you, I'm afraid."

"To be perfectly honest, Mr. Graham, I did want to ask you something."

"Yes?"

"I was going through the laundry the boarders set out Monday, logging the items and making sure all the pockets were empty, and I found something I think belongs to you."

Graham's brows furrowed, but Emma sensed no apprehension. "Indeed? I am not aware of missing anything."

Emma bowed her head slightly and looked down, then up at Graham. "I'm a bit embarrassed to tell you what it was," Emma paused.

"My heavens, I can't imagine what you could have found that would embarrass you, Miss Quinn. Please, tell me." Graham appeared genuinely at a loss.

"Well, all right, Mr. Graham. I'll just come out with it. I found an IOU from you to Mr. White for the amount of $112.00." Emma watched carefully for Graham's response.

Graham's expression melted, and his face looked flushed. He stood a little taller and stiffer, looking away from Emma. He reached back for the counter and leaned against it as he turned his eyes back to Emma. "You say you found this in my pocket?"

"Well, that's the odd thing. I could have sworn it was in Josiah's pocket that I had found it, but how could that be? I figured I was mistaken, and it had come from your pocket instead."

Graham stared into space and shook his head slowly. Once again, his brows furrowed. "I don't understand."

"I'm sorry, but what don't you understand, Mr. Graham?"

"I haven't seen the IOU since I signed it and handed it to Carson. I can assure you I was not in possession of it. I can only assume you were right, and it was in Josiah Turner's pocket that you found it, though why he would have it, I don't know." Graham continued staring off, looking for an answer.

Emma struck a lighter tone. "Well, I'm not sure it matters, really. With Carson's unfortunate death, the IOU is null and void, I'd imagine."

Graham expression brightened at the idea. "Yes, yes, you are quite right, Miss Quinn! It hardly matters at all!" a wide smile returned to his face. "Do you have the IOU?"

"Oh, no. It's back at the boarding house. I will have to give it to Levi, I suppose. If it wasn't in your pocket, then I was right that I found it in Mr. Turner's pocket. It is, perhaps, evidence relative to Carson's murder."

Graham considered what Emma said. "It is rather incriminating for poor Josiah, isn't it?"

"Perhaps, Mr. Graham." Emma paused, then added, "I am sorry I alarmed you, but I just wasn't sure what to make of my discovery. I do really love your shop here. Next time, I will make a purchase! Have a good morning."

Emma left Graham still wearing a vacant look on his face. She stopped at the Navajo Spring on her way back to the boarding house, which she would not have recognized at all were it not for the little sign posted. She looked upon the mineral deposits that had precipitated along the edge of the spring, forming a distinct border around the pool. She found a ladle lying off to the side of the spring, but she knew better than to use it to take a drink. She was less concerned about the water than she was about germs any previous user of the ladle may have left. So many people in Manitou and Colorado Springs were there because of poor health, particularly tuberculosis. She wasn't taking any chances. She walked over to the boulder that served as a landmark for the spring and leaned against it. The red rock had absorbed the heat of the morning light and felt warm against her back. She took a deep breath of the crisp, dry air and looked upon the rustic, undeveloped area. *"It is so gorgeous here—open and accessible and unspoiled. The arcade and the candy shop here in my time are quaint, but don't compare to the raw natural beauty now."* She closed her eyes against the sun on her face. Fountain Creek babbled, just as it had babbled all of her life, as it had for hundreds of years before her and would long after everyone she had ever known had died.

❀

"I did it, Claire!" Emma exclaimed. "I got a job!"

Claire came out of her bedroom to find Emma spinning around happily in the parlor. "Really? Where?"

"With Mr. Albright!" Emma clapped her hands together jubilantly, wearing an ear-to-ear grin.

"Mr. Albright?"

Emma caught Claire's incredulous tone. "Yes, Mr. Albright. It's on a trial basis for a month, but I have no doubt he will find me of value and keep me on afterwards."

"Doing what?"

"I offered to be his assistant as activities accelerate for the bath house project. I can type; I can do book-keeping *(I hope)* and other office-management tasks. I also said I could help him with the actual construction. I told him my father had been an amateur inventor, and I assisted him, so I know a bit about electricity. But really, all I needed was a chance to get my foot in the door. I'll figure out how to be valuable to him."

"Yes, that's what worries me." Claire sat on her sofa and brushed at the fur Lulu had left adhered to the pink velvet.

"What does that mean? Don't you see, Claire? I will be able to take care of myself, not rely on your kind generosity indefinitely." She also thought, *"I might also discover what's going on with the bath house project. I might find out why Mr. Albright missed that meeting and learn more about Carson's murder."*

Claire looked up at Emma and gave her a weak smile. "Yes, it may very well be a great opportunity, and of course, I am happy for you. Mr. Albright is a powerful, rich man. He's used to getting his way, Emma. Please, just be careful."

"Oh, I've worked with men all my life. I can take care of myself." Emma refused to have her moment dampened with vague cautions. "You'll see, Claire. Before the month is over, Mr. Albright will make me an offer of permanent employment. Now, do you know where I can find Levi? I have something to tell him."

"I believe he is in his suite," Claire answered, still worrying with the fur clinging now to her skirts. "Oh!" She called as Emma walked toward the door. "I need to go into town today. Would you like to join me?"

"No, thank you Claire. I need to talk to Levi about the case, and then I have my chores to do around here."

Emma walked up the stairs to the second floor and knocked on Levi's door. From the other side of the door, she heard a chair scrape across the wooden floor and footsteps approaching. The door opened and there stood Levi, wearing only his charcoal gray wool pants and a white cotton shirt, the top two buttons of which were unbuttoned, revealing a tuft of chest hair. His sleeves were rolled up to his elbows. He smelled of lye soap and pine trees. Emma's breath quickened, as did her heart rate.

"Emma?"

Emma stood stupidly silent. It took her a moment to remember why she was there. "Yes, Levi. Sorry to intrude on your privacy, but I have something to show you."

"Yes, all right. Give me a moment and I'll meet you in the parlor."

Emma nodded, and Levi gently closed the door. She had expected to be invited into his quarters and felt somehow chastised. Had she acted inappropriately, coming to his door? How else was she to let him know she needed to talk to him? Would she ever understand the social norms she now must live within?

❧ Chapter 27 ❧

Levi ran his hand through his wavy brown hair and rubbed his chin. *"My beard needs trimming,"* he thought, and ran a comb through his hair and beard. He ran around his sitting area, collecting his suspenders, vest, and tie, which were strewn over chairs and the footboard, and hastily finished dressing. He took a swig of brandy and swished it around his mouth, then opened his sitting-room window and spit it out. No one but Claire, Molly, and the men he shared the boarding house with had ever come to his door before. He had been surprised, and ill prepared, to find Emma standing in the hall. He gave his vest a tug and checked his image in his washstand mirror, straightening his tie. *"Now, let's go find out what brought the fair Miss Quinn to my door."*

Levi entered the boarding house parlor, where Emma was sitting, gazing out of the big front window. She turned to look in his direction when she heard him descending the stairs.

"I hope I didn't keep you waiting too long, Emma."

"No, not at all." Emma stood. "I wonder, though, if it would be better if we did this in Claire's quarters." She looked through the archway into the dining room and bent her head to look around Levi into the hallway. "I don't want anyone overhearing us," she whispered.

"Yes, all right, lead the way." Levi followed Emma into Claire's quarters. Emma shut the door behind him.

"Before I show you this, please promise you will hear me out before you react." Emma took the folded piece of paper out of her skirt pocket.

Levi shrugged his shoulders. "Very well, I promise."

Emma handed Levi the IOU she had found in Josiah's lapel pocket two days ago. "I found this in Josiah's pocket when I was helping Claire and Molly with the laundry Monday."

Levi opened the note and read it. He looked back up at Emma, who noticed the muscles in his jaws flexing. "I'm waiting," he said. "Please explain yourself."

"I didn't understand why Josiah would have it. I wanted a chance to think about it before I brought it to you, but then you came in and told us Josiah had been arrested and you had been ordered to discontinue the investigation. At the time, it seemed it would just further incriminate Josiah, and I knew if I gave it to you, you'd be duty-bound to disclose it to the prosecutor."

"That's exactly right, Emma." Levi's voice was a slow staccato. "I hope you say something that convinces me you are not guilty of suppressing evidence in a murder case."

"I confronted Josiah when I visited him in jail. He seemed genuinely mystified as to how it ended up in his pocket. I realize if he did murder Carson, and the IOU played a role, that he would lie about it, but I couldn't see how it figured in. It really doesn't prove anything at all, does it? I mean, so what if he has the IOU? It doesn't benefit him, and now that Carson is dead, the IOU is null and void. I think someone has made a mistake.

I think someone planted it on Josiah thinking it would incriminate him, but if anything, the IOU serves more to exonerate him. The real question is: who put it there? I thought it had to be someone from the boarding house, someone who had access to the clothes set out in the hallway for laundering. I eliminated you and Miss Sully as having the least reason to have done it. That left Willy and Peter. Between the two, Peter seemed the more likely one, so I stopped by his shop this morning and confronted him. He acted shocked that I had found the note, but I can't say he didn't put it there."

Levi tapped the folded note against his hand, considering what Emma had said. "There is a lot to what you have said. I agree Josiah's being in possession of this IOU is interesting, but not in and of itself incriminating, and does nothing to prove one way or the other his guilt. He must know that, so why would he lie about how the note came to be in his possession? Even if he came by it in the course of murdering Carson, there would be no reason to hide it. Carson could have given it to him for safe-keeping, and since the IOU clearly states to whom Graham owed the money, it would be of no value to the bearer now. Graham would have a better reason for lying. If he thought somehow that by putting the note in Josiah's pocket, it would point the suspicion away from him and toward Josiah, then he might do it."

"Does Graham have an alibi for the time frame when Carson was killed?" Emma asked.

"I didn't have a chance to find out before my investigation was called off." Levi and Emma shared a glance. Somehow, they would have to find out without the authority of a formal inquiry. In the meantime, Levi was obligated to turn the IOU over to the prosecutor, and that could only harm Josiah's case.

❁

Emma changed into her simple cotton dress and began doing her chores. It was an unusually mild day, so she wanted to finish her work at the boarding house and take a hike in the hills. She hoped to find Ancha, too.

When Emma entered the parlor to dust, she found Josiah sitting in the chair closest to the window, reading the newspaper. He folded it and set it on the occasional table when he stood to greet her.

"Good afternoon, Emma."

"Hello, Josiah. I'm surprised you are here this time of day. I thought you'd be at your office in town."

"I was this morning, but I have some design work to do, and I wanted to be on site for that. I had a very interesting morning, as it turned out."

"Yes?" Emma took a seat on the sofa and motioned for Josiah to resume his seat on the chair.

"Yes. It seems Mr. Albright has retained a lawyer for me. Edward Clark, a well-known lawyer out of Denver. He's far too high-priced for me, but he said Mr. Albright was paying his fees. I just wonder what it will end up costing me in the long run." He grinned ruefully. "Still, I am grateful, of course."

Emma frowned, trying to reconcile this news with Levi's belief that the influential men in town had pressured Sheriff Dana to arrest Josiah in the first place. It didn't make sense. "What does he make of your case?"

"He seems to think he will be able to get the case dismissed for lack of evidence. He will file the appropriate papers and request a hearing. He and the judge are well acquainted. He is optimistic." Josiah smiled.

"That's fantastic! Oh, it would be wonderful if they just dismissed the charges against you." Emma wondered if the IOU would ruin his chances at getting a dismissal.

"It would be better than being tried for murder, I agree. But dismissing the charges doesn't prove I'm innocent. It just means they can't prove I'm guilty. This business will tarnish my reputation, and I'm still not sure Mr. Albright can take the risk of keeping me on the bath house project."

"But he was insistent you commit to finishing the project, Josiah. I think he has confidence in you."

"He was, yes, but something is going on, Emma. Something behind the curtain. I don't know what it is, but I know the bath house project is at the center of it, somehow." Josiah paused. He glanced at the folded paper and cleared his throat. "Emma, I think we could both use a lift of spirit. I saw in the paper that the BeeBee house is having a hop on Thanksgiving Day. Would you like to go? The whole community will no doubt attend."

"A hop?"

"Yes, a hop—a dance. Not as formal as a ball. I find them more enjoyable for that reason, frankly. This one promises to be quite festive, since it will be the start of the holiday season."

Emma loved to dance, but she knew nothing about how they danced in the nineteenth century. She hesitated too long to answer.

"Of course, I understand." Josiah said, seeming to accept her refusal. "Perhaps it is too soon since you lost your family? Forgive me for being insensitive."

"No, Josiah, it's not that. You just caught me off guard." Emma wanted some fun. She wanted to have an evening just to enjoy herself. She threw caution to the wind. "I would like to go to the hop, thank you for asking me," she smiled.

✻

It was mid-afternoon by the time Emma ventured into Williams Cañon with her parcel of apples and two pieces of fried chicken. She could not hike for long, but she was full of nervous energy and looked forward to walking some of it off. She hadn't changed into her jeans—the cotton dress was comfortable enough—but she had donned the bear claw necklace, which she considered an amulet, especially now that she knew a shaman had made it.

"Ancha! Kwiyaghat!" Emma called when she arrived at the boulder. She waited a few moments and called again. When no one came, she put her fingers in her mouth and let out three quick, loud whistles. Again, no one came. She didn't want to leave the chicken on the boulder for fear it would attract predators, but she put the apples on the ledge for Ancha and then headed up the canyon path. She was disappointed he had not arrived, but she couldn't expect him to be waiting for her all the time, just in case she came.

She walked deeper into the canyon, reaching 'the narrows,' an area where the steep canyon sides closed in closely, then she turned back toward town. Perhaps she should set her sights on climbing up to Pikes Peak, she thought. She had done it a few times in her life, but now it would be different. No road for cars led up to the top along the west side. No cog rail made its way along the east side. It would be as though she had never hiked it if she did it now. Of course, she would have to wait until late spring or early summer, but it was something to look forward to. She was lost in these musings when she looked down the path and saw Ancha and Kwiyaghat some distance away, walking along the rocks above the path. She let out another shrill whistle. They stopped and turned to walk down to meet her.

"Hello, Ancha! Kwiyaghat!" Emma greeted them, reaching down to rub Kwiyaghat's head and ears. "I'm glad to see you both."

"I heard your loud noise from my dwelling. I was not sure it was you, but Kwiyaghat seemed to know." Ancha looked at his dog, his tone reflecting light amusement, yet he did not smile. Emma had never seen him smile.

"I thought it the best way to call for you. I hope it didn't offend you. If it didn't, I'll use the same signal in the future so you will know it's me."

"It works. I am not offended."

They turned to continue walking along the path. Emma felt peaceful and content having the company. It's as if they had always known each other, a familiarity for which there was no accounting, but Emma was grateful for it. For some time, they were silent. The only sounds were the wind in the pines, the dull thud of their footsteps on the dusty path, and the pat-pat-pat of Kwiyaghat's quicker pace as he pranced ahead and back to them, back and forth. A hawk screeched high above their heads. They stopped in unison to gaze in its direction, watching it soaring high in the sky, tipping its wings slightly to dip left and then right over the cliffs. They resumed their walk. The shadows were already forming deep in the canyon with the afternoon sun. When they reached the boulder, Ancha retrieved the apples.

"Oh, I have this for you, too," Emma said, untying the rag holding the chicken from around her waist. "I didn't want to leave it for animals to find." She handed it to Ancha.

"So you wore it like bait on your waist?" He took the bundle from her and shook his head.

"Humm, I didn't think of that." Emma confessed, sheepishly. "Here, let's sit so you can eat." She pointed to two rocks suitable for seats.

Ancha unwrapped the chicken and peeled off a chunk for Kwiyaghat, who swallowed it whole, wagging his tail happily.

He took a piece for himself and raised his eyebrows approvingly as he chewed the meat.

"Molly cooks for us. I thought you'd enjoy her fried chicken."

"Yes," Ancha swallowed. "It is very good. Thank you."

Emma reached for the bear claw around her neck with her left hand, the hand that bore the ring Paul had given her. It was an absent-minded gesture, but the moment her hand touched the bear claw, she had a vivid vision of both Ancha and Paul standing side-by-side. For the first time, Emma noticed a resemblance between them. Paul was taller, but their high cheekbones were similar, and their eyes were the same shape. In the vision, they both looked at Emma with a gaze that bore into her soul—like they were seeing the essence of her and approved. Then the vision just as quickly vanished. She let out a gasp.

Ancha looked at her inquisitively. "Are you well?"

Emma looked at Ancha, trying to see again the resemblance to Paul, but it was lost. "Yes, I just—it's nothing." Emma shook her head quickly. "It was just my imagination."

Ancha accepted her answer, but it was clear to him she was not telling him the whole truth.

❧ CHAPTER 28 ❧

Emma was glad that Claire was not at home when she returned. She did not want another confrontation about hiking in the hills, and she was still feeling unsettled from the vision she had had. After washing the trail dust from her face, she joined Molly in the kitchen.

"Hello, Molly. Can I do anything to help?"

"Oh, hello there, Miss Quinn! I suppose you can set the table. Dinner won't be ready for another hour or so, though, so there's no hurry."

"Please, Molly, call me Emma. Okay, I'll go ahead and set the table. I'll be in the big parlor afterwards if you need me to do anything else."

"Thank you, Miss . . . Emma." Molly smiled, turning back to the stove to stir her pot of stew.

After setting the table, Emma picked up the paper Josiah had left on the table earlier and settled onto the sofa to read. She smiled when she read the newspaper's title: *The Colorado*

Springs Gazette. The paper's name had been shortened to simply *The Gazette* in Emma's time, but it was familiar enough to give her some sense of home. She noticed the four-page paper featured national news on the first page. Manitou news, such as it was, was relegated to the last page. This is where she found the notice of the 'hop' Josiah had invited her to attend with him.

"Oh, the hop." Emma looked up and lowered the paper. *"What am I going to do? I don't know how to dance at this thing!"* Emma's stomach tightened at the thought.

"Ah! There you are, my dear!" Claire walked into the parlor from the entrance hall. "Molly said I'd find you here. Why the sour face?"

Emma returned the paper to the table. "Oh, Claire," Emma sighed, "Josiah invited me to the hop on Thanksgiving Day, and I said 'yes.' But I don't know how to dance—at least not the way you do these days."

Claire raised her eyebrows and, with a mischievous grin, said, "Josiah asked you to a hop?"

"Stop it. It's nothing serious. We both just thought it might be fun, and lord knows we could use a bit of fun. Normally, I'd be enthusiastic about a dance, but now I'm afraid I'll embarrass myself—and Josiah. I don't have a clue what to do."

"Well, it's simple, isn't it? I'll teach you. Maybe we can even get Levi to help."

Emma's stomach clamped even tighter.

❀

As had become a routine for them, Levi and Emma met in the reading room after dinner.

"I think we can safely eliminate Tommy White." Emma marked through Tommy's name on the table she had created on the butcher paper tacked to the wall. "You've verified he was at

205

the hotel during the entire window when Carson could have been killed."

"Yes, I agree. Tommy's not our killer." Levi stood next to Emma and pointed to the next name on the list. "I spoke to Graham today, informally of course. He said he was at the bookstore all day the day Carson was killed, including at the time of the earthquake. He described how the books had fallen off shelves and that he had to set the displays right afterwards because everything had moved out of place. He said no one was in the shop that afternoon, so no one can verify he was there precisely at that time. Although I did not sense subterfuge on his part, we can't eliminate him."

"Yes, and he does have the best motive as far as we know. He also had the means to put the IOU in Josiah's pocket. He's still our best suspect at the moment, I think." Emma wrote the highlights of Levi's discovery in the table.

"We can, however, eliminate Mr. Albright." Levi pointed to the next name. "I verified that he was called to the Colorado Springs Company board meeting. There's no way he could have killed Carson."

"Yes, but as we have already discussed, he may still be involved even if he wasn't the one who physically bashed Carson's head in." Emma sat the pencil down on the table and crossed her arms over her chest. "I hope to get some insight into Mr. Albright and his business now that I will be working for him."

"What?" Levi turned quickly from the wall and looked sharply at Emma.

"Yes! I went to Mr. Albright's office at the Manitou House today and persuaded him to give me a job. It's on a trial basis for a month, but it will give me a legitimate reason for poking around a bit to see if I can learn anything relevant to this case. I have to admit, I hope I don't find anything. I need the job."

"No."

"I'm sorry?"

"No, absolutely not, Emma. It's too dangerous, in many ways."

"What do you mean, Levi?"

Levi rubbed his eyebrows with this thumb and index finger, then pinched the bridge of his nose. He looked back at Emma. "Mr. Albright is one of the most powerful men in the area, Emma. You do not want to get on his wrong side, and there are many ways to get on his wrong side."

"I plan to be careful and discrete! If I find nothing suspicious, he will be none the wiser that I ever thought he was involved. It should have no bearing on my ability to develop a good relationship with him."

"That's my other concern. Just what do you think his motive was in agreeing to give you a job?" Levi raised his eyebrows, waiting for Emma to see what he was implying.

"Are you suggesting he has inappropriate intentions towards me?" Emma's voice raised in anger. "Do you think that's the only reason he could possibly have for giving me an opportunity?"

Levi shrugged and raised his palms up.

"Of course. What else could it be? I have no other value, right?" Emma said sarcastically, pressing her lips together. She tensed her crossed arms more tightly to her chest.

"That's not what I mean, Emma. I know you are intelligent and have much value to bring, but Mr. Albright cannot know that, yet. If he agreed so easily to give you a job, particularly on a trial basis, his reasons are suspect. Surely you see that."

Emma sat down and put her head in her hands. She felt foolish. She had come at the situation from the point of view of a professional woman in the twenty-first century—post "me too." She knew Levi was probably right, as had Claire been earlier in her warning. She had not considered the possibility that Mr. Albright's real motive may have been to have an excuse to be alone with her. Alone and in control. Her rage grew, but she knew it was misdirected at Levi.

"Damn it! You're right, Levi. I had not considered that Mr. Albright might have bad intentions." She lifted her head and looked at Levi. "But I will have to see it through and manage the situation. I can and will prove to him that I am valuable aside from his intentions. I can't walk away. I won't walk away."

Levi sighed and sat beside Emma, placing his hand on her arm. "All right, Emma. Just please, be careful."

❀

November 15, 1882

I was happy this morning when I thought I had cleverly convinced Mr. Albright to hire me, even if it was on a non-paying trial basis. I felt empowered. I felt it was possible for me to be self-supporting, even in 1882. Tonight, I feel silly and naïve. Both Claire and Levi have warned me about Mr. Albright—that he is a powerful man who is used to getting what he wants. And it's quite possible, even probable, that what he wants is not a smart, capable assistant, but an inappropriate relationship. How could I have been so blind? I may have walked right into a lion's den. Well, I've created this situation. It's up to me to make hay out of it, if I can. I have to be more mindful of what time I'm living in, though. My survival depends on it.

Emma put her journal away on the night table and retrieved her cell phone from the backpack under the bed. Her battery recharger showed that it only had 40% power left. Soon, her phone would be useless to her and the last connection to her previous life would be broken. She decided not to turn on her phone and flip through her pictures as she had done nightly since she arrived. Instead, she took out the bear claw necklace and brought the necklace to her heart and closed her eyes, hoping for another vision, if that's what it was, of Paul. She could imagine his face, but not in the same vivid, powerful way she had earlier that day in the canyon with Ancha. That had been different.

No vision came to her, but the necklace seemed to always give her a sense of calm, and she drifted off to sleep, still holding it against her chest.

❧ CHAPTER 29 ❧

"Come on, Emma, let's start your dance lessons." Claire said after they had finished cleaning up the breakfast dishes. "You've been moping about all morning. Perhaps a bit of dancing will improve your mood."

"Yes, maybe it would." Emma agreed. "I don't want anyone to see me, though. I don't want people knowing I don't know how to dance. It would be odd, wouldn't it, for me not to know?"

Claire was thoughtful. "Yes, I suppose it would be strange for you not to know basic things, like the waltz." She was silent for a moment as she continued to ponder. "I know! We could go up to the attic!"

"Is there music in the attic for us to dance to?"

Claire frowned at Emma. "No, but we wouldn't have music down here, either, if I'm dancing with you. If we can persuade Levi to help, I can play the piano while he dances with you. In the meantime, we'll have to sing." Claire smiled.

"Oh, right." Emma realized she had taken for granted a

phonograph or Victrola or something similar could provide music, but of course, none existed yet. "I have an idea! I'll be right back."

Emma went to her room and grabbed her cell phone. She decided it was worth using the power to play a few songs, and the thought of hearing her own music cheered her up.

In the attic, Claire opened the shutters to let in as much light as possible. The morning sun was still low in the sky and shone into the small windows sufficiently for their purpose.

"Where should I start?" Claire said, more to herself than to Emma.

"From the very beginning. I know there are dances called the waltz and foxtrot, but I don't know more than that."

"Humm. I've never heard of the foxtrot, but the waltz is fundamental. Let's start with that."

"Yes, okay." Emma stood in front of Claire, waiting for instruction.

"The waltz is done in 3/4 time: BA-ba-ba, BA-ba-ba, with the first beat being the one emphasized. The basic step is called the box step, and is forward, side, close, backward side close, like this." Claire sang "BA-ba-ba, BA-ba-ba, one, two, three, one, two, three," as she slowly demonstrated the box step for Emma. "Now, you will want to mirror my steps, stepping with the opposite foot in the opposite direction as my steps. Here, come here and I will lead as the man."

Emma stepped close to Claire, and they assumed a dance posture. "Ready?" Claire asked.

"Yes, ready."

"And, start: one, two, three, ouch!" Claire cried out.

"Sorry."

"Let's try again. Ready, and one, two, three, one, two three, one, two, ouch!"

"Damn it! Sorry Claire."

"Loosen up a little, Emma. Keep your knees soft."

After fifteen minutes, Emma thought she had bruised every toe on Claire's feet. "I don't seem to be getting the hang of this Claire. Maybe if we had some music?"

"I agree music would help, but I can't very well dance with you and play the piano at the same time. Besides, someone may walk in on us in the parlor, and I didn't think you wanted that."

"You're right, but I have another way. My cell phone can play music. It won't be very loud, but we will be able to hear it. I have a couple of songs that should work. Claire, prepare to be amazed!" Emma pulled her phone out of her pocket and did a search for "Perfect," by Ed Sheehan. She put the phone back in her pocket and the song started. Claire's eyes grew even wider than they usually were. She listened to the song until she found the beat.

"Ready and . . . one, two, three, one, two three," she counted out the beat quietly so they could still hear the song. "Very good, Emma!" They made it through four box steps without mishap. "Much better!" and Claire added a turn that Emma managed successfully. "Splendid, Emma!" Claire exclaimed.

When the song ended, both women separated and clapped with glee, laughing heartily.

"Oh, that was fun!" Emma laughed.

"Yes. What a remarkable thing to hear that song coming from your phone. It was an unusual song. I'm not sure what all the instruments were. The tempo was a bit slow, though."

"Well, let's try this one." Emma selected another song, this time "Kiss from a Rose," by Seal.

"I think you've got the hang of it, Emma," Claire said once the song was over. "Now all you need is a bit of practice."

"Oh! Can we do another one?" Emma was so happy to be dancing and hearing music. "Wait until you hear this one." She selected "Nothing Else Matters," by Metallica. The lead-in was long, and Claire, unsure of it, scrunching up her nose and shook her head back and forth. But then the melody started, and she picked up the beat. They danced around the attic slowly as Claire wore a look of wonder, listening to the heavy drumbeats and strings in the background as the male voice sang strange words to her ears. Emma began singing along, quietly, "Never care for what they know, and I know . . ." Then the electric guitar came in with a rift. "So close, no matter how far . . . And nothing else matters . . ."

When the song ended, Claire stood frozen.

"Are you okay, Claire?"

"Yes." Claire said, breathless. "That was the most remarkable thing I've ever heard. I *loved* it! It made me . . . feel things. I can hardly describe it."

Emma laughed. "Yes. The music is very different in my time." She stopped to consider what she was about to do, wondering if it was wise, but then she threw caution to the wind. "Let me show you how I dance in my day, Claire." Emma searched for one of her favorites, "Starboy," by The Weeknd. She turned up the volume as much as she dared and began doing her best hip-hop moves. She had the explicit lyrics version of the song, but Claire didn't seem to pick up on them. When the song was over, Emma was out of breath from trying to dance in the ridiculously long dress she was wearing.

"That was shocking! And utterly delightful!" Claire clapped, laughing.

Emma took a bow, then she remembered that she was nearly out of battery power. She reached back in her pocket to turn the phone off. "I have to conserve my power. I'm almost out. I won't be able to play any more music once I'm out of power."

They spent the rest of the morning on the galop, the polka,

and how hops generally opened and closed.

"There will be group dances, too, alternating between the couples' dances," Claire explained. "I'm sure the circle dance will be done. It's pretty easy to learn, especially when everyone else knows it."

Emma felt overwhelmed. She thought she could manage the waltz, and she knew she picked up line dances quickly, so she assumed she would do likewise with the circle dance. She struggled with the polka and was hopeless with something called the mazurka. The rituals associated with starting and ending the dance made her uneasy, and she was afraid she would be awkward at the hop. Still, the morning had been the most fun she had had since arriving in 1882. She looked forward to the dance.

❀

Emma placed the large plate of fried chicken on the sideboard. Her fellow tenants were all gathered for dinner, already queued to serve themselves the mashed potatoes, squash, fried chicken, biscuits and gravy that Molly had so competently prepared. The food was always simple and excellent at Maison La Salle. The smell of the chicken wafted into the air, making Emma's mouth water. She had skipped lunch and was famished.

"I can't believe it's almost the holiday season." Christina Sully said, taking her seat. "They say at the Manitou House that they are expecting a record number of winter visitors this year. I understand all the hotels that are open over the winter are nearly booked full through the end of the year." She placed her napkin on her lap and reached for her fork and knife. "I'm just glad there will be enough laundry to be done to keep me employed!"

"I second that, Miss Christina," added Willy. "Do you recall the year I had to head up to Leadville for the winter, Miss Claire? You were mighty kind to hold my room for me 'til I came back that April. I'd rather work at the livery any day than up in them dirty, dark mines."

"I was happy to do it, Willy. We are all family here, after all. We need to look out for each other." Claire smiled at everyone and took a fork full of mashed potatoes into her mouth.

"Yes, I usually close at the end of November, but I am now discussing with the owners the possibility of keeping the bookstore open at least until the end of the year," Peter added.

"It seems we are all prospering. I have recently secured a position with Mr. Albright." Emma chimed in.

"Indeed, Miss Quinn? What will you be doing for him?" Peter asked, stressing the words 'you' and 'him' just enough to make his insinuation clear.

Emma immediately regretted saying anything. "Well, it's on a trial basis for a month. He said he needed to think about what my duties would be. I start Monday."

"I dare say he does." Peter muttered, taking a drink of water.

"What are you implying, Graham?" Levi gave Peter a piercing glare.

"Nothing whatever, Levi." Peter gave Levi a reptilian grin. "It's wonderful that Miss Quinn has found a position under Mr. Albright." Again, Peter stressed slightly the word 'position' in his usual back-handed manner.

Emma felt her face turn hot and her mouth go dry. Dinner had been so pleasant until she had opened her mouth.

"Emma, I think it's grand that you will be working for Mr. Albright. I have always found him to be an upright fellow." Josiah offered.

"I heard Mr. Albright has retained a lawyer for you,

215

Josiah." Peter directed his bile-infused attention away from Emma. "It's understandable you would think well of him for being so generous to you."

"Peter, please. We have been enjoying a pleasant meal together. Why must you make everyone feel uncomfortable?" Claire did her best to rein Graham in and salvage the evening. "I suggest we retire to the parlor for some music and singing."

"I'd love to hear Miss Emma sing again!" Christina chimed in.

"Yes, Miss Emma. Yer purty voice would be a balm to my tired bones," Willy smiled wide.

Feeling somehow responsible for the tense turn dinner had taken, Emma agreed.

"I only know a couple of songs, Claire." Emma whispered as they carried the dishes into the kitchen.

"And you certainly cannot sing the songs you played for me today," Claire laughed. "Oh, it will be fine. I'll play a few sing-alongs for us all to sing, then you can sing a couple on your own. That will satisfy them."

Levi came in with a stack of dishes. "I swear to heaven, that Peter Graham provokes me," he said between gritted teeth. "Why do you tolerate him remaining here, Claire?"

"He pays his room and board on time, and he follows the rules, such as they are. Just because he is a bit disagreeable is no reason to ask him to leave, Levi."

"Well, I think you should consider the impact he is having on your other fine tenants. It isn't fair to them to have to tolerate his offenses. No matter how he tries to deny it, he provokes people on purpose."

Emma had to agree with Levi. It crossed her mind how convenient it would be to discover Graham had killed Carson and they could legitimately be rid of him. She silently scolded herself. Graham might be unlikable, but that did not mean he was a murderer. She must try to be objective, even if he was both unlikable and the best suspect they had.

The members of the boarding house, including Peter Graham, enjoyed their evening of song. Emma sang as a solo "Oh Susanna," "Beautiful Dreamer," and "Ruben and Rachel." She learned the words and melody to a few other songs that the group sang together. All in all, it had been a happy day.

That night, as Emma lay in bed, she made a resolution. She was not going to live without her cell phone. She needed her pictures and videos of her loved ones, her music, and her books. She needed a way to recharge her phone and Bluetooth earplugs. She knew there was no electricity infrastructure yet, and she didn't know when it would arrive in Manitou, but Alice had her 'electric bath.'" Emma assumed there was some source of electricity for that, so that's where she would start tomorrow morning.

⚘ CHAPTER 30 ⚘

Emma was getting efficient at her morning ritual. She had
become comfortable with using the chamber pot under her
bed at night. It was better than getting dressed and venturing
out in the cold, dark night. She was over the unpleasantness of
cleaning the pot out in the morning. It really wasn't any worse
than cleaning her cats' litter box. Molly was almost always there
when Emma woke, and she had water boiling on the stove,
ready for everyone to have hot water for their wash basins. The
lye soap was harsh, but effective. She had also grown
accustomed to using baking soda as tooth paste. Her hair was
still short enough that it did not require too much effort, and
she had learned to use cornstarch as a dry shampoo.

She also knew how to accomplish her morning chores
better. She gathered the eggs each morning, and a few days ago,
managed a decent batch of biscuits. She worked with Molly in
the kitchen without getting in the way as often and was busy
making the biscuit batter when Claire came into the kitchen.

"Good morning, Claire! Did you sleep well?"

"Well enough, thanks." Claire took a mug from the shelf and poured a cup of coffee from the pot on the stove. Her hair was more disheveled than usual, Emma noticed, as Claire sat at the table.

"I'm going to the bath house this morning after chores." Emma rolled out the biscuit dough and cut out each one, laying it on a greased baking sheet. "Alice had offered to show me her electric bath last week." Emma looked at Molly and considered her next words. "I thought I'd take her up on it today. Would you like to join me?"

"No, I have plenty to do around here. But please invite Alice to come over this evening, for dinner if she would like, or after. I have something to discuss with her." Claire took a big sip of coffee and let out a sigh of satisfaction.

"Yes, all right." Emma put the sheet of biscuits in the oven, then poured herself a cup of coffee and joined Claire at the table. The women sat quietly while Molly fried the bacon and eggs.

❀

The town was quiet that morning. Thanksgiving was a couple of weeks away, so the holiday tourists would be arriving soon, Emma thought. Tourists were the lifeblood of the village. Everyone depended on them, so Emma hoped for a good winter season, but she did enjoy the present calm, sparse population. In the distance, Emma heard a whistle as the train from Colorado Springs chugged into town. She stood on the foot bridge for a moment, taking it all in. It wouldn't be long before electricity and cars would forever change this place—and all places—irrevocably. Or maybe not. It would be interesting to see if the future in front of Emma now played out the way it had in Emma's original timeline. Emma shook her head, trying to sort out the ramifications of time travel was mindboggling. She continued on the path to Alice's bath house.

She saw smoke coming out of the vent in the roof above the office, as well as at the far end of the bath house, indicating that Alice was there and that she had her boiler going to heat the spring water for baths. She knocked twice quickly before entering the office, where she found Alice sitting at her desk, reading a journal.

"Good morning, Alice! I hope I'm not disturbing you." Emma greeted the doctor.

"Not at all!" Alice stood up and smiled warmly at Emma. "I am just getting caught up on some medical reading. It's quite exciting, really. A German doctor, Dr. Koch, has recently discovered that tuberculosis is caused by a bacterium. It is a revolutionary discovery. This article discusses the implications for treatment protocols." Alice stopped, seeing the flat expression on Emma's face. "Of course, this comes as no news to you, I suppose. Please tell me, do we find a cure?"

Emma looked down at the journal. She knew only two things about tuberculosis: an antibiotic could treat it, but it still existed and killed thousands of people in the world every year. "I'm not sure of the specifics, or even when advances happened, Alice, but this does lead to a much more effective way of dealing with the disease. I'm sorry I can't be more specific, even if I wanted to."

"It's good enough for me to know there is hope. Are you here for a bath this morning?"

"No. But before I get to the reason for my visit, Claire asked me to invite you to dinner tonight or, if you can't make dinner, to come by afterwards. She said she had something to discuss with you. She didn't tell me what it was about, though."

"That's curious. Well, yes, I'd be pleased to join you for dinner. Now, how can I help you, Emma?"

"Alice, I need a way to recharge my cell phone. It contains all of my pictures of loved ones and special places, my music, my books. It's all I have left of my life before I arrived here. I thought you might help me, since you are an 'electrician.'" Emma paused. "You mentioned an electric bath the other day. What do you use as your source of electricity? Do use batteries?"

"I do, yes. Come, I will show you my electric bath apparatus and we can discuss how to get you what you need."

Emma followed Alice down the narrow corridor to the last room. It was similar in most respects to the room where she had taken her hot spring water bath. The difference was the bathtub itself and the strange accessories hanging from pegs on the wall above the tub. The tub was metallic. Inside the tub was a wooden platform that resembled a crude lawn lounge chair.

"An electric bath uses an external battery to provide a low current that flows through the patient." Alice explained. "I place the patient in the tub's wooden insulated seat. The tub itself is insulated from the ground." Alice pointed to the wooden blocks the tub rested on. "I fill the tub with hot spring water, just as I do in the other baths. In the case of the electric bath, however, I add to it a solution to acidify the water in accordance with the ailment I am treating. I put the negative pole in contact with the tub here." Alice indicated the clamp affixed to the tub. "I then instruct the patient to hold the positive pole, thereby completing the circuit and allowing the current to run through the patient."

"What conditions do you treat with this?" Emma asked.

"Chronic pain, rheumatism, arthritis, nervous conditions, female discomfort, general degenerative ailments."

"Is it safe? Generally, it is a good idea to keep water and electricity away from each other."

"Yes, well, safety is the primary concern, of course. The current is low."

221

Emma was aware of some alternative medicine techniques that used low current electricity to diagnose things like allergies, and even traditional medicine used electrical stimulation for pain management. If it had been effective, though, Emma suspected it would be more widely used in modern days.

Alice sighed, seeing that Emma was skeptical. "Many doubt the efficacy of the treatment. I have added electric baths to attract business. The hard truth is that people do not flock to women physicians, and I struggle to maintain a viable practice. At least this way, people come to me and I have the opportunity to suggest other things that might provide more lasting relief."

Emma saw the resignation on Alice's face. She didn't fault Alice for finding a way to attract patients that she could genuinely help.

"I'm sure you've helped many people, Alice."

Alice relaxed, seeing that Emma did not judge her tactics harshly. "I use a Grenet cell for the electricity."

"That's perfect!" Emma said, remembering from her history of technology class that these electro-chemical batteries could provide sufficient power for her purpose. "I will need three of them, I think."

"I will order them from my supplier in Denver. I expect it will take a week or two to get them."

❋

Emma walked past the boarding house and continued up Cañon Avenue to Williams Cañon. She looked up the footpath to the Calhoun house and saw the maid on the side of the house, beating a rug. The maid's back was facing Emma, so she didn't shout out a greeting, but she saw a movement from the turreted room on the second floor and saw Anna looking out of the window. She waved, but Anna turned away, not seeing Emma's overture. *"It's just as well she didn't notice me"* Emma thought.

When she got to the boulder, she let out her whistle signal. A flock of blackbirds in a nearby tree took off in unison at the sudden shrill sound. Emma sat on a rock across the path from the boulder and waited. She breathed in the crisp, dry air that refreshed her at the same time that it dried out the inside of her nostrils and parched her throat. She let out a sneeze when a particle of the dusty earth tickled her nose. A quarter of an hour passed, and there was no sign of Ancha or Kwiyaghat. She resigned herself to the fact that they were not coming.

She climbed up to the ridge where she had first emerged from the cave and looked down on the town. She could see why Carson and Josiah had chosen that spot to meet with Mr. Albright to review the landscaping plans for the new bath house. Though some distance away, the slice of land between Cañon Avenue and Manitou Avenue was visible, and provided a bird's-eye view of what the area would look like once the project was done. She saw the sparsely sprinkled houses on the hills between the ridge and town, including the Calhoun house. Anna's room provided a panoramic view of the valley in which Manitou nestled and the hills where Emma now stood. The sun was at its highest point in the late fall sky, yet it cast long shadows behind Emma, giving her the sense that the hour was later than it was. The wind picked up, carrying with it a chill Emma had not noticed before. She returned to the boarding house before the unpredictable Colorado weather did something, well, unpredictable.

She walked into the main hall of the boarding house and immediately smelled apple pie, making her heart dance with joy. She looked in the parlor and saw Levi, who looked up from his newspaper at her.

"Hi, Levi!" She took another deep breath. "I can't wait for

dinner and that apple pie I smell."

"Good afternoon, Emma." Levi smiled and put down the paper. "I quite agree."

"It's getting cold outside." Emma looked out of the front window. "I wouldn't be surprised if we got a little snow. The clouds are gathering quickly with this wind that's picked up."

Just then Claire came in through the dining room.

"There you are, Emma! Did you give my message to Alice? Is she coming for dinner?" Claire set a bowl of apples on the occasional table.

"Yes, she accepted your dinner invitation."

"Ah, good." She turned to Levi. "Levi, it's unusual for you to be here this time of day. Say, if you're done for the day, maybe you could help Emma here with her dance lessons. I think we have the house to ourselves, aside from Molly, of course. I can play the piano for you."

"Dance lesson?" Levi turned to Emma. "You don't know how to dance?"

"I know how to dance to the music of *my* time very well, thank you. It's the waltz and the polka I need to practice."

"Yes, Josiah invited Emma to the dance at the BeeBee house on Thanksgiving Day." Claire nudged Levi playfully with her elbow, winking. "She needs to learn to dance, *tout de suite*. I told her you could help. You're a marvelous dancer, Levi." Claire beamed at Levi.

Levi held his gaze at Emma. "Josiah asked you to the hop?"

"Well, yes. He said it would be good fun, nothing fancy, and that everyone would be there." Emma didn't know why she felt she needed to explain. She only knew Levi's stare was making her uncomfortable.

Claire continued, oblivious to the tension in the room, "Come, Levi, Emma, I'll play a polka for you." She reached for them both to encourage them to assume the dance posture and then took her seat at the piano.

Levi put one hand on the small of Emma's back and took her hand with the other. She looked into his face, noticing his stern expression through his long eyelashes. She felt a tingle on her skin and a tightness in her chest. He did not look pleased, but his body was lithe and relaxed. She placed her hand on his shoulder, preparing and hoping she didn't embarrass herself with clumsiness.

"Ready? Three, two, one," Claire counted down and started playing an upbeat polka. Levi led Emma in the dance. She followed his lead effortlessly as he turned her back toward the front of the room. He was, indeed, a good dancer. He pranced her out of the room and into the hall, down the hall and back, then into the parlor again. Emma relaxed more into the movements; a broad smile bloomed unconsciously on her face. She looked up at Levi and saw his face had softened and he was smiling down at her. His shoulders were broad and hard. His hand held hers with a gentle strength that made her feel safe. She noticed him pulling her a little closer with the hand on her back.

They were both breathing fast when the music stopped. "Oh, that was marvelous!" Claire clapped happily. "Emma, you did very well, don't you think, Levi?"

"Most certainly, I do. Emma, you are a fine dancer." Levi smiled, looking down at Emma's beaming face.

"You made it effortless, Levi. I knew exactly what to do with you leading." Emma marveled at the difference it made, dancing with someone who knew what he was doing.

❦ CHAPTER 31 ❧

"My heavens, something smells divine!" Emma took in a deep breath as she walked into the kitchen. "What is that wonderful aroma, Molly?"

"Oh, you flatter me, Miss Emma," Molly grinned over her shoulder as she pumped for water at the sink. "It's just a simple roast beef with my own special herb dry rub."

"Well, it's making my mouth water and my stomach growl. I can't wait until dinner. I've been hungry since I walked in and smelled the apple pie. What can I do to help?"

"I've got it all under control, thank you. Just set the table and help me put the food on the sideboard when it's time. I understand Dr. Guiles will be joining us?"

"Yes. I'll take care of getting the dining room ready." Emma walked on to her little bedroom and shut the door.

She looked around the small quarters, wondering where she could set up the batteries for her phone. She would need three of them in series, she had calculated, and that was going to require more room than she had. *"I need my own living quarters. A place with more room and more privacy,"* Emma thought, which only made her more resolved to make a success of the internship she had negotiated with Frederick Albright. With income, she could secure her own place somewhere. She took a quick look at herself in the mirror over her washstand. She removed and replaced a couple of the hairpins she had used to try to keep her hair up and neat, and realized she was even less successful than Claire in managing her unruly locks. Finally, she gave up, waving her hands in frustration at her reflection, and ventured into Claire's parlor to look for her.

She found Claire in the reading room, reviewing a document intently. "Oh, I'm sorry. Am I interrupting you, Claire?"

Claire looked up at Emma and gave her a little smile. "No, I've looked this over several times already. I guess I'm just nervous that Alice won't agree." Claire gestured to the chair opposite her for Emma to have a seat.

"To what?" Emma took the seat.

"I've had a contract drawn up to lend Alice money to start her own bath house featuring those electric baths. I was furious when she told us the new bath house enterprise had excluded her. I just hope she isn't too proud to accept my offer."

Emma thought back to the day they had gone to tea at the Calhouns' when Claire had asked to speak privately with John Calhoun, Jr., and her recent trip to Colorado Springs. "Is that what you were up to with Calhoun that day at tea? And in town the other day?"

"Yes. I wanted to get the details sorted out and this contract drawn up so that it was all in place when I mentioned it to Alice. I thought she'd be less likely to refuse if all she had to do was sign the papers."

"That's very generous of you, Claire." Emma wondered just

how much money Claire had inherited from her family. Emma realized she knew nothing about Claire, really.

"Not so much generous as outraged at injustice, Emma, and if I can do anything to balance the scale, I will." Claire put the papers in order and placed them in their trifold binder, tying it shut.

Again, Emma marveled at how fortunate she was to have literally stumbled into Alice's and Claire's lives, and she felt ashamed that she had not been more curious to learn more about either of them. She had been so preoccupied with her own problems. She didn't know how to probe for more insight now, though, and Claire had moved on to another topic.

"Are you looking forward to the dance?"

"I would say I am more nervous about it than looking forward to it. I just hope I don't make a fool of myself."

"Your dancing is coming along fine, Emma, and we have several days yet to practice. You won't make a fool of yourself. Besides, it's all good fun; it's not meant to be taken too seriously."

"Yes, I know. I'll be fine. I am more looking forward to my new job with Mr. Albright." Emma said brightly. "I want so very much to make my own way."

"Yes, I know you do. I wish you all the success with your position." Claire looked down at the trifold, avoiding Emma's eyes. She gave the document a little touch and stood up. "I'm going to go see what I can do in the kitchen to help get dinner on the table."

"I'll be right out to get the dining room ready." Emma said, absently. Why weren't people being more encouraging to her about her new job opportunity? Was it so socially objectionable that she had a job in business?

❀

"Molly really outdid herself with dinner, Claire. Please tell her I thoroughly enjoyed it." Alice said, taking a sip of her after-dinner brandy in Claire's parlor.

"Oh, I will, Alice. I am blessed to have Molly, certainly," Claire agreed.

Emma sat apprehensively in the armchair opposite the one Alice occupied. Claire had asked Emma to join her and Alice after dinner, when Emma knew Claire planned to bring up the loan, but she wasn't sure why Claire wanted her there. "And for once, Peter Graham behaved himself. The company was very pleasant this evening," Emma added, trying to maintain the casual, relaxed tone of the post-dinner gathering.

Claire laughed. "Yes, lately Graham has been ruffling feathers, I'm afraid, but tonight he was almost charming." She sat her brandy snifter down on the occasional table. "Alice, dear, there's something I'd like to discuss with you. A proposition, of sorts." Claire folded her hands in her lap and smiled at Alice.

"A proposition?"

"Yes, and all I ask is that you hear me out before you say anything."

"All right, Claire. I'm happy to listen to what's on your mind." Alice leaned back in her chair.

"After you told us about losing your bath house, I started thinking about things. I'm sure you agree that from the very start, a few wealthy men—Palmer, Bell, Albright—have controlled this town. They literally own Colorado Springs and Manitou."

"Well, Palmer and Bell, certainly, yes."

"It isn't right, and it isn't good for our community to be completely controlled by so few men, even if their intentions are generally good. It isn't right that they are denying you your livelihood. You are a good doctor, and this community needs you."

"I am gratified you think so, Claire, but where are you going with all this?"

"I want to help you stay in practice. I want to help you continue offering your healing baths and treating patients. I have talked to my banker and lawyer, Alice, and I want to lend you the money to build a new facility of your own, to continue your electric baths and medical practice. I can't fund a facility as elaborate as the one Albright is building, obviously, but I can fund a modest one. I have the paperwork already drawn up. Please agree. People need what you offer, Alice." Claire paused and waited for Alice's reaction.

"Oh, Claire, I don't know." Alice frowned and slowly shook her head. "I appreciate your offer, but I don't feel comfortable borrowing money from you. I will figure something out."

"It wouldn't be a favor, Alice. The terms I suggest are that you have some period of time to get up and running, after which you would start repaying me, with interest. I would make a profit. It's a business decision on my part because I believe there is a need for your services."

Alice paused for several seconds. "I am concerned about what this would do to our friendship, Claire. We would no longer be on equal footing. What if I can't repay you? And I don't like the idea of being beholden to you."

"And if you don't accept my offer? What happens to our friendship then? Will you, William, and your children be able to stay here, or will you be forced to move to Denver or some other place? Then what becomes of our friendship? We need you here, Alice. I need you here."

Alice looked at Claire fondly and smiled. "You are a kind soul, Claire—maybe the kindest I've ever known. I won't say yes, but I won't say no, either, at least not tonight. Let me take the agreement. I'll look it over and think about it."

❧ Chapter 32 ❧

Emma was dusting the furniture in the boarding house parlor when she saw Josiah and a well-dressed middle-aged man walk through the front door into the hall. The men paused at the parlor doorway when they saw Emma.

"Good morning, Emma." Josiah greeted her, looking down at the hat in his hands. It was unlike him to be this demure, Emma thought. He then gestured to the man standing next to him. "This is my lawyer, Mr. Edward Clark. Mr. Clark, may I introduce Miss Emma Quinn, she is Mrs. La Salle's cousin, recently arrived from New Orleans."

"It is a pleasure, Miss Quinn." The solicitor dipped his head in greeting.

"Likewise, Mr. Clark." Emma paused, noticing the men were still standing in the doorway. She realized they were waiting for her to leave. "If you'll excuse me. I have things to attend to in the kitchen." Josiah gave her a grateful glance as she exited through the dining room.

In the kitchen, Emma took the teapot off the shelf, added a couple of spoons of tea leaves, and poured boiling water over them. She placed the tea settings and teapot on a tray and added a plate of Molly's oatmeal raisin cookies. The last Josiah had said, his lawyer was preparing to file for a dismissal of charges for lack of evidence. She wondered what had happened that they were meeting on a Saturday morning. She picked up the tray and went back to the parlor.

"Excuse me, gentlemen," Emma announced herself before entering. "I thought you might like some tea. I've also included some of Molly's cookies, Josiah." Emma sat the tray on the occasional table in front of the sofa. She tried to determine the men's mood. Josiah was leaning forward with his hands intertwined between his knees. Mr. Clark appeared to have just pulled out a file from his briefcase, which he was lying on the table as Emma walked in.

"Thank you, Miss Quinn. I'm glad you returned. Josiah was just informing me that you were the one who found Peter Graham's IOU to Carson White. I understand you turned it over to the authorities. Would you mind answering some questions about it?"

"Of course. I'd be happy to."

Josiah stood up and invited Emma to take his seat on the sofa nearest the chair Mr. Clark occupied. He moved to the opposite end of the sofa.

"I don't know how much Josiah has shared with you about his case." Mr. Clark looked at Josiah and hesitated.

"You may speak freely in front of Miss Quinn, Mr. Clark. I have nothing to hide."

"Very well. I must be perfectly frank, Miss Quinn. I was confident I could get the charges dismissed against Mr. Turner until the prosecution made me aware of the IOU you discovered and provided them. Now, I am less certain. I was hoping you could clarify some details that might help us."

"I'll do whatever I can to help, Mr. Clark. What are your questions?"

"Please, describe in as much detail as you can recall how you discovered the IOU."

"It was laundry day, and it was my task to collect the laundry each tenant had put out in the hall the night before and log the items so they could be returned after they were laundered. Claire, Mrs. La Salle, that is, instructed me to check all the pockets because tenants frequently leave items in them. When I went through Josiah's, Mr. Turner's, pockets, I found the IOU in the lapel pocket of his overcoat."

"And was anyone with you when you made this discovery?"

"Yes, both Mrs. La Salle and Molly, the cook, were in the kitchen with me when I found the note. But they were unaware of my discovery, and I did not tell them."

"Why not?"

"My first thought was that it would incriminate Josiah, but it was unclear to me the significance of my finding. I wanted to confront Josiah first, to learn if there was an innocent explanation. When Josiah denied knowing how it came to be in his pocket, I realized it didn't prove anything, really, and could in fact go some way to helping clear Josiah. So, I turned it over to Marshal Warwick."

"And would you be willing to testify under oath to all of this, if necessary, Miss Quinn?"

"Of course."

Mr. Clark turned to Josiah. "Josiah, were you wearing that overcoat the day Mr. White was killed?"

Josiah seemed to appreciate the significance of his answer before he gave it. "No! That day was mild. I only wear that overcoat on cold days."

"When and where, then, did you wear the overcoat

between the time Mr. White was killed and when Miss Quinn found the IOU?"

"I wore it each morning that I went into the Springs for work. It is cold early in the mornings, generally. And I wore it the day of the funeral. It was blasted cold that day. I also wore it to church that Sunday."

"Surely you didn't wear the overcoat while you were in the church or at the reception after the funeral," Mr. Clark commented.

"That's correct. I placed it on a hook in the church vestibule wall during the funeral service. I checked it with the clerk at the cloakroom at the Cliff House during the reception. I also placed it in the vestibule during Sunday service."

Mr. Clark leaned back in his chair and smiled. "I am relieved to learn these details. I will have no trouble at all demonstrating that the IOU proves nothing whatsoever. The real question is: who put it in your pocket, Mr. Turner? That's our killer."

❀

Emma was determined to find Ancha that afternoon. She still felt the impact of the vision she had had the last time she was with him, and she was eager to learn more about its significance. She gave her whistle signal three times at the boulder and wandered around it for nearly an hour. Still no Ancha. The tightness in her chest grew every moment that she waited and paced anxiously up and down the canyon path. Had something awful happened to him? She paused at the boulder and looked up at the rocky cliffs for any signs of movement in the direction from which she had sometimes seen Ancha emerge. She ventured up the rocky slopes in search of her friend.

She cursed freely as she struggled in her long dress and granny boots to navigate the rocky, gravelly incline. How was it that women were still tolerating clothes that did not serve them? She vowed to have clothes made that she could function in just as soon as her income allowed. She paused when she reached the top of the canyon wall, dusty and fatigued. As she caught her breath, she looked at the vista afforded by her high vantage point. The tightness in her chest released when she saw Pikes Peak to the west. She could not see Manitou, but she could see well down Williams Cañon to the north and knew it ran parallel with Waldo Cañon, where she had hiked so many times. A crow cawed high above her head. The love she felt for this land made her ache, and tears came to her eyes. She took a deep breath and let out the loudest whistle she could manage. This she repeated twice more. Then she waited.

"You do not give up."

Emma spun around, her heart now pounding with adrenaline for being startled. There stood Ancha and his ever-loyal Kwiyaghat, calmly staring at her. "For God's sake, Ancha. You scared me to death. Where on earth have you been? I've been worried sick about you!"

"You are too easy to sneak up on, Emma, and I did not realize you were my mother."

Emma felt the sting of his words. "Why are you being cruel? Don't you know how much I care about your well-being? I came the other day and missed you. When I couldn't find you today, I was concerned."

Ancha looked at her for several moments, silently. Emma was about to look away from his steady gaze when he said, "I am sorry. I did not mean to cause you pain. After the last time we met, I thought it best to keep my distance."

"Why?"

"Something happened that day. I felt it. When I asked, you

did not tell me the truth. A friendship must have trust. No trust, no friendship."

"So, you were going to withdraw, just like that? Without giving me an opportunity to explain or yourself an opportunity to understand? Somehow that does not seem very shaman-like of you." Emma realized her last statement was spiteful. "I'm sorry. I didn't mean to be that harsh."

"It made me think. What good can come of our friendship? You risk your reputation every time you come to meet me. I also am at risk. Most people do not want me here. They would welcome a reason to force me to leave."

"What about your vision? Your feeling that we are meant to be friends? I believe it, Ancha. I believe it because I think I've had a vision, too. That's one reason I wanted to meet you. I wanted to tell you what happened last time we met. I hoped you could help me understand it."

Ancha stood silently for a moment, then, apparently having made a decision, said, "Come, let us walk. You can tell me your vision." Ancha turned and waited for Emma to come along beside him. The ground was mostly dirt and rock, giving them room to walk together, side-by-side, along the high ridge. Kwiyaghat lifted his curled tail and pranced happily ahead of them.

"It happened when I touched this bear claw necklace you gave me." Emma lightly touched the necklace she wore around her neck. "I saw you and Paul, my fiancé, together. You seemed strangely similar. I didn't understand it. It seemed you were both looking through me. I felt you *knew* me and loved me, but not sexually. It was a way I'd never felt before, and it startled me. I've never had an experience like that, so I wasn't sure what it meant, if anything. But the effect it had on me has lasted. I wondered if it qualified as a vision and, if so, what the vision signifies."

Ancha was silent. Emma had learned to give him time. She was sure he had both heard her and listened, so she waited patiently for his response.

"There is one great Spirit. Spirit is everywhere, in all things. Spirit is timeless. This is true whether or not we see it," Ancha began. "Sometimes we see a moment of this truth in ways we almost understand. Mostly we do not know when we see such a moment, or we ignore it. I believe what you saw was such a moment."

"Was it a vision, then?"

"A very brief vision, yes." Ancha stopped at a sprawling evergreen bush, which had red berries still on it, and began picking the berries, placing them into the large leather pouch at his side. Emma recognized the plant, but knew nothing about it.

"What is this plant?"

"I think you call it bearberry," Ancha answered.

"Can you eat the berries?"

"Not like other berries. I use them for medicine, and on my meat. Bears seem to like them, though."

Of course, Ancha would know about using plants for medicine. He was a shaman. Emma wondered how long it had taken him to become one. She looked at Ancha's weathered face as he calmly harvested the berries. How old was he? It was hard to tell. He felt her stare and looked up at her.

"What is your question?"

"I was just wondering how long it took you to learn to be a shaman, and how old you are." Emma laughed a little, embarrassed by her admission.

"I came from a family of healers and shamans. I started learning as a boy and have studied all my life. I am not sure how old I am, but I know I am at least forty years. I remember when there were very few white men here."

From where they stood, they could see Colorado Springs, including the railroad leading north to Denver and south to Pueblo. Emma's heart ached at the knowledge that by 2019, the area would be an urban sprawl, almost meeting at the north with the even more aggressive sprawl of Denver, seventy miles away. "I am sorry, Ancha. I am sorry the white men have stolen your land." She dared not say more, even though Ancha's probing eyes seemed to wait for some assurance. When she remained silent, he gave her a sad smile and resumed picking the red berries.

"Do you think the bear claw necklace had anything to do with my vision?" Emma redirected the conversation back to the original subject.

Ancha stopped picking berries. Emma noticed he had only taken a few dozen, leaving the majority undisturbed on the bushes. "It is possible. It is a powerful object. You say you have only had one vision while touching it?"

"Yes, although it always seems to give me a sense of calm when I wear or hold it."

Ancha gestured to a low-lying rock for them to sit. "Come, Emma, I want to tell you something."

Emma sat next to Ancha on the rock. He rested his leather pouch on the ground and took her hands. "Emma, listen to me. You must be careful with visions. It is important to have the right mind, otherwise bad spirit can come just as easily as good spirit. You were lucky the first time. Do not try to have more visions."

"Will you teach me? Teach me to do it safely? I want to understand what I saw."

Ancha hesitated, still wearing a frown. Emma knew he was going to refuse.

"You gave me the necklace after having a vision. Maybe this is part of the plan, you teaching me. Please don't say no.

Please at least give it a chance. You mentioned the necklace is a powerful object. What makes an object powerful?"

"Power comes from the spirit of the object. The bear claw comes from the bear, who is powerful. A shaman can add power with his mind, his spirit."

"Do you make powerful objects? How do you do it?"

"It takes much practice—not something a student can, or should, do."

"Yes, I understand. Please, just explain to me about powerful objects."

Ancha sighed, still reluctant. "There are two kinds of powerful objects. One kind protects from harm. The other kind contains power that a medicine man can use with a purpose." He reached for the small pouch tied to his belt and from it pulled out a smooth rock that bore the shape of a crude turtle; a hairpin, still shiny, ending with a large cream pearl; a spotted feather; and a length of bright blue thread. "I have found these things, and they have power within them. The rock shaped like a turtle contains turtle power. The feather from the hawk contains hawk power, and so on. When I need these powers, I take the object that already has the quality I need, and I concentrate my mind on this quality. This makes that power greater. I keep these things in my medicine bag so I have the power when I need it." Ancha replaced the objects into his pouch. "It is getting late, Emma. You need to get back to town."

Emma knew better than to press Ancha for more that day. "Yes, you're right. Thank you, Ancha, for explaining to me. I have heard you. I will not try to have visions."

Ancha seemed to relax. He smiled gently and stood, reaching for Emma's hand to help her up. "I will show you an easier way back to town."

❧ CHAPTER 33 ❧

The way Ancha showed Emma was an easier descent, and it took her closer to town than the path she had forged earlier. It was late afternoon, nearly dinner time in fact, and Emma felt anxious that she was late for her evening duties at the boarding house. She dreaded having to make excuses for herself, where she had been—and with whom. Resentment rose in her body, making it tense. She had just passed the path to the Calhoun house when she saw, walking up the road, John Calhoun, Jr., and Anna.

"Good afternoon, Miss Quinn," John said, inquisitively.

"Good afternoon Mr. Calhoun, Miss Calhoun." Emma replied, smiling. She decided the least said the better and hoped their good manners would prevent them from asking questions and save her from having to offer an explanation of why she was traipsing down from Williams Cañon, alone. She attempted to just keep walking, hoping to avoid further conversation.

"I say, Miss Quinn, have you been wandering the

wilderness alone? It's not safe, you know?" John persisted.

"Yes, well, I was restless. If you will excuse me, I'm late for my evening chores. Have a good evening, Mr. Calhoun, Miss Calhoun."

"Of course. You, too, Miss Quinn." John said, bewildered at Emma's rudeness.

As Emma walked away, she heard Anna say tensely, "Someone must warn her, John! That filthy Indian could have molested her!"

Emma entered the boarding house from the kitchen, where she immediately met Molly.

"Heavens, Miss Emma! We've been lookin' for you for hours! Claire is down at the bath house now, thinkin' maybe you went there."

"I was out for a walk, Molly, and lost track of time. Really, I wish people wouldn't worry so much about me! I'll just go clean up and be right out to help you." Emma practically ran to her room and shut the door. *"I hope I don't have to hear too much about this,"* Emma thought as she washed her face and hands, brushed her hair and brushed off as much trail dust as she could from her dress. She came back to the kitchen and had just sat down at the table to peel the potatoes when Claire walked in. She looked up at Claire, who just glared at her. She suspected Molly's presence was keeping Claire from reading her the riot act, for which she was grateful.

Claire remained cool toward Emma all through dinner, and she declined to join the tenants in after-dinner entertainment, claiming she was tired and planned to retire early to bed.

"Well, how about a game of whist?" Josiah suggested after Claire had left the parlor. Willy declined, saying he had an early start at the livery the next morning to pick up tourists from Colorado Springs, but Graham and Levi were willing, and

Emma welcomed the distraction. Miss Sully was in her usual evening spot in the chair near the window, doing her crocheting. Josiah and Graham were still awkward with each other over the IOU, so Levi agreed to be Graham's partner, leaving Emma with Josiah.

"I saw you walking from the train depot with Mr. Clark this morning, Josiah. I trust everything is going well with your case," Graham, ever the instigator, said with a smirk.

"Graham, I hardly think Josiah's case is appropriate for us to discuss, under the circumstances," Levi cautioned. "Not only am I a man of the law, and it would not be wise for Josiah to say anything in my presence, but you are still suspected of planting that IOU in his coat pocket. He would be wise not to say anything about it to us."

"I quite agree, thank you, Levi," Josiah said, laying down the ace of diamonds and taking the trick. He led the king of diamonds. "I prefer to look forward to Thanksgiving. Claire said she has invited Dr. Guiles' and Molly's families to join us for dinner. That should be jolly. And then we have the dance afterwards." Josiah smiled at Emma.

Levi trumped Josiah's king. "I understand you and Emma will be going to the dance together."

"Emma's new in town, and I thought it would be a chance for her to get better acquainted with the community. Also, we could all use a bit of fun these days, don't you think, Levi? I assume you will be going as well? As Claire's escort?"

"I haven't spoken to Claire about it, but yes, I suppose so." Levi shuffled the cards and began dealing.

"Let's see, I believe we scored a point on that hand, right?" Emma, who was the score-keeper, asked. Everyone nodded assent.

"I hope the weather cooperates for the Thanksgiving celebration." Miss Sully said from her corner. "Willy asked me to join him at the dance," she giggled.

The players at the card table looked around at each other and smiled. Was there a romance blooming at the boarding house?

After the card game, Emma retired to her room via the door from the kitchen. She knew Claire was displeased with her, and she was in no mood for a confrontation. Claire's quarters were dark when Emma cracked the door to the reading room open, so she assumed Claire was asleep. Emma left the door open to let in as much heat from the parlor stove as possible. Lulu came running in and jumped on Emma's bed, circling several times before curling up at the foot with her tail over her nose.

"Make yourself at home, certainly!" Emma laughed at Lulu, reaching down to pet her rabbit-soft fur. Lulu rewarded her with loud purrs. Emma looked up through her window and saw lights in the upstairs rooms of the Calhoun house. She saw the silhouette of a woman in Anna's room, closing the curtains. "This town is too damn small, Lulu." Emma said, turning down her own lamp and settling under the covers.

❀

Claire was, indeed, a kind soul. She didn't stay angry, and she didn't hold a grudge. Emma thought how wonderful the world would be if it were filled with Claires. By the morning, Claire was acting perfectly normal, even cheerful.

"Emma, we have a lot to do today! We have to practice your dancing after church. I guess we will do that in the attic since we won't have the house to ourselves. And you must ready for your new job! This week is a big week for you!" Claire gave Emma a peck on the cheek as she walked through the kitchen. Emma put the biscuits in the oven and followed Claire to the dining room to help prepare the table.

"Yes, I admit, I am getting nervous about my new job." Emma pulled out the silverware from the sideboard drawer. "I hope you and the others are wrong about Mr. Albright, but I do appreciate the warning. Men and women routinely work together in my time, usually without incident, so I did not give it as much thought as I should have, given the times."

"In your time?" Graham asked as he walked into the dining room.

"You misunderstood, Peter. Emma said 'town,' not 'time,' and she's right. New Orleans is quite progressive in that respect." Claire gave Emma a wide-eyed look of warning. Emma was impressed with how quickly Claire provided cover for her slip-up. Graham frowned and went to the sideboard to serve himself eggs and bacon.

"Oh! The biscuits!" Emma cried and ran into the kitchen, pulling open the oven door just in time to prevent them from burning. She put them in a cloth-lined basket and brought them to the dining room. "I'm afraid they may be a little dry this morning. I forgot about them."

❀

"Good grief!" Alice laughed as the women told her of Emma's slip-of-the-tongue.

"Yes, I'm afraid I let my guard down. I will have to be more careful. I especially can't afford for Peter Graham to get suspicious. He strikes me as a vindictive sneak." Emma confessed.

"Oh, he likes to stir the pot, but I don't think he means any real harm, Emma." Claire chimed in as the three women walked to church. Emma thought to remind Claire he was still their number one suspect for Carson's murder, but before she could say anything, Claire continued. "Alice, will you and your family be joining us for Thanksgiving? I want to get a good headcount so I have enough food."

"Yes, yes, I am sorry I didn't confirm earlier. William was not sure he would have the day off at the mill, but he confirmed that he does, so we will all be able to come."

"Marvelous!" Claire held the church door open for the women to enter. They shed their coats and made their way to their pew.

"Where is Levi today?" Alice asked.

"He went hunting." Claire said flatly. Emma supposed she could only be mad at one of them at a time, and she secretly thanked Levi for taking the heat off of her.

"Well, it is a lovely, unseasonably warm day. 'Carpe Diem,' as they say." Alice settled into her seat, removed her gloves and put them in her reticule.

Emma's mind wandered throughout the sermon. She had no idea what it had been about, and had only the vaguest recollection of singing hymns, repeating the lord's prayer, and closing with the benediction. Her mind was on the up-coming week, but she was also keenly aware that progress on discovering Carson's murderer had completely stalled. She was beginning to think they would never know who killed the poor man. Perhaps the best they could hope for was getting the charges dropped against Josiah.

The Episcopal church was letting out just as they walked by. Emma saw Josiah escorting Anna Calhoun down the walkway. He waved to her and her companions as they approached. "Good morning, ladies! Isn't it a fine Sunday morning?" He beamed in greeting.

"Indeed, it is, Josiah!" Claire replied. "Miss Calhoun, it's good to see you."

"Thank you, Mrs. La Salle. Good morning Emma, Dr.

Guiles." Anna nodded at each of the women.

"We are off to the Cliff House for Sunday lunch." Josiah announced. "Do you mind if we walk with you?"

"Not at all," Claire beamed.

The group headed down Cañon Ave. "Emma, I hope you don't take offense, but I wanted you to be aware," Anna began, loud enough for everyone to hear. "I was concerned about you walking about the wilderness alone. You do know, do you not, that an Indian man lives amongst the foothills? He is a lone wolf. He refused to go when the last of the Utes were relocated to the reservation last year. Why the authorities allow him to linger, I do not know, but it simply isn't safe for you to explore the area alone. Not only is he out there, posing a threat, but of course, there are wild animals, too. One must be careful." Anna paused for effect. "You know, the more I think about it, the more I think *he* killed my dear Carson! He certainly had the opportunity and means, and obviously a motive. We would all be safer with him gone!"

Emma's blood ran cold.

∾ CHAPTER 34 ∾

"This is my fault!" Emma said angrily. "Seeing me coming down from the canyon planted that evil seed in Anna's head, and now Ancha is in danger." Emma pounded her fists on the reading room table and bowed her head. "You were right, Claire. I should have stayed away from Ancha for his own good." She rested her head on her folded arms and sobbed.

"It is not your fault, Emma." Claire bent over and wrapped her arms gently around Emma's bent shoulders and looked plaintively across the table at Alice. "Anna has always held animosity toward Ancha. She has wanted him forcibly removed from the beginning."

Emma hit her head against her arms several times and let out a frustrated scream between gritted teeth. Her sobs began sounding hysterical. Claire stood up and opened her hands, palms up, giving Alice another look begging for help.

Alice pulled out a chair abruptly and sat down. She put her hand firmly on Emma's arm. "Emma. Pull yourself together.

You are of no use to Ancha in this state. This is not your fault, and it is self-indulgent of you to think it is. Now, calm down so we can deal with this effectively."

Claire frowned at Alice. This was not the comfort she had hoped her friend would offer. To her surprise, however, Emma took a few deep breaths between bouts of sobs, and soon she had stopped crying altogether, the occasional stutter breathing the only remnant of the fit.

"Good. That's better." Alice gave Emma's arm three brisk pats and pulled away, leaning back in her chair. "Claire, perhaps some tea?"

Claire started, "Yes, of course. I'll go fetch some," and she walked through Emma's room for the kitchen with an urgent sense of purpose.

Alice sat silently with Emma while she collected herself. Shortly, Claire returned with the tea tray and began pouring cups for each of them. "Here Emma, my dear. I put extra sugar in yours."

Emma lifted her head and took the cup. "Thank you."

"Now, let's think like the intelligent women we are," Alice commanded.

Emma took a long drink of the hot tea. Embarrassment over her outburst was quickly replacing the fit of rage and fear. It was unlike her to lose control like that. She made another stutter breath as she inhaled to speak. "I am sorry. I don't know what got into me. Thank you, Alice. You are right."

"All right, we don't know if Anna just had this thought, or if it's something she's been suggesting for some time, so we don't really know the magnitude of the danger Ancha is in," Alice continued. "Also, she may not be the only one whose mind the idea has crossed. Frankly, I'm a little surprised it was not offered as the first theory with the number of people in town who would prefer to see Ancha relocated."

"I need to get a message to Ancha right away, warning him," Emma said, standing up. "We don't know how much time he has to hide."

"I'll go with you," Claire said. "If we are seen, it will not seem strange, and people will believe you have taken their cautions to heart, which will keep them from being suspicious of you."

"Yes, that's a good idea. Thank you, Claire. I'm going to write him a note, in case we can't find him."

"He can read?" Alice asked.

"Yes, he can read. And he speaks better English than many here in town," Emma said tersely.

She went into her room and pulled out a sheet of paper from her nightstand. She fished her gel pen and a pencil out of her backpack and returned to the reading room. Claire and Alice marveled at the pen as they watched Emma write the note:

Ancha,

You are in danger. Some in town think you killed Carson White near the cave on the day of the earthquake. You must hide well until the real killer is found. I have left a pencil for you. Use this paper. Let me know you got this message.

Your Student

"Come, Claire. I don't want to waste any more time." Emma folded the note, grabbed the pencil, and headed for the door. Claire ran after her.

"Your student?" Claire asked. "What is Ancha teaching you?"

"I'm not sure he is teaching me anything, yet, Claire, but I didn't want to sign my name. He will understand that it came from me this way." Emma walked as quickly as she dared without drawing undue attention from unknown observers.

"Let's try to act as natural and relaxed as possible." Claire said.

"I hope everyone is busy with after-church meals and observing the sabbath," Emma said, trying for some levity. Claire smiled.

"I meet Ancha at a special place. I think it's best to keep it a secret. When we get close, please stay behind and keep a look-out. I won't be long."

Claire agreed reluctantly. She had been keeping a look-out since they left the boarding house. So far, she had seen no one, but it was hard to tell who might be gazing out of their windows at them.

"Stop here," Emma commanded after they had walked some way into Williams Cañon. "I'll be quick."

Emma ran to the boulder and secured the note and pencil under a rock on a flat spot—the same spot she had used several times to leave food. She didn't even try to call for Ancha. She didn't want him exposed.

"I pray he finds my message and remains safe," Emma said to Claire as she rejoined her friend.

"You've done what you can for him."

❧ CHAPTER 35 ❧

The butterflies in Emma's stomach fluttered unabated. "Sit still, Emma!" Claire scolded as she struggled with Emma's hair. "Well, that will have to do," she sighed. "I have no more hairpins." She paused to inspect her work in the mirror and caught Emma's eyes in the reflection. "Don't look so pained. You will do fine today, dear. I know it." She smiled at her young friend and placed her hands upon Emma's shoulders.

"Thanks, Claire." Emma knew Claire thought she was nervous about starting her new job that morning, which she was, but her biggest anxiety was about Ancha's well-being. She still did not know if Ancha had received her message or if he had left one for her. She had not had the chance to check the boulder since she left her note. Claire had done her best to distract Emma by insisting on dance lessons in the attic, to tunes hummed by Claire as best as she could while instructing Emma. Emma's heart was not in her lessons, and her dancing was awkward and clumsy. But Claire had rightly pointed out that

Sunday afternoon was the last chance Emma would have to practice before the dance since she would be busy with her job during the day. Last evening, Claire helped Emma pick out her clothes for her first day at work.

"Nothing frivolous, but not too serious, either," Claire had advised. They had settled on the smart outfit Emma had worn after her hot mineral bath. It was Emma's favorite outfit. Wearing it made her feel confident.

Emma was buttoning her cloak, readying for her walk to the Manitou house, when a gentle knock came at the door to the boarding house main hall.

"Josiah! Come in!"

"Good morning, Claire." Josiah stepped through the threshold. He saw Emma and nodded. "Good morning, Emma. I am headed to the train depot, and I thought you might welcome a companion on your walk to the Manitou House."

"Yes, that would be nice, Josiah. I was just leaving." Emma joined Josiah.

The morning was crisp, but still. High wispy clouds in the sky foreshadowed a cold day. The town stirred awake as people engaged in their morning rituals. At the BeeBee House, a group gathered at the entrance while porters unloaded their luggage from a carriage.

"The holiday tourists are starting to arrive," Josiah said, making casual conversation. "I expect the train will bring many of them this morning."

"Yes, Willy mentioned that the livery prepared all of the hotels' wagons yesterday to bring guests from Colorado Springs. The trains were full, as well, he said."

"The town depends on a strong holiday season to get it through the winter. It virtually closes down between New Year's and April."

They paused at the end of the curved carriageway that led

to the Manitou House, where their ways parted. "Thank you, Josiah, for the company." Emma said, then laughed lightly. "I am rather nervous about starting this position with Mr. Albright and it was pleasant to be distracted."

"I am sure you will do well, Emma. As I've said, I've found Mr. Albright to be formidable in business, but a good man." Josiah tipped his hat and walked across Manitou Ave. to the train depot.

Emma turned to walk up the drive. *"Well, here goes nothing,"* she thought.

Emma heard the clock in the lobby strike 9 o'clock as she knocked on Mr. Albright's office door.

"Come in." Emma heard Mr. Albright say from behind the door. She let herself in.

"Ah, Miss Quinn! Good morning," Mr. Albright looked up from his writing, placing his dip pen in its holder.

"Good morning, Mr. Albright." Emma stood with her hands folded in front of her, waiting for instructions. She noticed that the room had been rearranged to accommodate a small spindle leg desk, situated at a right angle to Mr. Albright's and away from the wall just far enough for her to get behind it, where a simple wooden chair waited. On the desk was a manual type-writer. *"I told him I could type,"* Emma remembered, and she could—on a computer keyboard with a backspace button. Her stomach tightened.

Mr. Albright stood up and gestured to the sideboard behind him. "There's coffee. Would you like some?"

"Yes, thank you."

"How do you like it?"

"I drink it black."

Mr. Albright smiled, amused. "Somehow, that does not surprise me." He poured the coffee into a small bone china cup sitting on a matching saucer and reached over the table to offer it to Emma. He gestured to the small desk. "I know it's a bit crowded, but I had a desk and typewriter brought in for your use. I also put the telephone set on your desk. I'd like you to answer any telephone calls we get."

"Yes, all right. Thank you." Emma accepted her coffee and took a seat at the desk. She took a sip before setting the cup and saucer down. "What tasks would you like me to begin, Mr. Albright?"

"I am expecting a delivery from the stationers in Colorado Springs this morning—a file cabinet, file folders and other office supplies. These papers require a filing system." He pointed to a wooden box sitting against the wall next to the sideboard. "I've just been piling things up in there."

"Okay, I will start with that."

"And I have several correspondences to answer." Albright gestured to the inbox on his desk, which held several letters. "Can you take dictation?"

"I'm no stenographer, but I can take notes rapidly."

"Well, let's start there until the file cabinet arrives. I am taking the early afternoon train into the Springs, so you will have the office to yourself later."

Mr. Albright began dictating responses to letters. Emma kept up with the pace of his speech, but she didn't want to wait too long to type up the letters for fear she would forget the words behind her rapid scrawls.

"I believe that is the last of the correspondences I needed to respond to today," Mr. Albright looked at his pocket watch after dictating his fourth letter. "We have time for lunch before the train. Would you like to join me, Miss Quinn? They have excellent food here at the Manitou House."

Emma hardly felt at liberty to refuse. "Yes, I'd like that, Mr. Albright."

The dining room of the hotel was large. Windows lined the

two long walls. Against the windows were round tables seating six and four people, with the occasional two-topper. The room was simple and elegant. Each table had a white tablecloth and white napkins, folded into fans and tucked into high-stemmed crystal glasses. A wide path free of tables led from the broad double-door entrance to the narrower doors at back of the dining room, presumably to the kitchen. The maître d' greeted them and seated them at a table for two on the sunny side of the restaurant.

"The cream of asparagus soup is very good here, Miss Quinn," Mr. Albright recommended as he took the menu the maître d' handed him.

Emma was uncertain what to do. Did people typically eat a light lunch? "I would be glad for you to order for me, Mr. Albright, as you are familiar with the food here." She was glad to use the social convention of a man ordering for a woman, but it annoyed her to rely on it to avoid making a fool of herself.

"How are you finding our little village, Miss Quinn? I'm sure it's a big change from New Orleans," Mr. Albright said after they had placed their order.

"I love the scenery and the fresh air. I am just grateful to Claire for providing me a home, though things have been unsettled since I arrived, with Carson's murder and Josiah's arrest. You know he lives at Claire's boarding house. I understand you have retained a solicitor for him. That was very generous of you." Emma wanted to turn Mr. Albright's attention away from her and hopefully glean insight into why he had hired a lawyer for Josiah when Levi had suggested he might be behind the premature arrest.

"It's not generosity, Miss Quinn. It's business. The bath house must go ahead as planned and as quickly as possible. It must be open for the next season, and there are enough risks as it is."

"The rumor was that local men of influence pressured the sheriff to make a quick arrest, and since Josiah was the only viable suspect . . ."

"Well, it certainly wasn't me or anyone associated with the bath house behind Josiah's arrest." Mr. Albright interrupted Emma, emphatically. "It has been a serious burden to us."

"Your soup ma'am, sir." The waiter set the bowls on the table.

"Ah, I am famished! Enjoy, Miss Quinn." Albright seemed happy to end the discussion. He slurped his soup with relish.

❋

Mr. Albright left shortly after lunch for his train. Emma watched him walk across Manitou Ave. to the depot from the office window as she sat at her desk. The train was just pulling into the station, chugging to a slow stop. She mulled over what he had said at lunch. He had seemed sincere in his denial of having anything to do with Josiah's arrest. Given that he hired a lawyer to help clear Josiah, she was inclined to believe him. Who, then, had been pressuring the sheriff?

She looked skeptically at the typewriter in front of her and was relieved to find a pamphlet tucked under it that contained instructions. Emma perused it to get familiar with how to operate the contraption. She looked out the window for men delivering the file cabinet, which Mr. Albright said would arrive on the afternoon train. Instead, she saw Levi, walking with an older man, shorter than he, wearing a badge and carrying a rifle.

"Oh my God, is that the sheriff?" Emma felt a shock of adrenaline hit her heart. She jumped up and leaned over the sideboard to get a better view of the men walking toward town. She spun back around and leaned on the sideboard, hand over her mouth. What was the sheriff doing here? Was he looking for

Ancha? Emma wanted to run and follow Levi to find out, but she couldn't leave her work. All she could do was pray Ancha had received her note and was out of harm's way.

❧ CHAPTER 36 ❧

Emma was miserable. Soon after she had seen Levi and the badged man with the rifle, the delivery men had arrived with the file cabinet and office supplies. It was vital that she have a successful first day on the job, but every cell of her body wanted to run and discover if Ancha was in danger. She realized there was nothing she could do if he was. After instructing the delivery men where to put the heavy wooden file cabinet, she forced herself to figure out how to use the typewriter to type up the letters Mr. Albright had dictated to her. Under any other circumstances, she would have been happy to stay into the night to get a good start on the filing, but her typing had taken much longer than she had expected. She couldn't bear not knowing what was going on, so once she finished the last of the letters, she tidied up the office and left. She locked the door with the key Mr. Albright had provided her.

She burst into the boarding house and looked in the parlor, where Christina Sully sat near the window with her needlework.

"Good evening, Christina, have you seen Levi?"

"Good evening, Miss Quinn. He came in just a while ago and headed up to his rooms."

"Thank you, and please, call me Emma." Emma called as she ran up the stairs. She pounded on Levy's door and pushed her way in when he opened it.

"Emma! What's wrong?" Levi stepped out of her way.

She turned, brow furrowed, "I saw you and that law man this afternoon, arriving by train. Was he the sheriff? Has there been a development in Carson's case?"

"Come, let's go to Claire's rooms. It's not proper for us to be here alone. We can talk there."

Emma rolled her eyes. "That's ridiculous, but fine, let's go." She walked abruptly out of the still-open door. Levi grabbed his jacket and put it on as he followed her.

In Claire's parlor, Levi attempted to settle Emma. "Let's sit. Would you like a brandy?'

"Yes, I suppose." Emma plopped on the sofa. "Has there been a development, Levi?" She repeated.

Levi handed Emma her drink and sat with his drink in the armchair next to her. "Josiah's solicitor will probably win the motion to have the charges dropped against him."

"That's fantastic news!" Emma was uplifted. The expression on Levi's face remained serious, though, and just as quickly, Emma felt the pressure of dread on her chest. "There's more, isn't there?"

"Yes." Levi took a long sip of brandy. "Miss Calhoun and her brother went to the sheriff first thing this morning, insisting the Indian who lives in the hills was the killer. The sheriff came this afternoon to form a posse. We head out at dawn's first light tomorrow to find the Indian."

"His name is Ancha!" She shouted. So, Emma's fears had been justified. She fought to control the panic arising in her body. "I was afraid Miss Calhoun would act. She expressed her suspicions to me yesterday after church. Did she offer the sheriff any proof?"

Levi looked at Emma and huffed a cynical laugh. "It's endearing that you think proof is necessary, my dear. If they were willing to arrest an upstanding white man with nothing but weak circumstantial evidence, what makes you think they won't nail the In . . . Ancha to the cross similarly? Our law doesn't protect the likes of him. He will likely not survive to be arrested."

"There you two are!" Claire waltzed in. "Dinner is ready."

Levi set down his snifter and reached for Emma's hand to help her up.

"You go ahead. I'm not hungry." Emma's her stomach was in knots. Food was the last thing she was interested in.

Instead, Emma went to her room and changed into her "boy" clothes. She had very little light left, as the sun had already dipped below Pikes Peak, but at least the twilight would give her some cover.

She did not take Cañon Ave. to Williams Cañon. She sneaked between crevasses and low spots in the hills to avoid prying eyes, crouching low as she made her way cautiously and slowly to the boulder, taking the best care possible to remain unseen. By the time she got there it was almost dark. She quietly approached the boulder and looked for evidence Ancha had seen her note. She lifted the rock she had used to secure the message and found nothing under it. She prayed that meant he had seen it and acted on her warning. She looked around, hoping to find a reply, but the ledge was bare. Her heart fell. How would she know for sure he had seen her note? She stood for a moment, sweeping her eyes across the boulder one final time, when she noticed a thick stick poking oddly out of a crack over her head to the left. She could barely reach the stick, but when she touched it, the smaller piece of rock to the right of the stick moved just a bit. She needed longer arms and more leverage. She found a foothold on the boulder and lifted herself up, leaning on the stone for support. It gave her just enough additional height to wiggle the rock and discover it was not fixed to the boulder. She pried it away using the thick stick itself as a lever and discovered a small space behind it. In that space was Ancha's little medicine pouch.

Emma wedged the rock back in place and threw the stick away. She jumped down and crouched low as she found cover behind more crags and rocks. Just as carefully as she had come, she made her way back to the boarding house. She creeped around to the backyard, but when she heard noises and Claire's voice emanating from the kitchen, she backtracked to the side entrance. While Claire was busy with the dinner dishes, she returned to her bedroom and quickly changed into her dusty rose dress.

She sat on the edge of her bed and opened the medicine pouch and saw the note she had left Ancha. On the other side of her note, she read:

Student,

I am sad to hear Carson is dead. He was a good man. I hear your warning and am in a safe place. I found this near the cave the day after the earthquake.

Ancha

Emma looked in the pouch and pulled out its contents. She wasn't sure what significance it had, if any. She returned the note and the contents and placed the pouch in her backpack under her bed.

Feeling some comfort knowing Ancha had heeded her message, Emma ventured into the kitchen to offer Claire help.

"Did you go to see if Ancha got your note?" Claire whispered to Emma, handing her the last dish to dry.

"Yes," Emma whispered in reply. "He did, thank God. I just hope he can elude the sheriff's posse tomorrow."

"He may well be able to do so tomorrow, but for how much longer? He can't stay here and avoid them indefinitely." Claire looked sympathetically at Emma. "Anna and her ilk may get their way where Ancha is concerned either way."

Emma wondered if Ancha had reached the same conclusion. Had she seen the last of him so soon?

"Levi said he'd meet me in our parlor. He doesn't know anything about you and Ancha, and frankly, I think it best we keep it that way. It will be better for all concerned. Take the coffee tray in. I'll be right there." Claire poured the coffee into the pot and put it on the tray.

Emma decided Claire was right. She went through her room to the parlor, where she found Levi sitting, waiting patiently. "Claire is right behind me," she announced as she set down the tray and began pouring coffee for each of them.

"We all missed you at dinner, Emma. Are you feeling well? We were interested in hearing about your first day on the job."

"It was a tiring day, but I believe it went well. Mr. Albright was gone all afternoon. I did learn something interesting, though."

Claire walked in with another tray holding a plate of cookies, little plates, and napkins. She placed it alongside the coffee tray.

"Interesting, you say?" Levi asked, serving himself a cookie.

"Mr. Albright claims neither he nor his associates were behind pressuring Sheriff Dana to arrest Josiah. He said it was vital the bath house project be completed quickly and Josiah was needed." Emma still had no appetite. She just stared at the cookies.

"Well, it looks as though all will end well for Josiah, as things are turning out." Levi observed.

"Because they've found an even more vulnerable scapegoat?!" Emma looked up sharply at Levi. She sensed Claire's body tense up beside her on the sofa.

"Well, it is possible Ancha did it, Emma, surely you can see that." Levi paused, trying to decipher her reaction.

"I feel the same way about Ancha as I did about Josiah. There is no proof. He has no motive, so far as we know. And I could make an argument that he would be more motivated to avoid trouble, given his precarious place in society. He deserves due process and a fair trial, just as Josiah did."

"Ancha is not a citizen, Emma; Josiah is."

"What?" Emma stopped, stunned. She took for granted Native Americans were citizens, but she did not know their status in 1882. "Well, be that as it may, it's not about citizenship; it's about fairness. I thought you valued fairness, Levi."

"I do! But how I feel about it as a man is irrelevant. As a lawman, there is little I can do to prevent the sheriff going after Ancha."

"Well then, act as a man." And with that, Emma walked out.

❧ CHAPTER 37 ❧

"*God, please keep him safe,*" Emma thought as she looked through her little window at the posse on their horses, riding up Cañon Ave. The sheriff led a group of five men, including Levi—all of them brandishing rifles. The sun had not yet broken the horizon to the east. The blue-gray light was only just sufficient for the men to see their way. Two large hound dogs traipsed behind the horses. Emma's stomach clenched tightly. Her mouth was dry.

She didn't remember washing and dressing. She didn't remember helping Molly set breakfast out. She was sitting at the dining room table, picking at her eggs, when Claire came in, served herself, and sat down beside Emma.

"Can I fill your cup, Emma?" Claire asked gently.

Emma glanced carelessly at her empty coffee cup. "Yes, thanks." She took a sip of the warm liquid and felt it sooth her tight, dry throat. She looked miserably up at Claire, who gave her arm a gentle pat.

"Keep faith, Emma. You've done all you can. It's in God's hands now."

Emma felt a wave of irritation, but she knew her friend was just trying to comfort her. What's more, she knew her friend was right, and it didn't make her feel better knowing she was powerless to help Ancha.

"Please try to eat something. You skipped dinner last night."

Emma took a fork full of eggs and put it in her mouth. The eggs were cold, and she gagged. She took another sip of coffee.

Claire sighed and took a bite of her breakfast. The women finished their breakfast in silence.

❊

Emma arrived at work early. She wanted to be well underway with the filing project before Mr. Albright arrived to make up for not getting a start on it the day before. She ordered a coffee tray at the reception desk before letting herself into the office and was grateful for having work to do to keep her mind off the pack of men and dogs hunting Ancha.

"Good Morning, Miss Quinn." Mr. Albright greeted her when he walked through the door. His voice contained a tone of pleasant surprise, and he looked at her approvingly.

"Good Morning, Mr. Albright. There's fresh coffee on the tray." Emma lifted her chin toward the tray on the sideboard.

"You are an angel!" Albright walked over to the sideboard. "Do you already have a cup?"

"Yes, thank you."

Mr. Albright surveyed the papers Emma had strewn on her desk and on the floor around her area. "I had no idea there were so many papers."

"There's twice as many still in the box. The letters you

dictated are in that folder on your desk, ready to sign. I will get them mailed this morning. The carbon copies are here." Emma pointed to the small pile of papers on the corner of her desk.

"Thank you." Mr. Albright said brightly, seating himself behind his desk to read through and sign the letters. "Very fine work, Miss Quinn. I must admit, typed letters look much more professional than hand-written ones," he said as he signed the last of the letters. "I am off to Denver today. I won't be back until late tomorrow afternoon."

"I should be done with the filing by then. Do you have other tasks for me?"

"I expect when I get back that I will have plenty of tasks for you," He took his coat and hat from the hook on the wall. "Good day, Miss Quinn."

Emma felt uneasy about the cryptic comment Mr. Albright had made, apprehensive about what "plenty of tasks" might mean. *"You are letting your imagination run away with you."* She thought. *"He meant nothing in particular by it."*

Emma reached for the next document in the box and looked at it to determine in which category to place it. It was titled "Articles of Incorporation," and established the "Mineral Springs of Manitou Bath House and Park Company," with Mr. Albright as president and Dr. William Bell as a director. She did not recognize the names of the other directors and officers. She decided this belonged in its own category.

A dozen documents and an hour later (she couldn't resist reading each page), she picked up a fine ivory envelope. Inside she found a letter written in firm, confident script:

October 10, 1882

Dear Mr. Albright,

It has come to my attention that your enterprise plans to pipe mineral water from the Navajo spring to the new bath house for the purpose of filling the large plunge pool. I am writing to make you aware of concerns I and many in the community have.

First, the spring waters of Manitou were meant to be available, freely, to the public. Any attempt to deny the public fair access to this, or any, mineral spring in Manitou will be met with the strongest possible opposition.

Second, the amount of water required to fill and maintain the plunge pool in the bath house puts at risk the spring itself. I understand this large pool is planned to hold 35,000 gallons of water. What evidence do you have that this demand will not exhaust the spring?

Third, the very land you propose to build the bath house and park on is arguably in the public domain. Many who settled here did so with the understanding that the wedge of land between Manitou Ave. and Cañon Ave. would be kept as a public park area. Even the proposed name of your enterprise, "The Mineral Springs of Manitou Bath House and Park Company," acknowledges this in its very name.

I will be bringing my concerns to the town council. I plan to defend the interests of the people of Manitou to the utmost of my ability.

Yours Sincerely,

John S. Calhoun

So, John Calhoun opposed the bath house project. Emma thought back to her first day at the boarding house, when she overheard Mr. Albright and Josiah talking in the parlor. Mr. Albright had said, "now that the election is over, and it looks as though our people will prevail, our project can go forward." Levi had said John Calhoun had run for town council and lost. Would Mr. Calhoun have taken more drastic measures to prevent the bath house project from going forward? Did Carson figure into it somehow? Emma thought Mr. Calhoun himself was in Colorado Springs the day Carson was killed, but that did not mean he didn't have something to do with Carson's death. The more Emma tried to sort out the ramifications of the letter, the more muddled her mind became. She returned the letter to its envelope and put it in the drawer of her desk.

Emma missed lunch. She had become engrossed in classifying the papers and didn't notice the time until mid-afternoon when hunger finally demanded her attention. She had been so worried about Ancha when she left the boarding house that morning that it didn't even occur to her to bring anything with her to eat later. Emma's chest clinched as she thought of Ancha again. Was he okay? Had they found him?

Between worrying about Ancha and increasing hunger, concentrating on work became impossible. It was now three-thirty in the afternoon. Emma assessed her progress and decided she would be able to finish the filing by the end of the next day. She took the letter from the drawer on her way out, wishing she had her cell phone to take a picture of it rather than having to remove it from the office.

✽

"Is Levi back yet?" Emma asked Claire, whom she had found with Molly in the kitchen, preparing dinner.

"No, dear."

"Have we heard any word at all from the posse?"

"None."

Emma heaved a heavy sigh. She reached for an apron on the hook on the wall and tied it behind her. "What can I do to help?"

The women worked in efficient cooperation to finish dinner preparations. Emma had gone to the dining room to set the table when she heard someone enter through the front door. She ran to see if it was Levi.

"Oh, Mr. Graham. Good Afternoon." Emma greeted Peter Graham, trying to hide her disappointment.

"Good Afternoon, Miss Quinn. I smell something delicious."

"Dinner will be served soon. Molly made chicken pot pies."

"I'm looking forward to it. I'll be right back down." Graham turned for the stairs. Emma looked out the window. It was getting dark. Where was Levi?

❁

Despite Emma's hunger, she picked at her meal without relish. Levi still had not returned. Claire knew not to ask why she wasn't eating, and to distract her, made an attempt at conversation. "How was your second day on the job, Emma?"

"Hum? Oh, it was fine. I'm filing." Emma looked back toward the window.

"I suppose Levi and the posse are still out there looking for that Indian." Emma heard Graham's arrogant voice say. She looked over at him but otherwise did not respond.

"It's dark now. Levi should be back any time. I hope they found him. It frightens me that he's out there and dangerous," Christine Sully said innocently.

"He's not dangerous." Emma said tersely.

"Well, Levi and Willy both are missing a delicious chicken pot pie that Molly made." Claire said when she saw the looks on Graham and Christine's faces.

"How can you say that, Emma? He killed Carson! With his bare hands!" Christine persisted.

"We don't know that. There is no proof. There's no more proof that Ancha did it than there was Josiah did it. He's a convenient scapegoat, that's all. How long has he been here, living alone in the hills? Has he ever harmed anyone before? Why would he kill Carson?" Emma's tone increased in both volume and pitch as she spoke.

"I had no idea you were so sympathetic to Indians, Miss Quinn," Graham said condescendingly.

"I am merely applying the same standards to both Josiah and Ancha. I would have thought an *intelligent* man like you would do the same." Emma replied, pushing her plate away.

"I think it's highly more likely," Graham drawled, "that— what did you call him? Well, no matter. It's highly more likely the Indian did it than our gentle Josiah."

Emma's blood was in full boil. The only thing keeping her tongue in check was concern for Ancha's safety. She could not bear staying in the same room with Graham, though. "Excuse me. I will start the cleaning up, Claire. When Levi returns, please tell him I need to speak to him."

※

Emma was elbow-deep in dirty dish water when she heard Levi's voice coming from the hallway. She wiped her hands on her apron and rushed out to meet him. She intercepted him as he sat at the dining room table. He looked dusty and exhausted. Claire was preparing his plate at the sideboard and looked over her shoulder at Emma, smiling softly and shaking her head "no" ever so slightly. Emma's eyes darted back to Levi, expectantly.

"No, Emma, we didn't see any sign of Ancha. We ran out of daylight. We will head back out tomorrow morning."

Emma let out the breath she had been holding unconsciously all day. She would have to relive her anxiety all over again tomorrow, but for now she could relax.

After Levi ate, the three friends sat around the reading room table. "Surely this must have some bearing on the case!" Claire said after Emma had shown Levi and Claire Mr. Calhoun's letter.

"I don't know, Claire. While Calhoun made his objections known in this letter and tried getting on town council to influence things, I don't believe he had enough support from the townspeople. Everyone here relies on tourists, and the bath house will no doubt attract more visitors and extend the season. Most welcome it. Besides, killing Carson seems an extreme and uncertain way of sabotaging the project."

"But getting rid of Carson and then casting the blame on Josiah impairs the project significantly," Emma pointed out. "Perhaps Calhoun felt he just needed more time to persuade the town against the project. Also, he could have planted the IOU in Josiah's pocket at the funeral—or at church, for that matter."

"I'm still skeptical that it's a strong enough motive for murder, especially considering Carson was soon to be Calhoun's son-in-law."

"Well, you make a good point there, Levi," Emma admitted.

"Still, the IOU is a mystery, and goes a long way to casting doubt on Ancha being the killer," Levi conceded.

"YES! You're right!" Emma cried. "Surely you can point this out to the sheriff."

Levi sighed. "Emma, by now you must know the sheriff is

not concerned about finding the real killer. He just wants to keep his supporters happy."

Emma's face fell as she realized Levi was right.

"See here, Emma. Willy and I are joining the posse again first thing in the morning. I'll do my best to keep the posse from finding Ancha or, if we do find him, from killing him. I know it isn't much, but it's the best I can do under the circumstances."

"Thank you, Levi." She looked at him gratefully. "You are a good man," she said—and she meant it.

❧ CHAPTER 38 ❧

Emma hardly slept that night. She began readying herself for the day while it was still completely dark. In the kitchen, she got the cook stove fire started and put the big pot of water on it to boil. She realized she was hungry, having not eaten much to speak of the day before. She reached for an apple from the bowl on the table and took a bite.

"Why, good mornin' Miss Emma!" Molly said cheerfully, shedding her outer garments and hanging them on the row of hooks by the door. "You are up awful early. Are you feelin' all right?"

"Yes, I just couldn't sleep, and I thought I'd get up and make myself useful. I imagine you have a lot of work to do to prepare for Thanksgiving dinner tomorrow."

"You're a dear, to be sure, but my oldest daughter, Kate, and Dr. Guiles' daughter, Sarah, are coming this afternoon and tomorrow morning to help with all the preparations. It's going to be quite the feast!"

Emma's heart wasn't in the thanksgiving spirit. At the moment, she dreaded the feast tomorrow and the dance following it. How could she celebrate, dance, and sing while Ancha was running for his life and all alone?

Levi and Willy, who had also been recruited for the posse, came down for breakfast early. Molly fixed the early risers a quick breakfast and served it at the kitchen table.

"Tomorrow's Thanksgivin' Levi." Willy reminded him. "Ya reckon we'll have to search for that Indian tomorrow? I'm not sure the posse will want to take the holiday to do that."

Emma brightened at the thought of buying Ancha more time to escape. "Willy has a valid concern, Levi. Can you persuade the sheriff to resume the search on Friday, if you don't find Ancha today, that is?"

"I can make the case, certainly." Levi agreed, giving Emma a conspiratorial look. "Frankly, I don't hold out much hope we will find Ancha. He knows this land like the back of his hand. If he doesn't want to be found, we aren't likely to find him. By today, if we haven't found him, it should be clear to the sheriff that we probably won't, at least not anytime soon."

After finishing her breakfast, the first real meal she'd had in over a day, Emma returned to her room. Her heart felt lighter than it had in days, now that she had hope for Ancha. Before she left for work, she took out her cell phone (the battery was down to twenty percent) and used it to take a photo of John Calhoun's letter. She didn't know how she would use the information in digital format, but she did know she needed to get the letter back to the office before it was missed.

Emma got to the office as early as possible again. She wanted to have all the filing done before Mr. Albright returned that afternoon. She found it easier to concentrate that morning. It was amazing what lower anxiety and a good meal could do to improve one's faculties. She had even thought to bring a bacon and egg biscuit and an apple for her lunch.

Emma was labeling the last file folder when Mr. Albright returned on the late afternoon train. She saw him walking briskly from the depot toward Manitou House. The slight spring in his step indicated his business in Denver had gone well. She rushed around to tidy up the office, so it was in good order when he walked through the door.

"Good afternoon, Miss Quinn," Mr. Albright hung his hat and coat and surveyed the office. "It appears you have completed the filing."

"Yes, I have." Emma pulled out the top drawer of the file cabinet. "I've labeled all the folders and filed the papers in chronological order."

Mr. Albright inspected Emma's work. "Well done, Miss Quinn." He paused to read the labels. "The categories appear well-considered. I am impressed you organized all the papers in such a short amount of time."

"I'm afraid there's no coffee. I wasn't entirely sure what time you would be returning to the office this afternoon. Would you like me to call for a tray of coffee or tea?"

"No, I just stopped by to check on things and to tell you to go ahead and head home. Tomorrow is a holiday, after all. I imagine Claire could use your help at the boarding house."

"That's very kind of you, Mr. Albright."

"Do be here first thing on Friday, though. I have much to discuss with you then. You may leave now. I'll lock up."

"Thank you, and happy Thanksgiving."

Emma left Mr. Albright going through the correspondences sitting on his desk.

The reception area of the hotel was buzzing with activity. The visitors who had come in on the train were checking in at the reception counter; porters were unloading trunks from a wagon on the rounded drive outside the entrance; staff was busy decorating the lobby with branches of evergreen, gourds, and dried corn husks. The holiday season had begun.

Outside the early evening was cold. Clouds obscured the mountains. A light flurry of tiny snowflakes drifted and danced through the air, too light to land on the ground. Emma pulled her cloak more tightly around her and rushed down Manitou Ave., thankful that the wind was at her back. The shop-keepers had spent the day decorating their window fronts for the upcoming holiday. The air smelled of burning wood from the home hearths of the townspeople. As Emma took the fork in the road to Cañon Ave., two small boys ran by her, chased by a mutt terrier, nearly tripping her. She couldn't help feeling that she was living in a scene from a Currier and Ives greeting card, or a snow globe.

Emma's mood was festive when she walked through the front door of the boarding house and down the hall into the kitchen. She smelled pumpkin pie, her favorite. Molly and Claire were busy as usual in the kitchen. Emma went to her room and quickly shed her cloak, hat, and gloves and washed up. "What needs doing?" She asked when she returned to the kitchen.

"The usual. Get the dining room ready. We are having a light meal of soup and bread tonight, so we don't need the knives and forks." Claire instructed.

Emma went to the dining room and opened the silverware drawer. Some small pieces of paper sitting on the sideboard caught her eye. She picked one up. On it was printed in fancy type, *"Grand Spiritualistic Revival, Tuesday, December 5, 1882, 7:00 o'clock in the evening, Colorado Springs Opera House. Admit One."*

Emma looked up toward the ceiling and closed her eyes, her shoulders sagging. She had forgotten all about this event that Claire was so excited to attend. She had said she'd go to please her friend, but she had no interest herself. She suspected it was mere theater.

※

Levi and Willy were not as late for dinner that night. The boarding house tenants were still at the table eating when they returned from that day's search. Levi discretely shook his head with a little smile when Emma looked at him, letting her know they had still not found Ancha. The men were tired, dirty, and smelled of sweat and horse. Claire ushered them to their seats and served them both a bowl of soup. Levi did a masterful job of quickly satisfying Graham and Christina's curiosity. No, they hadn't seen any sign of Ancha. The trail was cold. The dogs were of no use at all because they didn't have a sample of Ancha's scent to go by. The posse had all agreed that there was no point in searching tomorrow because of the holiday. In fact, the search was called off altogether. Everyone agreed the Indian had escaped. The sheriff said "wanted" posters would be prepared and distributed. Ancha was officially a fugitive.

Emma contented herself with the temporary reprieve. They now had time to clear Ancha, though she didn't know how.

The boarding house residents all retired early. It had been a long day, and tomorrow was Thanksgiving Day.

✌ CHAPTER 39 ✍

Emma woke to sounds of laughter, pealing like Christmas bells, from the kitchen. She peaked out of her window and saw it was still dark, but the aromas emanating from the kitchen told her someone had already started cooking the Thanksgiving feast. The heat from the kitchen had taken the chill out of the air in her room, making her less reluctant to get out of bed and get dressed. Why had Claire not wakened her if there was work to be done? She ran a brush through her hair and pinned it up, tucked at her skirt to neaten it and went to the kitchen.

Molly, her daughter Kate, Claire, and Alice's daughter Sarah were all as busy as elves, peeling, slicing, rolling, and stirring. Kate, who looked about twelve, had flour on her chubby cheeks.

"Happy Thanksgiving, Emma!" Claire looked up from peeling potatoes and smiled warmly.

"Happy Thanksgiving! Why didn't you wake me so I could help?"

"Oh, I would have shortly, believe me!" Claire laughed. "But Molly and the girls arrived so early, and everyone just jumped in and started doing things. I had to get the operation under control first!" Everyone laughed.

"Where's Alice?" Emma looked around for the doctor.

"She'll be along later. She wanted to open the bath house for holiday visitors this morning."

"I see." Emma took a deep breath. "What is that wonderful smell?" She reached for an apron and tied it on.

"Oh, Miss Emma, this is my ol' punch recipe." Molly said from the pot she was stirring on the stove. "I only fix it on holidays. It has orange juice and lemon juice, sugar, cinnamon, cloves, and other spices. I keep the proportions a secret," she grinned.

"Like your cleaning powder?" Emma laughed.

Molly frowned at first, not getting the joke, but then brightened. "Yes, like that!"

Emma sat down at the table to help Claire peel potatoes. She soaked in the affectionate cooperation of the women and girls like a warm bath.

❁

"Oh, merciful heaven, I think my stomach is going to burst," Alice moaned, rubbing her tummy. "That was simply fabulous, ladies!"

"I completely agree!" chimed Josiah. "I don't believe I've ever had turkey that was so crispy and moist."

"I don't suppose anyone is ready for pumpkin pie yet?" Claire laughed. Everyone groaned and said no.

Thanksgiving dinner had been a success. The card table and occasional table had been used to accommodate Alice's and Molly's families. The boarding house guests were all stuffed from over-eating the turkey, potatoes, gravy, squash, and other delicacies the women had prepared. Molly's punch was all gone. Emma desperately wanted a nap. How would she muster the energy for the dance that evening when she was so full and sleepy now? And the clean-up . . . that had to be dealt with beforehand.

Her languor passed, however, and by the time she was dressed for the dance, she was feeling excited. She and Claire had retrieved the evening gown from the attic several days ago and had it laundered. They agreed the sky-blue watered silk would strike just the right tone: not too formal, not too casual. The color drew attention, unnecessarily, to Emma's dark blue eyes. Claire had done an admirable job with Emma's hair, using some of her best hair combs in the process. Yes, Emma was, indeed, all dressed up and ready to go. She walked into the boarding house parlor to meet Josiah.

He turned toward her when he heard the rustle of her skirt. "Oh, my. You look magnificent, Emma," he said, wide-eyed and awestruck. The sincerity on his face made Emma blush.

"Thank you, kind sir," Emma wanted to keep the mood light.

"Here, I brought you a 'bouquet de corsage,' I believe it's called." Josiah presented her with a corsage of three small, pink roses. "May I pin it on you?"

"Yes, it's beautiful, Josiah. Thank you." She was self-conscious as she stood still while he pinned the flowers to her lapel.

"Are you ready, Miss Quinn?" Josiah offered Emma his arm.

"I am. Mr. Turner." Emma smiled and tucked her hand into the crook of his elbow.

"I hope you don't mind. Willy and I arranged a carriage to take us to Saratoga Hall," He said, motioning her toward a simple carriage, where Willy and Christine were sitting tall and proper on the front bench. Willy held the reins in his hands, grinning from ear to ear.

"Good evenin' Miss Quinn, Josiah. You look lovely this evenin' Miss Quinn." Willy tipped his worn-out Stetson hat in an exaggerating fashion. Christine just beamed at them.

Emma couldn't help but giggle a little. She took the hand Josiah offered to help her into the carriage. As she settled in, she thought this must be what Cinderella had felt like the night of her infamous ball. Josiah tucked the rug over their laps.

It was a cold evening, so the rug was welcome, but it had hardly started warming them by the time they had gone the short distance to the BeeBee House, where the dance hall was located. Willy pulled up on the east side of the building. There, several other carriages and wagons were lined up to deliver their passengers.

Inside, the simple hall looked festive. Garlands of evergreen branches embellished the ceiling; gas-lit sconces lined the walls. A musical group, occupying one far corner of the room, was playing string music quietly. Cloth-covered tables were scattered around, situated close to the walls, where the older attendees could find seats. The younger men and women gathered in small groups, talking and drinking the flutes of champagne waiters offered them from trays.

"Ah, there's Miss Calhoun and John, Jr.," Josiah lifted his chin in their direction. "Shall we join them?"

"Sure,' Emma agreed.

"Good evening, Miss Quinn, Josiah," Anna Calhoun said pleasantly. Emma noticed the way Anna's eyes darted from Josiah to Emma and back. Anna's navy blue ensemble seemed too severe for the occasion. Emma thought Anna must still be in some phase of mourning attire.

"I hope you will reserve a spot for me on your dance card,

Miss Quinn," John Calhoun, Jr. said after the group had greeted each other.

"Oh, I'm afraid I don't have a dance card." Emma said, looking around helplessly.

Anna laughed. "Oh, this isn't formal enough for a dance card, Miss Quinn. John was being humorous."

"About the dance card, yes. About hoping you will dance with me, no." John added, smiling.

Emma looked over at Josiah, who seemed non-plussed. "I'd be happy to dance with you, Mr. Calhoun."

He waved his hand down casually. "Oh, please, can we all be on a first-name basis? This isn't Paris at season's opening."

They all laughed and agreed. Emma glanced at the entrance and saw Levi and Claire walk in. She caught Levi's eye and smiled, but he just looked at her. Claire, however, waved to make sure she had attracted Emma's attention and led Levi toward the group.

"Good evening everyone!" Claire said. "It looks like there will be a big turn-out tonight. Anna, is your mother here somewhere?"

"Yes, somewhere," Anna said, surveying the room. "She and Papa both. Ah! There they are." She pointed to a table near the band.

"Thank you. I want to make arrangements for us all getting to the event Tuesday. I'll be right back."

So, they were joining Mrs. Calhoun at the Spiritualism Revival. That surprised Emma a bit, but then, she had never asked Claire who frequented her reading room for card readings and seances. Now that she thought about it, Mrs. Calhoun seemed like just the sort that would.

"You will be joining us at the event on Tuesday, too?" Emma asked Anna.

"Yes. Mama has been interested in the occult since she lost

her first son, our brother, when he was but a child. We never knew him, but Mama has never gotten over the loss."

"I'm so sorry." Emma replied.

"I remain a sceptic. Mama has encouraged me to go with her though, suggesting I might get a message from Carson." Tears welled in Anna's eyes and she pulled out her hankie from her sleeve. Electric blue and iridescent green caught Emma's eye. It was the same hankie Anna had used the day of their tea party, the one with the embroidered peacock. Emma had a sense of déjà vu, but before she could consider it further, Claire returned.

"It's all set! The four of us will ride together Tuesday for the revival," she announced.

Just then the music stopped, and an announcer stood in front of the band, letting everyone know the dancing was commencing with a circle dance to "Old Susanna."

Emma smiled at Claire. Claire had prepared Emma for this very dance. She said the hops often started with a square dance to break the ice. Emma noticed Anna holding back.

"Aren't you coming, Anna?"

Anna looked appalled. "No! I'm still in mourning."

Josiah had taken Emma's hand and was pulling her toward the dance circle, sparing her from her faux pas.

After the circle dance was over, John Calhoun, Jr., approached Emma and, as a waltz started, reached his hand out to her, "May I have this dance, Emma?"

"You may," she smiled and took his hand. She glanced over John's shoulder and caught a glimpse of Josiah returning to stand by Anna. He bent down as she said something in his ear, and he laughed.

John was not as good a dancer as Levi, but Emma was still able to follow his lead. She noticed John looking displeased in Anna and Josiah's direction as they made a turn. The look passed quickly, though, when he turned his eyes to Emma, smiling. "How does Manitou suit you, Emma?"

"Very well. I have started a position with Mr. Albright that I am excited about, and I enjoy living at the boarding house with Claire."

"You are lucky to have such a wealthy relative. As you no doubt know, she is by far the biggest depositor at our bank. I have always found it curious that a woman as wealthy as she would choose to live in the manner she does. No one would ever dream how wealthy she is."

"Indeed, she lives to serve." Emma said, hoping to mask her surprise. She was aware Claire had some money from her family, but she had no notion how much. John suggested the amount was vast.

"Would you like some refreshment?" John asked when the song ended.

"Yes," and Emma walked with him to the table where hor d'oeuvres and glasses of lemonade were laid out for guests. Once again, Emma caught John looking disapprovingly in Josiah and Anna's direction. The couple were leaning toward each other in conversation.

"I'm sure Josiah and Anna have been of some comfort to each other since Carson was killed," Emma observed.

"Yes," John said grimly. "It is unseemly, though, that they have struck up such a friendship so soon."

"I imagine they were well acquainted already, given their mutual relationship with Carson."

"Not well, I don't think. In fact, I only saw them together once or twice while Carson was with us." John paused as though mentally counting the times he could recall.

"It's unfortunate no one saw anything the day Carson was killed," Emma continued. "I understand you had taken your mother to the dentist, and your father was at the bank?"

"I assume father was at the bank. Ordinarily when Mother comes to the Springs, she stops by the bank to see Father, but she was too groggy from the laudanum the dentist gave her after he pulled her tooth. So, I got her back home as soon as I could. I'm afraid she went straight to bed when we returned home, and when Tommy came to tell us about Carson, she was fast asleep. That left comforting Anna up to me. Father stayed in the Springs that night, as he often does when he works too late or has a business dinner."

"Emma, may I have this dance?" Josiah had walked over to her and offered his arm.

The band started playing "Camptown Races," and Josiah led Emma in a galop. Emma thought the dance should be called a gallop as she and Josiah hopped and skipped across the floor at a fast tempo. She was vaguely aware of Levi's somber face when she and Josiah danced quickly by where he stood.

They were both breathing fast when the song ended. The band went immediately into another waltz, slower in tempo than the one she had danced to with John. Josiah reached for Emma to begin dancing.

"May I cut in?" Levi asked. Josiah hesitated a moment, looked at Emma for some hint of what to do, then said, "of course," reluctantly.

Levi held her as close as her full skirt would permit. She noticed his hand was lower on her back than the other men's hands were on their partners'. The pressure of his hand on her back was firm, but gentle. She looked up at him and saw he was gazing steadily at her through his long lashes. She felt betrayed by her body's response. Paul crossed her guilty mind. She had to remind herself to be offended at the ritual of men passing her around like the town . . . well, passing her around as though her preference was immaterial.

"I'm sorry to butt in like that, Emma, but it looked like it was the only way I was going to get to dance with you this evening, between Josiah and John." His apology chipped away at her defenses.

Once again, Emma noticed how effortless it was to dance with Levi. As the song progressed, they both relaxed into the flow of their steps and the music. Emma felt free and smiled joyfully; Levi smiled back in response. Her heart felt ever lighter in her chest until she thought it might sprout wings and fly off altogether. In that moment, the only thing Emma was aware of was the song and the way she felt dancing in Levi's arms. They held their gaze a little too long after the music stopped. Emma looked away first, feeling a little naked.

Anna was facing away from Emma and Levi as they walked back to join their small group. The intricate updo Anna wore fascinated Emma. How many hairpins did it take to keep something like that in place? Emma counted at least ten pearl pinheads. *Pearl pinheads! Pearl pinheads and peacocks!*

"Oh, my God!" Emma gasped.

"What is it, Emma?" Levi stopped and turned to face Emma.

"I think I know who killed Carson." Emma whispered.

❋

She had wanted to consult Levi, but there was no opportunity with all the people at the dance. Toward the end of the evening, while Josiah went to fetch Emma's cloak from the cloakroom, Levi cornered her.

"We can't talk further tonight," Levi whispered.

"And I must be at work tomorrow." Emma groaned, frustrated.

"I'll come down early, then, before breakfast. We will have to sit tight until then."

Josiah returned and helped Emma with her cloak. "I'd offer you and Claire a ride in our carriage, Levi, but I'm afraid it's too small," he said amiably.

Emma thought they could make room, but before she could suggest it, Levi responded coolly, "Don't concern yourself, Josiah. I rather think Claire and I will enjoy the walk home."

✑ CHAPTER 40 ✑

As tired as Emma was, she did not sleep that night. She was too busy trying to piece together what knew. It still made little sense to her. She kept looking out of her window toward the Calhoun house. The lights from the windows had long since been extinguished. She looked to the hills, hoping she would not see any sign of Ancha, but compulsively watching just the same. On top of all that, she kept thinking about that dance with Levi . . .

It was clear to her she wasn't going to get any sleep, so she got up, washed, and dressed. She got the fire started in the cook stove in the kitchen and put a pot of water on to boil. She made a pot of tea and brought the tray into the reading room, where she sat with her paper and dip pen, making notes. She was thusly occupied when she heard a soft knock on the parlor door. She rushed to answer it before repeated knocks woke Claire.

"Good morning, Emma." Levi said quietly as she opened the door to let him in.

"Good morning," she whispered, leading him back to the reading room. "I've made tea," she said, gesturing to the tray sitting on the sideboard. "I've been making notes of everything we know, trying to see if there is something that would prove me wrong. So far I've found nothing." She sat back down at the table.

"You really think one of the Calhouns killed Carson?" Levi asked after looking at her notes.

"Yes, but I am no longer convinced I know which one. And even if I were convinced, there's no way to prove it." Emma sighed and leaned back in her chair. "We may never get closure on this case."

"Walk me through what you are thinking."

"Well, we've been through the letter John Calhoun, Sr., wrote. When his bid for town council failed, he may have decided to take more extreme measures. Perhaps he thought if he got rid of Carson, he could buy some more time to find a way to nix the bath house project. He has no alibi. John, Jr., said he assumed his father was at the bank that day, but he didn't come home that night. As far as we know, he could have been in Manitou at the time of the murder and returned to Colorado Springs for the night."

"Ok, I'll accept we don't know if has an alibi or not, but I still think you're suggesting a weak motive, especially given that his daughter was to marry Carson. Mr. Calhoun dotes on her. I have a hard time believing he would kill her fiancé on the off-chance it would derail the project."

"I admit it seems a weak motive, but people have killed for less, and maybe there is a more compelling reason he was so opposed to the project that we haven't discovered yet."

"Well, I suppose we can't rule him out completely. We do need to verify his whereabouts that day."

"Agreed. He may have an alibi. We just don't know."

"You have John, Jr., also listed here. He took his mother to the dentist in the city, remember?"

"Yes, but we haven't discovered *when* he took his mother to the dentist, and she was groggy on laudanum afterwards. She may not know when they got home. He may have had time to get her home and in bed and still have time to kill Carson." Emma took a sip of tea.

"You have a question mark by Anna's name. Surely you don't suspect her?" Levi gave her a dubious look.

"It's a mistake to underestimate Anna just because she's a woman. She's on my list because there is proof that she was in the area at some point." Emma went to her room and returned with the pouch Ancha had hidden for her at the boulder. She opened it and emptied its contents onto the table.

"A piece of blue thread and a hairpin?" Levi held the items in his hand. "How does this prove she was ever in the area where Carson was killed?"

"Ancha wrote a note, saying he found these things there the day of the earthquake."

"Ancha knows how to write? How did he leave you a note?"

"It's a long story for another time. The important thing is that this proves she was there at some point."

"Yes, but when? Just because Ancha found these the day of the earthquake does not mean that Anna left them there that day. And even if she did, it doesn't prove she murdered Carson. Besides, I don't see how a woman her size could over-power a healthy man like Carson and bash his head in. Why on earth would she kill him? By all accounts, she was besotted with him and looking forward to marrying him."

Emma put her head in her hands. "You're right." She looked up. "I just know it's one of them, Levi. Who else could it be?"

"What about the IOU? How does that fit into your theory?"

"It fits. Whoever killed Carson took it, maybe thinking it had value, or maybe out of panic. That was their mistake. Later, no doubt, they saw their error. They should have destroyed it at that point, but instead, they thought they could cast suspicion on Josiah, who was the last one to see Carson alive. I think they planted the IOU in his pocket at the funeral or at church when his overcoat would have been hanging on a hook and accessible to others."

Levi considered her scenario. After several moments, he asked, "Do you suppose it was Mr. Calhoun, Sr., who pressured the sheriff to arrest Josiah? Whoever was behind that has been a mystery since Mr. Albright hired a solicitor for Josiah, making it clear he wanted to clear Josiah so he could finish the project."

"Yes! In fact, it fits my theory of Mr. Calhoun, Sr's., motive, which was to derail the bath house project. Does Mr. Calhoun have that kind of influence?"

"Oh, yes. His bank is the largest in the area outside of Denver. He has considerable influence."

Emma heard a commotion from the kitchen. She looked out of the window and saw early dawn light. "I need to go help with breakfast and then head to work. Is there any way you can check on the senior Mr. Calhoun's alibi and maybe find out when Mrs. Calhoun and Junior were at the dentist?"

"I'll try. I don't want to make anyone suspicious that we are still investigating this."

❧ CHAPTER 41 ❧

So much had happened since she had last seen Mr. Albright that Emma forgot he wanted to talk that day about something. She remembered when she arrived at the office precisely on time, just as the lobby clock was chiming nine o'clock, to find Mr. Albright already there, sipping coffee behind his desk.

"Good morning, Mr. Albright. I hope you had a happy Thanksgiving." Emma said, removing her scarf, coat, and gloves.

"It was pleasant. Gen. Palmer was kind enough to invite me to join him and his other guests at his home for the feast."

Emma realized then, for the first time, that Mr. Albright was alone—no wife, grown children back east. She felt a moment of compassion for the powerful man and wondered if he was lonely.

"I looked at the filing system you created. It is quite good, I think."

"Thank you, Mr. Albright."

"Also, the letters you typed were error free. I have found that correct spelling and grammar are unfortunately rare. I also noticed you made minor revisions in my dictation that resulted in more elegant, clearer prose." Mr. Albright unlocked his top right drawer and pulled out a cash box, which he also unlocked and opened. He reached in and pulled out some cash. "I know you offered to work provisionally for a month before I decided whether to bring you on permanently, but you have demonstrated initiative, intelligence, and significant skill. It would be foolish of me to take undue advantage of you and risk losing you to another employer." He counted out bills and coins. "I hope you will find twenty dollars a week acceptable."

Emma's heart was racing—her first pay, and early! She could pay for the batteries Alice had ordered for her. She could begin repaying Claire. She could get her own place! She could buy books! She was elated. She opened her mouth to say, "Yes! Of course, it's acceptable." But, her experience in twenty-first century business had trained her to keep her cool, even when coming from a weak negotiating position. She wasn't sure what the strength of her position was, which in itself put her at a disadvantage. *"Buy time,"* she thought.

"I am honored that you are pleased with my work so far, Mr. Albright, and I greatly appreciate that you see my value and wish to treat me fairly," She paused for effect. "Perhaps twenty dollars a week is appropriate. One thing we were going to discover during the trial period is what my job responsibilities would actually be. Are you clear on what that is already? If so, I would like to have the benefit of your thoughts before I agree to a wage."

Mr. Albright looked at her, expressionless. Emma's heart pounded harder. Had she angered him? Had she botched the deal? All she could do was stand her ground and look calmly at him. Slowly, a half-smile appeared on his face, and he slowly shook his head. "Miss Quinn, I've never met a woman like you. You make a reasonable point." He paused, thinking. "Ok, yes, I have an idea of what I would like your job responsibilities to be. That brings me to the thing I wanted to talk to you about today."

So, her instincts had been right. Suddenly it was clear to Emma what Mr. Albright's game plan had been. He wanted her to agree to a wage, then require something of her that would support a higher wage. He was betting her desire for money would cause her to rush to that agreement. *"Point, Emma."*

"You may be aware of excursions that have come through Manitou. We had a party of 150 people last April from Boston. These excursions are vital to our local economy, obviously. The community leaders and businessmen here supported the bath house because they saw it as a way to draw more visitors and extend the season, benefitting everyone. I need someone to work with the railroad, the newspapers, and the local hotel proprietors to publicize Manitou, in general, and the bath house, in particular, and to sort out schedules and logistics to ensure the town can accommodate the people coming in on excursions."

"I see. That's an interesting and challenging task, and again, I am honored you have the confidence in me to consider me for that undertaking. May I suggest we agree on a base wage plus an incentive plan that would provide me an opportunity to make more money based on how successful I am in this undertaking? If you will give me the weekend, I can prepare an approach with the idea we can discuss it and modify it to reflect our agreement. In the meantime, I am prepared to honor my offer to work for you on a trial basis for the full month without wages."

"Well, how can I say no to that? I am intrigued with what you might propose. We will take this up on Monday, then."

❀

Emma spent the remainder of her workday taking dictation and typing it up. Mr. Albright had recommended that they close the office an hour early since there was no more immediate work to be done. The day was overcast, but Emma welcomed the muted daylight and hillsides obscured by low-lying clouds. It offered a different mood that felt more in keeping with the season to Emma.

Claire was crocheting an edge on a hankie, sitting on her sofa with Lulu curled up beside her, when Emma came into the parlor. "Oh, Emma! You're home early." She laid her work in a basket beside the sofa. "But I'm glad because I have good news and a surprise for you," she smiled.

"Really? What is it?"

"First, the good news. Alice signed the paperwork for the loan I offered her. She will begin planning her new enterprise after the new year."

"That is good news! She's made the right decision."

"And now the surprise. Come, I'll show you. We put it in the attic because there was no place to put it here." Claire led the way. When they got to the attic, Claire walked over to a short table on which was an object—or objects—covered with an old tablecloth. Claire removed the covering. "Ta-da!" she exclaimed.

It took Emma a moment to recognize what she saw, but then it dawned on her. "My batteries!" she clapped.

"Yes. Alice had it delivered directly here from the depot. It arrived midday."

Emma bent to get a closer look. "Wow, it looks like they are all wired up and ready to go. Where is the solution?"

Claire reached behind a crate and brought out a large jug

and gave it to Emma.

"I don't understand how this works. I will leave you to it."

"Thanks Claire," Emma said absently, her attention fully on the apparatus in front of her. The three Grenet cells rested in a wooden frame and were already wired together in series via metal strips along the top of the frame. Two wires led from the positive and negative conductive strips, ready to be connected to whatever the user wanted to provide power. Emma was elated that she wouldn't have to do that part. It looked like all she had to do was connect the wires to the recharger cord. She filled the three jars with the bichromate solution. Alice had thought to order large cells, so Emma felt sure they would provide sufficient current to power up her 24,000mAh recharger. She preferred to use her recharger to test with in case something went wrong. She did not want to damage her cell phone. The recharger could then charge her phone about eight times. *"Thank you, Paul."* She thought, grateful that he insisted she always bring the recharger with her when she travelled.

Emma ran downstairs and borrowed Claire's snipping scissors. She grabbed her recharger and cord and ran back up the stairs, eager to try things out. She stripped the insulation away from the cord with the scissors and wired the battery cells to the recharger. Then, she lowered each of the zinc plates into the solution in the jars. At first, she saw no indication that the recharger was receiving power, and her heart fell. She inspected the wiring; it looked secure, and when she looked at the display again, it showed it was recharging. *"Eureka!"* Emma clapped her hands together quietly. She wasn't sure how long it would take for the recharging to complete—probably until the next day. She covered the batteries and the recharger with the tablecloth. All she could do now was wait.

❀

December 1, 1882

I haven't been here a month yet, but it feels like I've lived a lifetime already, so much has happened. Despite it all, I feel empowered today. It looks as though I have a future with Mr. Albright—one that might actually be interesting and provide me with an adequate income. My batteries arrived today and I am charging my recharger as I write. I feel that I am able to have some influence over my future, and it's a great feeling.

My first hop was enjoyable. My dancing was adequate— I didn't step on anyone's toes, anyway. I like the custom of dancing with more than one partner. I especially enjoyed dancing with Levi. It's too bad the whole ritual of a dance has largely been lost in my time. Modern people are missing out on a lot of fun!

What I learned at the hop also helped me narrow down who killed Carson. I just don't know for sure which Calhoun it was, and I see no way to prove it. I won't give up, though, because Ancha's safety depends on clearing him completely.

I am afraid for Ancha. But if I am completely honest, what frightens me the most now is how swept away I feel. This place and time have demanded so much of me that I can hardly remember my life before, as recent as it was. This life already seems more real to me that that one—and I guess it is. I think of Paul often, and my friends and family, of course. It makes my heart ache. But I have found things here to enjoy and appreciate, and I am making good friends. All is not lost after all.

❧ CHAPTER 42 ❧

Emma was writing the first draft of her incentive proposal to Mr. Albright when Levi entered the reading room. Emma looked up when she heard him. "Hi there."

"Good Morning, Emma." Levi smiled. "I hope I'm not interrupting."

"Well, of course you are, but that's okay. Join me." She turned her papers over and pushed them aside. "I missed you yesterday. It's not like you to miss dinner," Emma laughed.

"I went into the Springs and stayed till late evening. I was following up on what we discussed in the morning."

"Oh, good! Did you learn anything?"

"Yes, but I'm afraid it doesn't simplify the matter. I found the dentist Mrs. Calhoun saw that day. She and her son arrived at noon, and she was there about an hour. The dentist verified that he gave her laudanum at his office, as well as a bottle to take home with her, so that part of John, Jr.,'s story seems true. I could not discover what they did after that. It's possible that they were home by the time the earthquake hit. If so, John, Jr., could have killed Carson, either to support his father's agenda or for some other reason we don't know yet." Levi poured himself a cup of coffee and refilled Emma's cup.

"Then, I went to the bank to check on Mr. Calhoun, Sr.,'s whereabouts that day. It was more difficult to do because I didn't want Mr. Calhoun to know I was nosing around. I struck up a conversation with the head clerk and learned Mr. Calhoun was in and out of the office all day. He was not there at the time of the earthquake, but he came in not long after to see if there was damage to the bank or injury to anyone."

"Not long after? What does that mean?"

"Indeed, the clerk couldn't be specific. He was distracted by the earthquake and assessing the aftermath himself. When I pressed him, he said it was probably between thirty and forty-five minutes."

"Did he say how Mr. Calhoun seemed?"

"Well, he was as rattled as everyone was. The clerk noticed nothing unusual given the circumstances."

"Humm. It's not conclusive, but it seems unlikely he would have had time to return from the meeting site where Carson was so quickly after the earthquake." Emma stopped and thought. "You're right. This does not simplify the matter. How are we ever going to solve this case, Levi?"

Levi didn't like to see hopelessness in Emma's blue eyes. As a lawman, he knew it was his duty to find the killer. He did not know why it was so important to Emma, but he could see that it was. That only gave him more reason to not give up. "I'm afraid the only way is for the murderer to confess, and . . ."

"Exactly! Of course!" Emma exclaimed.

"Of course? What are you thinking, Emma?'

"Shush, I'm trying to capture my thought." Emma felt an idea trying to emerge. Her eyes moved around the room as her mind hunted for it. Her eyes landed on the drawer where Claire kept her fortune-telling cards. "Yes," she mused. "Yes, I think it might work." She looked at Levi, "Come with me."

"Where are we going?" Levi jumped up to follow her.

"The attic."

❋

Emma led Levi to the table where her recharging station was safely hidden under the tablecloth. She had gone up the night before to check on progress and had discovered that the batteries were working, so she had plugged her phone into the recharger. That morning before breakfast, she had checked again and was thrilled to see her phone batteries were up to 60%.

"Turn around."

"Why?"

"Please just do it, Levi. Humor me."

Levi reluctantly turned his back to Emma. She got her cell phone, unlocked it, found a video of Paul talking about a foolish business associate. She put the phone in her pocket and hit the play button.

"That damn fool thought he could bluff me into agreeing to sell him our whole package at a 50% discount," Paul's voice came from her pocket. Levi spun around, wide-eyed, looking around the attic.

"What the . . ."

The sound of Paul's muffled laughter filled the room. Levi looked at Emma, alarmed. Emma turned the video off.

"Yes, I think this might work, Levi," she beamed and pulled out her cell phone.

Levi recognized the odd object in Emma's hand from the first day he met her. "Did that voice come out of this?" He took the phone from Emma and looked at it, amazed.

"Yes. Let me show you." Emma scrolled through her music, selected "Earned It," by The Weeknd, and turned the volume up. "May I have this dance, Mr. Warwick?" She lifted her arms. Levi's eyes widened again. He smiled and took her hand, listening for the beat. He began a waltz. Emma watched every change of his expression as he reacted to the slow tempo and musical tones he had never heard before, blended with the sound of string instruments familiar to his ears. The sensuality of the music and the words were not lost on him, and he held Emma closer than anyone in the nineteenth century would have thought proper. Their eyes locked together, each searching for the other's reactions. When the song was over, they were both breathing hard. Levi released Emma, cradled her head gently in his hands, and kissed her.

Emma lost herself in his full, warm lips. She had heard about weak knees before, but had always thought it was a cliché out of Harlequin romance novels. No longer. She feared her legs would fail her. She wrapped her arms around Levi's shoulders and welcomed his kiss with growing energy. Weeks of anxiety, fear, stress, grief, and who knows what else released like a volcano through her body.

Levi released his embrace and took a step back. He looked into her eyes. "I won't pretend to be sorry for that," he whispered. Then he cleared his throat.

Emma smoothed her hair with her hands, keenly aware of the flush on her chest and glad for the high neckline of her blouse. It was going to take her a while to be able to think straight.

❁

"There are about a thousand ways this could go wrong." Emma

admitted, rubbing her tired eyes. She was grateful that they had lots of details to sort out in their plan to trap Carson's killer. It gave them both something to focus on that required logic. Logic was safe.

"It is risky, but I believe it's our only shot. If we miss, though, we may have to accept that Carson's killer will never be brought to justice." Levi leaned back and rolled his head around in circles to relax his stiff neck.

"Which means I will never see Ancha again—never learn what the strange connection is between us," Emma thought. *"I may not see him again, in any case."* Then she said aloud, "We have nothing to lose by trying."

"I agree we shouldn't tell anyone else of our plan. The fewer people aware of what we are doing, the more likely it will work. Claire, in particular, is dismal at deceit."

"Yes, it's one of the reasons I love her!" Emma agreed.

Just then Claire walked in. "Well, I'm glad to see you both behaving normally." She opened the sideboard drawer to fetch a candle. "What on earth was going on over dinner? You were both so *stiff*."

They looked at each other and shared a smile.

❋

December 2, 1882

Ok, now I have a real problem (as opposed to the mere inconvenience of figuring out how to survive in 1882!). What am I going to do about that kiss between Levi and me? I have never in my life felt like that from a kiss. What does it mean? Is it just my body reacting to no sex for weeks? Is it more than that? Ugh, I can't deal with that right now!

Our plan is crazy. If it doesn't work, all is lost as far as finding justice for Carson and clearing Josiah and Ancha. And I risk exposing myself if our trick is discovered.

I used to look at movies set in the old west and wonder what people did to entertain themselves. I was a fool.

❧ CHAPTER 43 ❧

The first step of Levi and Emma's plan was easy. Claire had enthusiastically agreed to Emma's suggestion that they invite the medium Anna Eva Fay to be their guest at the boarding house and to conduct a seance for the locals. Anna Eva was one of the head-liners at the revival they were attending the next night and was well known in the spiritualism movement. Emma hoped she was more a performer than a medium. It was going to take a lot of acting to pull the plan off.

The next step, not as easy, was to get Anna Eva to agree, not only to visiting Manitou, but also to the séance—and the deception. They decided that Levi would have a better chance of persuading Miss Fay than Emma would, being a lawman (and a handsome one at that). His job was to meet with Miss Fay as soon as possible after she arrived in Colorado Springs and explain what they needed of her.

The last step for the plan to have a chance of working was to arrange that all of the members of the Calhoun family were present at the séance. Emma was confident Johns Sr. and Jr. would not be likely to come of their own accord. The best chance was if the séance was conducted at the Calhoun home. Emma suggested to Claire that Mrs. Calhoun would also be enthusiastic about the séance and that the Calhoun home could the perfect venue. Claire agreed and planned to pay Mrs. Calhoun a visit after church that day to propose it. Since Claire knew nothing of the plot, she was not at risk of being anything but herself in making the suggestion.

All of this was just phase one of their intricate plan . . .

❧ CHAPTER 44 ❧

As promised, Emma had her incentive plan ready to review with Mr. Albright Monday morning.

"The rationale is sound, Miss Quinn." Mr. Albright nodded in comprehension of the details. "I might debate the percentages depending on the overall margins, but I think we can sort that out. I am happy you have agreed to twenty dollars a week as a base wage." He put the agreement in his briefcase. "I have meetings in the Springs the rest of the day. If I get the opportunity, I will review this with the corporate accountant. If he has no objection, then I will agree to your proposal." He gathered his things and left for the train.

Emma should have felt elated. Instead, she was anxious and distracted. So far, good fortune had blessed her and Levi's plan. Mrs. Calhoun had thought Claire's suggestion "inspired," and readily agreed to hosting the event in her home. The two women had made a guest list and were busy letting people know to hold Thursday night open. They still needed to confirm with

Miss Fay. In an unexpected stroke of luck, Mrs. Calhoun had said her husband's bank was one of the patrons of the opera house, so Mrs. Calhoun felt sure Miss Fay would accept their invitation. Emma thought it would also increase the chances that all the Calhouns would be present. Yes, all of that had gone remarkably well. Her anxiety came from having to wait until this evening to learn if Levi had been successful.

❀

"Well? How did it go?" Emma's tone was urgent as she pulled Levi into the reading room and shut the door to the parlor. She had suffered through all the mundane dinner conversation and after-dinner chores, eager to talk to him.

"I learned from the opera house that Miss Fay and her troupe were expected this afternoon and that they were staying at the Colorado Springs Hotel, so I went there and waited." Levi began.

"Oh, for God's sake, cut to the chase. Did you get Miss Fay to agree?"

Levi frowned at her, frustrated that he wasn't allowed to recount the events on his own terms. "Yes."

"And?"

"Oh, now you are interested in the details."

"Levi, stop tormenting me. I've been waiting on pins and needles all day to find out how things went." Emma sat down at the table. "Now that I know our plan is on track, I am ready to hear the details, yes."

Levi joined her at the table. "I intercepted Miss Fay when she arrived at the hotel. I explained the situation and what we wanted of her. She was intrigued, but hesitant. I offered to take her to have coffee, and there explained in more detail. She took exception to the idea that she may have to do some acting, swearing that she never did that—that she was a genuine medium. I assured her I believed her, but the acting was justified under the circumstances since we were trying to find a killer and get justice for Carson. I also assured her that if we all stuck to the plan, no one but her, you, and me would ever know she had been acting. Her reputation would be safe. It took nearly two hours, but eventually I persuaded her."

"I bet Miss Fay dragged it out, enjoying your attention." Emma thought. She noticed Levi had made a special effort at his dress and grooming that morning. Still, she was very pleased he had garnered the medium's support. "Well done, Levi."

"When we returned to the hotel, a message was waiting for Miss Fay from Mrs. Calhoun. In it, Mrs. Calhoun invited her to visit Manitou as her guest and requested the opportunity to meet with Miss Fay before tomorrow's event."

"Yes, I knew she had stollen Claire's limelight." Emma made a disapproving smirk. "When Mrs. Calhoun heard the idea, she decided it would be better if Miss Fay stayed in her fine guest room instead of our humble boarding house."

"Well, she's committed to it then, that's fortunate." Levi pointed out. "At any rate, Miss Fay understood that this was part of the plan, so she sent a message back, agreeing."

Emma mentally reviewed all Levi had shared. "This plan just might work."

❧ CHAPTER 45 ❧

The party rode in the nicest carriage pulled by the best horses available at the livery. Mrs. Calhoun and Anne had dressed for the revival in fine, expensive clothes, just enough over the top to make the point they were "society" women. Claire wore a simple ensemble whose chief purpose was to keep her warm. Emma had followed Claire's lead.

"The Miller Brothers are well known in the spiritualism movement, but Anna Eva Fay is the real phenomenon," Mrs. Calhoun explained. "We are privileged to have her visit our community."

"Yes, it's so exciting!" Claire agreed. "You know, of course, that she has been proven *scientifically* to be authentic."

"How was she proven scientifically?" Emma was skeptical.

"William Crookes, a highly respected British scientist, conducted an experiment involving something called a galvanometer. The experiment proved that there was no way Miss Fay could have used her hands or body to perform deception or illusion when conjuring her spirit manifestations." Claire elaborated.

"Yes! She held a conductor, one in each hand. The galvanometer would detect if the circuit was broken and would fluctuate if she moved significantly. The galvanometer reading did not change while she went into a trance and summoned the spirits." Mrs. Calhoun concurred exuberantly. "Claire, it was ingenious of you to think of inviting Miss Fay as our guest in Manitou. This is the best opportunity I've ever had to speak to my dear, sweet boy, Charlie."

"Mama, please don't get your hopes up too high." Anna Calhoun, who had been silent until then, patted her mother's hand. "You have tried many times to make contact with Charlie. He was just a toddler when he died. Perhaps it is difficult for children to come through."

Emma suspected Anna was as skeptical as she was. She admired the gentle way Anna was attempting to protect her mother from disappointment. She caught Anna's eye and gave her a little smile of sympathy.

Playing on people's grief and hope was how charlatans got away with their deception. Emma was not a believer, yet she brought her bear claw necklace, hoping that Miss Fay might be tell her something about Ancha.

The gaslit street lights of Colorado Springs were shining into their carriage, dimly casting long shadows on the women's faces, making them resemble spirits themselves. The carriage came to a gentle stop in front of the opera house. The driver placed the step stool on the ground and offered the women his hand as they exited the carriage. Mrs. Calhoun reached in her reticule and pulled out the telegram Miss Fay had sent in response to her invitation, suggesting they meet her behind stage before the start of the event.

Inside the opera house, Mrs. Calhoun showed the telegram

to an usher and requested to see Miss Fay. The usher led them behind stage and to the door of Miss Fay's dressing room. He gently knocked on the door and when a sultry contralto voice said, "Yes, come in," he opened the door and announced the women. "You have visitors, Miss Fay. They showed me your invitation."

"Oh, yes, of course, let them in, Sammy."

The woman standing in front of them was lovely. She had dark blond hair, thick with loose curls arranged intricately and affixed high on the back of her head with filigreed hair combs. Her ice-blue eyes would have been harsh had they not been framed by full eyebrows. The gentle cleft in her chin drew attention to her well-shaped jawline. Her nose was narrow and regular. Her fine-boned frame, elegantly presented in a light green brocade gown, complemented her facial features. Emma thought back to Levi's long coffee with Miss Fay and wondered who had been the one to protract it.

"Miss Fay, it is such an honor to meet you. I am Mrs. Calhoun. May I present my daughter, Anna, and our friends, Mrs. La Salle and Miss Quinn."

"The pleasure is mine, I'm sure." Miss Fay smiled warmly, surveying each woman with her piercing eyes. She paused her gaze on Emma. A soft frown appeared between her brows.

"We are very much looking forward to your visit to our charming village." Mrs. Calhoun continued. Miss Fay reluctantly turned her eyes back to the matron.

"I have been to Denver a couple of times, but this is my first time to Colorado Springs. I look forward to visiting Manitou. I understand it is beautiful."

"Oh, indeed it is! We have made all the arrangements, Miss Fay. The carriage will pick you up and bring you to our home. Is tomorrow morning convenient for you, after you have enjoyed the fine breakfast at the hotel?"

"Yes, yes, that will be fine, thank you." Miss Fay looked back at Emma. "Pardon me, Miss Quinn, if I seem forward, but you quite intrigue me. I can't quite sort out why."

"Perhaps you sense the loss I have recently suffered," Emma offered.

"Perhaps."

"Well, no doubt we should leave you to finish preparing for the revival." Mrs. Calhoun, seeing that she was not the center of Miss Fay's attention, seemed content to shorten the visit. "We eagerly await your demonstration, Miss Fay."

"Thank you, you are most kind." Miss Fay gave Mrs. Calhoun a little bow. The women were in the narrow hallway leading backstage when she called out, "Miss Quinn? Could you come back a moment?"

Emma looked at her companions and shrugged her shoulders slightly, indicating she had no notion why the medium was calling her back. "I'll meet you at our seats."

Mrs. Calhoun looked enviously over her shoulder as Anna took her by the elbow to guide her to the front of the opera house.

"Yes?" Emma said back in Miss Fay's room.

Miss Fay stepped behind Emma and shut the door. "Miss Quinn, I wanted another moment with you. The energy I am picking up from you is something I have never felt before." She looked deeply into Emma's eyes. "There is something mysterious about you."

Emma seized the moment. She reached into her reticule for the necklace. The medium looked down and saw Emma's ring as Emma placed the necklace in her hand.

"This necklace was a gift. Can you tell me anything about the person who gave it to me? Is he well?"

Miss Fay closed her fingers over the necklace and closed her eyes. Emma waited patiently. After several moments, Miss

Fay's eyes flew open. "This necklace is very powerful, but it is not the only powerful object here." She looked again at Emma's ring. "May I hold your ring, too?"

Emma removed her ring and placed it in the medium's hand with the necklace.

Miss Fay closed her eyes again and took several slow, deep breaths. Finally, she spoke. "These objects are each magical. Together, their power is magnified. The man who gave them to you is very generous to part with such things."

"They weren't given to me by the same man." Emma said.

"I'm quite sure they were, Miss Quinn. Whoever gave them to you is very important to you—always has been, always will be."

"Is he safe? That's what I need to know."

"I don't know if he is safe, but I sense he is alive." Anna Eva handed back the items. "I am aware of the plan to catch a killer, Miss Quinn. We must talk further about it when I arrive in Manitou, but now must prepare for the revival."

Emma left to meet her companions, wondering what Miss Fay had meant. *That was a mistake. She's a fraud. Don't give it another thought.* But the medium had spoken so matter-of-factly, as though she didn't care if Emma believed her or not. Was that her tactic of deception? Emma was in this unsettled state when she found Claire and the Calhouns in the balcony seats reserved for patrons.

❀

The spiritualism revival was more a magic show than a spiritual experience. It had been well-performed and entertaining, but also was obviously—to Emma at least—an act. Miss Fay's stage persona was more dramatic and charismatic than the one she portrayed before the show. Emma still was not sure what to make of what Miss Fay had told her about the necklace and ring. She wanted desperately to believe Ancha was alive and safe, but she couldn't put stock in what the medium had said when she was so wrong about who had given her the items.

"Emma, my dear, you are very quiet." Claire said. Emma had said nothing on their way home except a vague agreement that the event had been a success. "Didn't you enjoy the revival?"

Emma had been aware of the conversation among the women in the carriage after the show but was too preoccupied to participate. "Oh, it was quite impressive. I am still sorting it all out."

"There is a lot to consider. How *did* Miss Fay know that word the audience member had picked on a random page in that book?" Mrs. Calhoun's eyes widened and she shook her head, still mystified.

"That was amazing, I concede, but the 'spirits' were obviously real people dressed as ghosts," Anna Calhoun added.

Emma's stomach tightened. She had hoped Anna would be less skeptical after the revival. The plan depended on everyone being at least a little open-minded.

❧ CHAPTER 46 ❧

There was a flaw in the plan. Levi and Emma needed some time with Anna Eva Fay to orchestrate the trap. Emma did not see when they would have that opportunity. Mrs. Calhoun clearly wanted to dominate the medium's time in Manitou. Emma was spending another difficult day at work trying to concentrate on her tasks while working out how to get Anna Eva alone.

"Did you hear me, Miss Quinn?" Mr. Albright asked.

"What? Oh, I apologize, Mr. Albright. I admit I am distracted. I am still mulling over the revival I attended with Claire and the Calhouns last night."

Mr. Albright looked steadily at Emma. "I imagine it is difficult for you, Miss Quinn, to have lost your family so tragically. I caution you on putting too much credence in these mediums, however. In my experience, one's time is better spent going through the grief and accepting the loss so one can move on. I have found one's faith in God useful in this regard."

"You're right." Emma genuinely agreed. "I will be more attentive."

Mr. Albright spent the rest of the day reviewing with Emma the various organizations and individuals involved in the excursions from the major cities back east.

Snow was falling steadily that evening on Emma's walk home. She still had not arrived at a way to have any time with Anna Eva, and time was running out. The séance was the next night. She found herself resenting that her job was interfering in her mission to expose Carson's killer, then scolded herself for her ingratitude. *"It will work out somehow,"* she told herself.

She was doing her part to get dinner served when Claire came into the dining room. "Emma, I'm so excited! Miss Fay arrived at the Calhoun's this morning, and this afternoon the Calhoun's maid brought me a message from Miss Fay. She requested to visit us tonight! Seems she learned from Mrs. Calhoun that I trained with Madam Bellefleur. She expressed an interest in learning more about my training. I had no idea Madam Bellefleur enjoyed such renown!"

"Bless Miss Fay's sneaky little heart." Emma thought. The woman knew they needed time to plan, and she had figured out the way to make it happen. "That is exciting! I look forward to her visit. Will she be joining us for dinner?"

"Yes. That's why I came in to tell you," Claire said, as though it was obvious. "Let's put her at the head of the table where I usually sit."

Emma put special effort into setting the table. She even folded the napkins like fans and placed them in the drinking glasses as she had seen done at the Manitou House dining room. She was adjusting the alignment of the knives and spoons when she heard a knock at the boarding house door.

"Oh, I'll get it!" Claire called merrily. Emma heard her rapid footsteps coming down the hall.

"Miss Fay! It's such an honor to have you as our guest!"

Emma joined Claire at the door. Miss Fay walked in, looking just as beautiful as she had the night before. "Good evening, Mrs. La Salle, Miss Quinn."

"Miss Fay! What a pleasant surprise!" Emma turned to see Levi walking down the stairs, beaming warmly at the medium. He reached for her hand and gave it a gentle kiss. Emma suddenly felt hot. "I had no idea you were joining us this evening," he said, shooting Emma a quick glance.

"Thank you, Mr. Warwick. I confess, I invited myself. I learned that Mrs. La Salle studied under the famous Madam Bellefleur, who in turn, learned from Mlle. Lenormand, who was unsurpassed, as everyone in the occult knows. I couldn't miss the opportunity to meet with Mrs. La Salle and pick her brain!" Miss Fay laughed. "It was shameless of me, I know."

"Nonsense!" Claire said. "We are honored to have you at our humble boarding house."

"Indeed, we are." Levi said huskily. Emma frowned at him as he put a hand on Anna Eva's back to guide her into the parlor.

※

One thing was sure: Miss Fay could read a room. Sensing not all the tenants were comfortable with spiritualism, she expertly steered the conversation over dinner to safe topics, like life on the road and which were her favorite cities. Emma suggested Miss Fay and Claire adjourn to Claire's quarters after dinner, where the two women could explore their common interests. Claire had asked Molly to stay and take care of the dishes after dinner, and Miss Sully had offered to help so that Claire could entertain her guest.

Miss Fay, Claire, and Emma retired to Claire's parlor, where Claire told the story of how she had met Madam

Bellefleur in New Orleans and had learned how to conduct séances and read fortune cards. "I have conducted several séances here for select believers, and I frequently read the cards for people seeking guidance. Would you like to see my reading room?"

"Most definitely, Mrs. La Salle." Anna Eva graciously accepted. As she followed Claire, she looked at Emma and raised her eyebrows, implying, *"When are we meeting?"*

A soft knock sounded at the door. Emma opened it to find Levi. She pulled him into the parlor and shut the door behind him. "Thank God you're here. I think we are going to have to tell Claire what we are up to. Otherwise, we may not get the chance to plan. She will keep Miss Fay occupied all night with card readings and so forth."

Levi sighed. "You're right," he agreed reluctantly.

They entered the reading room. "Claire, I'm sorry to interrupt, but we have something to tell you."

"Oh, I love this idea! It's quite inspired, Emma!" Claire, ever the good sport, accepted their plan without hesitation.

"We apologize for not telling you sooner, Claire," Levi said. "We thought the risk was lower if you didn't know."

"I understand, Levi, and agree. But now I think I can be of help, knowing the plan."

"If I may, I suggest we write the script for tomorrow night." Miss Fay focused them on the discussion.

"You are quite right, Miss Fay," Levi concurred, looking a little too long at Anna Eva's visage.

The four conspirators wrote out the lines for Miss Fay and the ghost of Carson.

"Mr. Warwick, will you be speaking as Carson? How will you fool the people in the room?

Levi, Emma, and Claire looked at each other. "We have some tricks up our sleeves, Miss Fay. I believe you can understand if we do not wish to divulge them." Emma said, finally. "If you come prepared with your role, we will be prepared with Carson's."

Miss Fay smiled, acquiescing. "Very well."

※

Emma and Levi were up late making preparations. Claire had made them a pot of coffee to help keep them alert until they had worked out every detail and practiced several times. Claire was invaluable, pointing out flaws along the way.

"I am simply exhausted," Claire said when the friends had finished preparing. "I bid you goodnight, what's left of it."

"It is late," Emma noticed. "Good night, Claire. Thank you for all your help."

"Miss Fay is a fascinating woman, isn't she?" Emma asked Levi when they were alone.

"That she is." He agreed.

"And very beautiful." She watched his face carefully.

"Indeed." He rubbed his eyes. "We need to be fresh tomorrow, and it is nearly two o'clock in the morning. Let's get some sleep." He stood, then leaned over and kissed Emma on the cheek. "Good night, my dear. I'll let myself out."

❧ Chapter 47 ❧

Adrenaline got Emma through her day. Her nerves were raw when she came home, and she snapped at Claire when she encouraged Emma to come to dinner. "I'm not hungry, and I have to make sure I'm prepared!" she had said. After reviewing plans with Levi for the sixth time, she agreed they had done all they could to be ready.

Josiah joined the group in the hallway as they were leaving for the Calhoun house.

"You are attending the séance, Josiah?" Claire asked as she adjusted her gloves.

"Yes. Anna invited me. She expects nothing will come of the night, but one never knows." He laughed nervously. "If Carson does make an appearance, I'd like to say farewell."

"Alice will meet us there." Claire added. The clock struck half-past six. "Come, let's go. We don't want to be late, and Miss Fay said she would start at seven o'clock."

The snow that had fallen the day before had mostly melted

on the dirt roads, but it was still pristine white on the hillsides, reflecting the moonlight. The night was cold and still.

"Welcome! Welcome all!" Mrs. Calhoun answered the door herself, gesturing them into the house with a wide flourish of her arm.

The octagonal parlor was dimly lit. The blazing fire in the fireplace made the room too hot. Emma could barely breathe. She perspired freely under her wool outfit. The room had been arranged for the occasion. Miss Fay's chair faced the sofa, and extra chairs from the dining room were set among the upholstered chairs to accommodate everyone. Emma needed something to drink and headed to the sideboard behind the sofa, where a tray of beverages reflected the firelight.

Emma looked to the entrance as she took a deep drink of lemonade. She waved at Alice and her daughter, who had just arrived.

"Please everyone, take a seat. We will begin shortly." Mrs. Calhoun announced.

There were about twenty townspeople gathered for the event. Among them was Tommy White, Carson's brother. A tall, lanky man with bushy eyebrows whom Emma did not know entered.

"Who is that man?" Emma asked Levi

"It's Frank Bowman, the proprietor at the billiards hall. I am surprised he is here. Come, let's find our seats."

Emma took her seat between Claire and Alice on the sofa, and Levi sat in a chair to the right of them, nearer the fire. Emma was glad for the dim lighting and the way the women's clothes filled the sofa with folds of material. Josiah and Anna sat next to each other on chairs to the left of the sofa nearer the entrance. Mrs. Calhoun, her husband, and son sat in a row to Miss Fay's right.

Miss Fay hit a little gong sitting on the accent table next to her seat. "Let us begin." She said with authority. "I realize we may have skeptics here tonight. I respect your skepticism. I don't ask you to believe, I merely ask that you keep an open mind so as not to block any entities that may want to come through tonight. Please, for the sake of those here who do believe and hope to be paid a visit from a loved one, follow my instructions." Miss Fay took a deep breath. "Several of you have provided me an item from your loved one. I have those here." She indicated a set of items sharing the table with the gong. "As the items call to me, I will use them to attempt to summon the dearly departed. Spirits can come through in various ways. Some move objects. Some speak through me. On very rare occasions, when a spirit is highly motivated, they will speak themselves. Of course, it's possible no spirits come through tonight." She took another deep breath. "Everyone, take three slow, deep breaths." When she had allowed sufficient time for the audience to do so she said, "Now, relax your mind, let go of your thoughts, surrender, surrender, surrender . . .   relax . . . relax . . . relax . . ."

Emma felt the tension in her body fade. She jarred herself back to alertness. She couldn't afford to relax!

Miss Fay picked up a little silver spoon and clasped it between her hands. She closed her eyes and breathed. "I sense a small child. A boy . . ." Emma saw Mrs. Calhoun grab her husband's hand. "His name begins with a C or a D . . ."

"That's my Charlie!" Mrs. Calhoun exclaimed. "Is he well? Charlie? Can you hear me, my dear boy?"

Miss Fay took a few long breaths. "Yes, he hears you . . ." She said slowly. "He wants you to know he is well and happy. He loves you both . . ."

Mrs. Calhoun looked at her husband, her eyes overflowing with tears. Emma felt sorry for the woman. She was being used as a prop for their subterfuge. She felt it was cruel and unnecessary.

"I feel him leaving us . . ." Miss Fay paused. "He is gone." She opened her eyes, replaced the spoon and picked up a hairbrush. She held it, closing her eyes and breathing deeply.

"I sense a spirit. Spirit, give us a sign." The room was silent, waiting. "Spirit, do you wish to speak?" Again, silence. Then, in a high, weak voice, entirely different from Miss Fay's sultry tone, the medium said, "Frraaannnk . . . Frraaannnk . . ."

"Gladys?" Frank Bowman said, his voice cracking.

"Yeeesssss . . ."

"Gladys, honey, it's Frank. Billy and I are doin' fine. Don't you worry about us." Frank cried out. "Are you all right, honey?"

"Yeeesssss . . ."

After several seconds, Miss Fay spoke again in her own voice, "the spirit is gone."

Tears ran down Frank Bowman's face, but he smiled.

Finally, the medium reached for the pouch Ancha had left for Emma. This was Emma's cue.

Miss Fay took more deep breaths. She began shaking. "There is much energy . . . sadness . . . disappointment . . . who are you? Who is coming through?"

Emma hit the play button on her cell phone, which was concealed in her skirt pocket. "Why? Why did you kill me?" The room gasped. Everyone turned to look at where the voice was coming from. Emma had recorded Levi's voice several times before getting just the right effect of a muffled, distant voice, hoping it would be convincing.

"Who are you, spirit?" the medium asked.

"Caaarrrssssonnn." Emma pressed the play button again. She heard Anna let out a little cry.

"Carson? Carson White?"

"Yeeesss." Everyone in the room was shocked at hearing the disembodied voice emanating from somewhere in the room.

"Carson, do you know who killed you?"

"Yeeesss."

"This is outrageous! What manner of trickery is this!" John Calhoun, Sr., bellowed.

"Stop, John! Let the spirit speak!" His wife cried.

Emma looked at John, Jr., who seemed not to know what to think. She turned to see Anna tightly grabbing Josiah's arm, her eyes wide with terror.

"Tell us, Carson! Tell us who killed you!" Miss Fay demanded.

"The one who owns the things you hold."

"Well, that's the Indian's, isn't it?" Anna exclaimed, her face pale and clammy.

Miss Fay opened the pouch and shook out the hairpin and blue thread.

"Anna, that is your hairpin!" Mrs. Calhoun looked with horror at the pearl-headed pin, then at her daughter. "What is the meaning of this?"

Emma hit the play button again. "Why did you kill me?"

"Stop at once! I demand it!" Anna's father commanded. But everyone was standing and looking at Anna.

Her eyes were bright with tears. She shook her head violently. "No! I, I didn't mean it! I didn't!!" She screamed.

"Stop talking, Anna!" her father ordered.

Josiah pulled away from Anna and looked at her, disbelieving his ears. "You killed Carson? Why? For God's sake, Anna, why?"

Anna looked at him and reached out, but he just pulled away farther.

"I didn't mean to! I was in my room, working on my embroidery and looking out my window. I saw you and Carson walking up the road to the canyon. Carson and I had been engaged for some time, but he would not set a date. I had the feeling he was beginning to regret our engagement, so I decided to follow you in the hopes I would hear something to help me understand his reluctance.

When I got near, I hid and listened. I heard him say how much he loved it here and wanted to stay. We had talked of going to Chicago! Or even New York, once he had the success of the bath house to launch his career. I didn't want to stay in this backwater town! I wanted to go somewhere where I could be respected in society. He promised me! Then, I heard you talking about the money that Mr. Graham owed him.

After you left, I confronted Carson. I reminded him that he had said we'd settle in a city somewhere. I said that with the money Graham owed him, we could set a date and begin our life together.

He said that's not what he wanted. He wanted to stay here. He had come to love the land and its beauty. He said if that's not what I wanted, he would release me from our engagement. I went into a rage and started screaming at him. And then the earthquake hit." Her hand went up to her mouth as the tears rolled down her cheeks. "A rock fell and hit Carson on the back of his head, and he fell unconscious. I was in such a fury, I picked up the rock and hit him with it, over and over again." She stopped and looked around the room for a sympathetic face. "I didn't mean to kill him! I was just so angry!"

"Was it you who planted the IOU in my pocket?" Josiah asked, wounded that she would incriminate him.

"Yes. Carson was holding the IOU when the earthquake hit. I took it, thinking it had value. When I got home, I realized I could not explain why I had it. I wasn't trying to incriminate you, Josiah! You must believe me. I thought as Carson's partner, you might collect on it . . . I thought perhaps that would encourage you to court me." She buried her face in her hands and sobbed.

Josiah turned his back on Anna in disgust. Anna's mother rushed to her and embraced her. John, Jr., still looked lost. Mr. Calhoun bowed his head in resigned shame. Everyone else in the room was standing in silent shock.

Levi walked up to Anna's father and said quietly, "I will have to arrest Anna, Mr. Calhoun. Give me your word she will not flee, and I'll wait until tomorrow to take her into custody."

Mr. Calhoun nodded. "I give you my word, Levi."

⚘ CHAPTER 48 ❧

"Here my good man, take this." Levi handed Josiah a whiskey. Claire and Emma guided him to Claire's pink sofa and sat on either side of him. He stared a long while at the glass in his hand, then took a sip.

"I'm so sorry, Josiah." Emma spoke first. "I imagine this is hard for you."

"I truly cared for her." Josiah took another sip. "When Carson was killed, I thought I might give her what he could not and that we might be happy together. I would have taken her anywhere she wanted to go. Turns out I was a fool."

"I know this stings, Josiah, but I don't think she could have made you happy in the long run." Levi poured two more drinks and handed them to the ladies, then served himself. "She killed Carson because he would not yield to her wishes. She remained silent when you were arrested. She actively blamed Ancha, knowing full well he was innocent. She is not an honest person."

"All that is true, Levi, but you are being harsh." Claire

countered. "Her parents spoiled her and created the selfish creature she has become."

"Nonsense Claire. She is a grown woman and responsible for her actions."

"The whole thing is tragic just the same." Emma intervened. "I don't believe she meant to kill Carson, and if the earthquake hadn't happened at just that moment, they may well have sorted things out with time."

A knock came to the outside door. Levi opened it and found Alice and Miss Fay, shivering on the little patio. Miss Fay was holding a large carpetbag.

"Oh my, come in, come in!" Claire jumped up to welcome the women. "You are frozen, the both of you. Stand here by the stove."

"Miss Fay did not feel comfortable remaining at the Calhoun residence. I knew she would be welcome here." Alice said, bluntly.

"Yes, of course you are, Miss Fay." Claire took the bag from the woman. "Make yourself comfortable. You've had quite a night yourself."

"I stayed behind for a while after everyone left to make sure Anna and Mrs. Calhoun were all right. They were both distraught, I recommended a sleeping draught for each of them." Alice poured herself a whiskey. "Miss Fay, would you like a drink?"

"Yes, please. I am rather worried about Miss Calhoun. There is no doubt she is distraught. And poor Mrs. Calhoun is worried sick about her."

Claire brought a chair from the reading room and placed it by the stove. Miss Fay and Alice sat to warm themselves.

"Miss Fay, was it necessary to fool Mrs. Calhoun and Frank Bowman into thinking their dead loved ones had come through? I agree it added authenticity to our trap, but it seemed cruel." Emma challenged the medium.

"Why do you think I was fooling them, Miss Quinn?" the medium asked, sincerely.

"Are you saying you weren't?"

"You seem to be under the impression that because I occasionally resort to theatrics, nothing I do is genuine."

"Of course that's not what Emma is saying." Claire dismissed the notion wholesale. Emma remained silent, puzzled by Miss Fay. Was she the real deal or not? "Miss Fay, I have a spare suite upstairs. You are welcome to stay there tonight. Let me just get the stove started to warm it up."

"I'll take care of it, Claire, dear." Levi sat his glass down. "Josiah, do you care to join me?"

"Yes, I'll come with you. Thank you, ladies. Goodnight." Josiah followed Levi.

"I apologize, Miss Fay." Emma softened her tone. "You did us a great service tonight. I didn't mean to be rude or ungrateful." She gave the medium a regretful smile.

"Don't give it another thought, I was happy to help."

"I do have a question for you, if you don't mind."

"Please."

"When I met you in your dressing room, you said the same man had given me both my bear claw necklace and my ring."

"Yes, that's correct."

"But it isn't. Why do you think it is?"

"The energy signature is the same."

"Energy signature?"

"It's like the unheard song emanating from each of us. Each unique. I can sense it, and the song emanating from those items is identical."

"Could it be because they are both mine? You are sensing my 'song?'"

"I sense your song, too, Miss Quinn. It is quite different,

and very unusual, I might add."

"This is fascinating!" Claire said. "I would love to learn from you, Miss Fay! Please, stay as long as you'd like."

Miss Fay smiled warmly. "I'm not sure this is something that can be taught, Mrs. La Salle, and as much as I appreciate your invitation, I have obligations." She sat down her glass. "I am feeling tired. If you don't mind, I'd like to retire now."

"Let me show you your room." Claire gestured for Miss Fay to follow her.

When the ladies had left, Alice said, "All right, Emma, tell me what in heaven's name has been going on tonight." She crossed her arms over her chest, waiting for an explanation.

Emma caught Alice up on the scheme that had led to Anna's confession. "I'm sorry, Alice. We thought the plan would have a better chance of working the fewer the people who knew about it."

"Amazing. I do feel left out, though I understand why you didn't tell me before."

Levi and Claire returned from upstairs.

"Our guest is settled in." Claire announced.

The four friends sat around the occasional table, sipping their whiskies.

"You have an unpleasant task in front of you tomorrow, Levi," Alice said.

"Yes, but I should think the Calhouns will recover from this. I don't believe Anna planned to kill Carson, and given her place in society and the fact that she is a woman, she may get off rather easy with a stint in a mental hospital."

"That's still rather dreadful." Alice noted.

"I'd like to know who pressured the sheriff to arrest Josiah. It seemed ill-conceived from the beginning." Claire wondered.

"I believe it was Mr. Calhoun, Sr. He wanted to sabotage the bath house project. When circumstances provided the opportunity for him to get rid of Josiah, he took it." Emma reasoned.

"I am confident you are right." Levi concurred, rubbing the back of his neck. "It has been a very long and trying night. I am going to bed. Good night, ladies."

He put his empty glass on the table and gave the women a quick nod. He closed the main hall door gently as he left, leaving a quiet stillness behind.

"Well, it's just the three of us, just like the first day you arrived, Emma," Claire mused. "Oh! Emma! I just realized! You've been with us one month today!"

Emma just shook her head. *"Unbelievable."* She thought.

❧ EPILOGUE ❧

On Saturday morning, Emma donned her blue jeans, flannel shirt, and jacket and headed to Williams Cañon. The dark cerulean sky was cloudless, the sun so bright it made her eyes water. She took deep breaths in cadence with her steps, walking with purpose to the boulder to leave a note for Ancha to let him know it was safe to return. She let out her whistle signal and waited, but not for long. Surely, he was not within earshot.

On the ridge by the cave where she had been born to this time, she saw the sun reflecting off snow-capped Pikes Peak, contrasting with the blue sky and rusty hues of granite. She sat on a rock and looked down on Manitou. Coping. That's all she had been doing since arriving in 1882. Life demanded her to survive and cope. She had done so. She had a place to live, a means of income, and friends. Her life before was far away, and she had no clear path back. The empty place it left inside her would last forever, but at least now she had time to mourn it. She let the ache in, and though she feared it would consume her, she surrendered to her sadness. She rested her head on her arms crossed over her knees as the tears rolled freely down her cheeks.

After the wave of grief passed, she opened her eyes and saw the bear claw necklace resting against her heart. Its powers were still a mystery to her, as was the insistent claim Anna Eva had made that the same man had given her both the necklace and her ring. That was impossible. Or was it? And if not, then anything might be possible, including finding a way back to her own time. She had been so focused on surviving that she had not yet applied herself to the task. Perhaps there was a way, and if so, Ancha might be the key. She stood on the rock and closed her hand—the one bearing Paul's ring—over the necklace and silently summoned Ancha. She was ready for her teacher to return.

Author's Notes

I got the idea for this book on August 23, 2011. I know this because it's the day that a 5.8 magnitude earthquake occurred southwest of Washington, D.C., and a 5.3 magnitude earthquake took place south of Colorado Springs, CO (although it occurred close to midnight on August 22, local time). The earthquake near D.C. damaged the Washington Monument, and for a couple of years, scaffolding obscured it while it underwent repairs. Being curious, I looked up the history of earthquakes in both regions and learned that the largest earthquake on record in Colorado occurred on November 7, 1882—election day. This one, estimated to be about 6.6 in magnitude, occurred near current-day Rocky Mountain National Park. It caused damage to the Boulder County depot and was felt as far away as Salina, Kansas, and Salt Lake City, Utah. I had been contemplating a mystery series set in the Colorado Springs area prior to this, but it was the events of this day, August 23, 2011, that inspired the idea of sending my hero back in time by way of earthquakes.

After making a trip to Colorado to begin my research and writing the first chapter of the book, life got in the way, and the book lay dormant until this year. Because of the COVID-19 shut down, I had to complete my research online. Fortunately, the resources available online have come a long way since 2011, and I was able to learn what I needed to write this book.

Manitou Springs, or Manitou as it was called in 1882, is a very real place. You can visit it, and I recommend that you do. You can explore Cave of the Winds, just as people did then, starting in 1881. I have done my best to be true to the history of Manitou, reading countless old newspaper articles, books, and online articles to get local details. I have consulted local historians and other experts to learn all I could about the town and its people. I have used some historically accurate names for context, though the details around them are pure fiction.

Miss Anna Eva Fay was a real person, and she traveled the United States doing demonstrations of her medium abilities around the time this story is set. I found no evidence that she was ever in Colorado Springs, but the Miller Brothers did, indeed, conduct a spiritualism revival at the Colorado Springs opera house in December, 1882.

The principal characters and all their circumstances are fictitious. I would, however, like to say a bit more about two of them:

Dr. Alice Guiles is inspired by Dr. Harriet Leonard. She was an actual person with a medical degree from the Keokuk School of Physicians and Surgeons in Keokuk, Iowa. She was an early resident of Manitou and lived there or Colorado Springs (with a few brief interruptions in Denver) until she died in 1907. She is buried in a local cemetery in Colorado Springs. She really was the proprietor of the original bath house in Manitou, and she really was not a part of the bath house underway in this book, but the reasons are of my own imagination. I deeply admire Dr. Leonard and her courage to become a physician in that time and to forge her way in the American West.

Ancha is inspired by the local legend of Emma Crawford. Emma lived in Manitou a few years later than 1882 and died in 1891 from tuberculosis, just before she was to be married. She claimed to have an Indian lover, whom she spotted in the foothills of Pikes Peak and whom she believed to be a ghost. I wanted a character to represent the Ute people in my story, so I invented Ancha. His name is taken from a list of Ute chiefs I discovered in the course of my research, so I hope it is authentic. Manitou and Pikes Peak was not just part of Ute territory; it was central to their origination story. They believed they had come from "Tava," or "Tavakiev," which means "Sun Mountain," their name for Pikes Peak. The Garden of the Gods was a sacred place for the Utes and other Native American tribes of the region. The springs of Manitou were also very important to them. I have found integrating Ancha's story the most challenging aspect of this book because it is difficult to confirm details of the Ute culture and language. I have done my best and beg forgiveness for any inaccuracies. I decided it was more important to have this point of view represented as best I could rather than not have it at all.